C. Desjardin

CW00448278

England, Canada and the Great War

C. Desjardins

England, Canada and the Great War

1st Edition | ISBN: 978-3-75233-031-1

Place of Publication: Frankfurt am Main, Germany

Year of Publication: 2020

Outlook Verlag GmbH, Germany.

Reproduction of the original.

ENGLAND, CANADA and the GREAT WAR

BY

Lieutenant-Colonel L.-G. DESJARDINS

PREFACE.

Even since the issue, last year, of my book:—"*L'Angleterre, Le Canada et la Grande Guerre*"—"*England, Canada and the Great War*"—a second edition of which I had to publish, a few weeks later, to meet the pressing demand of numerous readers—I have been repeatedly asked by influential citizens to publish an English edition of my work.

A delegate from Quebec to the National Unity—or Win-the-War—Convention, in Montreal, I had the pleasure of meeting a great many of the delegates from Toronto and all over the Dominion. Many of them insisted upon the publication of an English edition.

Having written that book for the express and patriotic purpose of proving the justice of the cause of the Allies in the Great War, and refuting Mr. Bourassa's false and dangerous theories, I realized that the citizens of Quebec, Montreal, Ottawa and Toronto, who strongly advised an English edition to be circulated in all the Provinces, appreciated the good it could make.

I consider it is my imperious duty to dedicate to my English speaking countrymen this volume containing all the substance matter of my French book, and the defense a truly loyal French Canadian has made of the sacred cause of Civilization and Liberty for the triumph of which the glorious Allied Nations have been so heroically fighting for the last four eventful years.

As I say, in the Introduction to this work, I first intended to write only an English resumé of my French book. But once at work writing down, the questions to consider were so important, and the replies to the Nationalist leader's inconceivable theories so numerous, that I had to double and more the pages I had thought would be sufficient for my purpose. I realized that many points, to be fully explained, required more comments and argumentation that I had at first supposed necessary.

Moreover, since writing my French book, most important events have taken place. To have the present English volume up to date, I had to consider recent history in its very latest developments, and reply to the Nationalist leader's last errors, which by no means were not the least. When once a man has run off the path of reason and sound public sense, he is sure to rush to most dangerous extremes, unless he has the moral courage to acknowledge that he was sadly mistaken.

I trust that the English speaking readers of this book, will not, for a single moment, suppose that I am actuated by the least ill-feeling against Mr.

Bourassa personally, in the severe but just denunciation it was my plain duty to make of his deplorable Nationalist campaign.

For many years past, I have ever been delighted in welcoming promising young men to the responsibilities of public life. I remember with a mixed feeling of pleasure and regret the occasion I first heard Mr. Bourassa, then a youth, addressing a very large public meeting held on the nomination day of the candidates to a pending bye-election for the House of Commons of Canada: Pleasure at the recollection of what I considered a fairly successful beginning of a political career; deep regret at the failure to justify the hopes of his compatriots and his friends through an uncontrollable ambition always sure to deter, even the best gifted, from the safe line of duty, well understood, and firmly, but modestly, performed.

Passion, aspiring and unbridled, is always a dangerous counsellor. Mr. Bourassa could have had a useful political life, if he had realized that public good cannot be well served by constant appeals to race prejudices, and by persevering efforts to achieve success by stirring up fanaticism.

The result of the unpatriotic course he has followed, against the advice of his best friends, has been to sow in our great and happy Dominion the seed of discord, of hatred, of racial conflicts.

Unfortunately, for the country, for his French Canadian compatriots, and for himself, he was deluded to the point of believing that the war would be his grand opportunity.

Instead of using his influence to promote the national unity so essential under the trying circumstances with which Canada and the whole British Empire was suddenly confronted, he exerted himself to the utmost to prevail on his French Canadian countrymen to assume a decisive hostile stand to the noble cause which Britain had to fight for, in order to avenge the crime of the violation of Belgium's territory, to protect France from German cruel invasion, and to prevent Autocratic power from enslaving Humanity.

Such a misconception of a truly loyal man's part was most detrimental to the good of Canada's future, to the destinies of the French Canadians, and to the political standing of the publicist who was its willing victim.

And to-day he finds himself in this position that he has no other choice but that of pursuing, at all hazards, his unwholesome campaign against all things British, or, boldly retracing his steps, to go back on all he has said and written to support inadmissible views, vain ideas, and passionate prejudices.

The latter course would certainly be the best to follow in the interest of his country, of his French Canadian countrymen, and of his usefulness as a public man. But, however much to be regretted, he seems utterly unable to overcome the prejudices which have taken such deep root in his heart and mind.

Prejudice, constantly cultured, soon develops into blind fanaticism, closing the intellect to the light of sound logic, to the call of duty, to the clear comprehension of what is best to do to promote the public good.

However seriously guilty he may be, the public man, so swayed by a fanatical passion, is sure not to rally to the defense of the superior interests of his countrymen when they are threatened by a great misfortune.

I cannot help deploring that after giving good hopes of a life patriotically devoted to the increasing welfare of Canada, by doing his share in promoting the best feelings among his countrymen of all races, classes and creeds, one of my kin, really gifted to play a much better part, has been so sadly mistaken as to exhaust his activities in forcing his way to the leadership of a group of malcontents unable to overcome their racial antipathies and listen to reason, even when their country and the Empire to which they have sworn allegiance are destructively menaced.

He has nobody else to blame but himself for the failure of his political career, due to his misguided efforts in thwarting the happiness and prosperity which our great Dominion would certainly derive from the persevering union of all the citizens enjoying the blessings of her free British institutions, to work out her brilliant destinies by their intelligent labours, their hearted patriotism in peace times, and with their undaunted courage and their self-sacrificing devotion in war days.

After a somewhat prolonged spectacular display in the House of Commons, as member for the electoral division of Labelle, he felt instinctively that he had exhausted what he considered his usefulness, and was doomed to a dismal failure. He retired from the Dominion political arena, to try his luck in the Legislative Assembly of the Province of Quebec. No wiser a man by experience, he challenged the Leader of the parliamentary majority to a truly duellist struggle on the floor of the House. He thrusted at his opponent with the vigour of a combatant certain to conquer. All those who witnessed this encounter, must remember how completely overbearing confidence, proudly asserted, was overcome by calm and superior argumentative power, sound and clear political sense. True parliamentary eloquence easily brought to reason pedantic and bombastic oratory. The first throw—*le début*—went decidedly against the Nationalist leader. A beaten fighter from this very first day, he met with as complete a failure in the provincial political arena as he had done in the federal one. Wisely indeed, he retired from parliamentary life, after realizing that debating power cannot be acquired by demagogic speaking.

4

The Nationalist leader next limited his efforts to the tribune, to the public platform. All remember the time when he was periodically calling great popular meetings held in *Le Monument National*, Montreal, where he preached his Nationalist gospel with vehement talking. This new experiment could not last. It soon subsided. And the Nationalist leader is since addicted to pamphleteering of the worst kind as I will show in this book.

Deeply moved by the dangers of a most mischievous campaign, I considered it my bounded duty to do my utmost efforts to prove how utterly wrong were the views which those pursuing it with passionate energy wanted to prevail, and to show the sad consequences it was sure to produce.

Having first addressed myself to my French Canadian compatriots to persuade them how much detrimental to their best future the Nationalist campaign was sure to be, I am to-day laying the case before my English speaking countrymen, at the urgent request of many of them, in order to fully acquaint them with the refutation I have made, to the best of my ability, of Mr. Bourassa's erroneous theories and wild charges against England and all those who patriotically support our mother country in the great struggle she has had to wage after doing all she possibly could to maintain the peace of the world.

I ardently desire that the reading of the following pages, will contribute to the restoration of harmony and good will, for a while endangered by the Nationalist campaign, in our wide Dominion, to whose happiness, prosperity and grandeur we, of both English and French origins, must devote our best energies and all the resources of our unwavering patriotism.

L. G. DESJARDINS.

Quebec, October 1st, 1918.

INTRODUCTION.

Canada, as one of the most important component parts of the British Empire, is going through the crucial ordeal of the great crisis which will determine her destinies jointly with those of the whole world. Instantly put under the strain, four years ago, by the outrageous challenge of Germany to human civilization with the criminal purpose of universal domination, she was fully equal to her unbounded duty. Conscious of her sacred rights, she at once realized that the constitutional liberties which she enjoyed in the freest Empire of all times, could not be more patriotically exercised than for the defence of the sacred cause which united in a gigantic effort England, France and Russia, soon to receive the support of Italy. By an almost unanimous and enthusiastic decision she rallied to the flag around which all the Dependencies of the Empire gathered from the five continents. Never a more inspiring array of loyal subjects, owing allegiance to a Sovereignty, was witnessed in the wide world.

Through the trying days of four full years of the greatest war which ever saddened the life of the human race, Canada has nobly, gloriously, done her duty. Several hundred thousands of her devoted sons have rushed to the front to fight the battle of Liberty, of Right, of Civilization. Thousands of them have heroically given their lives for the triumph of the cause which, if finally triumphant, will brighten with freedom, prosperity, human happiness and undying glory, the destinies of many generations.

The struggle is not over. The battle is not yet won. Victory is in sight but unfortunately still so far distant, that it is still calling forth the undaunted exertions of all those who have pledged their faith to rescue the world from the cruel thraldom of German militarism.

Two years ago, at the critical period which culminated in the undecided military operations which, though rendered illustrious by the glorious defence of Verdun, made it plain to the Allies that success would only be the reward of a much more prolonged effort of untold sacrifices, I undertook to write the book entitled in French: "*L'Angleterre, le Canada et la Grande Guerre.*"

Several of the most influential and widely circulated News-papers of Montreal, Toronto and Quebec, have kindly published highly appreciative Reviews of the French Edition of my book, concluding with the request of the publication of an English Edition, which, they affirmed, would be conducive to the public good. I have received many letters and verbal demands to the same purpose.

It is my duty to answer to a call daily becoming more pressing.

I now offer to the English reading public a condensed edition of my work, with the title "*England, Canada and the Great War.*" I concluded not to issue a complete English Edition of the French volume. Instead of translating my book, I considered it more advisable to write an English synopsis of its contents. Undertaking such a work, I realized more than ever how important it is for the Citizens of Canada to be able to speak and write the languages of the two great races of the Dominion. Knowing well my own deficiency in this regard, I hoped, however, to write the following pages with enough clearness to have my views well understood, trusting to the kindness of my readers to excuse the inadequacy of my command of English.

A few words explaining the reasons that prompted me to write the French book will, I am confident, be kindly appreciated by my readers. A close observer of the daily impressions which the events developed by the war were creating in Canada, I felt more and more deeply grieved at the persistent and unpatriotic efforts of the leaders of the Nationalist school of the Province of Quebec, and their henchmen, to sway my French-Canadian countrymen from the clear path of duty. I undertook earnestly to do my best to stem the threatening wave of disloyal sentiments and racial conflict they were stirring up throughout the land. "*England, Canada and the Great War*" was the result of the very careful study of the numerous questions therein considered and of the patriotic impulse which led me to publish it.

I dedicated the volume to my French-Canadian countrymen by a letter from which I translate the following:

"It would surely be vain to conceal how serious was the situation imposed upon our country by the sudden outbreak, in August, 1914, of the greatest war of all times. It was dominated by the supreme fact that Canada was a component part of one of the most powerful Empires whose destinies were to be determined, for good or ill, for many long years, by the terrible conflict suddenly opened, but, for a prolonged period, prepared by those who dreamt of conquering the world."

"Great Britain, our Sovereign Metropolis, had done her utmost to protect Humanity against the misfortunes which endangered her future, for the maintenance of peace. She had failed in her noble efforts. At the very moment when, against all the most critical appearances, she was still hopeful, she had, all of a sudden, to face the terrible alternative, either to submit to national dishonour by complying with the violation of solemn treaties which bound her as much as Germany, or to unite with France and Russia to avenge Justice outrageously violated, sworn international Faith, Civilization perilously threatened."

"Could she hesitate for one single moment?"

"Our Mother Country has done that which her most imperious duty commanded her to do. She accepted the challenge of Germany with the patriotic determination inspired by the most sacred cause. All the loyal subjects of the British Crown have applauded her decision to rush to the defence of invaded Belgium and France, to reclaim their national honour and her own, and to protect her Empire against the German armies."

"With the most inspiring unanimity and admirable courage, all the British Colonies have rallied around the flag of their Sovereign Metropolis to share the glory of the triumph of Right and Justice. At the very front rank, Canada has nobly done her duty. Her decision was most spontaneous and decisive. She was not deterred by fallacious subtilties, deducted from pretended conventions, out of age and opportunity, to hinder her laudable and patriotic course. Throughout the length and breadth of her vast territory, all minds shared the same view, all hearts were united and beating with the same powerful sentiment."

"The decision of Canada to participate in the present war was taken by the constitutional government of the country, sanctioned by Parliament, approved by public opinion, glorified by the hundreds of thousands of brave volunteers who courageously answered the call of duty."

"Views with which I cannot concur have been expressed and given full publicity. They challenge discussion. It is my undoubted right to criticize them."

"Since the beginning of the present war, Mr. Henri Bourassa, in addition to the daily publicity of his journal "*Le Devoir*", has developed, in two principal pamphlets, the theories of his "*Nationalism*". They are respectively entitled: "*Que devons-nous à l'Angleterre?*" "*What do we owe England?*" and: "*Hier, Aujourd'hui, Demain*" "*Yesterday, To-day, To-morrow*"."

"In earnestly searching out the real causes of the war, the responsibilities of the belligerent nations, their respective aspirations, the duty imposed by the irresistable course of events upon the British Empire and consequently upon Canada, I was incessantly called upon to consider the very strange propositions contained in those pamphlets."

"It was with great surprise that I read, for instance, as the heading of one of the chapters, the utterly false proposition that: "*The Autonomous Colonies are Sovereign States.*""

"And these most extraordinary affirmations that the *King of England has not the right to declare the State of war for Canada, without the assent of the*

Canadian Cabinet; that Canada could have participated in the present war as a Nation."

"It is my bounden duty to affirm that almost all the propositions contained in the two above mentioned pamphlets are wrong according to international law and to constitutional law, erroneous in their historical bearings, contrary to the true teachings of the past."

"Mr. Bourassa persistingly trying to convince his readers that the precedents of the Soudanese and the South-African wars have forced the British Colonies to participate in the present one, I considered it my duty to make, in two separate chapters, a special study of those military campaigns which, in both cases, were so felicitously terminated for all parties concerned."

"I cannot close this letter without expressing my profound regret that Mr. Bourassa has thought proper to use most injurious language adding outrage to the falsity of his opinions. At page 121 of his pamphlet: "*Yesterday, To-day, To-morrow*", any one can read, no doubt with astonishment, that Mr. Bourassa charges our countrymen of the British races with being *ignorant, assuming, arrogant, dominating and rotten with mercantilism.*"

"Such ridiculous and insulting words to the address of our countrymen of the three British races are surely not calculated to increase Canadian harmony."

"This book, written for the express purpose of assisting you to form for yourselves a sound opinion about the terrible events so rapidly developing, was inspired by my loyalty to the Empire whose faithful subject I glory to be, by my devotion to Canada and to my countrymen, by the affectionate recollection of France I will cherish to my last day.

"During the last fifty years, either as a private or as an officer of the Canadian Militia—my service as such having lasted more than forty years—as a member of the Legislative Assembly of the Province of Quebec, and as a member of the House of Commons of Canada, I have often taken the oath of allegiance to the Sovereign of Great Britain. From my early youth, I had learned that under the ægis of the British Crown, the citizen of the Empire could be true to his oath, and enjoy the precious liberty of expressing his opinion. But I had also soon realized that during the lifetime of a Sovereign State, days of peril might occur. I had easily come to the conclusion that in those trying moments the loyal duty could be very happily reconciled with the most sincere love of political liberty.

"In defending with the most sincere conviction the sacred cause of the Allies, I am doing my duty as a free subject of the British Empire, as a citizen of Canada and of the Province of Quebec, as a son of France, as a devoted servant of Justice and Right. I am true to my oath."

I desire to call the special attention of my readers to the complete sense of the last paragraph just quoted. I most decidedly wish its meaning to be fully understood by all, as I intended to convey it to my French Canadian compatriots. I have never concurred in the subtle distinction so often made between the several notions entertained by many respecting their duty towards the Empire and Canada separately. Having witnessed, for the last fifty years, the admirable evolution and natural growth of the British constitutional system over a fourth of the globe, developing into the freest Empire that ever existed, my mind was more and more impressed with the conviction that loyalty to the Sovereignty presiding over such a magnificent national heritage could not be of two different kinds. A free British subject, whether living in the United Kingdom, or in any one of the Dependencies of the Crown, cannot be at once loyal to the Empire at large and disloyal to any of its component parts; or, *vice versa*, loyal to the particular section of the State where he is living and at the same disloyal to the Empire. Such a false conception of the duties of loyalty, if it could be spread successfully throughout the Empire, would undoubtedly lead to its rapid dissolution and complete destruction. Genuine loyalty cannot agree with exclusive and rampant sectionalism, with local, racial or religious prejudices and fanaticism.

The few lines of the preceding closing paragraph of my letter dedicating the French edition of my book as aforesaid, express my own conception of the true loyalty of a faithful subject of the British Sovereignty, who has the clear vision of the meaning of his oath of allegiance. In consequence, first, I affirm my duty as a subject of the British Empire; second, as a citizen of Canada; third, as a citizen of my own Province of Quebec. And then, taking a wider range of the duty of any man towards his ancestors' lineage, I declare that under the cruel circumstances of the case, I also consider it is my duty to defend France against her deadly enemy. Further enlarging the vision of duty to its fullest extent, I say that I am bound to defend the cause of the Allies by proving that I am a loyal servant of Justice and Right.

Surely I could not emphasize in terms more pregnant my loyalty to the cause of the British Empire, of France, and their Allies, of Liberty and Civilization. I confidently hope they will persuade my readers that this book was written with the most sincere and patriotic desire to help rallying my French Canadian compatriots to the defence of the British, French and Canadian flags, which must together emerge triumphant from the gigantic fight against the most threatening wave of barbarism the world has ever had to contend with at the cost of so great and heroic sacrifices.

When the first French edition of this book was issued, in January of last year, matters respecting the prosecution of the war had not yet required the serious consideration by Parliament and the country of the question of conscription to maintain to their proper efficiency the Canadian divisions on the firing line. Consequently, I was not then called upon to consider that most important subject. When I had to decide about publishing a second French edition—the first being entirely exhausted—I at first thought of adding to my work a few chapters respecting the most notable events developed by the gigantic struggle shaking the world to its very basic foundation. Foremost amongst them were the Russian sudden Revolution, the solemn entrance of the United States into the great fight, the imperious necessity of the military effort of the Allies far beyond that which had been foreseen, in order to achieve the final victory which will be the only adequate reward of their undaunted determination not to sheathe the sword before Germany will agree to restore peace upon the only possible conditions which will efficiently protect humanity from any other attempt at brutal universal domination. The question of conscription in Canada was the natural outcome of the progress of the deadly conflict between Civilization and barbarism, constitutional Freedom and despotism, democratic institutions and autocracy.

I soon realized that I could not properly do justice to such grave subjects in a few pages added to my first book. After mature consideration, I considered it was my duty to undertake to write a second volume. I have so informed the public in the *Advertisement* which prefaces the second French edition of the first. This second volume I will soon issue, also intending to publish an English synopsis of it, if that of the first volume meets the kind appreciation I hope of my English speaking countrymen.

However, pending the publication of the second volume, I think it is my duty to express now my views, in a summary way, on that much discussed question of obligatory military service. Let me preface by saying that they are not new, having originated in my mind more than thirty years ago. The military necessities of the present war have, of course, given them more precision and clearness.

Deeply conscious of the sacred duty of all truly loyal British subjects through the present prolonged world crisis for the life or death of human Liberty, I had to consider conscription from the double stand-point of a free citizen of Canada and of my military experience acquired in the course of a service of over forty years.

Most strongly and convincingly opposed to the militarism of the atrocious German type—the curse of Humanity—I have always believed—and do still more and more believe—imbued, I hope, with the true sense and principles of democratic institutions, that the greatest boon that could be granted the world would be that the admirable Christian law of peace and good-will amongst men would prevail for all times, and save the nations from the cruel obligation of keeping themselves constantly fully armed at the great cost of the best years of manhood, and of their accumulated treasures. But unfortunately it has not yet been the good luck of man to reach the goal of this most noble ambition. Instead of a steady advance in the right direction, he has, for the last fifty years, experienced a most dangerous set back by the predominating influence of German militarism, developed and mastered by the most autocratic power to the point of threatening the liberties of the whole world.

Need I say that, as a purely philosophical question of principle, I most sincerely deplore that the political state of the world has been and is such that national safety cannot be, in too many cases, properly assured without the law of the land calling upon the manhood of a country to make the sacrifice of part of the best years of enthusiastic youth, and requiring from the nation, as a collective body, the expenditure, to an untold amount, for the purposes of defence, of the accumulated savings of hard work and intelligent thrift.

Fortunately, the two continents of America, so abundantly blessed by Providence, had, until the present war, been able to pursue their prosperous and dignified course free from the entanglements of European Militarism.

Even England, in all the majesty of her Imperial power, her flag gloriously waving over so many millions of free men, protected as she was by the waves which she ruled with grandeur and grace, had succeeded in avoiding the curse of continental conscriptionism.

Between permanent conscription, despotically imposed upon a nation under autocratic rule, and temporary military compulsion freely accepted by a noble people for the very purpose of saving Humanity from military absolutism, there is, every one must admit, a wide difference. I have been, I am, and will be, to my last day, the uncompromising opponent of autocratic conscription, which I consider as a permanent crime against Christian Civilization, and the ready instrument of barbarous domination. To temporary compulsion I can agree, as a matter of patriotic and national duty, if the circumstances of the case are such that without its timely use, my country which has the first and undoubted right to my most patriotic devotion, at the cost of all I may own and even of my life, for her defence, would fall the prey to despotism which would bleed her to death to sway the world.

Such is the ordeal through which Canada, the British Empire, in fact much the greater part of the universe, are passing with torrents of blood shed to rescue Mankind from the domination of German militarism.

If Germany could have her course free; if she could reach the goal of her criminal ambition, nearly the whole world would be, for many long years, in the throes of the most abominable conscriptionism.

If after the enthusiasm of voluntary military service has exhausted itself from the very successful result of its patriotic effort, is it not a duty for all loyal citizens to accept temporary compulsion, to save their country from the horrors of defeat at the hands of the most cruel enemy which has ever shamed the light of the sun since it shines over the Human race blessed with Christian principles and moral teachings.

To the present generation of young men, strong, healthy, brave, let us say: be worthy of the times you live in, be equal to the great task imposed upon you, accepting with patriotism the sacrifices you are called upon to make, never forgetting that temporary compulsion for you means freedom from permanent conscription for your children and children's children in years to come.

It is from the very height of such lofty considerations that I have made up my mind about this much vexed question which will, we must all earnestly hope, be more and more well understood and eventually settled to the everlasting good of the country once for all delivered from the exasperating menace of German despotism.

I must reserve for the second volume of this work, the fuller expression of my views of what should be the military system to be maintained in Canada, after the very wide experience we will have derived from the present great war. All I will add now is that ever since the early eighties of the last century, after many years of voluntary service in the Canadian Militia, I had fully realized that it is no more possible to make a real soldier by a few days yearly training, for three years, than you can make a competent lawyer of a young man studying law for a fortnight in the course of three consecutive years.

Since the federal Union of the Provinces we had spent much more than a hundred million of dollars for the training of our militia, with the appalling result that when came the day of getting ready for the fray, we had not two thousand men to send at once to the firing line. The first thirty thousands of the brave men who enthusiastically volunteered to go to the front had to be trained, at Valcartier and in England, several months before being sent to face the enemy whose waves of permanent divisions of armed men had overrun, like a torrent, Belgium and northern France. Of course, our boys fought and died like heroes, but nevertheless we at last learned, at our great cost, that soldiers no more than lawyers, doctors, merchants, transportation managers, bankers, business men of all callings, farmers, sailors, etc., can be qualified in a day.

When the time shall come to consider what will be the requirements of our military organization, after this terrible struggle is over, I hope none will forget that war is a great science, an awful and very difficult art, so that we shall not deceive ourselves any longer by the illusion that an army can be drawn from the earth in twenty four hours.

Our most efficient military commander cannot entertain the foolish delusion of Pompey, so crushingly beaten by Cæsar, at Pharsalia, that he can raise legions by striking the ground with his foot.

If our future national circumstances turn out to be such, after the restoration of peace, that we will not be called upon to make heavy sacrifices for defence —let Providence so bless our dear country—it will then be much more rational to save our money than to squander it on a military system which cannot produce military efficiency.

The future can be trusted to settle favourably its own difficulties. For us of the present generation, we have to attend to the imperative and sacred duty of the hour. Let no one shirk his responsibilities, waver in the heavy task, falter before the sacrifices to be patriotically and heroically accepted. To deserve the everlasting gratitude of future generations, we must secure to them the blessings of permanent peace in a renovated world freed from the tyranny of autocratic despotism.

Surely, I will be permitted to say that, undertaking to write *England, Canada and the Great War*, I fully realized my bounden duty to study all the questions raised by the terrible struggle, unreservedly, absolutely, outside of all party considerations, of all racial prejudices. A party man, in the only true and patriotic sense of the word, during the twenty-five years of my active political life, as a journalist and a member of the Quebec Legislature and of the Parliament of Canada, it became my lot in the official position which I was asked to accept and which I loyally filled, to all intents and purposes, for many years, to train my mind more and more to judge public questions solely from the point of view of the public good. I do not mean to say that partyism, well understood and patriotically practiced, is not productive of good to a country blessed with free institutions. But certainly in the course of a progressive, intelligent and eventful national life, ennobled by Freedom happily enjoyed, times occur when it behooves every one to rise superior to all other considerations, however important they may be, to serve the only one worthy of all sacrifices: the salvation of the country. Never was this principle so true, so imperative, than on the day when the world was so audaciously challenged by Germany to the deadly conflict still raging with undiminished fury.

That most important question of military obligatory service, brought up by the pressure of the imperious necessities of military operations, lengthening and intensifying to unforeseen proportions, was for many weeks considered by Parliament. Surely, no one for a single moment entertained the idea that, however desirable and imperative it was for the representatives of the people to be of only one mind so far as the prosecution of Canada's share in the war was concerned, constant unanimity of opinion was possible respecting the various measures to be adopted to that end. Parliament sitting in the performance of its constitutional functions, with all its undoubted privileges, could not be expected not to exercise its right to debate all the matters constitutionally proposed for its concurrence and approval. I must certainly and wisely refrain from any comment whatsoever upon the lengthy discussion of the Military Service Act in both Houses in Ottawa. Having received the Royal Assent, the Bill is now the law of the land. All will patriotically rejoice to see that without waiving their right to pronounce upon the deeds and the views of those who are responsible to them, the free citizens of Canada will cheerfully accept the new sacrifices imposed by the obligation of carrying the war to a successful issue, praying to God to bless their patriotic efforts, and even with the true Christian spirit, to forgive guilty Germany if she will only repent for her crimes, and agree to repair a reasonable part of the immense damages she has wrought upon trodden and martyred nations.

I hope,—and most ardently wish—that all my readers will agree with me that next to the necessity of winning the war—and, may I say, even as of almost equal importance for the future grandeur of our beloved country—range that of promoting by all lawful means harmony and good will amongst all our countrymen, whatever may be their racial origin, their religious faith, their particular aspirations not conflicting with their devotion to Canada as a whole, nor with their loyalty to the British Empire, whose greatness and prestige they want to firmly help to uphold with the inspiring confidence that more and more they will be the unconquerable bulwark of Freedom, Justice, Civilization and Right.

After having so fully expressed my profound conviction of what I consider to be my sacred duty as a loyal British subject, I feel sure I will be allowed to ask my English-speaking countrymen not to judge my French compatriots by the sayings and deeds of persons, too well gifted and too prone to injure their future and that of the whole country itself, but utterly disqualified and impotent to do them any good.

Need I affirm that my French Canadian compatriots are loyal at heart, a liberty loving and peaceful people, law-abiding citizens, fairly minded, intelligent, hard working, industrious. They have done, they are doing, and will do, their fair share for the progress and the future greatness of our wide and mighty Dominion. To all those who desire to appreciate their course in all fairness and Christian Justice, I will say: do not fail to take into account that like all other national groups they are liable, in overtrying circumstances, to be in a certain measure wrongly influenced by deficiencies of leadership, but depend that they cannot be, for any length of time, carried away by unscrupulous players on their feelings. Some of them were deceived by persistent efforts to persuade them that England was, as much as Germany, guilty of having precipitated the great war which has been the curse of almost the whole world for the last four years. The accumulated remembrance of their staunch loyalty and patriotism during more than a century and a half will do much to favour the harmonious relations of all Canadians of good will who, I have no doubt, comprise millions of well wishers of the glorious destiny of our country.

May I be allowed to conclude by saying that my most earnest desire is to do all in my power, in the rank and file of the great army of free men, to reach the goal which ought to be the most persevering and patriotic ambition of loyal Canadians of all origins and creeds.

And I repeat, wishing my words to be re-echoed throughout the length and breadth of the land I so heartily cherish:—I have always been, I am and will ever be, to my last breath, true to my oath of allegiance to my Sovereign and to my country.

CHAPTER I.

WHO ARE THE GUILTY PARTIES?

Any one sincerely wishing to arrive at a sound opinion on the great war raging for the last four years, must necessarily make a serious study of the causes which led to the terrific struggle so horribly straining the energies of the civilized world to escape tyrannical domination. The case having been so fully discussed, and the responsibilities of the assailant belligerents so completely proved, I surely need not show at length that the German Emperor, his military party, the group of the German population called JUNKERS, are to the highest degree, the guilty parties of all the woful wrongs imposed upon Mankind and of the bloodshed unprecedented in all the ages.

The German Empire had for many years decided that it would not alone attempt to dominate the world. It wanted a partner to share the responsibility of the crime it was ready to commit at the first favourable opportunity, but a docile partner which she could direct at will, command with imperious orders, and crush without mercy at the first move of resistance. That plying tool was found in the complicity of Austria-Hungary, for years under the sway of Berlin diplomacy.

No sane man, if he is sincere, if he is honest, can now, for a single moment, hesitate to proclaim that between Germany and Austria-Hungary, and the group of nations henceforth bearing the glorious name of THE ALLIES, Right and Justice are on the side of England, of France, of the United States, of Belgium, of Italy, of Canada.

Where is the man with a sound mind, with a strong heart, beating with the noble impulses of righteousness, with a soul dignified by lofty aspirations, who ignores to-day that for fifty years previous to the declaration of war, in August 1914, Germany had been perfecting her military organization for a grand effort at universal domination?

All my life a close student of History, I was much impressed by the constant Policy of England to maintain Peace during the last century. When the World emerged from the great wars of the Napoleonic Era, she firmly took her stand in favour of peaceful relations between the nations, trusting more and more for the future prosperity of them all to the advantages to be derived from the permanency of friendly intercourse, from the ever increasing development of international trade, prompted by the freest possible exchanges of the products of all the countries blessed by Providence with large and varied resources.

Her statesmen, so many of them truly worthy of this name, however divided they may have been with regard to questions of domestic government and internal reforms, were most united about the course to be followed respecting foreign relations. Perhaps more than all others having a say in the management of the world's affairs at large, they fully realized that no nation could prosper and successfully work out her destinies by systematically trying to injure her neighbours. No independent country can become wealthier, happier, and greater, by spreading ruin and devastation around her frontiers.

The most convincing evidence that England was constantly favourable to the maintenance of peace amongst the great Powers of the World, for the last hundred years, is found in her permanent determination not to be drawn into the vortex of European continental militarism, so powerfully developed by Prussianism. She could have organized a standing army of millions of men. She would not. True, during the few years which preceded the present hurricane, some of the most eminent of England's military officers, notably, foremost amongst them, Lord Roberts, seeing, with their eyes wide open, the aggravated dangers accumulating on the darkening horizon, warned their countrymen about the threatening waves which menaced the future of the world. But British public opinion, as a whole, would not depart from her almost traditional policy of "*non-intervention*". For nearly a century, Great Britain maintained her "*splendid isolation*", trusting to the sound sense which should always govern the world to protect Mankind against the horrors of a general war. Never was this great national policy better exemplified than during the long and glorious reign of Her Majesty Queen Victoria. For more than fifty years, she graced one of the most illustrious Thrones that ever presided over the destinies of a great Empire, with sovereign dignity, with womanly virtues, with motherly devotion, with patriotic respect of the constitutional liberties of her free subjects. When she departed for a better world, she was succeeded by the great King and Emperor—Edward VII.— who, during the few years of his memorable reign, proved himself so much the friendly supporter of harmony and good will amongst the nations that he deserved to be called "THE KING OF THE PEACE OF THE WORLD."

CHAPTER II.

THE PERSISTENT EFFORTS OF ENGLAND IN FAVOUR OF PEACE.

In 1891, Lord Salisbury, then Prime Minister of England, witnessing the constant progress of Prussian militarism on land and sea, and fully conscious of the misfortunes it was preparing for Humanity, ordered an official statement to be made of the extravagant cost of the European military organization, and sent it confidentially to the German Kaiser, who took no notice of it.

In 1896, Lord Salisbury lays before the Czar of Russia all the information he has obtained on the question of militarism in Europe. On the 28th of August, 1898, the Emperor of Russia addressed to the world his celebrated Manifesto in favour of peace. It urged, first, the necessity of a truly permanent peace; second, the limitation of military preparation which, in its ever increasing development, was causing the economic ruin of the nations.

The conferences of The Hague in favour of an international agreement for the maintenance of peace were the direct result of the initiative of the British Prime Minister, who foresaw the frightful consequences for Humanity of the enormous development of militarism by the German Empire.

All the great Powers of Europe and America, together with the secondary states, at once heartily concurred with the proposition of the Czar of Russia. Unfortunately, there were two sad exceptions to the consent to consider the salutary purpose so anxiously desired by those who valued as they should all the benefits the world would have derived from an international system assuring permanent peace. Germany and Austria, the latter already for years dominated by the former, opposed the patriotic move of the Emperor of Russia, suggested to him by Great Britain. They agreed to be represented at the Conferences for the only object of thwarting the efforts in favour of a satisfactory enactment of new rules of International Law to henceforth protect the world against a general conflagration, and to free the nations from the crushing burdens of a militarism daily developing more extravagant.

Ministerial changes in Great Britain in no way altered this part of the foreign policy of the Mother Country. In 1905, Mr. Campbell-Bannerman became Prime Minister of England. He was well known to be an ardent pacifist. Deprecating the mad increase of unchecked militarism, he said, in his ministerial program:—

"*A policy of huge armaments keeps alive and stimulates and feeds the belief that force is the best, if not the only, solution of international differences."*

On the 8th of March, 1906, Lord Haldane, then Minister of War, declared in the British House of Commons:—

"I wish we were near the time when the nations would consider together the reduction of armaments.... Only by united action can we get rid of the burden which is pressing so heavily on all civilized nations."

The second Conference of The Hague which took place in July and October, 1907, was then being organized. Russia was again its official promoter. Well aware of the uncompromising stand of Germany on the question of reduced armaments, she had not included that matter in the program she had decided to lay before the Conference. The British Government did all they could to have it placed on the orders to be taken into consideration. A member of the Labor Party, Mr. Vivian, moved in the House of Commons, that the Conference of The Hague be called upon to discuss that most important subject. His motion was unanimously and enthusiastically carried.

Informing the House that the Cabinet heartily approved the Resolution, Sir Edward Grey, Secretary for Foreign Affairs, said:—

"I do not believe that at any time has the conscious public opinion in the various countries of Europe set more strongly in the direction of peace than at the present time, and yet the burden of military and naval expenditure goes on increasing. No greater service could it (the Hague Conference) do, than to make the conditions of peace less expensive than they are at the present time.... It is said we are waiting upon foreign nations in order to reduce our expenditure. As a matter of fact, we are all waiting on each other. Some day or other somebody must take the first step.... I do, on behalf of the Government, not only accept, but welcome such a resolution as this as a wholesome and beneficial expression of opinion."

In July, 1906, a most important meeting of the Inter-Parliamentary Union took place in London. Twenty-three countries, enjoying the privileges, in various proportions, of free institutions, were represented at this memorable Congress of Nations. In the course of his remarkable opening speech of the first sitting, Mr. Campbell-Bannerman, Prime Minister, said:—

"Urge your Governments, in the name of humanity, to go into The Hague Conference as we ourselves hope to go, pledged to diminished charges in respect of armaments."

A motion embodying the views so earnestly pressed by the British Government was unanimously carried.

On the fifth of March, 1907, only four months before the opening of the

Second Hague Conference, Mr. Campbell-Bannerman, affirming the bounden duty of England to propose the restriction of armaments, said, in the British House of Commons:—

"Holding the opinion that there is a great movement of feeling among thinking people in all the nations of the world, in favor of some restraint on the enormous expenditure involved in the present system so long as it exists.... We have desired and still desire to place ourselves in the very front rank of those who think that the warlike attitude of powers, as displayed by the excessive growth of armaments is a curse to Europe, and the sooner it is checked, in however moderate a degree, the better."

Unfortunately, German hostility to reduced armaments prevented any good result from the second Hague Conference in the way of checking extravagant and ruinous military organization. There was sad disappointment in all the reasonable world and specially in England at this deplorable outcome. Mr. Campbell-Bannerman expressed it as follows:—

"We had hoped that some great advance might be made towards a common consent to arrest the wasteful and growing competition in naval and military armaments. We were disappointed."

Unshaken in her determination to do her utmost to protect Civilization against the threatening and ever increasing dangers of German militarism, England persisted with the most laudable perseverance in her noble efforts to that much desired end. But all her pleadings, however convincing, were vain. Germany was obdurate. Finally, on the 30th of March, 1911, speaking in the Reichstag, the German Imperial Chancellor threw off the mask, and positively declared that the question of reduced armaments admitted of no possible solution *"as long as men were men and States were States."*

A more brutal declaration could hardly have been made. It was a cynical challenge to the World. Times were maturing and Germany was anxiously waiting for the opportunity to strike the blow which would stagger Humanity.

Through all the great crisis of July and August, 1914, directly consequent upon the odious crime of Sarajevo, England exhausted all her efforts to maintain peace, but unfortunately without avail.

Knowing very well how much England sincerely wished the maintenance of peace, the German Government was to the last moment under the delusion that it could succeed in having Great Britain to remain neutral in a general European war. They were not ashamed to presume they could bribe England. Without blushing they made to the British Government the infamous proposition contained in the following despatch from Sir E. Goschen, the British Ambassador at Berlin, to Sir Edward Grey, the Secretary of State for

Foreign Affairs:—

Sir E. Goschen to Sir Edward Grey (Received July 29).

Berlin, July 29, 1914.

(Telegraphic.)

I was asked to call upon the Chancellor to-night. His Excellency had just returned from Potsdam.

He said that should Austria be attacked by Russia a European conflagration might, he feared, become inevitable, owing to Germany's obligation as Austria's ally, in spite of his continued efforts to maintain peace. He then proceeded to make the following strong bid for British neutrality. He said that it was clear, so far as he was able to judge the main principle which governed British policy, that Great Britain would never stand by and allow France to be crushed in any conflict there might be. That, however, was not the object at which Germany aimed. Provided that neutrality of Great Britain was certain, every assurance would be given to the British Government that the Imperial Government aimed at no territorial acquisitions at the expense of France should they prove victorious in any war that might ensue.

I questioned his Excellency about the French colonies, and he said he was unable to give a similar undertaking in that respect. As regards Holland, however, his Excellency said that, so long as Germany's adversaries respected the integrity and neutrality of the Netherlands, Germany was ready to give His Majesty's Government an assurance that she would do likewise. It depended upon the action of France what operations Germany might be forced to enter upon in Belgium, but when the war was over, Belgian integrity would be respected if she had not sided against Germany.

His Excellency ended by saying that ever since he had been Chancellor the object of his policy had been, as you were aware, to bring about an understanding with England; he trusted that these assurances might form the basis of that understanding which he so much desired. He had in mind a general neutrality agreement between England and Germany, though it was of course at the present moment too early to discuss details, and an assurance of British neutrality in the conflict which present crisis might possibly produce, would enable him to look forward to realisation of his desire.

In reply to his Excellency's inquiry how I thought his request would appeal to you, I said that I did not think it probable that at this stage of

22

events you would care to bind yourself to any course of action and that I was of opinion that you would desire to retain full liberty.

Our conversation upon this subject having come to an end, I communicated the contents of your telegram of to-day to his Excellency, who expressed his best thanks to you.

To the foregoing outrageous proposition, the Government of Great Britain gave the proud and noble reply which follows, for all times to be recorded in diplomatic annals to the eternal honour and glory of the Ministers who incurred the responsibility of, and of the distinguished diplomat who drafted, that memorable document:—

Sir Edward Grey to Sir E. Goschen.

(Telegraphic.)

Foreign Office, July 30, 1914.

Your telegram of 29th July.

His Majesty's Government cannot for a moment entertain the Chancellor's proposal that they should bind themselves to neutrality on such terms.

What he asks us in effect is to engage to stand by while French colonies are taken and France is beaten so long as Germany does not take French territory as distinct from the colonies.

From the material point of view such a proposal is unacceptable, for France, without further territory in Europe being taken from her, could be so crushed as to lose her position as a Great Power, and become subordinate to German policy.

Altogether, apart from that, it would be a disgrace for us to make this bargain with Germany at the expense of France, a disgrace from which the good name of this country would never recover.

The Chancellor also in effect asks us to bargain away whatever obligation or interest we have as regards the neutrality of Belgium. We could not entertain that bargain either.

Having said so much, it is unnecessary to examine whether the prospect of a future general neutrality agreement between England and Germany offered positive advantages sufficient to compensate us for tying our hands now. We must preserve our full freedom to act as circumstances may seem to us to require in any such unfavourable and regrettable development of the present crisis as the Chancellor contemplates.

You should speak to the Chancellor in the above sense, and add most earnestly that the only way of maintaining the good relations between England and Germany is that they should continue to work together to preserve the peace of Europe; if we succeed in this object, the mutual relations of Germany and England will, I believe, be **ipso facto** improved and strengthened. For that object His Majesty's Government will work in that way with all sincerity and good-will.

And I will say this: if the peace of Europe can be preserved, and the present crisis safely passed, my own endeavour will be to promote some arrangement to which Germany will be a party, by which she could be assured that no aggressive or hostile policy would be pursued against her or her allies by France, Russia, and ourselves, jointly or separately. I have desired this and worked for it, as far as I could, through the last Balkan crisis, and, Germany having a corresponding object, our relations sensibly improved. The idea has hitherto been too Utopian to form the subject of definite proposals, but if this present crisis, so much more acute than any that Europe has gone through for generations, be safely passed, I am hopeful that the relief and reaction which will follow may make possible some more definite rapprochement between the Powers than has been possible hitherto.

The British Government could not take a more dignified stand and express their indignation at the infamous proposal in stronger and more noble terms.

Let us now read the indignant protest of Mr. Asquith, the British Prime Minister, against the outrageous German proposition, addressed to the House of Commons, where it raised a storm of applause, proclaiming to the World the dogged determination of England to wage war rather than agree to the dishonourable German proposal:—

What does that amount to? Let me just ask the House. I do so, not with the object of inflaming passion, certainly not with the object of exciting feeling against Germany, but I do so to vindicate and make clear the position of the British Government in this matter. What did that proposal amount to? In the first place, it meant this: That behind the back of France —they were not made a party to these communications—we should have given, if we had assented to that, a free license to Germany to annex, in the event of a successful war, the whole of the extra European dominions and possessions of France. What did it mean as regards Belgium? When she addressed, as she has addressed in the last few days, her moving appeal to us to fulfil our solemn guarantee of her neutrality, what reply should we have given? What reply should we have given to that Belgian appeal? We should have been obliged to say that without her knowledge we had bartered away to the Power threatening her our obligation to keep our plighted word. The House has read, and the country has read, of course, in the last few hours, the most pathetic appeal addressed by the King of Belgium, and I do not envy the man who can read that appeal with an unmoved heart. Belgians are fighting and losing their lives. What would have been the position of Great Britain to-day in the face of that spectacle if we had assented to this infamous proposal? Yes, and what are we to get in return for the betrayal of our friends and the dishonour of our obligations? What are we to get in return? A promise—nothing more; a promise as to what Germany would do in certain eventualities; a promise, be it observed—I am sorry to say it, but it must be put upon record— given by a Power which was at that very moment announcing its intention to violate its own treaty, and inviting us to do the same. I can only say, if we had dallied or temporized, we, as a Government, should have covered ourselves with dishonour, and we should have betrayed the interests of this country, of which we are trustees.

After quoting and eulogizing the telegraphic despatch of Sir Edward Grey to Sir E. Goschen, dated July 30, 1914, Mr. Asquith proceeded as follows:—

That document, in my opinion, states clearly, in temperate and convincing language, the attitude of this Government. Can any one who reads it fail to appreciate the tone of obvious sincerity and earnestness which underlies it; can any one honestly doubt that the Government of this country in spite of great provocation—and I regard the proposals made to us as proposals which we might have thrown aside without consideration and almost without answer—can any one doubt that in spite of great provocation the right hon. gentleman, who had already earned the title— and no one ever more deserved it—of Peace Maker of Europe, persisted to the very last moment of the last hour in that beneficent but unhappily frustrated purpose. I am entitled to say, and I do so on behalf of this country—I speak not for a party, I speak for the country as a whole—that we made every effort any Government could possibly make for peace. But this war has been forced upon us. What is it we are fighting for? Every one knows, and no one knows better than the Government the terrible incalculable suffering, economic, social, personal and political, which war, and especially a war between the Great Powers of the world must entail. There is no man amongst us sitting upon this bench in these trying days—more trying perhaps than any body of statesmen for a hundred years have had to pass through, there is not a man amongst us who has not, during the whole of that time, had clearly before his vision the almost unequalled suffering which war, even in just cause, must bring about, not only to the peoples who are for the moment living in this country and in the other countries of the world, but to posterity and to the whole prospects of European civilization. Every step we took with that vision before our eyes, and with a sense of responsibility which it is impossible to describe. Unhappily, if in spite of all our efforts to keep the peace, and with that full and overpowering consciousness of the result, if the issue be decided in favour of war, we have, nevertheless, thought it to be the duty as well as the interest of this country to go to war, the House may be well assured it was because we believe, and I am certain the Country will believe, we are unsheathing our sword in a just cause.

If I am asked what we are fighting for I reply in two sentences. In the first place to fulfil a solemn international obligation, an obligation which, if it had been entered into between private persons in the ordinary concerns of life, would have been regarded as an obligation not only of law but of honour, which no self-respecting man could possibly have repudiated. I say, secondly, we are fighting to vindicate the principle which, in these days when force, material force, sometimes seems to be the dominant influence and factor in the development of mankind, we are fighting to vindicate the principle that small nationalities are not to be crushed, in defiance of international good faith, by the military will of a strong and overmastering Power. I do not believe any nation ever entered into a great controversy—and this is one of the greatest history will ever know—with a clearer conscience and stronger conviction that it is fighting, not for aggression, not for the maintenance even of its own selfish interest, but that it is fighting in defence of principles, the maintenance of which is vital to the civilisation of the world. With a full conviction, not only of the wisdom and justice, but of the obligations which lay upon us to challenge this great issue, we are entering into the struggle.

The German Government refusing to order their army to retire from the Belgian territory it had violated, at midnight, 4th to 5th August, 1914, the whole British Empire was at war with the whole German Empire.

Surely, there is not the slightest necessity to argue any more that in the terrific war raging for the last four years, Justice and Right are on the side of England and her Allies. No war was ever more just, waged with equal honour for the triumph of Liberty and Civilization, for the protection of Humanity against the onslaught of barbarism developed to the cruelty of the darkest ages of History.

CHAPTER III.

THE CALL TO DUTY IN CANADA.

Every one knows how the news of the State of War between the British and German Empires were received in our great Canadian Dominion, after the days of anxious waiting which culminated in the rallying of England to the defence of the cause of Freedom and Civilization. When the call for duty was sounded in the Capital of the British Empire, it rolled over the mighty Atlantic, spreading over the length and breadth of Canada, being re-echoed with force in our Province of Quebec.

At once called to prepare for the emergency, the Canadian Parliament met and unanimously decided that the Dominion would, of her own free will and patriotic decision, participate in the Great War. The course of events in Canada, for the last four years, is well known by all. It is recent history.

My special object in condensing in this book the defence which I considered it my duty to make of the just and sacred cause of the British Empire, and her Allies, in the great war still raging with undiminished fury, being to show how I did, to the best of my ability, try to persuade my French Canadian Countrymen where was the true path of duty, and how false and disloyal were the unscrupulous theories of "Nationalism", I must first review the successive movements of public opinion in the Province of Quebec.

In the preceding sentence, I have intently affirmed that the cause of the Allies was that of the whole British Empire. Surely, it should not be necessary to say so, as no truly loyal British subject would for a moment hesitate to come to that patriotic conclusion. Still, however incredible it is, the duty of the British colonies to rally to the flag to defend the Empire and participate in the deadly struggle between Civilization and barbarism, was challenged by the leaders of the "Nationalist school" in the Province of Quebec. Of course, that school never represented more than a small minority of thought and numbers. But, sad to admit, a fanatical minority, in days of trying sacrifices, can do a great deal of injury to a people by inflaming national and religious prejudices. We, French Canadians, have had much to suffer from the unpatriotic efforts of a few to bring our countrymen to take an erroneous view of the situation.

At the opening of the war, the general opinion in the Province of Quebec was without doubt strongly in favor of Canada's participation in the struggle. Any student of the working of our constitutional system knows how the strength of public opinion is ascertained, outside of a general election, in all cases, and more specially with regard to measures of paramount importance when the country has to deal with a national emergency.

The Parliament of Canada is the authorized representative of the Country. Called in a special session, at the very outbreak of the hostilities, they voted unanimously that it was our duty to participate in the war. All the representatives of the Province of Quebec heartily joined with those of all the other Provinces to vote this unanimous decision.

In the light of events ever since, who can now reasonably pretend that the patriotic decision of the Parliament of Canada was not entirely, even enthusiastically, approved by the Canadian people? The press, even in the Province of Quebec, with only one exception of any consequence, was unanimous in its approval of the action of Parliament.

The heads of our Church, the Archbishops and Bishops of the Ecclesiastical Provinces of Quebec, Montreal and Ottawa, in their very important Pastoral Letter on the duties of the Catholics in the present war, positively said:—

"We must acknowledge it—(nous ne saurions nous le dissimuler—): that conflict, one of the most terrific the world has yet seen, cannot but have its repercussion in our country. England is engaged into it, and who does not see that the fate of all the component parts of the Empire is bound with the fate of her arms. She relies upon our support, and that support, we are happy to say, has been generously offered to her both in men and money."

No representative of public opinion, of any weight, outside of Parliament, professional men, leaders of finance, commerce and industry, in the Province of Quebec, raised a word of disapproval at the Parliamentary call to arms.

Not one meeting was called, not one resolution was moved, to oppose the decision of the Canadian Parliament.

Not one petition was addressed to the two Houses in Ottawa against Canada's participation in the war.

Every one in the Province of Quebec knew that participating in the war would entail heavy financial sacrifices, and that the taxation of the country would have to be largely increased to meet the new obligations we had freely decided to incur for the salvation of the Empire and of Civilization.

The Government of the day proposed the financial measures they considered necessary to raise the public revenue which the circumstances required. Those measures were unanimously approved by Parliament. The taxpayers of the country, those of the Province of Quebec like all the others, willingly and patriotically accepted and paid without complaint the new taxes into the public treasury. During more than the three first years of the war, I visited a good part of the Province of Quebec, and addressed several large public meetings. Everywhere my attention was forcibly struck by the prompt willingness of my French Canadian countrymen to bear their share of the financial sacrifices Canada was called upon to make for the triumph of the cause of the Allies.

CHAPTER IV.

Recruiting By Voluntary Service.

No stronger evidence could be given of the determination of the country as a whole, and over all its component parts, to support Great Britain and her Allies to final success, than the truly wonderful record of the voluntary enlistment of more than four hundred thousand men, of all walks in life, to rush to the front.

Recruiting in the Province of Quebec indeed started very well. Several thousands of French Canadian youth rallied to the colors. I hope and trust that, sooner or later, it will be possible to make a more satisfactory statistical record of the number of French Canadians who enlisted. I am fully convinced that the total is somewhat much larger than the figures usually quoted. It would surely be conducive to a better understanding of the case, if such statistical information was carefully prepared and made public. It is easily conceivable that the pressure of the work of maintaining the splendid Canadian army renders it perhaps difficult to attend actually to the details of that compilation. So we can afford to wait for the redress of figures which may constitute a wrong to the race second in numbers but equal to any in patriotism in Canada.

Pending my remarks upon certain causes which have contributed to check recruiting amongst the French element in the Province of Quebec, I consider it important to mention those which were easy to ascertain and comprehend.

It is a well known fact that early marriages are a rule in the Province of Quebec much more than in the other Provinces of the Dominion. As a natural consequence, the available number of young unmarried men for recruiting purposes was proportionately less. I myself have known parishes in our Province where half a dozen of unmarried young men from twenty years of age and upwards could not be found.

It was easily to foresee that a comparison would be made between the number of Canadian-born volunteers in the English-speaking Provinces and that from the Province of Quebec. The degree of enthusiasm for enlistment in the other Provinces between the foreign born and the Canadian born has also been noticed. It has generally been admitted that most naturally the young men recently arrived in Canada were more strongly appealed to by all the sacred ties still binding them to their mother land. When generations have, for more than a century, enjoyed all the blessings of peace and lived far away from the turmoil of warlike preparations and military conflicts, is it to be much wondered at that the entire population is not at once permeated with the feeling of the dangers ahead, and do not rise rapidly to the full sense of the duty she is suddenly called upon to perform.

My daily personal intercourse with hundreds of my French Canadian compatriots allowed me to realize that many of them, even amongst the leading classes, were over-confident that the Allies representing at the beginning the united effort of England, France and Russia, soon to be reinforced by Italy, breaking away from the Central Powers, would certainly be equal to the task of being victorious over German militarism. Repeatedly, before public meetings and in very numerous private conversations, I urgently implored my hearers not to be so deluded, doing my best to convince them that it would be a fatal error to shut our eyes from the truth, that the military power of Central Europe, comprising the two great Empires of Germany and Austria, Bulgaria, with the help of Asiatic Turkey, and the undisguised support of baneful teutonic influences and intrigues at the courts of Petrograd and Athens, was gigantic, and that the terrible conflict would surely develop into a struggle for life and death between human freedom and barbarism.

This feeling of over-confidence was passing away, when it became evident that to triumph over the modern huns and their associates was no easy task; that the goal of freeing humanity from the threatening universal domination would require the most determined effort of the nations who had heroically undertaken to reach it.

CHAPTER V.

INTERVENTION OF NATIONALISM.

The great struggle being waged with increased intensity, it was daily becoming more and more evident that the Allied nations were bound to muster all their courage, perseverance and resources to successfully fight their determined foe. It was just at the thick of this critical situation, calling forth the devotion and patriotism of all, that the "Nationalist" campaign of false theories and principles was launched with renewed activity in the Province of Quebec.

Mr. Henri Bourassa, ex-member of Labelle in the House of Commons, was, and still is, the recognized leader of the "Nationalist School" in our Province, and wherever it finds adherents. His personal organ, *"Le Devoir,"* is daily expounding the doctrines of that School.

In October, 1915, Mr. Bourassa issued a pamphlet of over four hundred pages entitled:—*"What do we owe England?"*—in French:—*"Que devons-nous à l'Angleterre?"*

In the long overdrawn and farfetched argumentation of this volume, the author's effort is to try and prove that Canada owes nothing to England, that all those who favour the Canadian participation in the war are "revolutionists," that we are unduly paying a large tribute to the Empire.

In 1916, Mr. Bourassa supplemented his first book with a second pamphlet, entitled:—*"Yesterday, To-day, To-morrow,"* in French:—*"Hier, Aujourd'hui, Demain,"* in which he amplified the views expressed in the preceding volume.

I undertook to read Mr. Bourassa's works, and I must say that I was astonished at what I found therein. I felt very strongly that his erroneous views—without questioning their sincerity—were bound to pervert the opinion of my French compatriots, to enflame their prejudices, and to do a great deal of harm in promoting the ever dangerous conflict of race fanaticism. Over forty years of experience of public life had taught me how easy it is to introduce a prejudice in a man's mind, but how difficult it is to destroy it when once it has taken root.

CHAPTER VI.

What Do We Owe England?

To this question raised by Mr. Bourassa, and argued at length by himself in the negative, I answered by a chapter of my book:—"*L'Angleterre, le Canada et la Grand Guerre*"—"*England, Canada and the Great War.*"

Great Britain, ever since she came to the conclusion that the days of the old colonial policy were passed, and agreed that we should freely govern ourselves, with ministerial responsibility, within the powers set forth in our constitutional charter, has scrupulously respected our political liberty. We have administered our own affairs at our own free will. The Imperial Government never attempted to interfere with the development of our federal politics. They would surely have declined such interference, if it had been asked for.

As long as we form part of the British Empire, it is evident that we owe to England that loyalty which every colony owes to her mother-country. Granted by the Sovereign Power ruling Canada the freest institutions, having the best of reasons to be fully satisfied with our relations with Great Britain, we are in duty bound to be loyal to her flag. We must be true to our allegiance.

We have freely decided to incur the sacrifices we are making for the war. We have so decided because we considered it of the greatest importance, for the future of Humanity, that the German ambition for universal domination be foiled; that the British Empire be maintained; that France should continue a first class Power, as expressed by Mr. Asquith; that before all, and above all, the eternal principles of Right, Justice and Civilization, shall not be trampled upon by the terrific assault of teutonic barbarism. Moreover, we are also in duty bound to judge with fairness England's part in the great society of nations, and, especially, that she plays in the great events of the present crisis. Beyond doubt, a truly loyal Canadian must refrain from poisoning foreign opinion and that of his fellow British subjects against Great Britain in attributing her course to selfish interests, wilfully taking no account of her broad and admirable foreign policy, ever inspired by the steady desire to maintain peace.

In the first mentioned work, Mr. Bourassa lays great stress on the fact that for nearly a century and a half, previous to the South African War, Canada did not participate in the wars of the Empire. He extensively quotes from the documents and the discussions between Canada's representatives and the

Imperial Government, respecting the defence of our country, and that of the Empire herself. He concludes by pretending that the result of all these negotiations and conventions was the agreement that Canada would have only to attend to her own defence, and that Great Britain was always obliged to protect us against all outside attacks. From these pretensions he draws the startling conclusion that all those who do not stand by the conventions he did his best to emphasize are doing revolutionary work.

The answer to such extravagant notions is rather plain and easy. There was not the slightest necessity for the Nationalist leader to multiply lengthy quotations to prove what mere common sense settles at first thought:—

First:—That any country, whether it be independent or a colony, must defend itself when attacked by an enemy.

Second:—That a Sovereign State is bound to defend all the territory under its authority and covered by its flag.

But all this has nothing whatever to do with the very different question of Canada's participation, outside her own territory, in a war in which Great Britain is engaged, which participation Canada has freely, deliberately approved and ordered. Such was the case in 1914. The Parliament and the people of Canada at once realized that in the gigantic conflict into which Germany had drawn all the Great Powers of Europe, our future destiny as much as that of England herself was at stake. Without the slightest hesitation, unasked and unsolicited by the Mother Country, we decided that we were in duty bound to do our share to defend the great Empire of which we are a very important component part, and to help saving the world from tyrannical domination.

Much too often giving to words a meaning which they positively cannot convey, Mr. Bourassa argued at length to prove that the agreements, conventions, and understandings arrived at between the Imperial and Canadian Governments, at different dates, were a *solemn treaty*.

How false and untenable such a pretention is, surely needs no lengthy argument. International Law knows no treaties but those made between Sovereign States. It is most absurd to pretend that a Sovereign State can make a treaty between herself and its own colony. Where is the man with the slightest notion of Constitutional Government who would pretend, for instance, that the British North American Act is a treaty between Great Britain and Canada. It is an Act passed by the Legislative authority of the Sovereign State to which we belong, enacting the conditions under which Canada would enjoy the rights and privileges of constitutional self-government, participating in the exercise of Sovereignty within the limits of the powers enumerated in the Act creating the Dominion. It was precisely because we knew we were acting within the limits of those powers, that we decided to join with England and her Allies in the great war.

CHAPTER VII.

CANADA IS NOT A SOVEREIGN STATE.

As long as Canada will remain under the flag of Great Britain—and for one I hope it will yet be for many long years,—it is evident that it will not be a *"Sovereign State"* in the full sense of the word.

One can hardly believe that the Nationalist leader, at page 17 of his pamphlet —*"Hier, Aujourd'hui, Demain"*—*"Yesterday, To-day, To-morrow,"* opens a chapter with the title: *"Les Colonies autonomes sont des Etats Souverains."*—*"The autonomous colonies are Sovereign States."*

Mr. Bourassa was evidently led to the grievous error contained in the preceding title by a complete misapprehension of the true meaning of the word *"autonomous."* He took *"autonomy"* for *"Sovereignty,"* being under the delusion that the two are synonymous.

Any student of History knows, or ought to know, that after the war which culminated in the independence of the United States, England adopted an entirely new colonial policy. She was the first Sovereign Power, and has ever since remained the only one, to realize that the old system was doomed to failure, that it was worn out. Her leading statesmen, who always ranked amongst the most eminent the world over, were more and more convinced that the only safe colonial policy was that which would grant *"self-government"* to the colonies, trained to its harmonious working, for their interior management. The true meaning of this new policy was that several of the colonies were, by acts of the Imperial Parliament, called to the exercise of a share of the Sovereignty, well defined in their respective constitutional charters. Canada was one of the first British colonies to enjoy the advantages of such a large part of the Sovereign rights.

Such *"autonomous colonies"* as Canada, Australia, New Zealand, South Africa, Newfoundland, have been, and are to the present day, do not transform them into *"Sovereign States,"* enjoying full *"Sovereign powers."* They are not *"Independent States"* in the full sense of the word.

That Canada is not a Sovereign State is proved beyond doubt by the very fact that she could not amend or change her constitutional charter by her own power and without a new Imperial law. If the Nationalist leader's pretention was sound, any member of the House of Commons, or of the Senate, in Ottawa, could propose a bill to repeal the British North America Act, 1867, and to replace it by another constitutional charter. The very supposition is absurd. Can it be imagined that His Excellency the Governor-General could be advised by his responsible Ministers to sanction, in the name of His Majesty the Sovereign of Great Britain, a bill repealing an Act of the Imperial Parliament? Still it is exactly what Mr. Bourassa's theory amounts to.

Our constitutional charter does not only provide what is called our Federal,— or National—autonomy, but also the Provincial autonomy. The powers of both are well defined in the Imperial Act. The Provinces of the Dominion also exercise that share of the Sovereign rights delegated to them by the Imperial Parliament. Would the Nationalist leader draw the extravagant conclusion that the territory of any one of the Provinces cannot be declared in the "State of War" with a Foreign Power, by His Majesty the King, without the assent of the Ministers of that Province? Still that absurd proposition would not be more so than that affirming the necessity of the assent of the Canadian Cabinet, to a declaration of War involving Canada in an Imperial struggle.

The Sovereign right of declaring war to, and of making peace with, another independent State, is vested in the King of Great Britain, acting upon the advice of his responsible Ministers in the United Kingdom. To the Imperial Parliament belongs the constitutional authority to deal with the Imperial Foreign Affairs.

It is plain that when Great Britain is at War with another Sovereign State the whole territory of the British Empire is in the "State of War" with that Nation.

It is inconceivable that Mr. Bourassa has seriously pretended that Canada was not at war with the German Empire the very moment the British Empire was so in consequence of the violation by Germany of Belgian neutrality. One can hardly believe that he has propounded the fallacious constitutional doctrine that His Majesty "*the King of England hath not the right to declare Canada in the State of War without the assent of the Canadian Cabinet.*"

Where and when has the Nationalist leader discovered that the Canadian Ministers have the right to advise His Majesty upon all the questions pertaining to the Imperial Foreign Affairs? Any one conversant with the constitutional status of Canada knows that the Canadian Ministers have the right to advise the representative of the Sovereign only upon matters as defined by the British North America Act, 1867, and its amendments.

I was indeed very much surprised at the attempt of Mr. Bourassa to use the authority of Sir Erskine May in support of his erroneous pretension that the autonomous colonies of Great Britain were Sovereign States.

To all the students of the Constitutional History of England, Sir Erskine May is a very well known and appreciated writer. I have read his works several times over for many years. I was certain that he had never written anything to justify the Nationalist leader in quoting him as he did.

Here follows the paragraph of May's Constitutional History quoted by Mr. Bourassa in support of his own views:—

Parliament has recently pronounced it to be just that the Colonies which enjoy self-government, should undertake the responsibility and cost of their own military defence. To carry this policy into effect must be the work of time. But whenever it may be effected, the last material bond of connection with the Colonies will have been severed, and colonial states, acknowledging the honorary sovereignty of England, and fully armed for self-defence, as well against herself as others, will have grown out of the dependencies of the British Empire.

I must say that I am absolutely unable to detect one single word in the above quotation to authorize Mr. Bourassa to affirm that Sir Erskine May was of opinion that *"the autonomous colonies were Sovereign States."* The true meaning of the above extract is surely very plain. What does it say? It declares, what was a fact, that the British *Parliament has recently pronounced it to be just that the Colonies which enjoy self-government should undertake the responsibility and cost of their own military defence.*

Would the British Parliament have deemed it necessary to express such an opinion, if the Colonies had, then, been Sovereign States, consequently obliged, in duty bound, to defend themselves *alone* against any possible enemy. Surely not, for the obvious reason that Great Britain would have had no more responsibility for the defence of territories no longer covered by her flag and under her Sovereignty.

The very fact that the British Parliament thought proper, *under the then circumstances*, to say that the Colonies enjoying self-government should undertake to defend themselves, is the convincing proof that they were not Sovereign States.

The following sentence of May's quotation says:—*To carry this policy into effect must be the work of time.*

It is clear that the *policy* requiring the work of time to be carried into effect was not actually existent at the time Sir Erskine May was writing.

The extract quoted by Mr. Bourassa concludes by declaring that when such a policy *has* been finally adopted, the Colonies will have developed into Colonial States having *grown out of the dependencies of the British Empire.*

Evidently, when the Dominions of Canada, Australia, South Africa, New Zealand, will have grown out of the dependencies of the British Empire, they will no longer be Colonies of Great Britain. But when will that very important event take place? Surely, Sir Erskine May could not foresee. Even to-day Mr. Bourassa cannot say more than any one else. Pending that unforeseen outcome, the Dominions will remain parts of the British Empire under her

Sovereignty.

The above quotation was taken by Mr. Bourassa from the edition of Sir Erskine May's "Constitutional History" published in 1912. But they were first edited by the author in 1863. When has the Imperial Parliament adopted the above mentioned "*Resolution*"? It was voted in 1862—the 4th of March— more than fifty-six years ago. Quoted as it has been by Mr. Bourassa, it appears to have been only very recently adopted. The fact that it is more than half a century old, and was carried before the Federal Union of the Provinces, is a convincing proof that it has no bearing whatever upon the conditions of Canada's present colonial status. By the aforesaid "*Resolution*," the British House of Commons was only expressing the opinion that the time had come for the Colonies to undertake the responsibility and the cost of their defence. The "Resolution" does not say that Great Britain would no longer be called, in the exercise of the rights and duties of her Sovereignty, to defend her Colonial Empire.

By what reasoning can a mere expression of opinion by the English House of Commons be interpreted as at once transforming the Colonies into independent Sovereign States?

Any one somewhat conversant with the political events that led to the Federal Union of the Provinces knows that in applying to the British Parliament for the new Constitutional Charter, the Legislature of United Canada had a twofold object:—first, the settlement of the constitutional difficulties then pending between Upper and Lower Canada; secondly, a broader development of Canada and also of the British Empire. Such was the purpose of the coalition government formed in 1864. All the members of that Cabinet were strongly in favour of the maintenance of Canada's union with Great Britain. I have heard them expounding their views on what the future of Canada ought to be. I am positive that neither Sir John A. Macdonald, Sir Georges Cartier, the honorable Georges Brown, nor any of their colleagues, of both political parties, ever said a word which could be construed as expressing the opinion that the proposed Federal Union would make of Canada an independent Sovereign State. It is incredible that Mr. Bourassa should have so erroneously understood their real views so as to pretend that they favoured Confederation for that very purpose.

As a proof of his pretension, he quoted the following words of Sir John A. Macdonald, in the Legislative Assembly of old United Canada:—

"*With us the Sovereign, or, in this country the representative of the Sovereign, can act only on the advice of His Ministers, those Ministers being responsible to the people through Parliament.*"

Mr. Bourassa used the foregoing sentence in support of his contention that the King of England could not declare war without the assent of the Canadian Cabinet. It is impossible to understand how such a notion can be seriously held and expressed. His Majesty cannot ask nor accept such an advice, if it was tendered, for the very reason that the Canadian Cabinet has not the constitutional right to advise the King respecting the international relations of the Empire. And why? Precisely because the Canadian Ministers would not be responsible for their advice to the Imperial Parliament and to the electorate of the United Kingdom.

The true meaning of the above quoted sentence of Sir John A. Macdonald is very plain. Ministerial responsibility was the fundamental principle of the old Constitution, as it is of the Federal Charter. Sir John A. Macdonald was perfectly right in affirming that *"in Canada, as in England, the Sovereign could act only on the advice of His Ministers," that is to say on the advice of His responsible Ministers within the constitutional powers of our Parliament on all matters respecting which they had the constitutional right to advise His Majesty.*

Sir John A. Macdonald never said—he could not possibly say—that as Prime Minister of Canada, under the new Constitution, he would have the right to advise the Sovereign on all matters within the exclusive constitutional jurisdiction of the Imperial Parliament, for instance respecting the exercise of the Royal prerogative of declaring war against, or of making peace with, a foreign independent State. He has never propounded such an utterly false constitutional doctrine.

Mr. Bourassa went still further. He quoted the following sentence from Sir John A. Macdonald:—*"We stand with regard to the people of Canada precisely in the same position as the House of Commons in England stands with regard to the people of England."*

I was indeed most astonished to read Mr. Bourassa's inference from those words that Sir John A. Macdonald *had affirmed the absolute equality of powers of the Imperial and the Canadian Parliaments.*

If the opinion expressed by Sir John A. Macdonald could be so interpreted, he would have affirmed—what was radically wrong—that under the new Constitution, the Canadian Parliament would have, *concurrently with the Imperial Parliament*, absolutely the same powers. What did that mean? It meant that the Canadian Parliament, just as the Imperial Parliament, would have the right to edict laws establishing Home Rule in Ireland, regulating the government of India and the Crown Colonies, granting constitutional charters for the good government of the Australian and South African Dominions, &c., &c.

Surely it is not necessary to argue at any length to prove that Sir John A. Macdonald never for a moment entertained such an opinion. What he really said, in the above quoted words, was that within their constitutional jurisdiction, within the limits of their respective powers, the two Parliaments stood in the same position, *respectively*, with regard to the people of England and to the people of Canada. It was equivalent to saying—what was positively true—that the British Ministers and the British Parliament were responsible to the people of England, and that the Canadian Ministers and the Canadian Parliament were responsible to the people of Canada,—both of them within the limits of their respective constitutional powers.

If the Canadian Legislature had enjoyed all the constitutional powers of the British Parliament, she would not have been obliged to pass addresses asking the latter to enact a new charter creating the Federal Union of the Provinces. She could have repealed her then existing constitution and enacted the new one by her own authority. But that she could not do. She could not repeal the old, nor enact the new charter.

But the most extraordinary is that Mr. Bourassa went so far as to declare that Canada should have participated in the present war only as a *"Nation,"* meaning, of course, as an independent Sovereign State.

On reading such a preposterous proposition, at once it strikes one's mind most forcibly that if Canada had really had the power to intervene in the world's struggle as a "Nation," she would have had the equal right to the choice of three alternatives.

First:—Declare war against Germany and in favor of the Allies.

Second:—Remain neutral.

Third:—Declare war against Great Britain and fight for Germany.

For it is obvious that all the Sovereign States—and Canada like them all if she had been one of them—had the Sovereign Right to fight for or against Great Britain, or to remain neutral. Of course, I am merely explaining in its entirety the Right of a Sovereign State. I surely do not mean to say that Canada, had she really been such a State, would in any way have been justifiable in joining with Germany in her dastardly attempt to crush Civilization in the barbarous throes of her domination.

What would His Excellency the Governor-General have answered his Prime Minister advising him to declare war against England, he who represents His Majesty at Ottawa? Would he not have told him at once that the Canadian Prime Minister had no right whatever to give him such an advice; that Canada, being a British Colony, could not declare war against her Sovereign

State; that for the Canadian people to take up arms against England would be treasonable revolt?

It is absolutely incredible that a public man, aspiring to the leadership of his countrymen, can have been so completely lost to the sense of the Canadian constitutional situation as to boldly attempt to pervert their mind with such fallacious notions. He might as well pretend that the State of New York, for instance, has the Sovereign Right to declare war against the Government of the United States.

I, for one, cannot help wondering that any one can seriously think that a colony, always pretending to remain loyally so, can wage war against her Sovereign State. I feel sure that all sensible men do share my views on that point.

CHAPTER VIII.

GERMAN ILLUSIONS.

When Germany threw the gauntlet to the Powers of the "Entente," she labored under the delusion that the war would most surely break down the British Empire. She was determined to do her utmost to that end. But she utterly failed in her criminal efforts.

Strongly bound by ties of affection and constitutional freedom, the great autonomous Dominions and Colonies at once rallied with courage and patriotism to the defence of the Empire, of Justice, of Right and Civilization. India,—that great Indian Empire—to the utter disappointment of Germany, has stood admirably by Great Britain ever since the outbreak of the War, by her noble contributions of man-power and her munificent generosity of very large sums of money, in one instance amounting to $500,000,000.

The Crown Colonies have also done their share of duty with great devotion.

The admirable result which for the last four years has been shining bright and glorious all over the world, is that, contrary to teutonic expectations, the war, far from breaking asunder the British Empire, has wonderfully solidified her mighty edifice, by an intensity of loyalty to her free institutions, to her glorious flag, which the enjoyment of the blessings of peace would not have proved so easily possible.

CHAPTER IX.

THE NATIONALIST ERROR.

The leaders of our Nationalist School have for years strenuously laboured to pervert the mind of our French-Canadian compatriots by the false pretensions that we were, in some mysterious way, coerced to participate in the European War. Even previous to the days of the South African conflict, they boldly took the stand that Canada should, on no account, and under no circumstances whatever, participate in what they called the Wars of the Empire—*les guerres de l'Empire*. Canada, they affirmed, had only to defend her own territory if attacked.

Fully appreciating how insidious and dangerous such theories were, I endeavoured to show, as forcibly as I could, that there had been no attempt by England at coercion of this Dominion to help her in the struggle against Germany. Of course, as previously explained, Great Britain being at war with the German Empire, the whole British Empire was at war. But no one in England ever intended to propose to force the colonies to engage actively into the fight. The Imperial Parliament would certainly not have taken into consideration any such proposition.

But is it not plain and beyond discussion that we, *ourselves*, had the undoubted right to intervene in the war to the extent that we would consider it our bounden duty to do so?

Evidently we could not remain neutral in the great conflict. At the very moment that Great Britain was at war with Germany, Canada, a British Colony, was part and parcel of the belligerent Sovereign State, the British Empire. By an incredible misconception, the Nationalist leaders confounded *neutrality* with *non-participation* in the war, if we had so decided.

To be, or not to be, neutral, was not within our constitutional rights. If Germany, either by land or by sea, had attacked our territory, as she had the undoubted belligerent right to do, would it have availed us an iota to implore her mercy by affirming that we were neutral? Could we have pretended that she was violating neutral territory?

No one with the least notion of International Law would for a moment hesitate to give the true answers to those questions.

But the very different question to participate, or not, in the war, was for us alone to decide according to our constitutional charter. We have freely, deliberately, decided to do our share in the great war. We continue and persevere in our noble task, freely and deliberately.

It is admitted by all that under the actual constitutional organization of the Empire, the Imperial Parliament could not require the autonomous colonies to participate in the war. But no one can assuredly deny to that Parliament the right, in the case of an imminent peril, to formulate the desire that the autonomous colonies would help Great Britain to conjure the threatened calamity.

But, in the present case, the Imperial Parliament has not even been under the necessity of expressing such a legitimate wish, for the obvious reason that the colonies at once took their patriotic stand in favor of the cause of England and her Allies. If the colonies had not so decided, of their own free will, it is most likely that the Imperial Parliament would not have expressed the wish for the assistance of the Dominions overseas.

The hearty support granted by the colonies to Great Britain, to develop its full value, had to be spontaneous, enthusiastic. Such it was, such it is, and such it will be to the last day of the conflict which victorious conclusion we are so strongly determined to achieve.

CHAPTER X.

HAD CANADA THE RIGHT TO HELP ENGLAND?

Not satisfied to do the best it could to persuade our French-Canadian countrymen that they had been coerced into the war by England, our "Nationalist School" extensively used the argument that Canada had not the right to intervene into the European struggle. I refuted this erroneous pretension by the following propositions, the very essence of our constitutional rights and liberties:—

1.—The Canadian Cabinet had the undoubted constitutional right to advise His Excellency the Governor-General to approve the measures to be taken to give effect to their decision to participate in the war, decision and measures for which they were responsible to the Canadian Parliament and to the Canadian Electorate.

2.—The Canadian Parliament had the undoubted constitutional right to approve or disapprove the decision and the measures of the Cabinet. Parliament approved that decision and those measures, acting within their constitutional right.

3.—Even at the time I was writing, it could evidently be affirmed that the Canadian Electorate had approved the stand taken by both the Canadian Cabinet and the Canadian Parliament according to well known and defined constitutional usages.

Was it not proved beyond reasonable controversy, that the Canadian people heartily approved the decision of their Parliament to help in the great war?

Let me summarize the evidence as follows:—

1.—The war policy of the Cabinet, at the special session called in August, 1914, for that very purpose, was unanimously approved by Parliament, no Senator and no Member of the House of Commons moving to censure the responsible ministers for their decision to have Canada to participate in the war. The two great political parties have solemnly sanctioned that decision.

2.—Public opinion was also very strongly proved by the almost unanimity of the public press patriotically supporting the stand taken by Parliament. The exceptions were so few, that, as usual, they contributed to emphasize the soundness of the general rule.

3.—During the three years following the decision of the Canadian Parliament, a great number of large public meetings were held throughout Canada, and addressed by many leading and influential citizens all approving the action of Parliament. The meetings enthusiastically concurred in the powerful indorsation of the war policy of the speakers.

In a few public gatherings some disapproval was expressed, but not one meeting would go to the length of passing "Resolutions" censuring the Cabinet and the Parliament of Canada, or declaring that our Dominion should not have interfered into the war.

4.—Not one petition against the Canadian intervention into the war was addressed to Parliament.

5.—Leading Clergymen, of all denominations; leaders of political associations almost of all shades of opinion; financial, industrial, commercial leaders, all of them approved the patriotic interference of Canada into the war.

6.—The evident general approval of the unanimous decision, taken in 1916, to extend the Parliamentary term.

7.—The wonderful success of the public loans raised for war purposes.

8.—The enlightened and generous patriotism with which the country has accepted and paid war taxation.

9.—But, above all, the voluntary recruiting of four hundred thousand men of all social conditions who have rallied to the flag of the Empire for the defence of her existence and for the triumph of Civilization and Justice.

I, therefore, drew the undeniable conclusion that, contrary to the "Nationalist" pretension, Canada was participating in the war in the most regular constitutional way, without even the shadow of a breach of our Canadian autonomy, of our constitutional rights and liberties.

CHAPTER XI.

The Duty of Canada.

Having affirmed that Canada had no right to interfere in the war, the "Nationalist" leaders at once concluded that she was not in duty bound to do so. That most discreditable inference was, of course, the natural sequence of the wrong principle aforesaid. They further drew the conclusion that it was no part of the duty of Canadians to join the Colors to help winning the war.

It was in flat contradiction of those erroneous notions that I positively declared, in my letter dedicating my book to my French Canadian compatriots, that *"in defending with the most sincere conviction the sacred cause of the Allies, I am doing my duty as a free subject of the British Empire, as a citizen of Canada and of the Province of Quebec, as a son of France, as a devoted servant of Justice and Right."*

Very narrow minded indeed is the man who has no higher conception of his duty than the one limiting him to the observance of positive and negative laws enacted by the legitimate authority to protect society and every one of its members.

When England, together with the other leading nations, was brutally challenged by Germany, and threatened in her very national existence, it is beyond comprehension that Canada, and all the British colonial possessions overseas, could so mistake their bounden duty as to refuse rushing to help the Mother Country in such a trying occurrence. Moreover, have we not, merely as men, duties to perform to protect Civilization against the deadly attack of barbarism, to have Justice and Right triumphant in international relations?

It is a matter of deep wonder to me that any one could have been so blind as not to perceive that in joining with Great Britain to defend the cause of the Allies, we were surely defending our own territory, our own soil, our own homes. How incredible was the "Nationalist" contention that we should have waited for the actual German attack of our land before mustering our resources of resistance. Who could not see, at a glance, that if Germany had, as it fully expected, easily triumphed over the combined forces of France, England and Russia, it would have been sheer madness to attempt resisting the victorious onslaught of a few hundred thousands of her veteran soldiers, whose valour would have been doubled by the enthusiasm of their European conquest.

After mature consideration of the possible results of the disastrous defeat of the combined efforts of the Allies, both on land and sea, the conclusion was forced upon my mind that Germany, ferociously elated by such a wonderful success, would no doubt have exacted from England the cession of Canada to her Empire. So that without even firing a gun against our territory, our wide Dominion would have been instantly transferred from the British to the German Sovereignty. I shuddered at such a vision, and still more deeply realized how much we, Canadians, were all in duty bound to help the Allies in crushing Prussian militarism.

CHAPTER XII.

THE SOUDANESE AND SOUTH AFRICAN WARS.

In the two previously mentioned pamphlets, Mr. Bourassa argued at length to prove that Canada had been led to intervene in the great European war as a consequence of her intervention in the South African War. It is well known throughout the Dominion that the South African conflict was the occasion chosen by the "Nationalist" leader to proclaim his doctrine that the autonomous colonies should have nothing to do with the wars of the Empire —LES GUERRES DE L'EMPIRE. He then strongly opposed Canadian support of Great Britain in her struggle in South Africa.

In one of his pamphlets, Mr. Bourassa affirmed that the Government of Sir John A. Macdonald had, in 1884, refused the request of the Imperial Government to interfere in its favour in the Soudanese war. Well aware of the events of this struggle, I positively knew that the "Nationalist" leader's assertion was not borne out by the facts, and was historically false. I considered it my duty, in a special chapter, to explain fully the circumstances of the case to my French Canadian countrymen.

It should be well remembered that England was brought into the Soudanese conflict on account of her relations with Egypt, which she had delivered from the Turkish yoke.

Mr. Bourassa prefaced his above mentioned affirmation by recalling the fact that it was in consideration of the Soudanese difficulties that *"for the first time in the history of the Colonial Empire of Great Britain, offers of armed support were made by the autonomous colonies."*

Is it not evident that if—as was true—such offers were made spontaneously by the Colonies, it cannot be pretended that the proffered armed support was asked by England. If England did not solicit such support, it is plain that Sir John A. Macdonald and his Cabinet could not refuse what was never applied for.

What are the true historical facts?

In November 1884, General Laurie, who has represented one of the electoral divisions of Nova Scotia at Ottawa, who has also held a seat in the British House of Commons, took the initiative to propose to raise a Canadian regiment for the campaign in the Soudan. In the regular official way, General Laurie's offer was addressed to the Secretary of State for the Colonies, Lord

Derby. The Imperial Government declined the offer.

On the 7th of February, 1885, on hearing the news of the disaster of Khartoum, which caused great excitement in England, and naturally created a strong public feeling to avenge the outrage, General Laurie, always enthusiastic, tendered anew his services. He was not the only Canadian officer wishing to go and fight the cruel Soudaneses. A member of the Canadian Parliament, Colonel Williams, commanding the 46th volunteer battalion of Durham-East, also desired to take part in the African campaign with his regiment. On the 9th of February, 1885, he tendered his proposition to Sir Charles Tupper, then High Commissioner in London, who sent it to the Colonial Office.

On the 10th of February, His Excellency the Governor General, Lord Lansdowne, cabled to the Colonial Secretary that the offers of military service were very numerous. This spontaneous movement, so rapidly spreading, was the forerunner of those of 1899 and 1914. Thirty years ago, and long before, there were brave men in Canada. There always have been and ever will be.

These news were no doubt very encouraging for the Imperial authorities.

Lord Derby, thanking Lord Lansdowne, begged him to say "*Whether they* (the offers of service) *are sanctioned and recommended by the Dominion Government.*"

On the 12th of February, Lord Lansdowne answered Lord Derby that the Dominion Government was ready to approve recruiting in Canada for service in Egypt or elsewhere, provided that the men would be enlisted under the authority of the Imperial Army Discipline Act, and the expense paid by the Imperial Treasury.

It consequently follows from the above despatches that the Soudanese campaign offered to many officers of our volunteer Militia the long wished for opportunity to freely tender their services to the Imperial Government; that the British authorities never applied to the Canadian Government, then presided by Sir John A. Macdonald, for armed support in Soudanese Africa; that, on being officially informed of the offers of service received by His Excellency the Governor General, the Colonial Secretary, before accepting or declining them, enquired if the Canadian Government sanctioned and recommended them; that the Governor General answered him in the affirmative, the recruiting to be made according to the Imperial Military Act at the expense of the Imperial exchequer.

On the 16th of February, the War Minister, then the Marquis of Hartington, informed the Colonial Secretary that he had come to the conclusion to decline with thanks the offers of service from Canada, for the reason that it would have taken too long a time to recruit and organize the regiments offered by General Laurie and Colonel Williams.

Was I not right, when I refuted Mr. Bourassa's assertion, in saying that if a *refusal* was *then* given, it was by the British Government who had received the freely tendered services, and not by the Canadian Government, to whom no demand of armed support had been made by Great Britain?

If it is indeed very astonishing that Mr. Bourassa should have taken the responsibility to affirm that the Government of Sir John A. Macdonald had refused to help Great Britain in the Soudanese campaign, it is easy to understand his object in so doing. His purpose was to convince his French Canadian readers that the political leaders at the head of the Government, in 1899 and 1914, together with the Canadian Parliament, had, in a revolutionary way, reversed the traditional policy of Canada of non-intervention in the "wars of the Empire"—*les guerres de l'empire*. And to achieve his end, so detrimental to the best interests of the Dominion, he did not hesitate to draw an absolutely erroneous conclusion from undeniable historical facts.

The "Nationalist" leader was very anxious to charge the chieftains of the two great political parties with an equal responsibility for what he terms a "Revolution" in our relations with the Mother Country. With this object constantly in view, he pretended that the intervention of Canada in the South African War created the precedent which brought about the Dominion participation in the European war, in 1914. In order to stir up to the utmost the prejudices of the French Canadians, he boldly qualified the South African conflict as an *infamous crime* on the part of England.

Unfortunately, the true history of the difficulties which culminated in the Boer War of 1899, was at the time little known throughout Canada, and even less particularly in the Province of Quebec. At the outbreak of the struggle, wishing to form a sound opinion of the causes of which it was the direct outcome, I made an exhaustive study of the South African question, beginning at the very inception of the Dutch settlement dating as far back as 1652, the year during which the Dutch East India Company occupied Table Bay. Six years later, in 1658, French Huguenots reached South Africa, joining with the Dutch Reformists, who rather energetically did all they could to assimilate them. Still later on, besides some few German immigrants, a third group of Europeans settled on the African coast. They were Englishmen.

All the Europeans, on landing in South Africa, few in numbers, had at once to contend with the black race numbering many millions. The history of the long struggle between European civilization, represented by the English and Dutch immigrants, and African barbarity, is indeed very interesting. Carefully read and studied in all its bearings, it strongly impressed upon my mind the conviction that had it not been for the timely armed protection they often solicited and received from England, the Dutch Boers would certainly have been annihilated by the tribes of the black race. They could not hope to successfully resist the onslaughts to which they were repeatedly submitted. They were saved from utter destruction by the strong arm of Great Britain, occupying an important strategical position by her Cape Colony. The British Government had favoured the settlement of the sons of England in South Africa, for the purpose of assuring, by a powerful naval station, the freedom of communication with the great regions soon to develop into her vast Indian Empire.

How, and under what circumstances, was British Sovereignty established in South Africa? I considered this question the most important to ascertain, in order to judge fairly the history of the last century in those regions. It was settled by the Peace Congress of Vienna, in 1815. All the European nations represented at that congress, have sanctioned British Sovereignty in South Africa upon the condition of the payment by England to the Kingdom of the Netherlands, of which Holland was then a part, of the sum of $30,000,000. Consequently the Sovereign Rights of Great Britain in South Africa were henceforth undeniable.

In my French book, I somewhat extensively summarized the development of the British and Dutch groups of settlers in South Africa. It is well known that the Boers are of Dutch origin. That a rivalry did develop between the two national elements, is not to be wondered at by any one having some knowledge of the history of the world.

I do not consider it necessary to go at any length in relating the vicissitudes of the conflict between the aspirations of the Boer element and the undoubted rights of British suzerainty. As a rule they are sufficiently well known by my English readers.

But I wish to emphasize the two undeniable facts: first, that throughout this protracted contest, England did perseveringly try to favour South Africa with the largest possible measure of political liberty. Second, that the crisis was finally brought about by the persistent determination of the Government of Pretoria to refuse justice to the Uitlanders and to the British capitalists who, at the urgent request of President Kruger, had invested many millions in the development of the very valuable mines recently discovered in the Transvaal territory.

Though England had agreed to the establishment of the two Republics of the Transvaal and Orange, she had maintained her suzerainty on those territories, which suzerainty the Government of Pretoria had again recognized by the

Convention of 1884.

The most convincing proof that England did not intend any unfair design against the South African Republics, is the fact that she did not prepare to resist the armed attack of the Government of Pretoria which could be easily foreseen by the intense organization they were evidently making to impose Boer supremacy in South Africa.

In his very unjust appreciation of the policy of Great Britain in South Africa, Mr. Bourassa kept no account whatever of the very important fact that war was declared against England by the South African Republic. How could Great Britain have been guilty of a hideous crime in not bowing to the dictate of President Kruger and his Government, as the "Nationalist" leader said, is beyond comprehension.

England was absolutely within her right in accepting the challenge of the Government of Pretoria, and fighting to maintain her flag and her Sovereignty in South Africa.

Fortunately, the South African War, characterized by deeds of heroism on both sides, has had the most satisfactory conclusion. It is to be hoped that for many long years the future of that great country is settled with all the blessings that political liberty and free institutions will surely confer on that important part of the British Empire. The Boers themselves have fully recognized that their own national development cannot be better guaranteed and safeguarded than by the powerful Sovereignty pledged to their protection, on the only condition of their loyal allegiance to the flag waving on the fair land where they can multiply in peace, prosperity and happiness. The enthusiasm and the admirable courage with which they have rallied to the support of Great Britain and her Allies in the present war, is the best evidence how much they appreciate the advantages of their new conditions in the great South African Dominion destined to such a grand future.

I most sincerely deplore the persistent efforts of the "Nationalist" leader to pervert more and more the mind of my French Canadian countrymen by his so very unfair appreciation of the nature of the South African conflict. It was with the hope of counteracting them that I introduced a special chapter in my French edition explaining, as fully as I could, though in a condensed form, the South African question.

The assertion that the participation of Canada in the present European war was the sequence of the precedent of our intervention in the South African struggle, is also most injustifiable and untenable. Had Canada taken no part whatever in the South African War, it would not have made the least difference with regard to the decision of the Canadian people to support Great

Britain and the Allies in their gigantic effort to put an end to Prussian terrorism. The assertion which I most emphatically contradict could have no other object but to prejudice the public mind against Canadian intervention in any of the wars of the Empire—*les guerres de l'empire.*

CHAPTER XIII.

BRITISH AND GERMAN ASPIRATIONS COMPARED.

In the attempt to justify his opposition to the Canadian armed support of the Allies' cause, Mr. Bourassa repeatedly asserted that Great Britain was as much as Germany aspiring to rule the whole world. He pretends that there is no difference between Anglo-Saxonism and Germanism.

How unjust and dangerous is such a doctrine is evident to any fair minded man. It was no doubt calculated to prejudice the French Canadians against Great Britain, by telling them that the sacrifices they were called upon to make were imposed upon them only to favour the British determination to reach the goal of her ambition:—universal domination.

I strongly repudiated such assertions and vindicated England's course and policy.

To accuse Great Britain to aspire to universal domination is a most unwarranted charge, contradicted by the whole history of the last century during which she was the most determined supporter of peace.

Though one of the great Powers of the world, England never undertook to organize a large standing army. How could she aspire to the world's domination without a complete military organization comprising many millions of men, is what I am unable to understand.

Mr. Bourassa's argument to prove his assertion is based on the efforts of England to maintain and develop her naval forces so as to guarantee her supremacy on the high seas of the world. How he failed to realize that Great Britain, on account of her insular position, close to the European continent, is by nature itself bound, of sheer necessity, to protect herself by the strength of her military naval power, is beyond comprehension. Supremacy on the seas is for the Mother Country a mere question of national existence,—to be or not to be. But supremacy on the seas cannot, and will never, permit England to attain anything like universal domination. And why? For the obvious reason that Great Britain is not, and never can become, a continental Power, in the exact sense of the word.

I explained, conclusively, I believe, that the case would be very different if Germany succeeded in her efforts to supplant England's supremacy on the seas. When the Berlin Government undertook to build a huge military fleet, Germany was the greatest continental military Power. What were her expectations when she adopted that threatening naval policy? The Berlin authorities were very confident that when they would decide to bring on the great war for which they had been strenuously preparing for half a century, they would in a few months have continental Europe at their feet and under their sway. Triumphant over Europe they would have at once dominated Asia and a great part of Africa. The next surest way for the German Empire to reach universal domination was to break England's power on the seas. What is impossible for England to accomplish, on account of her insular position, Germany, being a continental Empire, could achieve if she became mistress of the seas.

The present war is the proof evident that the mighty power of England on the seas has been the salvation of her national existence and, almost equally, that of France and Italy. It kept the oceans open for the trade of all the Allied and neutral nations. He is willingly blind, intellectually, the man who does not see that deprived of the matchless protection of her naval forces, Great Britain could be starved and subdued in a few months by an enemy ruling the waves against her.

Is it possible to suppose that any man aspiring to help moulding the public opinion of his countrymen, ignores that with the relatively small extent of the territory it can devote to agricultural production, Great Britain can never feed her actual population of over forty-five millions, most likely to reach sixty millions in the not very distant future. Consequently how unjust, how extravagant, is it to accuse England of any aspiration to dominate the world by means of the sacrifices she is absolutely bound to make for the only sake of her self-defence, her self-protection.

If he does not know, I will no doubt cordially oblige the "Nationalist" leader by informing him that Great Britain, usually importing food products to the amount of seven to eight hundred millions of dollars, for many years past, required as much as a billion dollars worth of them in the war year of 1915. It is so easy to foresee that the continual increase of the population of the United Kingdom, by the new large developments which will surely follow the war in all industrial, commercial and financial pursuits, will cause a relative increase in the importations of food products likely to reach, and even exceed before long, an average total annual value of a billion and a quarter dollars.

None of the European continental Powers has the same imperious reasons as England to take the proper means to guarantee her control of the seas. How is it then that Germany is the only Power to object to England's policy, if it is not for the ultimate object to attain universal domination by the overthrow of Great Britain's ascendency on the wide oceans, which would permit her to realize her long cherished aim by the combined powerful effort of her gigantic military forces both on land and sea.

With regard to England's naval supremacy, the "Nationalist" leader is also committed to other opinions which I strongly contradicted. He entirely forgets that beyond the sea coast limits, well defined by International Law, no Sovereign rights can be claimed on the high seas. The navigation of the ocean is free to all nations by nature itself. Has any Government ever entertained the foolish idea that the broad Atlantic could, for instance, be divided into so many parts as the European, Asiatic, or American continents, over which several States could exercise Sovereign powers? No Chinese Wall can be built on the seas.

My own view of the case, which I believe to be the correct one, is that England's naval supremacy means nothing more nor less than the police of the seas, and the protection of the flags of all the Nations navigating them, besides being, of course and necessarily, the guarantee of her National existence.

Blind also, intellectually, is the British subject not sufficiently inspired by the true sense of the duties of Loyalty, who does not understand that once Great Britain's maritime power would be crushed and the United Kingdom either conquered or obliged to an humiliating peace which would ruin all her future prospects, the Colonial Empire would equally be at the mercy of the victorious enemy of the Mother Country.

With the most earnest conviction, I have tried, to the best of my ability, to persuade my French-Canadian compatriots of the inevitable dangers ahead if the false views which were so persistingly impressed upon their minds were ever to prevail, and the aim they undoubtedly favour to be realized.

Another argument widely used by our "Nationalist" School to influence the opinion of the French Canadians against Canada's participation in the war, was that Great Britain herself was not doing what she ought to win the victory. I have personally heard this false objection repeated by many— unconsciously of course—who were influenced in so saying by the "Nationalist" press.

No more unfair charge could have been made against England. I could not help being indignant at reading it, knowing as I did, by daily acquired information what an immense effort the United Kingdom had been making, from the very beginning of the hostilities, to play its powerful part in the great war into which it had nobly decided to enter to avenge its honour, to defend the Empire and the whole world against German barbarous militarism.

I have already commented on the immense service guaranteed to the Allied nations by the British fleet. To illustrate the wonderful and admirable military effort of Great Britain, I will quote some very important figures from the most interesting Report of the British War Cabinet, for the year 1917, presented to Parliament by Command of His Majesty.

Under the title *"Construction and Supply"* the Report says:—

During the past year the Naval Service has undergone continual expansion in order to enable it to meet every demand made upon it, not only in the seas surrounding these islands, but in the Mediterranean, the Persian Gulf, the Red Sea, the Arctic Ocean, the Pacific, and the Atlantic, where it has co-operated with the Naval forces of the Allies. The displacement tonnage of the Royal Navy in 1914 was 2,400,000 tons. To-day it has increased by 75 per cent. (—**making a total of 4,200,000 tons** —). The ships and vessels of all kinds employed in the Naval Service in September, 1914, after the whole of the mobilisation had been completed, had a tonnage of just over 4 million; now the figure is well over 6 million. Transports, fleet attendants and overseas oilers and similar auxiliary vessels at the outbreak of war numbered 23; the Admiralty to-day control nearly 700 such craft. The strength of the personnel, which was 145,000, has been increased to 420,000.

From these brief particulars regarding the ships and their manning, an estimate can be formed of the expansions that have been made in the auxiliary services, such as guns, torpedoes, munitions, and stores of all kinds, anti-submarine apparatus, mines, &c., and some idea is gained of the demands that have been made upon the great army of workers on shore, the men in the Royal dockyards and arsenals, in the shipyards, the engine shops, and the factories, without whose help the Fleet could not be maintained as a fighting force.

As regards warship and auxiliary ship construction, the output during the last 12 months has been between three and four times the average annual output for the few years preceding the war.

The Admiralty now control all the dry docks in the country,...—250 merchant ships are being repaired each week, either in dry dock or afloat.

Since the beginning of the war, 31,470 British war vessels have been placed in dock or on the slips (—**as many as 225 being repaired in one week**—).... These figures do not include repair work carried out to the vessels of our Allies....

The Transport Service is of the highest importance in carrying on the war. What has been the achievement of England on that score? Under the title: —*"Transportation"* the War Cabinet Report proves its immensity as follows: —

The record of what has been done by the transport services for the Armies of the Allies shows a stupendous amount of work accomplished, which constitutes one of the brilliant achievements of the war. There had been transported overseas up till the end of August, 1917, the last date for which complete statistics are available—some:—13 million human beings —combatants, wounded, medical personnel, refugees, prisoners, &c.; 2 million horses and mules; 1/2 million vehicles; 25 million tons of explosive and supplies for the armies; ... 51 million tons of coal and oil fuel for the use of our Fleets, our Armies, and to meet the needs of our Allies.

The operations of the seas are on such a large scale that it is difficult to realize all that is involved in sea transportation; for example, over 7,000 personnel are transported, and more than 30,000 tons of stores and supplies have to be imported daily into France for the maintenance of our own army. About 567 steamers, of approximately 1 3/4 million tons, are continually employed in the service of carrying troops and stores to the Armies in France and to the forces in various theatres of war in the East.

We all know that the Berlin Government expected that the submarine campaign would result in an early final victory for the Central Empires. Herr von Bethmann Hollweg, then the Imperial Chancellor, said:—"*The Blockade must succeed within a limited number of weeks, within which America cannot effectively participate in the operations.*"

How he was mistaken, and extravagant were his expectations, events have proved. This sentence is also proof evident that he realized how effective the United States effort would become, if the submarine campaign did not succeed within a few weeks.

The iniquitous submarine campaign, re-opened early in the year 1917, "*added materially to the responsibilities of the Navy. To meet this new and serious menace drastic steps had to be taken to supplement those adopted in the previous December and January.*"

The Report adds:—

A large number of new destroyers have been built and at the same time auxiliary patrol services have been expanded enormously so as to deal with the nefarious submarine and minelaying methods of the enemy. Before the outbreak of the war there were under 20 vessels employed as minesweepers and on auxiliary patrol duties. To-day the number of craft used for these purposes at home and abroad is about 3,400, and is constantly increasing.

A new feature of the means adopted for the protection of trade against submarines has been a return to the convoy system as practised in bygone wars. It has been markedly effective in reducing the losses. During the last few months over 90 per cent. of all vessels sailing in all the Atlantic trades were convoyed....

The Royal Naval Air Service at the outbreak of war possessed a personnel of under 800; at the present moment the numbers approach 46,000 and are continually increasing.... Mention must also be made of the great value of the air services in combating the submarine menace round our coasts.... Illustrating their extent it may be stated that in one week the aircraft patrol round the British coasts alone flies 30,000 miles.

The general result of the German attack, therefore, though serious enough, is far from unprecedented. In the two years after Trafalgar, when our command of the sea was unquestioned, we still lost 1,045 merchant ships by capture, and in the whole period from 1794 to 1875 we lost over 10,000 merchant ships.

Nor should we lose sight of the very heavy losses sustained by the enemy in the present war. At the commencement of hostilities, Germany had 915 merchant ships abroad, of which only 158 got home safely; the remainder within a few days were cleared from the oceans, either captured or driven to shelter in neutral ports. In the aggregate the German Mercantile Marine consisted of over 5 million tons of shipping; at the present time nearly half of this has been sunk or captured by ourselves or our Allies, while the bulk of the rest is lying useless in harbour.

Let me now refer to the military effort of Great Britain. Under the title: —"*Strength of the Army,*" &c., the War Cabinet Report gives the following most inspiring figures.

The effort which the British nations have made under the one item of "Provision of Men for the Armed Forces of the Crown" amounts to not less than 7,500,000 men, and of these 60.4 per cent. have been contributed by England, 8.3 per cent. by Scotland, 3.7 per cent. by Wales, 2.3 per cent. by Ireland, 1.2 per cent. by the Dominions and the Colonies, while the remainder, 13.3 per cent., composed of native fighting troops, labour corps, carriers, &c., represent the splendid contribution made by India and our various African and other Dependencies.

Royal Artillery.—The personnel of the Royal Artillery increased 17.6 per cent., between August, 1916, and August, 1917.

In the first nine months of 1917 the supply of modern anti-aircraft guns in the field increased 44 per cent., that of field guns 17 per cent., of field-howitzers 26 per cent., of heavy guns 40 per cent., of medium howitzers 104 per cent., of heavy howitzers 16 per cent., and of heavy-guns on railway mountings 100 per cent.; these last have an increased range of about 35 per cent.... We have also supplied large numbers of heavy guns and trench mortars to our Allies in different theatres of war.

The Medical Service has continued to expand with the growth of the Army and its strength is now largely in excess of our whole original Expeditionary Force.... More than 17,000 women are employed as nurses and over 28,000 others are engaged in military hospitals on various forms of work.... Hospitals in the United Kingdom now number more than 2,000.

The health of the troops in the United Kingdom is actually better than the peace rate; the same is the case in France, excluding admissions to hospital by reason of wounds.

The above quoted figures prove that out of a total of 7,500,000 men for the Armed Forces of the British Crown, Great Britain—the United Kingdom—had contributed, at the end of last year, 5,625,000, out of which number the shore of England and Wales amounted to 4,800,000. The British Colonial Empire's contribution had been 1,875,000.

At the date of the current year—August, 1918—I am writing, I can safely calculate that the number of men for the Armed Forces of the British Crown —using the words of the Official Report above quoted—has reached, at least, *the grand and magnificent total of 8,000,000.* The percentage of respective contributions of the United Kingdom and the Colonial Empire no doubt remaining the same, the relative number of each of them is,—for the United Kingdom 6,000,000; for the Colonies 2,000,000.

I consider the War Cabinet Report of 1917 so interesting, so encouraging, that my readers will, I am confident, kindly bear with me in a few more very important quotations, the full Report itself having had only a very limited circulation in Canada.

TRANSPORT.

In addition to the prodigious Naval effort of England, both military and mercantile, previously illustrated, Great Britain has most powerfully contributed to the fighting operations on land by an immense improvement in transportation facilities by railway construction in all British theatres of war.

The Report says:—

> In all these theatres railways have come to play a more and more important part. In France a vast light railway system has been created, involving the supply during the present year of approximately 1,700 miles of track and the whole of the equipment.... Exclusive of these light railway systems, the total amount of permanent railway track supplied complete to all theatres of war is about 3,600 miles. In Egypt the railway crossing the desert from the Suez Canal has now reached and passed Gaza. In Mesopotamia the rapid and successful movements of our troops have only been made possible by the construction of a whole series of lines since the beginning of 1917. The development of road-building has been on a similar scale, and the shipments of material, equipment and stores for these two purposes during the last nine months have averaged 200,000 tons a month. Much labour has also been spent in the organisation of an Overland Line of Communication through France and Italy to the Mediterranean in order to save shipping. This line was opened for personnel traffic in June, 1917, and for goods traffic early in August.

In France the conveyance of supplies of all kinds to our armies along the French rivers and canals is performed by a large fleet of tugs, barges, and self-propelled barges. The fleet thus employed in France consists of over 700 vessels, and the tonnage carried by it averages over 50,000 tons per week.

THE AIR SERVICE.

In a recital indicating generally what steps have been taken in matters of administration and control, the Report says:—

> From the point of view of defence, the new arm presented problems pregnant with at least equal importance. The proud and ancient inviolability of these islands was being challenged in a new and startling fashion, and the seriousness of the problem was added to by the fact that the geographical position of the capital of the Empire rendered it particularly inviting to attack from the air.

Respecting the supply of Aircraft, the Report says that:—

In endeavoring to describe the measures taken to meet the aircraft needs of the Navy and Army, the writer is at once confronted by the fact that the information desired by the country is precisely the information desired by the enemy. What the country wants to know is what has been the expansion in our Air Services; whether we have met and are meeting all the demands of the Navy and of the Army, both for replacement of obsolete machines by the most modern types, and for the increase of our fighting strength in the air; what proportion of the national resources in men, material and factories is being devoted to aviation; what the expansion is likely to be in the future. These are precisely the facts which we should like to know with regard to the German air service, and for that reason it would be inadmissible for us to supply Germany with corresponding information about ourselves by publishing a statement on the subject.

It can be said that the expansion of our Air Services is keeping pace generally with the growing needs of the Navy and the Army.

In Chapter VIII, under the heading:—"*The Ministry of Munitions in 1917*," the following is read:—

The number of persons engaged in the production of munitions in October, 1917, was 2,022,000 men and 704,000 women, as compared with 1,921,000 men and 535,000 women in January. They have thus been increased during the past six months at the rate of 11,000 men and 19,000 women per month. These numbers include those employed in Government and in private establishments, in the principal munition industries, chemical and explosive trades, engineering and munition plants, furnaces and foundries, in shipbuilding and in mining other than coal-mining. The total represents approximately two-thirds of the total labour occupied on Government work in industry.

The preceding official statistics prove most conclusively that actually, and ever since the beginning of the third year of the war, more than *twelve millions* of men and women—more than the fourth of the total population of the United Kingdom—have been either in the Armed Forces of the British Crown—Navy and Army—or in the shipbuilding yards, in munitions factories, in transportation on land and sea, in the Medical Service, in the Air Service, &c., employed for the success of the cause of the Allies.

THE FINANCIAL EFFORT OF GREAT BRITAIN.

The gigantic military effort of Great Britain, in all the branches of its wonderfully developed organization, as above illustrated, was only rendered possible by a corresponding financial contribution.

During the financial year preceding the outbreak of the war, the total expenditure of the Government of Great Britain was $987,464,845. The hostilities have imposed upon the United Kingdom vast expenditures. "For that period"—again quoting the War Cabinet Report—"from the 1st April, 1917, to the 1st December, 1917, the total Exchequer issues for expenditure (including Consolidated Fund Service and Supply Services) were £1,799,223,000,—($8,796,115,000) representing a daily average for that period of £7,344,000 ($36,720,000)."

At this rate of expenditure, the total for the year equals at least $13,500,000,000. But the financial charges entailed by the war being constantly on the increase, they can be calculated at a daily average of no less than $40,000,000 until the close of the conflict.

England has not only incurred very heavy financial obligations, met both by an enormously increased taxation and the issue of large National loans, to pay the cost of her own war expenditure, but she has also generously helped her friends whose financial resources were not so abundant as her own. To the 1st December, 1917, she had made advances to the Allies amounting to no less than $5,930,000,000. In addition to this large amount, the advances she had made to the Dominions for the same period summed up $875,000,000.

ACHIEVEMENTS OF DOMINION, COLONIAL AND INDIAN TROOPS.

Under the above title, the War Cabinet Report concludes a general review of the past year's effort by paying high tribute to the value of the services rendered by the whole British Colonial Empire, in the following elogious terms:—

In the above sketch of military operations during the past year, it has not been possible to distinguish between the particular services rendered by the various nations and nationalities of the Empire. But it must not be forgotten that during the war the forces of the Crown have become welded into a true Imperial army, representative of every part of the world-wide British Commonwealth, and a brief note may be included as to the special services of the various overseas forces.

The share of the Australian, New Zealand, Canadian, South African and Newfoundland contingents in the successes of the 1917 campaign are well known. The capture of Vimy Ridge in April, the prolonged and bitter fighting around Lens during the whole summer and autumn, and the capture of Passchendaele were carried out by the Canadian Corps, which has thus proved itself as excellent in offensive as its splendid defence of Ypres in 1915 had shown it to be in defensive fighting. The New Zealand

and Australian contingents have corresponding achievements to their credit in their share of the battle of Messines and in the long sustained and bitterly contested fights in the Ypres salient from July to November. The South African brigade sustained the brilliant reputation which it won last year at Delville Wood by the devoted services it rendered on the battlefields of Arras and Ypres. Finally, the Newfoundland Regiment took a glorious and costly part in the same two battles. The troops of all the Dominions have shown themselves throughout the campaign of 1917 to have maintained the historic standards of the British Army and have been worthy rivals of the United Kingdom troops in every military effort and achievement.

This testimony to the services rendered by the Dominions would not be complete without some reference to the part played by South Africa in German East Africa, where her troops have borne, under the brilliant leadership of General Van Deventer, a conspicuous share in a peculiarly arduous campaign.

The smaller Colonies and Protectorates have naturally been unable to play so great and conspicuous a part in the World War, but in their own spheres they have contributed their full share to the military effort of the Empire. Labour and fighting troops were freely drawn upon for the Mesopotamian and East African theatres. West Africa, British East Africa, Uganda, Nyasaland and Rhodesia have all sent contingents to fight in German East Africa. 16,000 men from the West Indies have been sent across the Atlantic; and labour corps from the Eastern Colonies have been sent to the Mesopotamian and East African fronts, and, despite unfavourable conditions, to the Western theatre. A large number of individuals from overseas possessions, such as the Malay States and Hong Kong, have also joined the Imperial forces.

Finally, India's contribution, both in man-power, material and money, has steadily increased throughout the year. India has taken a very important share in the victorious campaign in Mesopotamia. The great majority of the troops in this theatre of war are Indian. They have fully sustained the high reputation of the Indian Army for gallantry and endurance. India has been responsible for much of the supply, medical and transportation system by water and on land. Indian forces have also rendered conspicuous service in France, Egypt and East Africa. The question of the supply of officers, especially medical officers, has been solved; commissions have been granted to Indians, and a voluntary Indian Defence Force is now being organised and trained. Special mention should be made of the loyal and effective assistance of the Indian ruling princes and chiefs, from the smallest to the greatest.

The Indian Government has moreover generously contributed $500,000,000 towards the cost of the war.

The foregoing quotations of official figures, of facts undeniable, of achievements really most extraordinary, constitute the unanswerable refutation, complete and crushing, of the Nationalist charge that England, while not doing her own duty with regard to the war, was using undue influence to coerce the British Colonies to participate in the conflict far beyond the fair proportionate effort to be expected on their part; that an illegitimate pressure of Great Britain's Government on her Colonies was being practised, as insidiously alleged, to promote her Imperialist ambition of the World's ascendency.

Unfortunately, those false and most unjust notions had taken deeper root in many minds, even in some who should have been much above such an unfair misconception, than was at first supposed. Hence the importance of setting the matter right, and the necessity of proving that England's war achievements, in every branch of the Military Service, were far exceeding what had, at first, been expected of her, and was ever considered possible. British pluck and manliness were equal to the direst emergency that ever called them forth. Patriotism, courage, determination, perseverance, rising superior to any increased difficulties, have truly worked miracles of manly efforts and self-sacrifices inspired by the noble cause which brought Great Britain in the World's struggle.

CHAPTER XIV.

THE VERITABLE AIMS OF THE ALLIES.

After doing their utmost to persuade the French Canadians that the Allies, more especially England and Russia, were equally responsible for the war, together with Germany and Austria, our "Nationalist" leaders moreover asserted that they were hostile to a just and lasting peace on account of their unfair claims. In support of their pretension, they repeatedly affirmed that the Allies were pledged to the complete destruction of the German Empire. No more unfounded charge could be made against the Nations suddenly challenged in a gigantic struggle for life or death.

It was very important to protect my French Canadian countrymen against views which, if not proved to be absolutely wrong, were calculated to bias their mind against the Allies. With this patriotic object strongly impressed upon my mind, I fully explained what were the veritable aims of Great Britain, France, Russia and Italy, in fighting their deadly enemy. When I issued my French book, the United States had not then entered the contest. Their declaration of war against Germany, in the spring of 1917, after the outrage of the sinking of the Lusitania, and the numerous criminal provocations of the submarine campaign, clearly emphasized, once more, what the Allies had been strenuously struggling for from the outbreak of the hostilities. They had taken up the gauntlet savagely thrown to them, declaring to the world that they would battle to the last to put an end to German militarism, always threatening general peace, to protect the small nations, notably Belgium and Servia, against the onslaught of mighty and tyrannical conquerors, to save Humanity, Civilization and Freedom from the crushing ascendency of autocratic rule. The great American Republic rallied with them to the defence of this most sacred cause. Need I refer to the numerous and eloquent messages of President Wilson, to the writings of the American press, and to the declarations of all the leading public men of the United States, in both Houses of Congress, or before public meetings, in support of the contention which was proved beyond controversy for all fair minded men.

Mr. Bourassa, whether from sheer misconception, or blindly carried away by incomprehensible German sympathies, having their root in his prejudiced hostility to England, could see no difference between a war policy aiming at putting an end to Prussian militarism, and one having for its object the dismemberment of the German Empire. Nor could he conceive that fighting for human liberty was a nobler purpose than struggling for autocratic tyranny.

Though ever posing as the champion of the small nationalities, he would not utter a word of sympathy for martyred Belgium, barbarously conquered Servia, oppressed Poland, since the beginning of the war.

The great conflict once begun under so terrific conditions, every one somewhat posted with the immense resources of the belligerents, their respective warlike spirit and enduring qualities, could easily foresee that, unfortunately, it was most likely to last for several years, the contending parties being so far apart in their respective aspirations. Elated beyond all reason by her triumph over France, in 1870, which had for its first very important result the final creation of the German Empire, proclaimed to the world from Versailles,—the bleeding heart of her vanquished foe,—the new great Power, dominating Central Europe, lost no time in setting all its energies to the task of perfecting the most gigantic military organization ever seen. To all clear sighted men, Germany could not be supposed to accept the heavy sacrifices required for such an end with the sole purpose of maintaining peace. Further conquests were evidently her inspiring aim.

Who can forget how Humanity was staggered by the rapidity of the onslaught of the Teutonic hordes let loose against nations whose greatest wish was to keep the peace of the world? In a sudden rush, the waves of the torrent overran Belgium and Northern France dashing direct towards Paris.

The wonderful plan of campaign, so scientifically conceived and matured, could then be understood as it was boldly and powerfully developed. The Berlin military staff, knowing that France was not sufficiently prepared for the struggle, that England, if forced to intervene in honour bound, by the criminal violation of Belgium's neutrality, would require a couple of years to organize an army of millions of men, decided to strike the first blow with such an overpowering strength as to conquer Belgium in a victorious run and crush France out of the fight. A couple of months were to be sufficient to that most coveted end. Meantime Austria was to face and resist the Russian attack, to allow Germany the necessary time to settle victoriously the western part of the campaign, so cleverly planned and successfully carried out, before transferring her glorious legions to the Eastern theatre of the war. Russia was not supposed to be able to properly organize her armies in less than many months, when it could no longer expect to triumph over the enthusiastic Huns.

In the depressing darkness of those anxious days, the great Marne victory came like the brilliant sun piercing the heavy clouds, pledging final success as the reward of the persevering courage and heroism to be long displayed to deserve it. Germany's first dream of conquering universal domination by military operations even overshadowing those of the illustrious Napoleonic Era, and of Cæsar's marvellously laid deep foundations of Roman grandeur, was shattered to pieces.

Before the Teutonic armies could be reorganized for another great offensive, England's forces and those of her Colonies would be in a position to enter the struggle; France's resources would be brought to bear with all their strength; Italy would break away from the Central Empires and heartily join the Allies.

Then the conflict turned to that weary trench fighting which to the sadness of its trials added new evidence of the inevitable lengthening of the war. No wonder that the longing for peace was intensified under the pressure of conditions becoming more and more trying. Without doubt all true friends of human prosperity and happiness, in their limited possible worldly measure, were fervently praying to God in favour of the restoration of harmony between the warring Nations. But they saw with undeniable clearness that there were two essential—sine qua non—conditions to the peace of the future. To be of any value it must be *Just* and *Durable*. If it could become permanent, much more the better.

Unfortunately, outside the legions of the true friends of an honourable peace, there were found, in the Allied countries, faint hearted men getting tired of the worries and sacrifices consequent upon the prolonged struggle. The moment they began to show their hands, was the signal for the ultra Revolutionists of Russia, finally organized into the disastrous bolshevikism, for the paid traitors of France, for the disloyal elements of the British Empire, to rally around them to set in motion, with accrued force, a current of opinion clamouring for peace almost at any price. To quiet this unpatriotic longing of the disheartened, the political leaders of the Allies publicly explained their war aims, positively affirming that their objective was that *Just and Durable* peace to which alone they could and would agree.

Canada had also her *pacifist* element. So far as the French Canadians were concerned, it was, though small in numbers, almost entirely recruited in the ranks of the supporters of "*Nationalism*." I feel I must explain that our "*Nationalism*," as it has been repeatedly propounded, does not in the least represent the sound views of the very large majority of my French Canadian countrymen.

As was to be expected, Mr. Bourassa was again the outspoken organ of our French Canadian *pacifists*. He laid great stress on what he gave out as a fact: that if peace negotiations were not at once entered upon and brought to a successful conclusion, it was on account of the Allies' unreasonable claims, pointing especially to England's determination not to surrender her supremacy on the high seas, to develop more and more what he termed her *imperialism* for the purpose of dominating the world *economically*.

In my French work, I strongly took issue with the views of our *pacifists* as expressed by their leader and their press. Addressing my French Canadian countrymen on the bounden duties of all loyal British subjects, it was my ardent purpose to tell them the plain truth. Writing, as I did, in 1916, I was then, as I had been from the very beginning, firmly convinced that the conflict would be of long duration, that it was very wrong—even criminal if disloyally inspired—for any one to delude them by vain hopes, or deceive them by false charges.

Having some knowledge of military strategy and tactics, I saw with the clear light of noon day that, despite the gigantic efforts put forth by the Allies, and the admirable heroism of their armies—our Canadian force brilliantly playing its part—final victory would be attained only by indomitable perseverance, both of the millions of fighting men and of the whole Allied nations backing them to the last with their moral and material support. That profound conviction of mine I was very anxious to strongly impress on the minds of my French-Canadian readers, imploring them not to be carried away by the "Nationalist" erroneous pretentions that peace could easily be obtained, if the Allies would only agree to negotiate. I told them plainly, what was absolutely true, that the war aims of Germany were so well known and inadmissible that there was not the least shadow of hope that peace negotiations could lead to a reasonable understanding realizing the two imperious conditions of *Justice and Durability* in a settlement to which all the Allies were in honour pledged. I explained to them that it was no use whatever to be deluded by expectations, however tempting they might appear, because under the then conditions of the military situation—time and events have since brought no favourable change but quite the reverse—there was not the slightest chance of an opening for a successful consideration of the questions to be debated and settled before the complete cessation of the conflict. There was only one conclusion to be drawn from the circumstances of the case, and, however sad to acknowledge, it was that the fight must be carried on to a final victorious issue, any weakening of determination and purpose being sure to bring about humiliating defeat.

THE ONLY POSSIBLE PEACE CONDITIONS.

Whenever representatives of the belligerents shall meet to negotiate for peace, there will of course be many questions of first class importance to consider and discuss. But the one which must overshadow any other and of necessity carry the day, is that peace must be restored under conditions that will, if not forever, at least for many long years, protect Humanity and Civilization against a recurrence of such a calamity as ambitious and cruel Germany has criminally imposed upon the world. I urged my French Canadian readers to consider seriously how peace due to a compromise, accepted out of sheer discouragement, would soon develop into a still more trying ordeal than the one Canada had willingly and deliberately undertaken to fight out with the Allies. I forcibly explained to them that if the present war did not result in an international agreement to put an end to the extravagant and ruinous militarism which, under Prussian terrorism, was proving to be the curse of almost the whole universe, all the sacrifices of so many millions of lives, heroically given, of untold sufferings, of so much treasures, would have been made in vain if Germany was allowed to continue a permanent menace to general tranquillity.

It was a wonder to me that any one could fail to understand that an armed peace would be only a truce during which militarism would be spreading with increased vigour and strength. It was evident—and still daily becoming more and more so—that Germany would only consent to it with the determination to renew, on a still much larger scale, her military organization with the purpose of a more gigantic effort at universal domination.

Then was it not plain that labouring under the inevitable necessity of such an international situation, the Allied nations,—the British Empire as much as France, the United States and Italy—would by force be obliged to make the sacrifices required to maintain their military systems in such a state of efficiency as to be always ready to face their ambitious foe with good prospects of success. Such being the undeniable case, I affirmed—I am sure with the best of reasons—that Great Britain could not return to her ante-war policy of the enlistment of only a small standing territorial army, trusting as formerly to her Naval strength for her defence and the safe maintenance of her prestige and power. Like all the continental nations, England would have to incur the very heavy cost of keeping millions of men always fully armed.

I firmly told my French Canadian countrymen that it was no use deluding themselves with the "Nationalist" notion that peace being restored under the above mentioned circumstances, the British Colonies would not be called upon to share, with England, the burdens of the extensive military preparations necessitated for their own safety as well as for that of Great Britain and the whole Empire. The very reasons which had prompted Canada and all her sister Dominions to intervene in the present war, would surely induce them to cooperate with the Mother Country to maintain a highly and costly state of military preparedness in order to be ever ready for any critical emergency.

Could it be believed that after the sad experience of the actual conflict, the Allied nations—Great Britain perhaps more than any other—would blindly once again run the risk of being caught napping and deceived by an unscrupulous and hypocritical enemy, unsufficiently prepared to at once rise in their might to fight for their very national existence and the safety of Mankind against tyrannical absolutism. If such abominable pages of History as those that for the last four years are written with the blood of millions of heroes defending Human Freedom were, by fear of new sacrifices, allowed to be repeated, shame would be on the supposed civilized world having fallen so low as to bow to the dictates of barbarism. Let all truly hearted men hope and pray that no such dark days shall again be the fearful lot of Humanity. Let them all resolve that if the world can at last emerge free from the present hurricane, they will not permit, out of weakness and despondency, the sweeping waves of teutonism to submerge Civilization and destroy the monuments of the work of centuries of the Christian Art.

After showing the dark side of the picture, and what would be the fearful consequences of a German victory, or of an armed peace pending the renewal, with still much increased vigour and resources, of the conflict only suspended, I explained to my French Canadian readers the great advantages to be derived by all, Germany included, from the restoration of peace carrying with it the untold benefits to be derived from the cessation of extravagant military organization, yearly destroying the capital created by hard work and the saving of the millions of the working populations. If an international agreement could be arrived at by which militarism would be reduced to the requirements of the maintenance of interior order and the safeguarding of conventional peace amongst the Powers, then many long years of material prosperity, in all its diversity of beneficial development, would surely follow. Canada, like the other British Colonies, would not have to incur any very large expenditure for military purposes, devoting all her energies to the intelligent building of the grand future which her immense territorial resources would certainly make, not only possible, but sure.

How much could material development be conducive to intellectual, moral and religious progress, if the Nations of the Earth would only sincerely and permanently abide by the Divine teachings of Christianity.

Considering all the conditions of the military situation, at the end of the summer of 1916, I clearly perceived the imperious necessity of the Allies— Canada as well as all her associates—to fight to a finish. That duty I did my best to impress on the minds of the French Canadians. Events have since developed in many ways, but they all tend to strengthen the conviction that ultimate victory will only be the price of unshaken perseverance, of undaunted courage, of more patriotic sacrifices.

CHAPTER XV.

JUST AND UNJUST WARS.

In one of his pamphlets Mr. Bourassa favoured his readers with his views on the justice and injustice of war. He affirmed that a Government could rightly declare war only for the three following objects:—

1.—For the defence of their own country. 2.—
To fulfill the obligations to which they are
     in honour bound towards other nations.
3.—To defend a weak nation unjustly attacked.

I have no hesitation to acknowledge the soundness of those principles, as theoretically laid down. I took the "Nationalist" leader at his own word, wondering more than ever how he could refuse to admit the justice of the cause of the Allies.

Looking at the case from the British standpoint, was it not clear as the brightest shining of the sun that England had gone to war against Germany for the three reasons assigned by Mr. Bourassa as those which alone can justify a Government entering a military struggle.

Great Britain was by solemn treaties in honour bound to the defence of Belgium whose territory had been violated by Germany, the other party to those treaties which she threw to the winds contemptuously calling them *"scraps of paper."*

Even outside of all treaty obligations, it was England's duty, according to the third principle enunciated by Mr. Bourassa as authorizing a just declaration of war, to rush to the defense of Belgium, a *"weak nation" most dastardly attacked by the then strongest military Power on earth.*

The British Government, being responsible for the safety of the British Empire, would have been recreant to their most sacred duty, had they failed to see that if the German armies were freely allowed to overrun Belgium, to crush France and vanquish Russia, Great Britain and her Colonies, unprepared for any effective resistance as they would have been, had they remained the passive onlookers of the teutonic conquest of continental Europe, would have been the easy prey of the barbarous conquerors. Consequently, in accepting the bold challenge of the Berlin Government, that of England also did their duty for the defence of Great Britain and the British Empire.

But the whole British Empire being at war with Germany for the three above enumerated causes combined, were the free autonomous Colonies of England not also in duty bound to help her in vindicating her honour and theirs, and to do their utmost to support the Mother Country in her efforts to oblige the Berlin Authorities to respect their treaty obligations! Were they not also in duty bound to participate with England in the defence of invaded weak, but heroic, Belgium! Were they not in duty bound to at once organize for their own defence, sending their heroic sons to fight their enemy on the soil of France, instead of waiting the direct attack upon their own territories!

The British Parliament dealing exclusively with the Foreign Affairs of the Empire, the international treaties which they ratify are binding on the whole Empire. If such a treaty is violated by the other party or parties who signed it, violently obliging England to stand by her obligations, are not the Colonies also bound to uphold the Mother land in the vindication of her treaty rights?!

Looking at the same question, in the full light of the sound principles of the justice of any war, from the German standpoint, what are the only true conclusions to be drawn? To satisfy Austria's unjust demands and maintain peace, Servia had, in 1914, at the urgent request of England, France and Russia, gone as far as any independent nation could go without dishonour. Not only backed, but no doubt inspired, by the Berlin Government, Austria would not consent to reduce by an iota her unfair pretentions against Servia.

It was plainly a case of a great Power unjustly threatening a weak nation. Consequently, according to the "Nationalist" leader's principle, Russia was right and doing her duty in intervening to protect the menaced weak State. Instead of hypocritically resenting Russia's intervention in favour of Servia, it was equally Germany's duty to join with her to save this weak nation from Austrian unjust challenge. Had it done so, Austria would certainly have refrained from exacting from Servia concessions to which she could not agree without sacrificing her independent Sovereignty. The Vienna Authorities backing down from their unjust stand, there would have been no war. And Germany, together with Russia, would have deserved the gratitude of the world for their timely intervention, prompted by a clear sense of their duty and a sound conception of their international right.

It is well known how the very opposite took place. Russia, to be ready for the emergency of the declaration of war by Austria against Servia, ordered the mobilization of that part of her army bordering on the Austrian frontier, answering to the Berlin request for explanations that she had no inimical intention whatever against the German Empire, that her only object was to protect weak Servia against Austria's most unjust attack. The Kaiser's government replied by requesting Russia to cancel her order for the mobilization of part of her army. And in the very thick of this diplomatic exchange of despatches, whilst England and France were sparing no effort, by day and night, to maintain peace and protect Mankind from the threatening calamity, Germany suddenly threw the gauntlet and declared war against Russia.

Foreseeing clearly that France was consequently in honour bound to support Russia, in accordance with her international obligations towards that great Eastern Power—in strict conformity with the second principle enunciated by Mr. Bourassa and previously quoted—, Germany took the initiative of a second unjust declaration of war, and this one against France.

The military operations against France being very difficult, and certainly to be very costly in a fearful loss of man-power, before the strongly fortified French frontier could be successfully overrun, Germany, after a most shameful attempt to bribe England into neutrality, decided to take the easy route and ordered her army to invade Belgium's neutral territory, in violation of her solemn treaty obligations. That treacherous act filled the cup of teutonic infamy, and brought Great Britain, and the whole British Empire, into the conflict.

So Germany was guilty of the most outrageous violation of the three sound principles laid down by the "Nationalist" leader qualifying a just war against an iniquitous one, whilst England and France won the admiration of the world by their noble determination to stand by them at all cost.

Still Mr. Bourassa, by an incomprehensible perversion of mind in judging the application of his own loudly proclaimed principles, has not to this day uttered one word openly condemning Germany's war policy and eulogizing that of England and France. On the contrary, he has tried to persuade his readers that both groups of belligerents were equally responsible for the war, more especially giving vent to his, at the least, very strange hostility to England and scarcely dissimulating his teutonic evident sympathies. He never positively expressed his disapproval of Austria's unjust attack against Servia, but condemned Russia for her intervention to protect that weak country, concluding that the Petrograd Government was the real guilty party which had thrown the world into the vortex of the most deadly conflict of all times.

One of the most damaging and unfair arguments of Mr. Bourassa was that in intervening in the struggle, England was not actuated by a real sentiment of justice, honour and duty, but was merely using France as a shield for her own selfish protection. And when he deliberately expressed such astounding views, he knew, or ought to have known, that by her so commendable decision to avenge outraged weak Belgium, Great Britain had at once, by her command of the seas, guaranteed France against the superior strength of the

German fleet, kept widely opened the great commercial avenues of oceanic trade, the closing of which by the combined sea power of the Central Empires, would have infallibly caused the crushing defeat of France by cutting off all the supplies she absolutely required to meet the terrible onslaught of her cruel enemy. He knew, or ought to have known, that the navigation of the seas being closed to her rivals by Germany, Russia would have been very easily put out of the fight, her only available ocean ports, Vladivostock and Arkhangel, through which supplies of many kinds, especially munitions, could reach her eastern coast, at once becoming of no service to her.

He knew, or ought to have known, that if Great Britain had remained neutral, Japan, Italy, Portugal, would not have declared war against either Germany or Austria.

As such consequences of British neutrality were as sure as the daily rising of the sun, was I not right when I drew the conclusion that if a shield there was, it was rather that of Great Britain covering France, all her allies and even the neutral nations, with the protection of her mighty sea power. With such a conviction, the soundness of which I felt sure, I told my French Canadian countrymen that, for one, I would, to my last day, be heartily grateful to England to have saved France from the crushing defeat which once more would have been her lot, had she been left alone to fight the Central Empires. Heroic, without doubt France would have been. But with deficient supplies, with much curtailed resources, with no helpful friends, heroism alone, however admirable and prolonged, was sure to be of no avail against an unmatched materially organized power, used to its most efficiency by the severest military discipline, by national fanaticism worked to fury, and by soldierly enthusiasm carried to wildness.

In a single handed struggle with Germany, in 1914, France would have been in a far worse position than in 1870. The extraordinary development of the new German Empire—the outcome of the great war so disastrous to France— in population, in commerce, in manufacturing industry, in financial resources, in military organization, made her fighting power still more disproportionate. To her wonderful territorial army, she added her recently built military fleet, then much superior, in the number of vessels carrying thousands and thousands of skilled seamen, to the French one. Moreover Austria, with another fifty millions of people, Bulgaria and Turkey, with more than thirty millions, were backing Germany, whilst, in 1870, France had only Prussia to contend with.

All those facts staring him like any one else, how could Mr. Bourassa reasonably charge Great Britain with using France merely as a tool for her own safety. Under the circumstances of the case, such a preposterous assertion is beyond human comprehension. I, for one, cannot understand how he failed to see that, had England been actuated by the selfish and unworthy motives to which he ascribes her intervention in the war, she could have then, and at least for several years, wrought from Germany almost all the concessions she would have wished for. Could it not, by an alliance with the Central Empires, have attained the goal of that dominating ambition which the "Nationalist" leader asserts to be her most cherished aim.

But such a dishonourable policy England would not consider for a single moment. She indignantly refused Germany's outrageous proposals, stood by her treaty obligations, and resolutely threw all the immense resources of her power in the conflict which, at the very beginning, developed into a struggle for life and death between human freedom and absolutist tyranny.

I am sure, and I do not hesitate to vouch for them, all the truly loyal French-Canadians—they are almost unanimously so—are like myself profoundly grateful to Great Britain for her noble decision to rush to the defense of Belgium and France in their hour of need. Comparing what took place with what might have been, moved by all the ties of affection that will ever bind them to the great and illustrious nation from which they sprung, they fully appreciate the inestimable value of the support given by their second mother-country to that of their national origin. They ardently pray that both of them will emerge victorious from the great conflict to remain, for the good of Mankind, indissolubly united in peace as they are in war.

A "Nationalist" Illogical Charge Against England.

Our Nationalists, after charging England with using France merely as a shield against Germany, have been illogical to the point of reproaching her for not having intervened in favour of her close neighbour, in 1870. It is most likely that, had she done so, they would have pretended that she would have been actuated by the same selfish sentiment that prompted her, for the only sake of her own protection, to enter into the present conflict.

How is it that Mr. Bourassa, so fond of charging England with ambitious views of constant self-agrandizement, of worldly domination, can suddenly turn about and accuse her of having shamefully sacrificed France, in 1870, to the overpowering German blow?

The circumstances of the two cases—1870 and 1914—were very different. The conflict of 1870 had, apparently at least, a dynastic cause. The House of Hohenzollern had been intriguing to have a Prussian prince of her own elevated to the Spanish Throne. The Imperial Government of Napoleon III strongly objected to such a policy. The diplomatic correspondence which ensued did not settle the difficulty. France declared war against Prussia. Many years later it was discovered that by a falsified diplomatic despatch, Bismark had succeeded in his satanic design to bring the government of Napoleon III to attack Prussia, thus shamefully throwing upon France the responsibility of the war.

In 1870, England was at peace with all the European Powers, as she had ever been since 1815, with the only exception of the Crimean War. During the diplomatic correspondence that led to the hostilities, what reason would have justified England to break her neutrality? What would the present critics of her course have said if she had sided with Prussia? Would they have pretended that she would have used Prussia as a shield against France?

I personally remember very well the tragic events of the terrible year, 1870. The crushing military power of Prussia as proved by the triumphant march of her victorious armies, was a revelation for all, for France still more than for others. True Prussia had beaten Austria in the short campaign ended at Sadowa. The Prussia France was then fighting was not the giant Empire against which she is battling with such heroism for the last four years. France was at the time the leading continental Power. The general opinion was, when war was suddenly declared, that France would easily triumph over her enemy.

It must not be forgotten that, in 1870, England was even less ready than in 1914 to engage in a continental conflict. Her standing army was not large, and then partly garrisoned in the colonies. Some of her best regiments were stationed in Canada. She could have been a really important ally of France only as a strong support of another continental power joining with her against Prussia, for instance Russia or Austria, or both of them.

If England had been able to send 500,000 men in a few days to the very heart of France, incessantly followed by another half million, it is almost certain that the Prussian army would not have entered Paris. But England had not that million of trained men. It would have taken at least a year to organize such a large army.

I will speak my mind openly. After Sedan, any attempt at saving France by force would have been vain and useless. Even Russia and Austria were unprepared for such a task. Their intervention, coming too late, would most likely have given Prussia a chance to win a much greater victory. France out of the struggle, Prussia would then have had the opportunity to achieve, as early as 1870, what she has ever since prepared for, and tried to accomplish by the war she has brought on in 1914.

What then becomes of the "Nationalist" pretention that Great Britain has ever been aiming at dominating the world, when it is so easy to understand that without a very large territorial army, which she persistingly refused to organize, she was unable to take an important part in any continental war. The days were passed, after the extraordinary development of Prussian militarism, when she could brilliantly hold her own on the continent with a small standing army backed by generous subsidies to the European powers. The present war is surely proof evident of it, since England, instead of the two hundred thousand men she was expected to send over to France, as her man-power contribution, has had to raise a total army, with all the auxiliary services, of 6,000,000 officers and men, exclusive of the 2,000,000 contributed by the whole British Colonial Empire.

The Nationalists accusing England to have abandoned France to her sad fate, in 1870, was only another instance of their campaign to arouse the feelings of the French Canadians against Great Britain.

OTHER "NATIONALIST" ERRONEOUS ASSERTIONS.

Mr. Bourassa has had his own peculiar way of explaining the real determining cause of the war. Some men are—by nature it is to be supposed—always disposed to judge great historical events from considerations inspired by the lowest sentiments of the human heart. In the "Nationalist" leader's view, the great war was brought about by the treacherous alliance of British and German capitalists speculating together, in actual partnership or otherwise, in the production of war material: cannons, rifles, munitions, war shipbuilding, &c.

In my humble opinion, such views are lowering to a very vulgar and lamentably repulsive cause—if it could be true—events of immense significance, the result, on the one side, of criminal aspirations which, however guilty they may be, have not yet been degraded to the profound depth of abjection they suppose; on the other, by the most noble sentiments which can inspire nations to make the greatest sacrifices to avenge outraged Justice and Right.

Autocratic German ambition, such as it has proved to be, is bad enough. Still the cause of the war, such as asserted by Mr. Bourassa, would have been far worse. National aspirations, however wrongly diverted from their legitimate conception, will never be as contemptible as the nasty greed of individual speculators treacherously sucking the very life blood of their countrymen for the sake of squeezing millions of dollars at the cost of their country's honour and future.

Unfortunately, illegitimate "profiteering" has taken place in the course of every war. Of course it must be severely condemned and firmly prevented, to the utmost, by governmental authority strongly supported by public opinion which must, however, be cautious not to be unduly influenced and carried away by the wild charges of some who denounce others with so much apparent indignation for the only reason that they themselves are not succeeding as they would like to do in their speculative attempts.

Illegitimate "profiteering" is one of the deplorable effects of a war; it is never its real cause.

What are the true causes, humanly speaking, of the cataclysm so violently shaking the world? They were of two kinds. The first was the disordered ambition of a nation having reached, by prodigious efforts, such a power that she fatally determined to dominate everywhere, militarily and politically. To this first cause was added that of secular race rivalry.

The two causes of the first kind—which can properly be called *offensive*, were followed by the noble one of the resistance to oppression, of the defence of the honour of threatened nations, of the energetic determination to avenge violated international treaties, and to save the civilized world from a new barbarous invasion.

If the Allies had humbly bowed to the odious German claims, there would have been no war.

Consequently, the two evident causes of the war are, on the one hand, German ambition to universal domination; on the other, the absolute necessity on the part of the Allies to prevent by all possible means the success of such a tyrannical enterprise.

However much guilty they have been in bringing on the most terrible war of all times, it is still injurious for the Berlin Government to suppose that in assuming this weighty responsibility, they were playing the part of an unconscious instrument of the most diabolical thirst of money making by shameless "profiteers."

But such a charge is absolutely inexplicable when one accuses France, England and Belgium to be, in their admirable and heroic campaign for the world's deliverance and freedom, the pliant tools of contemptible speculators in the production of war materials.

Governments and nations are, as a rule, far from having dropped to such a low state of incurable corruption. For many of them, there yet exists bright summits, shining with the clear light of Justice, Right and Honour, which in those times of sufferings and burning tears, are the pledge of better days and the promise of the world's resurrection.

INCREDIBLE "NATIONALIST" NOTIONS.

Can it be possibly believed that the "Nationalist" leader has asserted that when the British capitalists and bankers invested the savings entrusted to their safe keeping, they were principally actuated by the desire to create in Canada a financial influence which would, in due course, assist with force in dragging the Dominion to participate in the Imperial wars against her better judgment? Yet, so he has positively written and developed the wild argument.

Any man, with the slightest business experience, knows that, in all cases, would-be borrowers go where money is to be lent. I have not yet learned that one of them ever went to the North Pole in search of millions for railway building and all kinds of industrial and commercial enterprises. Daring explorers who ventured thither, facing so many risks, were stimulated by a laudable thirst of fame and the desire of scientific progress. They did not imagine, for a moment, that they were likely to discover, in these far away regions, great financial markets amply provided with millions of accumulated capital waiting for safe and profitable investments.

Canada, a young country, as large as all Europe in territorial extent, with wonderful undeveloped resources of the agricultural soil, of the mines, of immense forests, of mighty rivers, of large and breezy lakes, could not progress without labour and capital. The large natural increase of the population, supplemented by immigration, was sure to supply the labour. Capital, to the amount of hundreds of millions, could not be provided by the only savings of our people. Immigration of capital was even more pressingly required than that of men. The Governments of Canada, federal and provincial, city corporations, railway companies, industrial concerns, wanting money, all went where it could be found. It happened that London, the capital of the British Empire, was by far the largest financial market of the world. No wonder then that instead of going to Lapland, Canadian borrowers crowded in London, where they met with those of nearly all the nations of the world, gathering in the same city for the same purpose.

Two incontrovertible economical truisms are, without the shadow of a doubt, the following:—

1. That a would-be borrower wishes to get the money he wants in the easiest way at the lowest interest charge;

2. That a wise lender wishes to secure for his money the safest investment carrying the highest possible rate of interest; the rate of interest being however subordinated, in his mind, to the safety of the investment.

Such were the sound economical considerations which settled for the Canadian borrowers of all sorts, and the British investors, the conditions of all the loans made on Canadian account.

Any one merely hinting to the British saving public that the money invested in Canada was sent over to our shores for the object of creating a financial influence which would force the Dominion into costly wars, could not have adopted a more unwise course to destroy the best chances of the success of a loan. Canadian credit was of first class order, because the British investors knew our grand possibilities; because they were aware that Canada had always been a safe debtor, honouring with clock regularity her interest charges and the payment of maturing loans; because also, and in a very large measure, they realized that we were not in the same position of so many nations of the Old World, exposed to frequent warring necessities likely to exhaust our means and to jeopardize our bright prospects.

Confidence being the sound basis of good credit, we got all the money we wanted for all the purposes of our national economical development, the true interest of Canada and of Great Britain being equally well served by the financial intercourse between the wealthy mother-country and her progressive colony.

CANADIAN FINANCIAL OPERATIONS IN THE UNITED STATES.

Our "Nationalists," so eager to discourage Canadian effort in the war, and, with this object, always prone to magnify German warlike achievements and the difficulties confronting the Allies, were rather nervous at the increasing prospects of the United States joining the *Entente* Nations. Their leader seized every opportunity to argue that they would be mistaken in doing so. During the weary months when the President of the neighbouring Republic was

85

prudently feeling his way before taking the bold stand which he has ever since so brilliantly and bravely upheld, the "Nationalists", through successive ups and downs in their expectations, could scarcely help hiding their desire that the United States would not intervene in the struggle. Those of us who had not been moved by the horrors of the Belgian invasion, by the murder of so many innocent victims of teutonic savageness, by the brutal killing of Edith Cavell, by the Armenian massacres, by the wanton destruction of admirable works of Art, could not be expected to thrill at the barbarous sinking of the Lusitania, sending to the bottom of the ocean hundreds of American citizens of the neutral American Northern Republic. They were anxious that the Washington Government should condone the outrageous offence and all the subsequent ones perpetrated by the German submarines against our neighbours. How much they were dismayed at the sudden close of Mr. Wilson's apparent hesitation, and at the proud declaration of war from Washington to Berlin. Though rejoicing at it, they did not consider that the Russian bolsheviki's collapse could compensate for the additional military and financial resources the Allies were sure to derive from the United States participation in the war.

Canada having to borrow many millions to sustain her warlike effort, and the British money market being closed to further outside investments, had two sources left for her successful financial operations: her own market and that of the United States. The Washington Authorities had generously decided to help financially the European Allies in pressing need of money. The Ottawa Government, before making a grand appeal to the Canadian public, applied to Washington for a loan. Mr. Wilson's cabinet, however much they would have liked to meet the wishes of the Canadian Government, had to answer that, having such a large war expenditure to incur, and such big sums to collect to assist their less wealthy European associates in the struggle, they could not see their way to grant Canada's demand.

Acknowledging the value of the reasons given for not complying with their request, the Canadian Ministers then applied to Washington for the permission to negotiate a loan in the open American market. This was readily granted.

It was, of course, well understood that going in the open market, Canada, to secure the required sum of money, would have to pay the then current rate of interest increasing, as usual, in proportion to the increased pressure of the demand of funds.

It is utterly incredible—but still it is true—that Mr. Bourassa did denounce in his newspaper *Le Devoir*, the Ottawa Cabinet's action in borrowing money from the American saving public. In severe terms he blamed the Washington

Authorities for not having lent millions to Canada at the low rate of interest they had agreed to accept from France and Italy. He asserted that this refusal on their part was a testimony of ill-will against the Dominion. And in the most violent terms he charged all those who favoured Canadian borrowings in the American market with being traitors selling their country to the United States.

It is hard to say whether the charge is not more ridiculous than contemptible. It is the repetition, in an aggravated form of absurdity, of the argument accusing the British investing capitalists to have had for their only object in lending us their money to help coercing Canada into the Imperial wars.

Was Mr. Bourassa ignorant of the fact that the building of the magnificent railway system of the United States, that their great industrial development, were due to the billions of British capital which for the last eighty years have flowed, in rolling waves, towards the shores of the Republic, invading, in the most peaceful and friendly way, her large territory, and drawing from its immense resources the greatest immeasurable accumulation of wealth ever created by the labour of man? I am not aware that any American writer ever ran the risk of being crushed by ridicule in accusing all the United States borrowers in the English market, governmental and others, of the hideous crime of selling their country to Great Britain. It would have been sheer madness to say so in the broad light of the marvellous economical progress of our neighbours. They knew very well that the billions of dollars invested by the British saving public for the development of their territorial riches, were producing returns much larger than the rate of interest paid to their British creditors.

No one in the United States ever apprehended, for a single moment, that because the Republic had borrowed enormous sums from Great Britain, she was likely to lose her State independence through the financial influence of the holders of her securities of all sorts.

Such "Nationalist" notions, as above exposed and contradicted, can only create very wrong and deplorable conclusions in the public mind, were they allowed to follow their course without challenge and without the refutation proving their complete absurdity.

CHAPTER XVI.

"Nationalist" Views Condensed.

After refuting at length the "Nationalist" theories, I thought proper to condense them in a concrete proposition, and challenge their propagandist to call a public meeting in any city, town, or locality, in the Dominion,— Montreal for instance—and to find a dozen of citizens of standing in the community, to consent to move and second a *"Resolution"* embodying their doctrines.

This condensed proposition, I translate as follows:—

"Whereas England has unjustly declared war against Germany;

"Whereas Great Britain has done nothing to maintain the peace of the world;

"Considering that His Majesty King George V. *had not the right to declare the state of war for Canada without the assent of the Canadian Cabinet*;

"Considering that Canada, as an autonomous colony, *is a Sovereign State*;

"Considering that British Sovereignty over Canada *is only a fiction*;

"Considering that Canada, interfering in the present war, *should have done so as a Nation*;

"Whereas Canada should only have fought on her own account, like *Belgium, Servia, Italy or Bulgaria.*

"Whereas *the maintenance of a compact British Empire is the most permanent provocation against the peace of the world*;

"Considering that the supremacy of England on the seas is unjust;

"Considering that Great Britain's aspiration, for a long time past, has been universal domination by means of her military naval power;

"Whereas England is unfair against France in using her as a shield against German invasion;

"Considering that England is exercising by all possible means a strong pressure upon the Colonies for her only benefit;

"Considering *that all the social leaders have united to demoralize the conscience of the people, to poison their mind, to set their vigilance at sleep, and to represent to them as a national duty what would formerly have been considered as a betrayal of national interests*;

"Considering *that England is trying to crush Germany, being afraid of her colonial expansion and her maritime and commercial competition*;

"Whereas our compatriots of the British races have many faults; *that they are ignorant, assuming, arrogant, overbearing and rotten with mercantilism*;

"Considering that they have acquired *many of the worst vices of the Yankees*;

"Considering that Canada should never participate, outside of her own territory, in the wars of the British Empire;

"Considering that the Canadian Cabinet and Parliament are criminally guilty of having ordered the organization of a Canadian army to go and fight against Germany on the French territory, and in authorizing the payment of the cost of this military expedition;

"Be it "Resolved", that this meeting energetically protest against the declaration of war against Germany by His Majesty King George V, *without the assent of the Canadian Cabinet*, to defend Belgium's territory invaded by Germany violating solemn treaties;

"That this meeting is of opinion that, for the purpose of favouring the restoration of peace as soon as possible, England should notify all the Powers that she abdicates for ever her supremacy on the seas, which supremacy Germany could hereafter safely exercise;

"That this meeting being absolutely convinced that *the maintenance of a compact British Empire is the most permanent provocation against the peace of the world*, is strongly of opinion that Great Britain should, in order to quiet the fears of the Nations friendly to peace and opposed to militarism, like pacifist Germany, dissolve her Empire, at once acknowledging the immediate independence of India and of all her autonomous Colonies;

"That this meeting's formal opinion is that the Canadian Parliament's imperious duty is to order without delay the dissolution of the British bond of connection, *which would be a public benefit*, and to proclaim the immediate independence of Canada;

"That a copy of the present "Resolution" be addressed to His Excellency the Governor General, to the Members of the Federal Cabinet, to the Senators and to the Members of the House of Commons."

The italics in the above draft "Resolution" and "Preamble" are quoted from Mr. Bourassa's writings.

The "Preamble" and "Resolution" emphasize, in their true and complete meaning, the "Nationalist" doctrines perseveringly propounded for years past to poison French Canadian mentally. That such teachings can only produce disloyal feelings, stir up national prejudices and hatred of the Mother Country, and be most detrimental to the best interests of the Province of Quebec, of the Dominion of Canada, and of the British Empire as a whole, every one must admit with sadness.

My challenge, which is still maintained, has not been taken up yet. All may rest assured that it will never be. The most ardent "Nationalist" knows that no responsible citizens would move the adoption of such views.

CHAPTER XVII.

LOYAL PRINCIPLES PROPOUNDED.

To the foregoing "Nationalist" proposition, I opposed one condensing, in a concrete form, the views and principles of the truly loyal Canadian citizens. I also translate it as follows:—

"Whereas, since 1870, the German Empire had been a permanent menace against the peace of the world by her threatening military policy;

"Whereas England, throughout the same period, and more especially during the twenty years previous to 1914, had done her utmost efforts to maintain peace;

"Considering that Great Britain had, in many ways, solicited Germany to agree to the limitation of armaments, especially of the building of war vessels;

"Considering that she had persisted in her attempts with the German Government to save the nations from the ruinous system of excessive armaments, in spite of the latter's refusal to accede to her demands;

"Considering that though in honor bound, like England, by three solemn treaties, to respect Belgium's neutrality, the German Government have, in August 1914, ordered their army to violate Belgian territory in order to more easily invade France to which they had declared war;

"Whereas Great Britain, in honour bound, could not permit the crushing of Belgium by the German Empire;

"Considering, moreover, that Germany, after mutilating and destroying Belgium, by the deprivation of her independence, after triumphing over France which she would have once again dismembered, would have undertaken to beat England to deprive her of sea supremacy, in order to obtain, by this last conquest, her domination over Europe and almost all the world;

"Considering that the defeat of England might very likely have resulted in the cession of Canada to Germany;

"Considering that the world at large is greatly interested in the maintenance of England and France as first class Powers on account of their services in favour of Human Civilization and Liberty;

"Considering that the German armies have accompanied their military operations with untold barbarous acts, by the murder of priests, of peaceful citizens, of wounded soldiers, of religious women, of mothers, of previously criminally outraged young girls, of old men, of young children, with the destruction by fire and otherwise of Cathedrals, Churches,—monuments of the Christian Art,—of libraries—sanctuaries of Science—of historical monuments, the legitimate glory and pride of Human Genius;

"Whereas the German Government is guilty of the murder of thousands of persons, men, women and children, by the sinking of merchant vessels—the Lusitania, for instance—by its submarine ships, without giving the notices required by International Law;

"Whereas from the very beginning of the war, the Allied Nations, England, France and Russia, have jointly agreed, in honour bound, to require, as the essential peace condition, the cessation by all the belligerent Powers of the crushing and ruinous militarism prevailing before the opening of the hostilities, by the fault of Germany's obstination to constantly strengthen her military organization both on land and sea;

"Considering that England and her Allies are struggling for the most venerable and sacred cause:—*outraged Justice*—; that, being a British Colony, *Canada is justly engaged in the present cruel and deplorable conflict, for the defence of the Right and the true Liberty of Nations; that our Canadian soldiers are valiantly fighting with those of England, France and Belgium for the great cause of sovereign importance—the protection of the world threatened by Germanism*;

"Considering that England, to which the political life of Canada is bound, and France, to which the French Canadians owe their national existence, *have to fight for sacred interests in a war of endurance* requiring the incessant renewal of all the energies of the most ardent patriotism, the victims of which falling on the field of honour have the merit of giving their lives *for Justice*";

"Considering that, though wishing the restoration of peace as soon as possible, and earnestly praying Divine Providence to favour the world with the blessings of peace, more and more urgently needed after this assault of abominable barbarism against Christian Civilization lasting for the last four years, the Allies are absolutely unable to terminate the war by giving their consent to conditions which would not protect Humanity against the direst consequences of the militarism fastened by the German Empire on the Nations so anxious to bring it to an end;

"Be it "Resolved":—

"That this meeting approves of the free and patriotic decision of the Federal Parliament to have Canada to participate in the so very Just War which England, France, Belgium, the United States and Italy are fighting against the

German and Austrian Empires, allied in an effort to dominate the world;

"That this meeting's strong opinion is that, on account of the terrible crisis menacing the British Empire and Civilization, it was the bounden duty of Canada to intervene in the war for the safety of the Mother Country and her own, for the salvation of Liberty and *of the sacred cause of outraged Justice*;

"That this meeting desires to express her admiration and profound gratitude for the braves who enlist in the grand army which the Canadian Parliament has ordered to be organized for the defence of the cause of the Allies, which is also that of the civilized world;

"That this meeting also concur in the opinion that Canada is in duty bound to continue to participate in the present war until the final victory of the Allies, which will guarantee to the world a lasting peace and put an end to German militarism which has been the direct cause of so much dire misfortunes for Humanity."

The italics of the above draft "Resolution" are quoted from the writings and speeches of leaders of French Canadian Roman Catholics.

There was no need of calling meetings to adopt the preceding "Resolution" with its well defined preamble. It had been approved, in all its bearings, at the outset of the hostilities by the unanimous decision of the Canadian Parliament, by the almost unanimous consent of public opinion, by the religious, social, commercial, industrial and financial leaders of the country. It had been so approved by the four hundred thousand brave Canadians who rallied to the Colours; by the subscribers, by thousands, to the national war loans.

Since writing the above draft "Resolution", its full substance has been almost unanimously approved by the Canadian people in general elections, the two contending political parties entirely agreeing so far as the Justice of the cause of the Allies was concerned, differing only as to the best means for Canada to adopt to achieve final victory.

Without entering into any considerations respecting the divergence of the views of the leaders of political thought, in the still recent electoral campaign, —from which it is more advisable for me to abstain in the interest of the cause I am defending—I may be allowed to remark that only a small remnant of the "Nationalist" element dared to reaffirm his hostility to Canada's intervention in the conflict and to avow his opinion *that the country had done enough*.

What did those irreconcilable "Nationalists"—so few in numbers as the event ultimately proved—mean by their assertion that *Canada had done enough for the war?* According to its literal wording, it must have signified that no more sacrifices should have been incurred for the triumph of the Allied cause. If it was so, the conclusion to be drawn from such sayings was that, to put an end to any further Canadian contributions, orders should be given to bring back the Canadian Army from Europe, and to send home all the forces still on Canadian soil. It is plain that even if the new Canadian Parliament had decided not to increase our contribution of man-power, in order to maintain the efficiency of the Canadian divisions at the front, large sacrifices would have had to be made to keep on the theatre of war the forces which were still in the field.

To refuse to participate in the war would have been deserting the flag at the hour of danger, and a total misconception of our plain duty.

Giving up the fight, once engaged in the struggle, before triumphant victory, or irremediable defeat, in the very thick of the battle, so heroically carried on by the Allies, would have been sheer cowardice—bolchevikism of the worst kind.

Whether they meant it or not, those few "Nationalists" dared not openly propose the recall of our troops. The solitary "Nationalist" candidate who had the nerve to face the electorate was defeated by a very large majority.

No better proof of the weakness of the hold of the doctrines of "Nationalism," on sound public opinion, is required than the decision of its most outspoken advocate and leader, Mr. Bourassa, to refrain from being a candidate in any constituency, and to advise all his supposed friends to do likewise. No one was deceived, with regard to this decision, by the reasons, or rather excuses, given to explain it.

Evidently, if the "Nationalist" group and their leader had been confident of the support of the large number of electors whose opinion they pretended to represent, they would certainly not have lost the chance to show their strength, and the opportunity to elect many candidates of their persuasion to enter Parliament free from any party allegiance but that of their own element. But any one somewhat posted with the currents of public opinion in the Province of Quebec, knew very well that if pure "Nationalist" candidates had been nominated in all the constituencies of the Province, running between the regular party nominees,—ministerial and opposition—the average number of ballots cast for them would scarcely have reached ten per cent. of the French Canadian votes, less than two per cent. of the whole Canadian electorate.

It was moreover highly probable that, had they tried the game, they would not have even succeeded, in two-thirds of the constituencies, in inducing citizens of sufficient standing to accept their nomination and their political program.

Once engaged in such a hopeless electoral contest, they would have had either to humbly retire from the field, or to await the doomed day by nominating men of no weight whatever. Both alternatives would have led them to an equally disastrous defeat.

UNJUST "NATIONALIST" GRIEVANCES AGAINST ENGLAND.

At the end of the very first page of Mr. Bourassa's pamphlet, entitled:—*What do we owe England?*—in French:—Que devons-nous à l'Angleterre?,—The following lines are found:—(*Translation.*)

> British Imperialism, in its concrete and practical form, can be defined in ten words: **the active participation by the Colonies in the wars of England**. It is almost precisely the definition I gave of it as early as the days of the African war. It is exact. Considered from a larger point of view, from its profound causes and far reaching consequences, British Imperialism calls for a more ample definition. Its object is to have Great Britain dominate the world by means of the organization and concentration of all the Military Forces of the Empire—both Sea and Land Forces—; it means the gradual annihilation, or at least the enslaving of all the divers nationalities constituting the British Empire, in order to bring about the World's supremacy of the Anglo-Saxon race, of her thoughts, of her language, of her political conceptions, of her commerce and her wealth. Its object is to crush all competitions, all internal and external oppositions. It is the German Ideal; it is the Roman Ideal. It is the Imperialism of all countries, at all times, enlarged to the limits of the monstrous pretensions of Pan-Anglo-Saxonism.

All the propositions of the above quotation do not bear, for one single instant, the light of historical research, of reason, even of common sense.

I challenge Mr. Bourassa, and any one else, to read the speeches and the writings of all those who have studied the great question of the future of the British Empire, and to detect therein one single word to justify the assertion *that the organization and concentration of all the Military Forces of the Empire have for their object to help England to dominate the world.*

I have already abundantly proved that England never aspired to dominate the world. I answered Mr. Bourassa's unfounded propositions as follows:—

1—I will surely be allowed to say that for nearly the last fifty years, I have done my best efforts to keep myself well informed with the opinions expressed by the most authorized political men of the Mother Country—of all parties—by the most renowned publicists, by the most distinguished writers of the great English press. I have yet to read one sentence leading me to suppose that the mind of any one of them was haunted by the foolish hope of

Great Britain's domination of the world. Many of them have spoken and written to persuade their countrymen of the growing urgency to consider the most effective measures to be adopted to defend the Empire, in view of the efforts of other nations—notably Germany—to strengthen their military organizations. No one advised them to incur the most heavy sacrifices *in order to dominate the world*. They had too much political sense to believe that such a ridiculous scheme could ever be carried out.

2—What the "Nationalist" leader calls British Imperialism never had for its objective *the gradual suppression, or at least the enslaving of the divers nationalities constituting the British Empire.*

Such an assertion is nothing less than a stroke of the imagination which recent history utterly refutes, proving, as it does, the very reverse, as follows:—

A—The creation, by Imperial Charters, of the great autonomous federal Canadian, Australian, South African Dominions.

B—The federal system adopted for the Dominion of Canada purposely for the protection of the French Canadians whose special interests are entrusted to the Legislature of the Province of Quebec.

C—The South African Union Charter is the guarantee of the Boers' control of the future of that vast stretch of country, by means of the two fundamental principles of the British constitutional system:—government by the majority combined with ministerial responsibility.

No Empire in the world grants as large a measure of freedom as the British Empire does, to the various national groups living under the protection of her flag.

3—British Imperialism, contrary to Mr. Bourassa's assertion, was never deluded by the wild dream *of a world wide supremacy of the Anglo-Saxon race, of her thoughts, of her language, of her political conceptions, of her commerce and her wealth.*

Surely, I have yet to learn that Great Britain has dreamt, and is dreaming, to impose *by Force* her "mentality," her language, her political institutions to China, to Japan, to Russia, to France, to all the South American Republics, to Italy, to Spain, to Germany, to Austria-Hungary, to Turkey, &c., which, considered as a whole, represent, any one must admit, a pretty large part of the universe.

4—Mr. Bourassa's assertion that England aspires to dominate the world, *economically, commercially*, is most positively contradicted by the history of the last eighty years. Who does not know—and I cannot for a moment suppose that Mr. Bourassa ignores it—that, nearly a century ago, Great

Britain, finally rallied in favour of a Free Trade Policy, has opened her market free to the products of all the nations of the world. Is that not a rather strange way of aspiring to an economical domination! And whilst all the countries of the earth, the British colonies as well as foreign nations, can freely sell their goods in the British market, they protect their own markets by high customs duties—in some cases almost prohibitive—against British goods.

National commercial statistics are opened to the "Nationalist" leader's perusal as to any one else. If he had referred to them, he would have learned that the Foreign Trade of Great Britain, in 1913, the year preceding the outbreak of the war, amounted to $7,017,775,335; exports were valued at $3,174,101,630; imports totalized $3,843,673,695, exceeding the exports by the large amount of $669,572,065.

By looking at the figures, Mr. Bourassa would only have had to call upon his common sense to draw the conclusion that England was certainly not moving along an easy road to the commercial domination of the world by maintaining a policy resulting in an import trade larger, by an annual average of nearly twenty per cent., than her exportations.

Before the war, Germany, by rapid strides, had succeeded in attaining the second rank amongst the great trading nations, coming next after Great Britain. In the same year—1913—her Foreign Trade totalized $5,351,500,000, divided as follows:—Imports $2,801,675,000; exports $2,549,825,000.

The really wonderful industrial and commercial expansion of Germany, during the last forty years previous to the war, offered another opportunity to Mr. Bourassa to show his spite against Great Britain. He would have been sorry not to make the best of it. Calling into play his fertile imagination, he unhesitatingly charged England with deep rooted jealousy of Germany's trade success and the guilty intent to crush it out of existence.

To this absurd assertion—not using the word offensively, being always determined to be courteous in any discussion I engage—I answered by quoting the figures of the reciprocal relative external British and German trade. In 1913, Great Britain sold to Germany goods to the amount of $203,385,150, and bought German products for a total value of $402,055,285. Great Britain's exports to Germany were then only about fifty per cent of her imports from the same market. It is indeed difficult to detect in such trade relations between two nations any sign of the intent, on the part of the country buying from the other double the value of her sales to her, to dominate her people commercially.

Any one knowing all the circumstances and the causes that imposed upon

Great Britain the duty of taking part in the European struggle, cannot help being shocked at Mr. Bourassa's accusation *that England has incidentally been brought into the conflict only through the frantic desire of her business men to use it to crush the commercial competition of Germany.* No serious men could have entertained such strange notions. And the "Nationalist" leader certainly charged the political leaders and the business community of England with sheer madness.

With all right minded men, the world over, I have long ago reached the sound conclusion that universal economical domination is only a chimerical idea absolutely outside of all possible realization. England does not indulge in any such extravagant dream, being too well aware how vain it would be.

May I ask my readers—and Mr. Bourassa has been one of them,—to join with me in a short general review of the economical progress of the world, in its broadest lines, rising, for this purpose, as should be done in all cases, superior to all national and local prejudices. A grand natural scenery is always better appreciated from the mountain top. Equally so, questions of universal import must be considered from the heights of the noblest principles inspiring the Christian desire to promote the general good of Mankind. Considered from this elevated standpoint, very short-sighted indeed is the man who fails to see THAT THE ECONOMICAL PROGRESS OF THE WORLD, AGRICULTURALLY, INDUSTRIALLY, COMMERCIALLY, IS BOUND UP WITH INTELLIGENT, ENERGETIC AND PERSEVERING LABOUR; THAT IT IS THE OUTCOME OF THE IMPROVEMENTS OF ALL THE MEANS OF PRODUCTION, TO THE CONSTANT INCREASED PERFECTION OF THE AGRICULTURAL AND INDUSTRIAL ARTS, TO THE ENLARGEMENT OF THE RESOURCES OF CAPITAL, ACCUMULATED BY JUDICIOUS SAVINGS. It is bound with the improvement of means of transportation by land and sea; with the much enlarged facilities of the exchange of all kinds of products; with the superior management,—the result of a much wider experience—of all the institutions distributing credit; with the energetic development of all the resources which generous Providence has profusely provided the earth for the good of Humanity. It is more than useless to expect economical progress from disastrous armed conflicts which, in the course of a few years, nay, only a few months, destroy the accumulated wealth of many years of incessant labour.

War is productive of untold material losses. As a general rule, it cannot make the nations of the world richer. Many successive generations have for a long time to bear the crushing burden which they inherit from guilty ambitious Rulers as the only result of their thirst of vain glory. Materially, a nation may profit by an unjust war, resulting in the defeat of a weaker rival, but the riches thus acquired by the one, either by territorial acquisitions, or by the payment to her of war contributions and indemnities, or both, from the other, are merely transferred from the vanquished to the victor. The great society of nations, instead of gaining anything by it, is only losing, as a whole, the total amount of the financial cost of the military operations, of the squandering of hard earned savings, of diminished labour and production, of the waste of productive capital, of the loss of so many long days which could have been so much better employed. But most deplorable is the loss entailed by the warring nations, and the universe at large, by the sacrifice of the younger generations, of early youth and of strongly developed manhood, for the success of tyrannical and criminal purposes.

There can be but one justification—and it is a noble, a glorious one—of the sacrifice of so many valuable lives and so much material wealth: the sacredness, the sanctity of the cause for which a nation, or a group of peoples, take up arms against an enemy, or enemies, only intent on crushing weaker rival, or rivals, by all the illegitimate means at his, or their command, for self-aggrandizement, for unjust domination. Such is the present war: sacred and just on the Allied side; abominable, brutal, barbarous on the German side, enhanced in its guilt by the ferocious Turks and the shameful submission of the enslaved Austrians to the overpowering will of their teutonic masters. It will not have cost too much if it has the result of freeing Mankind from the horrors of German militarism, assuring to the world a long reign of justice and moral grandeur.

England can rightly claim a very large part of the merit accruing to all those who have contributed to the immense material progress of the world during the last century. She has actively and most intelligently worked for it by her vigorous industrial and commercial development, by the very numerous billions of dollars she has contributed, all over the world, to railway building and oceanic navigation. She has contributed to it by her extraordinary amount of savings which allowed her to supply the capital required for so many varied enterprises over all the continents. She has played the very important part of universal banker, distributing her immense treasures to foster production of all kinds everywhere. She has most largely contributed to the economic phenomenon of the gradual diminution of the universal rate of interest.

If, according to Mr. Bourassa's strange notion, all this is to be considered as equivalent to economical domination, the more the whole world will enjoy it the better, more prosperous it will be, and future generations will have so much more cause for rejoicing at its increased development, and to be grateful to England for it.

The witnesses who, for the last sixty years, have lived with their eyes opened, preferring the full shining light of the bright days of universal economical development to the darkness obscuring fanatical minds only intent on stirring up local, sectional and national prejudices, and miserable petty ambitions, have rejoiced at the greatly varied advantages Humanity has derived from the gifts of Providence favouring her with the great scientific discoveries which have worked, are still, and will for all times, work wonders for her material prosperity. The regular tendency of those natural forces recently applied to production is an increased movement towards the unification of the industrial, commercial and financial interests of the world. The vital energies of all peoples have more or less been stimulated by the same causes, operating everywhere, reaching until lately unknown and undeveloped regions. Engineering genius, broadened by the new scientific resources at its command, has triumphed over all difficulties. The gigantic locomotive, drawing palatial passenger coaches, and sometimes as much as a hundred heavily loaded freight cars, run by thousands and thousands daily through luxurious prairies. They cross giant rivers, ascend with alertness the highest mountains, or rush through tunnels which the skill and hard work of man has pierced through them, backed by the financial power of millions of money. Automobilism covers the whole universe, multiplying intercourse and human relations, and making possible, in a few days of marvellous organization, a glorious military victory like that almost miraculously carried at the Marne.

Giant steamers, of fifty to sixty thousand tons—of a hundred thousand in the near future—ply, day and night, over the high seas. In mid-ocean they scatter human thoughts through the air to very distant points. They carry within their large skulls immense quantities of the most varied products.

Means of transportation have become so numerous, so improved, so rapid, that the surplus agricultural production of the most fertile regions do reach, in a few short days, the countries which, on account of their numerous industrial and commercial population, have to import a large quantity of food products. The equilibrium between production and consumption becomes yearly more easily obtainable. Famine by the inequality of agricultural production is very much less to be apprehended. Millions of human beings are no longer, as hitherto, threatened to die by starvation at the same time that more favoured regions had a surplus of food products which they could not use, sell, or export.

Without a most powerful capitalization of savings—totaling, in some cases, billions of dollars—without the marvellous development of the great transportation industry by land and sea, could the Canadian and American western grain crops be delivered, within a few days' time, with an astonishing rapidity and at very small cost, on all the markets where they are absolutely required for daily consumption.

Every country on earth is multiplying her efforts to develop her manufacturing interests by an active and intelligent use of the raw materials with which her territory has been favoured by Nature.

To this intense economical development of the world, all the peoples are contributing their shares in various proportions, of course:—In Europe, Great Britain, France, Germany, Russia, Austria, Italy, Belgium, &c.; in the two Americas, the United States, Canada—Canada with the sure prospects of such a grand future—the Argentine Republic, Brazil, &c.; in Asia, Japan, China, and the so very large Asiatic regions of Russia; in Africa, the British colonies, Egypt, Algeria, &c.; and Australia, so recently opened to the glories of Christian Civilization, blooming in the Pacific ocean washing her shores, fertilizing her lands nearer to its refreshing breeze.

Who does not see that all this development tends naturally to the economical unity of the world. If Humanity is ever effectively delivered from the dangers of wars like the one actually desolating her so cruelly, she will have to be grateful for this great boon to the unification, on a larger scale, of the general interests of all the nations requiring permanent peace for their regular and harmonious growth.

To the wonderful material prosperity achieved as above explained, England has contributed her legitimate share, without trying to dominate economically the universe which derived all the great advantages which her business genius has so largely developed.

It must not be supposed that I lose sight of the inconveniences which material prosperity may entail. One of them is the tendency to bend the national aspirations to materialism. This can be counteracted by the national will to apply material development to the more important intellectual, moral and religious progress of the people at large.

Any nation aspiring to dominate the world by brute force or by the power of wealth, would be guilty of attempting an achievement just as vain as it would be criminal in its conception.

Any nation is within her undoubted right and duty in aspiring to the legitimate influence of her material progress, of her intellectual culture, of her moral development, of her religious increased perfection. Happy indeed would be the future of Humanity if all the Nations and their Rulers understood well, and did their best efforts to practice Christian precepts in the true spirit of their Divine teaching.

CHAPTER XVIII.

IMPERIALISM.

Mr. Bourassa is apparently so frightened by what he calls *Imperialism* that the horrible phantom being always present to his imagination, he shudders at it in day time, and wildly dreams of it at night. Judging by what he has said and written, he seems to have worried a great deal, for many years past, about the dire misfortunes which, he believed, were more and more threatening the future of the world by the strong movement of imperialist views he detected everywhere. It is the great hobby which saddens his life, the terrible bugbear with which he is ever trying to arouse the feelings of his French Canadian countrymen against England.

The deceased British statesman, called Joseph Chamberlain, by his efforts to promote the unity of the Empire, inspired Mr. Bourassa with a profound fear which he wanted his compatriots to share by all the means at his command:— public speeches, newspaper editorials, pamphlets. He charged him with the responsibility of the *infamous crime* he brought England to commit in accepting the challenge of President Kruger and the then South African Republic, and fighting for the defence of her Sovereign rights in South Africa. According to the Nationalist leader, a vigorous impulse was given by the South African war to the political evolution which he termed *British Imperialism*. Nothing was further from the true meaning of this important event.

In refuting Mr. Bourassa's assertion, I showed that the South African war was not the outgrowth of Imperialist ideas, and that it has in no way resulted in a dangerous advance of the kind of Imperialism which so much frightens him and all those who experience his baneful influence.

As I have previously proved, the South African campaign was imposed upon England by the then aspiration of a section only of Boer opinion, led by the unscrupulous and haughty President Kruger, imprudently relying on the support of the German Kaiser who had hastened to congratulate him for his success in the Jameson Raid. It resulted not in favor of Imperialism of the type so violently denounced by Mr. Bourassa, but in a most beneficent expansion of Political Freedom by the granting of the free British institutions to the new great South African overseas Dominion. It is only the other day that ex-Premier Asquith, on the occasion of a great public function, has declared that Premier Botha, the former most prominent Boer General, was now one of the strongest pillars of the British Empire.

It being so important to set the opinion of the French Canadians right respecting that question of Imperialism, so much discussed of late, and by many with so little political sense and historical knowledge, I would not rest satisfied with a refutation of the special Bourassist appreciation of the causes and results of the South African conflict. I summarized, in a condensed review, the divers phases of the political movement which can properly be called *Imperialism*, tracing its origin as far back as the organization of the first great political Powers known to History: the Persian, the Egyptian, the Greek Empires, &c. More than ever before, Imperialism was triumphant during the long Roman domination of almost all the then known world. Every student of History is impressed by the grandeur of the part played by the Roman Empire in the world's drama. Constantine struck the first blow at Roman Imperialism —unwillingly we can rest assured—in laying the foundations of Constantinople, and dividing the Roman Empire into the Western and Eastern Empires. At last, after repeated invasions, the Northern barbarians succeeded in smashing the Roman Colossus.

After many long years during which European political society passed through the incessant turmoil of rival ambitions, Charlemagne sets up anew the Western Empire, being coronated Emperor in Rome. Ever since, amidst multiplied ups and downs, Imperialism has swayed to and fro by the successive edification and overthrow of the Holy Roman Empire, the short lived Napoleonic European domination, the recently organized North German Empire.

So far as Imperialism is concerned, all those great historical facts considered, how best can it be defined? Is it not evident that from the very birth of political societies for the government of Mankind, a double current of political thoughts and aspirations has been concurrently at work, with alternate successes and retrocessions: one tending towards large political organizations, uniting a variety of ethnical groups; the other operating the reverse way to bring about their dissolution in favour of multiplied small sovereignties. Each of the two opposing political systems has had its ebb and flow tides; the waves of the one, in their flowing days, washing the shores of the other until they had to recede before the pressure caused by the exhaustion of their own strength and the increased resistance of internal opposition.

Viewed from this elevated standpoint, Imperialism is not new under the sun. It is as ancient as the world itself. Mr. Bourassa has been uselessly spending his energy in breaking his head against a movement which is in the very nature of things, developing the same way under the same favourable conditions and circumstances.

Are the days we live so fraught with the dangers of Imperialism as to justify the fears of the alarmist? The answer would be in the affirmative, the question being considered from the point of view of Germany's autocratic Imperialism, if the free nations of the world had not joined in a holy union to put an end to its extravagant and tyrannical ambition. But how is it that Mr. Bourassa, the heaven-born anti-imperialist, so frightened at the supposed progress of British Imperialism, is so lenient towards Teutonic Imperialism? How is it that from the very first days of the gigantic struggle calling for the most heroic efforts of the human race to emerge safe and free from the furious waves powerfully set in motion by the most daring absolutism that ever existed, he has not thought proper to chastise as it deserved the worst kind of Imperialism that he could, or any one else, imagine?

Taking for granted that the present economical conditions of the universe, likely to intensify, are working for great political organisations, from the causes previously explained, any intelligent observer could not fail to see that for the last century four great imperialist evolutions have been concurrently— or rather simultaneously—developing themselves; they were the British, the Teutonic, the Russian, the Republican in the United States. Let no one be astonished at seeing the two words *Imperialism* and *Republicanism* coupled together. In their true sense, they are easily conciliated.

The Roman Republic, by the grandeur of its part, was Imperialist as much as the Empire to which she gave birth. Cæsar, without the imperial crown was Emperor as much as August. He was more so by his genius, and by the eminent position he had acquired by one of the most brilliant careers in History.

Bonaparte, General and First Consul, in the closing days of the first French Republic, was Emperor as much as he became on the day of his Coronation, at Paris, by the Sovereign Pontiff.

Imperialism being a great historical fact through all the ages, and most certainly destined to further developments, is it to be judged favourably or alarmingly?

No doubt the problem is of the greatest possible political importance. The question can, I consider, be at the outset simplified as follows:—Would the prosperity, the freedom, the happiness of the world be better served by great political Powers, or by the multiplication of small sovereignties? It is just as well, and even better, to admit at once that a unique, a dogmatic, answer cannot be given to that question. Independent nations, sovereign societies, are not created at will by men, merely according to their fancy, to their variable and very often undefined wishes. History teaches that they are the outgrowth of various circumstances, of many divergent causes,—the most important, the one inscrutable, being always the action of Divine Providence directing the destinies of peoples as well as those of every human being. Different causes produce, of course, different results. Large and small political communities can surely be productive of much good for their populations. Much depends upon the intelligence, the wisdom, the devotion, the patriotism of the rulers and the governed. They can also do much harm. Unfortunately, the readers of past events have too much reason to deplore that both large and small political organizations have been equally guilty of maladministration, of ambitious cupidity of their neighbours' possessions, of unjust wars. As an uncontrovertible example, can I not point to the present German Empire, whose origin dates back to the days of the very small Prussia of two centuries ago, fighting her way up to her actual greatness by successive, unfair, and often criminal aggressions.

After reading much of the history of past ages, I have not been able to come to the conclusion—and the more I read, the less inclined I am to do so—that the days when England, France, Central Europe, Italy, &c., were subdivided into numerous small political organizations, almost always warring, were preferable to ours, even darkened and saddened as they are by the present trials and sufferings.

If, on the other hand, the causes which at all times have tended to the creation of large political sovereignties are gradually acquiring an increased momentum of strength and activity, from the changed conditions brought about by the great scientific discoveries so wonderfully developing the commercial relations of the nations, is it not more advisable to study the true nature of the evolution and the good it can produce, rather than to shiver at the supposed prospects of an Imperialist cataclysm so certainly to be averted if public opinion is sound and Rulers wise. Crying on the shores of the St. Lawrence, against the advance of the rolling waves, would not prevent the tide from running up. The mad man who would try it, and persist in remaining on the spot, displaying his indignant and extravagant protest, would surely be submerged and drowned.

Political developments, like many others, obey natural laws which no true statesman can ignore nor overlook. Because the limits of a political organization are extended, does it necessarily follow that only deplorable consequences can be expected from their enlargement? Surely not. One might as well pretend that unity, cohesion, strength, grandeur, are only productive of baneful results. Is it not a certainty that they can be equally beneficial or harmful, according to the intellectual and moral qualities of those who are called upon to apply them to the best interests of those they govern.

German Imperialism, for instance, was not *per se* a public misfortune. It became such because instead of using its instrumentality for the general good of the world as well as that of Germany, it was applied to a barbarous and criminal purpose to satisfy unjust and senseless aspirations.

In the same years, all the resources of British Imperialism,—so abhorrent to Mr. Bourassa and his Nationalist adepts who view with such meekness the Teutonic type—have been brought into play for the freedom of the world and the protection of the small nationalities—notably Belgium.

Bulgaria was a small State. Was it on this account less ambitious and troublesome for its neighbours? Any one conversant with the recent Balkan history knows that Bulgaria has from the start aspired to dominate the Balkan States. When the Berlin Government struck the hour which was to throw not only Europe, but three-fourths of the universe into the worst horrors of war, has Bulgaria rallied to the defence of her weak neighbour, Servia? Has she proved any sympathy for treacherously crushed Belgium?

I emphatically declare that I would oppose Imperialism with all my might, if I thought that it is by nature a necessary producer of absolutism, of autocratic tyranny. But, the British precedent considered through all its beneficial developments, I must recognize that true Imperialism is not incompatible with the just and wise exercise of political liberty, with respectful protection of the rights and conditions of the divers national elements under its ægis.

I pray to remain to my last day a faithful friend of the political liberties of the people. Knowing, as I do, how hard it is to apply them to the government of nations—great or small—I am not bewildered by vain illusions. But I cannot conceive—and never will—that the justice of the real principles of Political Liberty is to be denied on account of the difficulties of their satisfactory working, certainly obtainable when applied in conformity with the dictates of moral laws owing all their power to their Divine origin.

The best political institutions which can work out such great advantages for the populations enjoying them, are too often diverted from their beneficient course by the vicious passions of those who are charged with, and responsible for, their administration. It would be most illogical to draw the inference that good institutions become bad by their guilty management.

Free and autocratic governments are essentially different in their natural structure. Though liable to mismanagement by unscrupulous politicians, free institutions can, under ordinary favourable conditions, be trusted to be productive of much good for the peoples living under their protection. Autocracy—the whole human history proves it—by nature engenders absolutism. Crowned or revolutionary despots as a rule are not imbued with the patriotism nor purified by the virtues required for the good government of a country. Kaiserism, Terrorism and Bolshevikism are equally despicable and unfit to contribute to the sound progress which liberty, practiced by sensible and wise men, can develop.

Reverting to the Nationalist bugbear, which does not in the least move me to despair of Canada's future, I consider that Imperialism, sensibly appreciated, is of two kinds: Autocratic Imperialism; Democratic Imperialism:— Absolutism is the foundation stone of the former; Political Liberty that of the latter. I am energetically opposed to the first. I sincerely believe that the second can do a great deal for the prosperity of the countries where it has regularly and justifiably been developed according to the natural laws of its growth.

Autocratic Imperialism, in contemporaneous history, is almost exclusively typified by its Teutonic production. A general review of the world shows that for the last century, and more, with one sad exception, all the nations have been moving along the path leading to a greater freedom of their institutions. Even Japan and China have joined in the race. Russia had deliberately done so. Much was expected from her first efforts, and much would certainly have been reaped in due course had not the calamitous war still raging at first opened an opportunity for the reactionary Russian element, strongly influenced by German intrigues, spies and money, to check, through the Petrograd Court, the forward movement of Russian political liberty, and to impede, for Germany's sake, the success of the Russian military operations. Under those circumstances—as was also to be expected—the advancing wave of the aspirations of the great Russian people for more political freedom, was bound either to recede before the autocratic outburst, or to rush impetuously against the wall Germany was to her best helping to raise against it. The latter prevision happened, history once more repeating itself.

Even barbarous Turkey, in recent years, had been somewhat shaken by a sudden desire to remove some of her secular shackles. The young Turks movement might have had some desirable results had the Ottoman Empire, as every national and political considerations should have induced her to do, sided with France and England.

Germany is actually the only country in the world where Autocratic Imperialism has been flourishing during the last century. We all know the extent and the grievousness of the calamity it has wrought on the universe.

During the same last century, Democratic Imperialism—using the term in its broadest and most reasonable meaning—has had two distinct beneficial developments:—the Monarchical Democratic Imperialism, and the Republican Democratic Imperialism.

The Monarchical Democratic or free Imperialism—it is scarcely necessary for me to say—is that of Great Britain.

The Republican Democratic or free Imperialism is that of the United States of America, of the Argentine Republic, of Brazil.

Happily the two great and glorious countries which are favoured with the advantages of the Democratic type of Imperialism are united in a grand and noble effort to destroy the German Autocratic Imperialism in chastisement of its criminal aspirations to universal domination.

The two types of Democratic or free Imperialism the Monarchical and the Republican—can be better illustrated by a comparative short historical study of their development in Great Britain and her colonies, and in the United States. I summarize it as follows, beginning by the last mentioned, as it requires a shorter exposition.

CHAPTER XIX.

AMERICAN IMPERIALISM.

The still recent and wonderful growth of the two American continents, in population and wealth, is almost an incredible marvel. It is none the least politically.

The two Americas, by the extent of their areas, the vastness of their productive lands, the length and largeness of their mighty Rivers, the broadness of their Lakes, the grandeur of their scenery, seem to be most adapted to great developments of many kinds. It is difficult to think of small conceptions originating in the New World, which the genius of Columbus discovered and the combined genius of all the great races of the Old are united in developing.

Let me first put the question:—when the leading European nations undertook to colonize the new Continents, were they not, consciously or not, throwing the Imperialist seed in a fertile land where it was sure to take root and blossom? Spain, France, and, last, England were certainly not obeying the dictates of our "Nationalist school" when they brought under their Sovereign authority such vast stretches of American territory.

That Christian Civilization was to be extended to the new great Hemisphere, goes without saying. That the riches, then unknown, of the New World, were to be extracted from the land so full of them, was one of the duties of the discoverers, all will admit. The European Governments in extending their Sovereignties to America unfortunately adopted the mistaken Colonial Policy then still too much prevalent. Their error was to stick to the wrong conception that a colony was important only in the measure that it could be favourable to the interests of the Metropolis. History proves that this colonial system is bound to lead to unfair treatment of the colonies. Absolutism, then dominant in Europe, could not be expected to show any tender leniency towards the Colonials who were above all to work for the wealth and glory of the Metropolis. Spain proved to be the worst promoter of that Regime. Her failure has been most complete. She has had to withdraw her flag from the very large part of America over which it might have been kept waving, if sounder and more just political notions had prevailed in the narrowed minds of her Rulers.

England, treading along the wrong path of Colonial oppression, but in a much less proportion, had to face a like result in the revolt of her American Colonies. Fortunately for her, for America and the world at large, the event widely opened her eyes. In acknowledging the independence of the young Republic of the United States, she was destined to be proud of her offspring in witnessing the astonishing development of the child to whom she had given birth. Could she have then foreseen that the day would come when at the hour of her dire trial, the daughter who threw off her motherly authority, too stringently exercised, would rush to her support for the defence of the very principles of Political Liberty for which she, the child, had fought for her independence, how soon would England have forgotten the sufferings of the parting and blessed Providence for them!

The American Revolution, successfully carried out, was the occasion for England to revolutionize her Colonial Policy. She was the first nation—and I am sorry to say she has remained alone—to understand with great clearness that the old Colonial Regime, fraught with such disastrous consequences, must be done away with and replaced by the new one which called the colonies to the enjoyment, to the largest possible extent, of the free institutions of the Mother Land.

Like every new born child, whose laborious birth was critical, the American Republic experienced great difficulties the very moment she commenced to breathe freely. So true it is always that national development, like personal success, cannot be achieved without struggle.

The United States offer the example of the best development of the Imperialist evolution in the world. It dates as far back as the proclamation of the Independence of the Republic. When she was admitted into the international society of Sovereign States, she had at first to settle her political organization. The framing of a constitutional charter proved to be a very arduous task, at times almost desperate.

Three sets of divergent opinions were fighting at close range during the protracted and solemn deliberations which at last reached a happy conclusion. Thirteen American British Colonies had coalesced to wring their Independence from England. The goal once attained, a first group of opinion was favoured by the supporters of the dissolution of the temporary union organized to secure the Independence of the whole, but to revert, they said, if successful, to their previous separate status. Had this view prevailed, at the very start North America would have been cumbered with thirteen Sovereign States. Many were alarmed at the creation of so many small Republics. More reasonable persons suggested to organize three or four of them, instead of thirteen, meeting as much as possible the wants natural to geographical conditions. It was no doubt an improvement on the first mentioned scheme. It met with the hearty support of devoted adepts.

It is much to be hoped that they will forever receive from the successive generations of their countrymen the reward of the gratitude they deserve, the true statesmen who, at this important juncture, stepped on the scene and bravely took their stand in favour of the maintenance of the Union which had conquered Independence, and of the establishment of only one great Republic. The celebrated Hamilton was their trusted leader. They knew they were undertaking an herculean task. At that time, the population of the thirteen original States, scarcely four millions in number, was scattered over a vast territory, and located, for the most part, on the lands near the Atlantic coasts, two thousand miles in length, from North to South. Transportation was in a very primitive stage. Many years had yet to run before the whistle of the locomotive, powerful and struggling, would be echoed by the solitude of immense forests. No one foresaw that, in less than a century, the overflowing tide of European immigration would roll its waves so powerfully as to cross the whole continent and the Rocky Mountains to reach the coast of the Pacific Ocean.

With such conditions, so unfavourable to the aspirations of only one new Independent State, moulding together political groups so far apart, interests apparently so hostile, the local point of view, local prejudices, were sure to dominate. They inspired the strong current of opinion in favour of the dissolution of the temporary Union, and the organization of every one of the old provinces into a separate Sovereign State.

How, under such circumstances, the friends of a unique National American Union succeeded in the marvellous achievement of carrying their point by a prodigy of persuasive demonstration, will forever be a wonder for the student of the Republic's history. Few in numbers when they boldly threw their challenge, they encountered the shock of local fanaticism heightened by their offensive. Everything seemed to predict their utter failure. If ever Founders of States have proved the heroism of their convictions, the American Federalists have most gloriously done so. Undoubtedly, the force of the argument was with them. But what can logic, reason, good sense, too often do against inveterate prejudices? Were they, in this particular instance, destined to be powerless?

The Federalists—such is their historical name—were not to be disheartened by the formidable obstacles thrown in their way. An *Imperialist* inspiration was certainly the basic foundation of their demonstration finally triumphant. They told their countrymen that if they were to erect thirteen small Republics upon the burning ruins of the first Union to which they owed their Independence, they would prepare a very sad future for their children and children's children. European immigration was setting in, slowly but surely. They predicted that the World, this time, would witness, not a barbarous invasion like that which overthrew the Roman Empire, but one which the Old World would overflow to the New Continents. This surplus European population would bring over to America Christian Civilization, the training of hard work, large hopes, courage, experience in many ways, persevering energy, which would transform the boundless regions which could become their national heritage—until then the domain of the wandering Indian—into one of the greatest and wealthiest countries on earth. Would they commit the irreparable error to destroy the certainty of such a magnificent National Destiny, by creating thirteen separate governments, with the sure result of renewing in America, by such race groupings, the atrocious military conflicts which, for centuries, have flooded the European soil with human blood.

Hamilton and some of his most distinguished friends published that work, entitled: *"The Federalist"*, which will ever live as one of the broadest and most elevated productions of Political Intelligence. To all, and especially to the "Nationalist" theorists, I strongly recommend the reading of that book, a monument of the genius of great statesmen.

In short, after a lengthy discussion characterized by their brilliant eloquence and their argumentative strength, the supporters of the Federal Union of the thirteen States, under one Sovereignty, carried the day. They had well deserved their glorious triumph. The Republic of the United States of North America was founded under the ægis of the free constitutional Charter which has done so much for her prosperity and her grandeur.

Such was the initial move of the evolution of American Imperialism. Those amongst us who desire to learn more about its developments have only to look over the boundary line. The thirteen original States, federally united, have increased to number forty-four, with three more territories gradually developing into Statehood.

The actual population of the Republic is already much over a *hundred million*, living in unrivalled prosperity and contentment on a territorial area of more than *three millions and a half square miles*, larger than all the European Continent. The sun of the present century will set upon a people of more than 250,000,000, with a splendid situation in a world to the destinies of which they will contribute in many admirable ways, if they are only true to the Christian principles which alone can assure Civilization and Progress.

If the term *Imperialism* truly means what the word implies,—*Sovereignty being exercised over a large population and a vast territory*, this political evolution, so decried by some, has most undoubtedly achieved a great success amongst our neighbours to the South.

In all sincerity, may I not ask every unprejudiced mind:—has not the whole

World every reason to be much elated at witnessing the beneficent results of the triumph of the American Federalists? Evidently, it has been *Imperial* in its nature, in its proportions. It is so in its promises for the future greatness of the Republic. It has maintained, with only one exception, peace and harmony during nearly a century and a half, between the descendants of the European nationalities who have trusted their future welfare to the Sovereignty of the United States. Instead of wasting their energies in endless conflicts, such as numerous small States would have infallibly occasioned, thanks to the unity of the Sovereign Power binding into an admirable whole territories larger than Europe, they have learned to consider themselves as citizens of the same free country, as the free subjects of the same governmental authority. The temporary rupture of the Union, caused by the war of Secession, was but a vain reactionary action against the powerful current driving the Republic towards her grand future.

It is most unlikely—I can say *impossible* without the slightest hesitation—that the United States, after taking such a grand and glorious part in the present war, will abandon the broad and felicitous policy by which they have grown to be one of the greatest independent nations of the world, to drop so low as to adopt the blinding notions of a narrow, sectional, prejudiced and fanatical "Nationalism", such as the type which would ruin the future of our own Dominion, if ever it was allowed to prevail. They know too well, by the happiest experience, that the only true *"Nationalism"* is that which by the united effort of the intelligence, the culture, the strength, the patriotism of citizens of divers races has wrought for them their present admirable national status so full of the brightest promises. When peace shall have been restored, the great and mighty American Republic will be one of the leading Powers on earth, owing her unrivalled prosperity in a very large measure to her appreciation of the wonderful results obtainable by the union of all her subjects, of whatever racial origins, working with the same heart and devotion for the grandeur of their common country.

I am not unduly enthusiastic, I am only speaking the plain truth, when I affirm that the Republican Imperialism of the United States has been most beneficent, having guaranteed to Mankind the inestimable boon of laying deep and strong in a virgin soil, providentially gifted with the most varied, the most abundant, the richest resources, the destinies of a great Sovereign Nation comprising numerous ethnical groups. This liberal, progressive, peaceful, harmonious Imperialism, it is a duty to approve wishing it to achieve new triumphs for the general good of Humanity.

Republican Imperialism is also making its way—contaminating it, our "Nationalists" would say—in Southern America. This large and splendid half of the New World has been for too many years the theatre of civil troubles which appeared endless. A great change for the better has taken place since the beginning of the concentration movement which has united almost the entire Southern American Continent into eight Sovereign States, two of which with really Imperial proportions.

The Brazilian Republic has a territorial area of 3,218,991 square miles, with a population of more than 24,000,000 increasing at the average rate of six or seven hundred thousand a year. With the great natural resources at her command, she will certainly develop into one great Power. The day is not so far distant when it will have a population exceeding *fifty millions* living in comfort on a soil of luxurious wealth.

The Argentine Republic has a territory of 1,153,119 square miles in extent. Her population is over 8,000,000, having doubled during the last twenty years. At this rate of a yearly increase of five per cent, it is easily foreseen what large total it will reach in a few years. It is wealthy, doing the best with her splendid resources, already contributing extensively to feed the population of Europe.

The other Southern American Republics—the Bolivian, the Chilean, the Colombian, the Peruvian, the Venezuelan—have all territorial areas double in extent of those of the Great Powers of Western and Central Europe.

In Southern America, like everywhere else, the rising tide is not running in favour of a multiplicity of small Sovereignties, always in a warring frame of mind. Since her political reorganization, South America, as a whole, has enjoyed the advantages of peace and of a large material progress.

In reality the same political phenomenon is to be found in the five continents forming the whole earthly globe. Let the "Nationalists" call it *Imperialism* if they like, I cannot help concluding that it is the outgrowth of natural causes operating in the sense of larger political units, giving to the Nations getting so constituted, prestige, power, grandeur, favouring public order and, in many instances, the development of free institutions.

CHAPTER XX.

BRITISH IMPERIALISM.

Let me now consider the wonderful development of what I have called Monarchical Democratic or free Imperialism. It has so far been exclusively of British growth. It is the typical form of Imperialism which has been honoured with the most violent, the most unjust, denunciations of our "Nationalists".

How did it deserve such an hysterical reprobation? Such is the question to which I shall now endeavour to give a decisive negative answer.

I have previously once said that British Imperialism, like American Imperialism, has Political Liberty as its foundation stone. I think this can easily be proven.

Any close observer of political events, will agree with me, I am confident, that Imperialism is also "OFFENSIVE" and "DEFENSIVE" in its expansion. The meaning of these two terms is clear.

For the last fifty years, "OFFENSIVE" IMPERIALISM has been the GERMAN DESPOTIC IMPERIALISM. The present war—its criminal work—is the convincing evidence in support of the charge.

I have, I believe, proved to the satisfaction of every fair minded man, that during the same last fifty years England's constant efforts have been to maintain peace. Consequently, I am authorized to draw the conclusion that British Imperialism was not intended to be, and has not been "OFFENSIVE".

The Imperialist effort OFFENSIVELY, AGGRESSIVELY and VIOLENTLY tending to the continuous and unmeasured expansion of a Sovereign Power, with the objective of universal domination by all possible means, however unjust, immoral and savage they may be, is a most guilty effort deserving the severest condemnation. Such is the German autocratic Imperialism.

On the contrary, the DEFENSIVE Imperialist effort, having for its only object the protection of an Empire, the maintenance of her standing in the society of nations, and of peace so essential to the general prosperity of the world, is meritorious, beneficent and laudable. Such has been the British Monarchical democratic Imperialism.

It is from this elevated standpoint that I will consider the negotiations which, for the last few years, have taken place between the Metropolis and her autonomous Colonies, respecting Imperial defence. While admitting the right of all the free citizens of Canada to appreciate them, and entertaining a real respect for the sincerity of opinions which I cannot conscientiously share, I cannot help considering that many amongst us have fallen into a serious error in judging the nature of these negotiations.

Is it truly, as has been asserted, in obedience to a powerful wave of "OFFENSIVE IMPERIALISM" that Great Britain has of late convened representatives of her free Colonies to meet, in London, to confer about the best means to adopt for the general security of the whole British Empire?

Is it, as also asserted, with the unworthy design to entrap the Colonies that their self-appointed delegates have been called in secret conclaves where the political leaders of England would, by unfair and foul means, prevail upon them to agree to unjust sacrifices on the part of the peoples they represented?

I am absolutely unable to share such erroneous views, I must admit with all candor that I have not yet been brought to the conclusion that British Statesmen are all contaminated with "Machiavellism". A free country like the United Kingdom is not a land where such deplorable principles are likely to blossom.

What are then the extraordinary events which have recently taken place to justify the assertion of the "Nationalist" leader that, in the course of the last few years, a complete REVOLUTION has been wrought in the relations of the autonomous Colonies with their Metropolis? Of such a Revolution, cunningly promoted to bring the colonies against their will to participate in the Imperial wars—*les guerres de l'empire*—I do not perceive the smallest shadow of traces.

As everybody else, living with their eyes not closed to the light of day, I clearly saw, principally during the last twenty years, that important developments were taking place under the sun; that European equilibrium upon the maintenance of which universal peace so much depended, was rapidly breaking asunder; that the German Empire was more and more unmasking her guilty ambition to dominate an enslaved universe; that, to reach that goal, she was organizing an army formidable by its millions of warriors, their superior training, their ironed discipline and their unrivalled armament. I knew that the sadly famous Kaiser Wilhelm II. was determined, at all cost, to increase the power of his Empire by the addition of a military fleet in such proportions as to be able, in a successful naval battle, to conquer the supremacy of the seas.

Under such circumstances, was it to be supposed that the Statesmen responsible for the government of Great Britain would be so careless and so blind as not to see the dark spots crowding on the horizon!

The problem of Imperial defence was then once more raised, not by a mere caprice of vain glory on the part of England, but by the inevitable outcome of the initiative of would-be opponents, if not actually declared enemies. The overseas colonies being more and more likely to be attacked, in a general conflict, was it surprising that the British Government was induced to confer with them for their common defence under the new conditions which were surely not of their own metropolitan or colonial creation.

All the representatives of Great Britain, of Canada, Australia, South Africa, New Zealand, at the London conferences, took part in those solemn deliberations with the full sense of their responsibility. None of them was so mistaken as to consider the question, of paramount importance, of the DEFENSIVE organization of the Empire, as futile, merely to be used by the astuteness of some and the guilty complicity of others, joining together to sacrifice the future of their common country. The odious imputation, the shameless charge, were equally unjust and calumnious for the British ministers and the colonial public men who, in their turn, went to London to deliberate on subjects so vitally interesting all the component parts of the Empire.

CHAPTER XXI.

The Situations of 1865 and 1900-14 Compared.

Our "Nationalist" opponents of all colonial participation in the Imperial wars, affirm that Canada should have abided with the convention of 1865. Are they not aware that, since that year, a great deal of water has run along the rivers; that the world, although perhaps not wiser, has at least grown half a century older; that so many ancient conditions have radically changed; that nations, like individuals, to be progressive, cannot go on marking time on the same small hardened spot?

Any man sincerely desirous to form for himself an enlightened opinion on the question of Imperial defence, must first admit that two national and general situations, totally different, create widely different duties.

Let us compare for a moment, 1865 and 1900-14—*yesterday and to-day*—as the "Nationalist" leader says.

Fifty years ago, the German Empire was non-existent. Nothing pointed to the early birth of this terrible child destined to grow so rapidly to such colossal proportions.

The French Empire was the leading continental Power; Great Britain, then as now, the leading naval Power, both military and mercantile.

Those two nations, without a formal alliance, had been united ever since the days when Lord Palmerston favoured the advent of Napoleon III.

The Union of England and France was doing much to maintain the peace of the world.

The United States were just emerging from the trials of their great Civil War. They had to solve the very difficult problem of their national reconstruction. Their population did not exceed thirty-five millions.

How different was the situation of 1900-14!

The German Empire had become formidable with her population of 68,000,000, her soldiers numbering more than 7,000,000, with 1,000,000 of men permanently under arms, ever ready for an offensive campaign, with her fleet much enlarged yearly at the cost of enormous financial sacrifices; allied to Austria-Hungary, with her population of 50,000,000, to Italy, with her 36,000,000—then being one of the Triple Alliance—supported by Turkey and Bulgaria,—in all a combined strength of 150,000,000 bodies and souls; with the Germans exalted to the utmost by persistent appeals to their feelings and to their ambitious dreams.

The American Republic grown to the rank of a first class Power, with a population of 100,000,000 and a magnificent military fleet.

Was it even sensible to pretend that such altered worldly conditions did not make the revision of the understanding arrived at in 1865 an imperious necessity.

They are living in an imaginary world those of us who assert that Canada could remain a British Colony under a permanent agreement—never to be amended—by which the Mother Country would be bound to defend her, at all costs and all hazards, whenever and by whomsoever attacked, Canada in the meantime refusing, whatever the perils of England might be, to spend a dollar and to send one man for her defence. There could be but one issue to the consideration of such propositions: the dissolution of the British Empire. I regret to say that Mr. Bourassa has audaciously declared that such has been the objective of his oppositionist campaign to the Canadian participation in Imperial wars.

If Canada, through its constitutional organ, the Ottawa Parliament, had signified to England, in 1914, that she would not take the least part in the war imposed upon her by Germany, nor do anything to help her Allies, France and Belgium, could she, without blushing with shame, have claimed the protection of the British flag, if her territory had been attacked.

Would not England have been fully justified in taking the initiative to break the bond which could henceforth but be disastrous to her, our shameless attitude towards her, at the hour of her peril, being most favourable to her mortal enemy.

Have I not every sound reason to conclude that Canadian participation in the present war was in no way whatever the outcome of an Imperialist attempt to drag her, against her will, in the conflict into which she so nobly hastened to enter with the determination to fight to the last, and to deserve her fair share of the glory which will be but one of the rewards that will accrue to all those who will have united together to save Liberty and Civilization from the German barbarous onslaught.

CHAPTER XXII.

BRITISH IMPERIALISM NATURALLY PACIFIST.

According to its "Nationalist" opponents, British Imperialism has always been of a conquering nature, like that of the Roman type and those of ancient history.

This opinion is formally contradicted by a long succession of undeniable historical facts. Undoubtedly the splendid structure of the British Empire was not erected without armed support. The creation, without an army organization, of a Sovereign State comprising a fourth of the Globe, which component parts, themselves of colossal proportions, situated in all the continents, separated by the immensity of the seas, would have been more than marvellous.

I will not pretend that always and everywhere the expansion of British Sovereignty has taken place according to the dictates of strict justice. Still I do not hesitate to say that, on the whole, it has developed under conditions which were never the outcome of a mere conquering ambition.

With much reason, English citizens are proud of the fact that their Empire is the result of a NATURAL GROWTH. When the call to arms had to be made, it was oftener for DEFENSIVE WARS.

The British Empire, outside the United Kingdom, comprise, for the most important part, Canada, Australia, the South African Dominion, and India. It is easy to explain, in a few lines, under what general circumstances those immense regions were brought under the British flag. I shall, of course, begin this short historical review by the acquisition of Canada by England.

The great event of the discovery of the New World, at the end of the fifteenth century, tempted the western European nations to acquire vast colonies in the new continent. Spain, France, Portugal, Holland, were the first in the field. If the craving for large colonies in the new Hemisphere was of Imperialist inspiration, England does not appear to have been one of the first Powers infested with the disease so dreaded by our "Nationalists". She was rather late to catch it. Hollanders settled in New York before the British.

As all ought to know, Spain took hold of the whole of Southern America. France displayed her flag on the larger part of Northern America, commanding the St. Lawrence and Mississippi Rivers, and the Great Lakes. Those immense regions, extending from the cold north to flowery Louisiana, were called NEW FRANCE. Later on, that part of North America bordering on the Atlantic, from Maine to Virginia, became British, and was subdivided into thirteen provinces, or separate colonies. For such a dominating Imperialist, as some pretend she has ever been, it must be admitted that England was rather in a modest frame of mind with regard to her colonial enterprises. The British Government itself was slow in moving towards the Imperialist goal which was stirring up Spain and France to a much greater activity. The first British emigrants were Puritans looking for that religious liberty, under a new shining sun, which was denied to them by their native land in those days when fanaticism was unfortunately too much triumphant in many countries.

As it was inevitable, the European Colonies in America, all satellites of their metropolis, fell victims to the political rivalries of the nations who settled them. Not satisfied with fighting in Europe, those Powers also decided to gratify the New World with a specimen of what they could do on the battlefields. The Seven Years War did not originate in America, as it was the outcome of secular European international difficulties.

If the European nations, in taking possession of America, were making a conquest, it was that of the white race over the yellow one of the New World. Spain and France, in raising their flags over four-fifths of the American continent, were surely strengthening Imperialism. Will our "Nationalists" accuse them of having unduly saved the New World from the secular Indian barbarism?

More especially, Spanish Imperialism in America was most despotic. By a very false political conception, Spain undertook a great settlement work in America with the sole object of bleeding her colonies to her only profit. It failed disastrously as it deserved to. It is because she persevered in her fatal error that, in 1898, she was forced out of Cuba. The last stone of her immense colonial edifice was cast away.

England shared Spain's error, but much less heavily. Like Spain, she reaped what she had sowed. The thirteen British American colonies revolted and conquered their Independence. Alone French Canada remained loyal to England.

If the French Canadians had sided with the British Colonies to the South in the contest for their Independence, the Canada of those days would certainly have been included in the American Republic when England was forced, by the fate of war, to acknowledge the new Sovereign nation. Her offspring then violently broke away from the parental home, but has recently hastened to her defence, at the hour of danger, only remembering the first happy years of her childhood.

Following the loyal advice of their spiritual leaders, and of their most trusted civil chieftains, the French Canadians remained true to England, refusing to desert her, thus maintaining her Sovereign rights over the Northern half of the Continent destined, a century later, to develop into the present Dominion, enjoying the free institutions of the Mother Country.

As previously stated, the American Revolution brought for ever to an end British absolutism in the new continent. Henceforth, liberty and autonomy were to be the two foundation stones of a new colonial Policy which, far from disrupting the Empire as the autocratic one had done, was to cement its union so strongly as to make possible the gigantic military effort she has displayed for more than the last four years.

The Treaty of Paris brought the Seven Years War to a close. Once more the peace of the world was temporarily restored. By the Treaty of Paris, Canada was ceded to England, our "Nationalists" say. If so, how can they pretend that the extension of British Sovereignty over the regions which have become the great autonomous Dominion of Canada was an undue manifestation of British conquering Imperialism?

An intelligent and impartial student of the early settlements of the two continents of America can only draw the conclusion that the New World has not been the theatre of the operations of British Imperialism. Its first real attempt was tried—with much laudable success—in 1867, by the federal union of the Canadian provinces, decreed by the Sovereign legislative power of the Parliament of Great Britain, at our own request and in accordance with our own freely expressed wishes.

Australia is the second autonomous colony of England in extent and importance. It comprises nearly all the territory of the Oceanic continent, so called from the geographical position, in the Pacific Ocean, of the Islands forming it. New Zealand is the second group of these Islands. It is another autonomous British colony, called, since 1907 "THE DOMINION OF NEW ZEALAND".

Those two Dominions have a combined territorial area of more than 3,000,000 square miles—almost as large as the whole of Europe—with a population of six millions rapidly increasing. Their two largest cities, Sydney and Melbourne, each having a population of 700,000, are great commercial centres.

If British Imperialism has had anything to do with the bringing of Australia and New Zealand under British Sovereignty, it must be admitted by all fair minded men that it has worked its way in the most pacific manner. Deservedly renowned British explorers—Cook, Vancouver, and others—

discovered and took possession of the Oceanic continent in the name of their Sovereign. Welcomed by the aboriginal tribes, they raised the British flag over the fair land of such a promising future in the latter end of the eighteenth century—Cook in 1770. It has ever since been graciously waving, by the sweet breeze of the Pacific, over one of the happiest peoples on earth, enjoying the blessings of interior peace and all the advantages of the political liberties conferred upon these great colonies, more than half a century ago. As a matter of fact, England has organized her Australasian possessions into free autonomous colonies at the very dawn of their political life, dating from the middle of the last century, when they began that splendid progressive advance developing more and more every year.

Is it not evident, beyond the shadow of a doubt, that the settlement of the Australasian colonies by England, so satisfactory and so promising, has not been brought about by the illegitimate ambition of an unmeasured Sovereign aggrandizement by a guilty sort of Imperialism.

The establishment of British Sovereignty in the Indian country, immense in extent, wealth and population, is one of the greatest events of the historical development of the British Empire.

I shall not say that all that took place in the government of India deserves a blind approval. That British authority was much too long left in the control of a company was a misfortune. Under such a regime abuses were sure to develop and increase. They did and were energetically denounced—more especially on that day when Sheridan rose to such an eloquence, in the House of Lords, that a motion of adjournment had to be carried, to allow the peers to recover the free control of their minds before rendering judgment in the case brought before their tribunal, impeaching Warren Hastings.

The rule of the Indian Company was abolished, in 1858, by *The Government of India Act.*

In 1876, the illustrious Disraëli—Lord Beaconsfield—took the statesmanlike decision of adding a new prestige to the British Crown and to the Sovereign wearing it. He had Parliament to adopt the *Royal Titles Act*, by which Her Majesty Queen Victoria was proclaimed EMPRESS OF INDIA.

Such, in due course, and without any trouble, was accomplished that great political evolution which substituted, for populations numbering more than three hundred millions of human beings, an Imperial system in place of the deplorable government by a company. For the last sixty years, the new regime has given peace, order and prosperity to India.

A French publicist wrote as follows:—

After troubles of nine centuries duration, India has recovered peace under the tutelage of England, the best colonizer of the peoples of Europe. England has rendered an evident service to India. She has freed her from the intestine wars tearing her since her historical origin; she has given her a police and an administrative system.

Nations, like individuals, are not perfect. To judge equitably, impartially, the government by a Metropolis of the regions under her Sovereignty, one must not only be scandalized at her failings, but must take the broader view of her whole history in appreciating its final good and commendable results. So judging the government of India by England, every impartial mind must conclude that, on the whole—and more especially for the last sixty years—it has been beneficient. It promises to be still more so, as a consequence of the admirable share India is taking in the present war.

Egypt and the Soudan have a territorial area of 1,335,000 square miles, with a population of 15,000,000. I pride to be one of those who congratulate Great Britain to have freed the ancient and glorious Egyptian country from Turkish tyranny. A proclamation, dated the 18th of December, 1914, has finally placed Egypt under England's protectorate with the agreement of France.

In the chapters respecting the Soudanese and South African wars, I have shown how satisfactory has been the rule of Great Britain in those African countries.

It being ever true that the earth was Providentially created for men to live in the legitimate enjoyment of the blessings of peace multiplied by the fruits of their labours, the Egyptians and the Soudaneses have every reason to congratulate themselves for their liberation from the Turkish barbarous yoke, and for the protection they receive from one of the most civilizing nations.

I sincerely believe that this short review of the respective situation of five of the principal component parts of the British Empire, is sufficient to form the honest conviction that if England has practised Imperialism, she has done so for the real benefit of the peoples living under the ægis of her Sovereignty, the most favourable to colonial political liberty.

CHAPTER XXIII.

BRITISH IMPERIALISM AND POLITICAL LIBERTY.

British history, for the last century and more, proves that Imperialism is not naturally incompatible with Political Liberty, nor with the respect due the national aspirations of divers ethnical groups. The unity and the consolidation of the Empire made their greatest strides since the close of the war which resulted in the independence of the neighbouring Republic. As previously explained, they were the outcome of the very wise and statesmanlike change of colonial policy then adopted by England. The days were to come when they would be put to the severest test and would prove more than equal to its greatest strain. Those are the days which the British Empire is living through, with brilliancy and heroism, amidst the dazzling lightning and the roaring thunder of an unprecedented military conflict, with every prospect of surviving its sufferings and sacrifices with a still stronger political structure.

The same evolution by which Great Britain was to reach the summit of Political Liberty by the final triumph of the new constitutional principle of ministerial responsibility, was spreading to her far overseas Colonies. Canada, Australia, New Zealand, South Africa, Newfoundland were successively granted constitutional charters based on the same principles as those of the institutions of the United Kingdom.

As I have already said, Imperialism becomes dangerous and deserves the severest condemnation, only where and when it is the instrument of autocratic absolutism. It causes me no alarm whatever when it is developed under free institutions, guaranteed and protected by ministerial responsibility.

Whatever said to the contrary, by prejudiced and designing writers, imbued with the extravagant notions of a narrow and fanatical "Nationalism", Canada, the most important of the autonomous Colonies of the British Empire, is freer than ever. Like all the other nations, she suffers from disastrous events shaking the whole worldly edifice, but she is none the less the absolute mistress of the initiative of whatever efforts she considers her duty to make under those trying circumstances. England has imposed nothing upon Canada, has asked nothing from Canada, since the beginning of the war. She has, of course, accepted, with much pleasure and gratitude, the help we have freely offered and given her. Let our "Nationalists", in their inspired unfairness, say, if they like, that Canada, like all the Allies defensively fighting, was forced in the conflict by the imperious necessity of the situation created by those who expected to reach the goal of their ambition. But they have no right to charge Great Britain to have coerced the Dominion, against her will, to join in the struggle which the British Government had done their utmost to prevent.

If it was not giving to this work too wide a range, I would like to undertake an historical sketch of all the good the British constitutional system has produced in the United Kingdom and in the Colonies. I shall quote only a few of the most important examples.

In my opinion, the one development in England's history, since the close of the eighteenth century, most interesting to the French Canadians, is certainly that which resulted in the emancipation of the Roman Catholics of the United Kingdom.

To persuade my French Canadian countrymen of the good to be wrought by the patriotic use of the British institutions, I explained to them that at the beginning of the last century, the Roman Catholics of the United Kingdom enjoyed no political rights. They were neither electors, nor eligible to the House of Commons. They asked that justice be done to them. True statesmen, high and fair minded, admitted the justice of their claims and supported them. The ensuing political contest lasted more than twenty years.

To obtain the proposed change in the long standing laws of the realm from an exclusively Protestant electorate, was indeed a great task to accomplish. The public men supporting the Roman Catholics' claims were courageous and eloquent. They carried the day. Have not the true friends of political freedom every reason to congratulate themselves that a great measure of justice granting political rights to Roman Catholics was voted by an Electorate and a Parliament exclusively Protestant.

King George IV, through fear that his Royal prerogative might be impaired by the change, was hostile to it. He was persuaded to agree to the measure by Sir Robert Peel, the life long opponent of Roman Catholic emancipation. Whatever were the religious convictions and feelings of Sir Robert Peel, he was a statesman of a high class. As all the leading public men of England, he had a broad conception of the duties of the chief adviser of the Crown, and of the true spirit of the British constitution. The voice of the nation having spoken in no uncertain sounds, the national will must be followed. He plainly said so to His Majesty who yielded. Then, in a most admirable speech, he— Sir Robert Peel—moved himself the passing of the bill granting justice to the Roman Catholics, carried it through the two Houses of Parliament and had it sanctioned by the King.

A great act of national justice always receives its due reward. The Roman Catholics have been faithful and loyal subjects. George IV and his successors have lived to see many evident proofs of their loyal devotion, more especially since the opening of the present war.

The final success of the free discussion of the question of granting to the Roman Catholics of the United Kingdom all the rights enjoyed by the British subjects of all the other religious denominations, carried in spite of difficulties not easily overcome, is certainly one of the greatest and most honorable triumphs that Political Liberty has ever obtained. I was often deeply moved at reading the historic account of that most interesting debate in Parliament, on the public platform and in the press. More and more, the conviction was firmly impressed on my mind and soul that a great people accomplishing a grand act of justice gives a most salutary example to posterity deserving the admiration and gratitude of all generations to come.

I was only appreciating with justice and fairness the part played by England in Canada, in telling my French Canadian countrymen that they enjoyed the political rights of British subjects many years before the same privileges and justice was granted to the Roman Catholics of the United Kingdom. That much in answer to the charge of our fanatical extremists that England and her Government always wanted to oppress the French Canadians on account of their religious faith.

Without going back to the eventful days of *Magna Charta* and of the *Bill of Rights*, both embodying the fundamental constitutional principles which were finally bound to overcome the last pretentions of absolutism of yore, I considered a short review, in broad lines, of the work performed by the British Electorate and the Imperial Parliament, during the last century, would help in destroying in the minds of my French readers the prejudices forced upon them by "Nationalist" writers. That great work is principally illustrated by eight important measures of general interest.

I have just mentioned that most honourable one emancipating the Roman Catholics of Great Britain.

Shortly after, it was followed by that abolishing the Corn Laws after a protracted and very interesting discussion. That important measure was also carried on the proposition of the same Sir Robert Peel, for a long time its determined opponent. The manufacturing population, increasing so rapidly, would soon have been starved by the continuously augmenting cost of bread. Sir Robert Peel foresaw the fearful consequences sure to ensue, if no relief was granted to millions threatened with hunger. He was, as I have already said, too much of a statesman to hesitate in doing his duty. He gave up his own opinion and advised his Sovereign to do away with the Corn Laws, the repeal of which he had Parliament to vote.

With the advent of Queen Victoria, ministerial responsibility for all the acts of the Sovereign became definitely the fundamental principle of the British constitution.

Complete ministerial responsibility, once fully recognized in Great Britain, was without delay granted to all the British colonies having representative institutions.

The abolition of slavery all over the British Empire is, every one must admit, a political development of first magnitude, one doing the greatest possible honour to the great nation having first taken the glorious initiative of granting to the black race the justice ordered by Christianity. It is undoubtedly a very valuable reform to the credit of England.

The Imperial Parliament realized that the constitutional regime of the United Kingdom could not bear all the fruits to be expected from it with an electorate restricted to privileged classes. To support such a splendid edifice, admirable in structure and strength, a larger basic foundation, more solid, laid deep in the national soil, was required. After a long political struggle, freedom was once more triumphant in the Motherland. The first great Reform Bill of 1832 was the starting point of successive legislative enactments, enlarging the franchise, calling to the exercise of political rights various classes of the people, bringing up the British electorate to the glorious standard of being one of the freest, the most enlightened, and most independent in the world. The crowning measure of this extensive political reform has been the Bill of 1917 providing for the addition of some 8,000,000 voters to the roll, including about 6,000,000 women.

The rotten boroughs of old were abolished and replaced by a much better redistribution of electoral divisions.

Dating from 1867, great autonomous federal colonies, with full Sovereign rights in the administration of all their interior affairs, have been created by Imperial charters. The Canadian, Australian, South African, and New Zealand Dominions, of a total territorial area exceeding 7,000,000 square miles, with a total population of over 25,000,000, nearly 20,000,000 of which belong to the white race, have commenced their new political career with all the confidence and the hopes inspired by their free institutions.

Finally, the Imperial Parliament passed a law granting Home Rule to Ireland. Unfortunately, the war, so disastrous in many ways, prevented the immediate carrying out of the will of Parliament, certainly representative of that of the nation. But this vexed question must at last be settled once for all. It is to be hoped that the day is not far distant when it will be removed from the political arena by a solution satisfactory to Ireland, to England and to the whole

Empire.

Besides all those very important measures of political reform, the British Parliament has passed many laws of urgent social improvement.

The crowning act of the Imperial Parliament has been its determined attitude for the maintenance of peace through a long series of years.

If all the above enumeration of measures of widespread influence for the general good is to be called Imperialism, I say without hesitation that it is an Imperialism worth favouring. The world will never have too much of it.

CHAPTER XXIV.

IMPERIAL FEDERATION AND "BOURASSISM".

The leader of our "Nationalists," always frightened, apparently at least, with the supposed dangers of further Imperialist encroachments detrimental to the best interests of the British autonomous Colonies, seems alarmed at the prospects to follow the close of the hostilities. Consequently, it has been a part of his campaign to bring the French Canadians to share his fears for their future.

Not in the least worried by such apprehensions, it was also my duty to try and persuade my French Canadian compatriots not to be unduly disturbed by the sayings of a publicist magnifying the errors of his excited imagination.

That there will be after-the-war problems to consider, is most likely. What will they be? It is very difficult to foresee just now with sufficient definiteness. So much will depend upon the general conditions of the restoration of peace. However, broad lines have, for the last four years, been outlined with fair clearness permitting a general view of what is likely to happen.

Let us for a moment examine the traces of the initial phases of the constitutional developments likely to be the outcome of the joint effort of the whole Empire to win the war.

The second chapter of the Report of the War Cabinet for the year 1917—already quoted somewhat extensively—deals with the new aspect of Imperial Affairs more especially the consequence of the war. The opening paragraph partly reads as follows:—

The outstanding event of the year in the sphere of Imperial Affairs has been the inauguration of the Imperial War Cabinet. This has been the direct outcome of the manner in which all parts of the Empire had thrown themselves into the war during the preceding years. Impalpable as was the bond which bound this great group of peoples together, there was never any doubt about their loyalty to the Commonwealth to which they belonged and to the cause to which it was committed by the declaration of war. Without counting the cost to themselves, they offered their men and their treasure in defence of freedom and public right. From the largest and most prosperous Dominion to the smallest island the individual and national effort has been one of continuous and unreserved generosity.

After mentioning that during 1917 "great progress has been made in the organisation both of the man-power and other resources of the Empire for the prosecution of the war," and that "the British Army is now a truly Imperial Army, containing units from almost every part of the Empire," the Report says:—

The real development, however, of 1917 has been in the political sphere, and it has been the result of the intense activity of all parts of the Empire in prosecuting the war since August, 1914.

It had been felt for some time that, in view of the ever-increasing part played by the Dominions in the war, it was necessary that their Governments should not only be informed as fully as was possible of the situation, but that, as far as was practicable, they should participate, on a basis of complete equality, in the deliberations which determined the main outlines of Imperial policy.

Accordingly, a Special War Conference was convened to meet in London, where for practical convenience it was divided into two parts: one, "known as the Imperial War Cabinet, which consisted of the Oversea Representatives and the members of the British War Cabinet sitting together as an Imperial War Cabinet for deliberation about the conduct of the war and for the discussion of the larger issues of Imperial policy connected with the war." The other "was the Imperial War Conference, presided over by the Secretary of State for the Colonies, which consisted of the Oversea Representatives and a number of other ministers, which discussed non-war problems connected with the war but of lesser importance."

On the 17th May, 1917, the British Prime Minister, giving "to the House of Commons a short appreciation of the work of the Imperial War Cabinet," said in part:—

I ought to add that the institution in its present form is extremely elastic. It grew, not by design, but out of the necessities of the war. The essence of it is that the responsible heads of the Governments of the Empire, with those Ministers who are specially entrusted with the conduct of Imperial Policy should meet together at regular intervals to confer about foreign policy and matters connected therewith, and come to decisions in regard to them which, subject to the control of their own Parliaments, they will then generally execute. By this means they will be able to obtain full information about all aspects of Imperial affairs, and to determine by consultation together the policy of the Empire in its most vital aspects, without infringing in any degree the autonomy which its parts at present enjoy. To what constitutional developments this may lead we did not attempt to settle. The whole question of perfecting the mechanism of "continuous consultation" about Imperial and foreign affairs between the "autonomous nations of an Imperial Commonwealth" will be reserved for the consideration of that special Conference which will be summoned as soon as possible after the war to readjust the constitutional relations of the Empire. We felt, however, that the experiment of consulting an Imperial Cabinet in which India was represented had been so fruitful in better understanding and in unity of purpose and action that it ought to be perpetuated, and we believe that this proposal will commend itself to the judgment of all the nations of the Empire.

The preceding are words of political wisdom, worthy of the best form of British statesmanship. Were they the dawn of a new era, dissipating the clouds accumulated by the trials of a long period of military conflict, and showing in a future, more or less distant, the rising constitutional fabric of a still greater Imperial Commonwealth, not so much in size, than in unity, in freedom and strength? Time will tell. But can we not at once note with confidence that the fundamental principle upheld by all the leading British public men is that, whatever constitutional developments may be in store for us all, they will not be allowed to infringe "in any degree the autonomy" presently enjoyed by the Oversea Dominions.

The Imperial War Conference held in London, last year, passed the following very important "Resolution" dealing with the future constitutional organisation of the Empire:—

"The Imperial War Conference are of opinion that the readjustment of the constitutional relations of the component parts of the Empire is too important and intricate a subject to be dealt with during the war, and that it should form the subject of a special Imperial Conference to be summoned as soon as possible after the cessation of hostilities.

"They deem it their duty; however, to place on record their view that any such readjustment, while thoroughly preserving all existing powers of self-government and complete control of domestic affairs, should be based on a full recognition of the Dominions as autonomous nations of an Imperial Commonwealth, and of India as an important portion of the same, should recognise the right of the Dominions and India to an adequate voice in foreign policy and in foreign relations, and should provide effective arrangements for continuous consultation in all important matters of common Imperial concern and for such necessary concerted action, founded on consultation, as the several Governments may determine."

We can await without the slightest alarm the holding of the proposed "*special Imperial Conference to be summoned as soon as possible after the cessation of the hostilities.*" The fundamental principles upon which "*the readjustment,*" if any one is made, "*of the constitutional relations of the component parts of the Empire*" are to rest, are well defined in the above "Resolution":—*through preservation of "all existing powers of self-government and complete control of domestic affairs;—full recognition of the Dominions as autonomous nations of an Imperial Commonwealth, and of India as an important portion of the same*";—the admission of "*the right of the Dominions and India to an adequate voice in foreign policy and in foreign relations.*"

Upon that large and strong basis, I, for one, am ready to wait with patience and confidence the result of the deliberations of the future special Imperial Conference. With regard to the proposed Conference, I cannot see any reason for anyone to indulge in the "Nationalist" hysterical fears of an oppressive Imperialism devouring, as the old mythological god—Saturn—his own children.

As I have said, the work of the special Imperial Conference will be rendered more or less easy by the conditions of the future peace. I pray, with all the fervour of my soul, that the war shall not end by a hasty compromise—as wished for by our blind, if not really disloyal, pacifists—by which the world would be doomed to another disaster far worse than the one it is straining every nerve to overcome, and that after years of the most costly warlike preparations. Such a peace would be the saddest possible conclusion of the present conflict, and much worse than the sacrifices yet to be borne by the prosecution of the war to a finish. We must all implore Providence to save Humanity from such a cataclysm.

A special Imperial Conference meeting under such disheartening circumstances would indeed have a most difficult task to accomplish. It was evidently an act of wisdom on the part of the Imperial War Conference of last year to express the opinion that the special Imperial Conference should be summoned only after the cessation of hostilities.

When peace shall have been restored with the only conditions which can be satisfactory to the Allies and to the world at large, a special Imperial Conference will be in order, having for its object to consider the readjustment of the constitutional relations of the component parts of the Empire, in conformity with the requirements of the new situation which will have grown out of the necessities of the war. However important the task, the tranquility of the world being, let us hope, assured for many long years, there will be no reason for the Conference to proceed hastily to any insufficiently matured conclusion. The representative public men who will meet in London from all over the Empire will not forget, we may rest confident, that the safest way to a good working readjustment will be, as it has always been in the past, that which will follow the straight line of natural growth. Dry cut resolutions, imprudently adopted, and pressed upon unwilling populations would have ninety-nine chances out of a hundred to be more injurious than profitable.

Every sensible man must acknowledge that the war has in an extraordinary manner hastened the rapidity of the advance towards the turning point in the Constitutional organization of the British Empire. The day is near at hand when the problem will have to be faced with courage and broadness of mind. Very blind indeed, and far behind the times, is he who does not realize that TO BE, OR NOT TO BE, for the Empire, is confined to two clear words: CONSOLIDATION or DISSOLUTION. The tide has either to ebb or flow, the wave to advance or recede. The edifice must be strengthened or left to decay. Like any living being, a political society, be it great or small, after its birth, more or less laborious, grows to a prosperous and healthy old age, or crumbles down prematurely. Very much depends, for either course, on the wisdom or extravagance of the way of passing through life. Unmeasured ambitions, wild expectations, are too often, alike for the individual and the nation, the surest road to a lamentable ruin. Wisdom, the outcome of sound moral principles, and wide experience, is, on the other hand, the safest guarantee of longevity, of bright old days full of contentment, honour, prestige and true grandeur.

Grave will be the responsibility of those who will meet in solemn conclave to lay down the foundations of the future British Imperial Commonwealth. No less serious will be the responsibility of the populations, scattered over the five continents, who will be called upon to pronounce, freely and finally, upon the propositions which will be submitted to their approval or disavowal. Consequently undue haste would be more than ill-advised.

For instance, the paramount question to be considered by the new Imperial Conference will most likely be that of the future military organization of the

Empire. Is it not evident that this problem will be much more easily settled if the Allied nations succeed in carrying the point they have the most at heart:— The reduction of permanent armaments as the safest protection against any new outburst of savage militarism flooding the earth of God with human blood. If this *sine qua non* condition is the top article of the future peace treaty, the great Powers having agreed, in honour bound, to maintain the world's tranquillity and order, will all be afforded the blessings of a long rest from the ruinous military expenditures too long imposed upon them by the mad run of Germany to conquer universal domination. The British Empire, as a whole, will, as much as any other nation, enjoy the full benefits of such a favourable situation. She will, like her Allies, return to the pursuits of peace, with millions of veteran soldiers who, for the next ten years at least, would, in large numbers, certainly join the Colours once more, if need be, to defend their country in a new just war. Then, under such circumstances, why should the peoples of the whole Empire be immediately called upon to incur more expenses for military purposes than absolutely necessary for the maintenance of interior order, and to meet any sudden and unforeseen emergency.

The liquidation of the obligations necessarily accumulated during the war will be the first duty of all the Allied nations. The task will no doubt be very large, most onerous. Still I trust that it will not be beyond their resources of natural wealth, of capital and labour, of courageous savings.

As the "Resolution" adopted by the Imperial War Conference says, "the readjustment of the constitutional relations of the component parts of the Empire is too important and intricate a subject to be dealt with during the war." When taken up after the war—even if just *as soon as possible*—it will be none the less IMPORTANT AND INTRICATE. Such a subject should not be dealt with without matured consideration and given a hasty solution. If the peace treaty satisfactorily settles the world's situation for a long future of general tranquillity which will certainly bless all the nations with many years of unprecedented prosperity, plenty of time will be afforded to deliberate wisely upon the paramount question of the building of a "new and greater Imperial Commonwealth." Our frenzied "Nationalists" can quiet their nerves. The imperialist wild bear will not be growling at the door. Because we are all likely to be called upon to consider how best to promote the unity and the future prosperity of the Empire, we will have no reason to fear that we shall be, from one day to the other, forcibly thrown into perilous adventures by the Machiavellic machinations of out and out Imperialist enthusiasts.

I have already said that it is becoming more and more evident that TO BE, or NOT TO BE, the British Empire must either CONSOLIDATE or DISSOLVE. I must not be understood to mean that with the restoration of peace under the happy conditions all the Allies are fighting for, the Empire, as she will emerge from the tornado, could not, as a whole, resume, for more or less time, her prosperous existence of *ante*-war days. What will be best to do, it is too early to foresee. Then it is better to wait for the issue of the war, trusting that all the truly loyal British subjects will then join together to pronounce upon whatever questions of imperial concern will claim their urgent consideration.

But there is a certainty that can be at once positively affirmed. All the peoples living and developing under the ægis of the British flag are determined that the British Empire is to be. Whenever a special Imperial Conference sits in London, all the representatives of the many component parts of the British Commonwealth will meet in the great Capital surely to deliberate over the most practical means TO CONSOLIDATE THE EMPIRE. We may all depend that no one will propose to destroy it.

How best to consolidate the Empire, such will be the important question. To be sure, the future special Conference will not likely be wanting in propositions from many outside would-be constitutional framers. Schemes may be numerous, some worth considering, others useless if not mischievous. No reason to feel uneasy and to worry about them. We can confidently hope that British statesmanship will be equal to the new task it will be called upon to perform. Our Canadian public men will have much to gain by closer intercourse with their Imperial colleagues, and by judging great questions from a higher standpoint.

Let there be no mistake about it: the true secret of the most effective consolidation of the Empire was discovered by the British statesmen the day when they realized that henceforth free institutions and the largest possible measure of colonial autonomy were the only sure means to solidify the structure of the British Commonwealth. Such is the opinion of the Imperial War Conference outlining in their previously quoted "Resolution" what must be the fundamental basis of any future "READJUSTMENT OF THE CONSTITUTIONAL RELATIONS OF THE COMPONENT PARTS OF THE EMPIRE."

CONSTITUTIONAL DEVELOPMENT OF INDIA.

As a preliminary to the prospective readjustment of the political status of the Empire, it is worth noting the advance of India towards political autonomy. It was made manifest by the significant step of inviting India to the deliberations of the Imperial War Cabinet, and by the "Resolution" adopted by the Imperial War Conference that India must be fully represented at all future Imperial Conferences.

Respecting India, the Report of the War Cabinet, for the year 1917, says:—

It was clear, however, that this recognition of the new status of India in the Empire would necessarily be followed by substantial progress towards internal self-government. Accordingly, on August 20th, the following important declaration of His Majesty's Government on this subject was made in the House of Commons by the Secretary of State for India:—

"The policy of His Majesty's Government, with which the Government of India are in complete accord, is that of the increasing association of Indians in every branch of the administration and the gradual development of self-governing institutions with a view to the progressive realization of responsible government in India as an integral part of the British Empire. They have decided that substantial steps in this direction should be taken as soon as possible, and that it is of the highest importance, as a preliminary to considering what these steps should be, that there should be a free and informal exchange of opinion between those in authority at home and in India. His Majesty's Government have accordingly decided, with His Majesty's approval, that I should accept the Viceroy's invitation to proceed to India to discuss these matters with the Viceroy and the Government of India, to consider with the Viceroy the views of local Governments, and to receive with him the suggestions of representative bodies and others. I would add that progress in this policy can only be achieved by successive stages. The British Government and the Government of India on whom the responsibility lies for the welfare and advancement of the Indian peoples, must be the judges of the time and measure of each advance, and they must be guided by the co-operation received from those upon whom new opportunities of service will thus be conferred and by the extent to which it is found that confidence can be reposed in their sense of responsibility. Ample opportunity will be afforded for public discussion of the proposals, which will be submitted in due course to Parliament."

In accordance with this declaration, the Secretary of State left for India in October, and has since been in consultation with the Government of India and deputations representative of all interests and parties in India in regard to the advances which should be made in Indian constitutional development in the immediate future. No reports as to the results of these discussions had been made public by the end of the year.

Another important decision relating to India was that whereby the Government abandoned the rule which confines the granting of commissions in the Indian army to officers of British extraction. A number of Indian officers, who have served with distinction in the war, have already received commissions.

Who, only twenty years ago, would have believed that the day was so near at hand when this Asiatic vast and populous country, called India, would be most earnestly considering, through numerous representatives, in consultation with the British Government, the proper steps to be taken "FOR THE GRADUAL DEVELOPMENT OF SELF-GOVERNING INSTITUTIONS WITH A VIEW TO THE PROGRESSIVE REALIZATION OF RESPONSIBLE GOVERNMENT IN INDIA AS AN INTEGRAL PART OF THE BRITISH EMPIRE." In every way, it is a most extraordinary political evolution. If it reaches the admirable conclusion aimed at—for which success every true friend of Political Liberty will fervently pray—it will have realized one of the greatest constitutional achievements of modern times.

Behold just now how safely and wisely this Indian evolution is proceeding under the experienced direction of British statesmanship. It is "TO BE ACHIEVED BY SUCCESSIVE STAGES", declares the Secretary of State for India, speaking in the name of the whole British responsible Cabinet. Such have been accomplished all the constitutional developments which have wrought so much perfection for British free institutions.

True progress, in every form, is never revolutionary. And why? For the very reason that instead of fighting for destruction by brute force, it aims at perfecting by regular advances in the right direction, by successive improvements which experience justifies, which reason, intelligence and wisdom approve, which political sense recommends, which sound moral principles authorize and sanction.

A country favoured with the free British constitutional regime is not the land where bolshevikism of any grade or stamp, can flourish and bear fruits of desolation and shame.

The wonderful Indian country, for so many centuries tortured by intestine troubles, at last rescued by England from that barbarous situation, given a reorganized administration able to maintain interior peace, favoured by British business experience and capital with material progress in many ways, specially in transportation facilities, may soon see—let us hope—the dawn of the glorious days of a large measure of political freedom and responsible government.

Far away indeed from the perilous Imperialism abhorred by our much depressed "Nationalists" is India safely moving.

CHAPTER XXVII.

THE FUTURE CONSTITUTIONAL RELATIONS OF THE EMPIRE.

Though very difficult to say what they will be, I thought proper, for the better information of my French Canadian readers, to consider some of the suggestions which of late years have been repeatedly made.

Mr. Bourassa, in his recent pamphlets, reviewing the situation from his wrong and prejudiced standpoint, has decidedly come out in favour of Canadian Independence. The least that can be said is that the time was very badly chosen to raise the question. To select the moment when the Motherland was engaged in a fight for life or death, to propose to run away from the assailed home where we had lived many happy years, was certainly not an inspiration of loyal devotion and gratitude. I am glad to say that the wild proposition met with no countenance on the part of our French Canadian compatriots.

To the point raised in England, some years ago, that it was not to be supposed that the British Empire was destined to exist forever, one of the leading British statesmen of the day, then a member of the Cabinet, answered that, though it was likely to be true that the British Commonwealth would not be eternal, like many other great political societies of times gone by, it was surely not the particular duty of a British minister to do his best to hasten the day of the final downfall of the country he was sworn to maintain. The rejoinder was no doubt peremptory. It can very properly be used in answer to Mr. Bourassa's plea for the independence of Canada.

However, the question having been so unwisely raised, to say the least, for the obvious purpose of disheartening the French Canadians from their present situation and raising in their minds extravagant hopes of a change for the better, I believed it advisable to tell them not to be carried away by dreams of a too far distant possible realization.

In all frankness, I must say that I have never taken any stock in the suggestion made from time to time, for the last fifty years, in favour of Canadian Independence. It always seemed to me that our destinies were not moving along that way. In my opinion, which nothing has happened to alter, the steady growth of the consolidation of the Empire was yearly working against the assumption of the prospective independence of the Dominion.

But even supposing that the course of events would change and put an end to British connection, could we pride ourselves with having at last, though in a very peaceful way, achieved our national independence? I am more and more strongly impressed by the paramount consideration that, nominally independent, Canada would be very little so in reality. Situated as she would be, she could not help being under the protectorate of the United States. I have always thought so. I think it more firmly than ever, when I see looming larger every day on the American political horizon the fact that the neighbouring Republic will come out of the present war with flying Colours, taking rank as one of the most powerful nations on earth.

Be that as it may, there is every certainty that the question of Canadian Independence is not within the range of practical politics. Mr. Bourassa's proposition is doomed to the failure it deserves.

Consequently, it is much better to try and foresee what the future political conditions of Canada are more likely to be after the close of the hostilities. And this must be done with the only purpose of wisely, and patriotically,—in the larger sense of the word—contributing our due share to the sound and solid framing of the changes, if any, which the best interests of the Empire, generally, and of all her component parts, in particular, may require.

We have not, and I most earnestly hope and pray that we shall not have, to consider what new political conditions would be as the consequence of the defeat of the Allies, or even as necessitated by a peace treaty due to a compromise. We must only look ahead for the encouraging days to follow the victory won by the united efforts and heroism of the nations who have rallied to put an end to Prussian militarism.

One certainty is daily becoming more evident. All loyal British subjects will applaud the triumphant close of the war with the desire to do their best to maintain and consolidate the Empire they will have saved from destruction at the cost of so much sacrifices of heroic lives and resources.

NO TAXATION WITHOUT REPRESENTATION.

The great objection raised by Mr. Bourassa against the participation of Canada in the wars of the Empire is that the Dominion is not represented in the Parliament to which the British ministers, advising the Sovereign on all matters of foreign relations, are responsible. He draws the conclusion that the Colonies are called upon to pay for the war expenditures of Great Britain in violation of the constitutional principle:—NO TAXATION WITHOUT REPRESENTATION. The principle is no doubt true. But it is altogether wrong to pretend that so far it has been violated to coerce the Dominion to participate in the wars which England has been obliged to wage. Our "Nationalists" would be right in their opposition if the Imperial Parliament had attempted to pass laws compelling the autonomous Colonies to contribute men and money to a conflict. Had they claimed the right to raise revenues in Canada by an

Imperial statute, we would certainly have been entitled to affirm that not being represented in the British House of Commons, we could not be taxed in any way for any Imperial purpose—war or others.

Nothing of the kind has ever been done, ever been attempted, even ever been hinted at.

The argument falls entirely to the ground, shattered to pieces, from the fact that Canada has only participated in the wars of the Empire of her own free will, in the full enjoyment of her constitutional rights. Whatever sums of money the Dominion has to pay for the conflicts into which we have freely and deliberately decided to intervene, are perceived by the Canadian treasury in virtue of laws passed by our federal Parliament upon the advice of our responsible Cabinet.

Last year, the people of Canada were called upon to elect new members of our House of Commons. The citizens of the Dominion had the undoubted constitutional right to pass condemnation on the ministers and on the members of Parliament who had voted for the participation in the war with men and money. They could have elected a new House of Commons to discontinue such participation and recall our army from Europe. But had they not the equally undoubted right to do what they have done by such a solemn expression of a decided and matured opinion:—approve and order to fight until victory is won?

In accepting with deep gratitude the noble and patriotic support we, Canadians, were giving her in the most terrible crisis of her Sovereign existence, was England in any way violating any of our cherished constitutional privileges? No sensible, no reasonable, no unprejudiced man can so pretend. The case being such as it is, there is not the shadow of common sense in the assertion that Canada is taxed without representation for Imperial war purposes.

COLONIAL REPRESENTATION.

If the question of Colonial representation is raised at the special Imperial Conference to be held as soon as possible after the war, Mr. Bourassa and his friends will not be welcomed to cry if it is settled very differently from their wishes, after their unwise clamour for an excursion into the unknown.

The question of the readjustment of the constitutional relations of the component parts of the Empire, when duly brought up, will very likely take a wide range, so far at least as consideration goes. What will be the conclusions arrived at, nobody knows.

Pending that time, any one is allowed to express his own views. I thought proper to explain mine in my book dedicated to the French Canadians. I now summarize them as follows:—

Would it be advisable to have the Colonies represented in the present Imperial Parliament? After full consideration of the question, I must say that I have finally dismissed it from my mind as utterly impracticable. Can it be supposed for a moment that the electors of Great Britain would agree to have the Dominions overseas and India represented in their House of Commons, to participate in the government of the United Kingdom for all purposes? With representation in the present British House of Commons, would the Colonies be also represented in the British Cabinet, to advise the Crown on all matters respecting the good government of England?

Would the Colonies be represented according to their population in the British House of Commons? If they were, India alone would have a number of representatives five times larger than all the other parts of the Empire

Is it within the range of possibility that the people of Great Britain would consent to colonial representatives interfering, even controlling the management of their internal affairs, whilst they would have no say whatever in the internal government of the Colonies?

Would the colonial ministers in the British Cabinet be constitutionally responsible to the people of the United Kingdom without holding their mandate from them?

Such a system would be so absurd, so radically impossible, that it is not necessary to argue to prove that it would not work for one single year.

In my opinion, Colonial representation would be practicable only with the creation of a new truly Imperial Parliament, the present British Parliament to continue to exist but with constitutional powers reduced to the management of the internal affairs of the United Kingdom. If such is the scheme of the "Nationalists," then they are converts to that Imperial Federation which they have vehemently denounced for years, and to the largest measure possible of that Imperialism which has been cursed with their worst maledictions.

If ever complete Imperial Federation becomes an accomplished fact, how will it be organized? Will the new Imperial Parliament consist of one Sovereign, one House of Lords—or Senate—one House of Commons?

Would the Sovereign be King or Emperor? I, for one, would prefer the word EMPEROR. He might be titled His Majesty the Emperor of the British Commonwealth and the King of Great Britain.

With Imperial Federation—a regime of complete Imperial autonomy—the word "colonies" would no longer apply. Would Canada, Australia, South

Africa, India, New Zealand be called Kingdoms, like Prussia, Bavaria, Saxony, Wurtemberg, of the German Empire?

Evidently, the constitutional powers of the new Parliament would be limited to external relations, to strictly Imperial affairs.

The new constitutional organization of the British Empire would combine Imperial, National and Provincial autonomy, each operating within the well defined limits of their respective privileges and attributions.

Under such a regime, there would be three sorts of responsible Cabinets: The Imperial Cabinet responsible to the whole Imperial electorate; the National Cabinets of the component Kingdoms of the British Empire responsible to the electorate of each one of those Kingdoms respectively; the Provincial Cabinets responsible to the electors of each province respectively.

The Royal—or rather Imperial—Prerogative to declare war and to make peace would be exercised upon the responsibility of the Imperial Cabinet.

To the new Imperial Parliament would undoubtedly be given the right and the duty to provide for Imperial defense. They would have to organize an Imperial army and an Imperial navy for the protection of the whole Empire.

The whole of the reorganized Empire would have to pay the whole of the expenditures required for Imperial purposes, defense and others, on land and sea, out of revenues raised by laws of the Imperial Parliament.

Under the new Imperial constitutional regime, would the Imperial Parliament be given the authority to regulate Imperial trade and commerce, the Imperial postal service, &c.?

Would the new Parliament have the exclusive right to approve commercial treaties sanctioned by His Majesty the Emperor, upon the advice of his responsible Imperial Cabinet, without reference whatever to the National Parliaments of the component Kingdoms?

How easily is it ascertained that numerous questions of paramount importance are at once brought to one's mind the moment the vast problem of a new and greater Imperial Commonwealth is considered. Shortsighted and inexperienced are the politicians and the publicists who imagine that it could be given a satisfactory solution after hasty and insufficient deliberations. It is very reassuring to know that the matter necessarily being suggested for consideration at the Imperial War Conference, last year, it was immediately decided, by a "Resolution," adopted on the proposition of the Canadian Prime Minister, "THAT THE READJUSTMENT OF THE CONSTITUTIONAL RELATIONS OF THE COMPONENT PARTS OF THE EMPIRE IS TOO IMPORTANT AND INTRICATE A SUBJECT TO BE DEALT WITH DURING THE WAR."

What would be the real meaning of such a radical change? It is worth while to enquire at once.

The British Empire would no longer comprise a Metropolis holding autonomous Colonies and Crown Colonies, but would be organized in a new Sovereign State with an Imperial Parliament to which all the component parts —or Kingdoms—would send representatives.

Indeed it would be a grand, a magnificent, political edifice. But to find shelter under it, Canada would have to renounce her right to decide alone, and freely, to participate, or not, in the wars of the Empire, to determine alone what her military organization should be, to raise ourselves, without the intervention of a superior Parliament, the revenue which we consider proper to apply to Imperial purposes.

I, for one, do not foresee that such an important constitutional change, if ever it is made, will be suddenly brought about, in the dark, as the result of the machinations of a most mischievous Imperialism inspiring our "Nationalists" with shivering terror. It is positively sure that no one holding a responsible political position, or having a responsible standing in the British political world, will ever be mad enough to propose, suggest, or even hint, to build a new Imperial structure without the solid foundation of the deliberate consent of all the Colonies, of all the would-be component parts of such a vast Commonwealth.

How many years of serious discussion, of earnest consideration, did it not take to bring about the creation of the Canadian, Australian and South African Dominions. It cannot be reasonably imagined that the creation of the new and greater Imperial Commonwealth will be a much easier task to accomplish with the necessary conditions of successful durability.

I also thought proper in my French book to write a few lines on the important question respecting the mode of ascertaining the deliberate consent of the Colonies to any intended readjustment of the constitutional relations of the component parts of the Empire, specially if it was proposed to rear a new and larger political fabric. I did so because of late it has been frequently suggested to use the *plebiscit* or the *referendum* as the most opportune way to consult public opinion.

I must say that, without going to the length of denying that a public consultation may, in a particular case, be advantageously made by way of a *plebiscit* or *referendum*, I am not a strong believer in the efficiency of either proposition, and why? Because I cannot help considering them as more or less contrary to the solid constitutional principle of ministerial responsibility which they would gradually undermine if frequently appealed to.

144

I feel specially adverse to the *plebiscit*, because History proves that, by nature, it engenders DESPOTISM, CÆSARISM. Contemporary history offers two striking examples never to be forgotten.

Napoleon the First, whose power was the legitimate result of his wonderful genius and of his eminent services to France, wanted his dynasty to rest on the *plebiscitary* foundation. Millions of votes—almost the unanimity of French public opinion—answered enthusiastically to his call. He was not such a man as to refuse the chance offered him to exercise a supreme power so manifestly tendered to him. All know that he very soon unbridled his devouring ambition and ruled France with all the might of an absolutism strengthened by the glories of military campaigns truly marvellous. To any attempt at freedom of criticism, he could reply that his Imperial power—mightily supported by his commanding genius—was strongly entrenched on the unanimity of opinion of the French nation expressed by the result of the plebiscit.

Napoleon III, favoured by the immortal prestige of his glorious uncle, but far behind him in genius, though intellectually well gifted, as he proved it during his Presidential term of the second French Republic and during the first years he occupied the Imperial Throne of France, used the plebiscit to have his famous *coup d'Etat* of the second day of December 1851, prepared with consummate skill and carried out with great energy, ratified by the nation by an overwhelming majority of several millions of votes. He lost no time in drawing the final result of this first great success and in reaching the term of his ambition. The tide of popular enthusiasm was all flowing his way, carrying him to the Throne elevated for his uncle who had lost it after the hurricane which exhausted its strength at Waterloo. On the second of December of the following year—1852—the second French Empire was proclaimed to the international world. Following the example and the precedent of the first Bonaparte, Napoleon III also decided to use the plebiscit to legitimate his Imperial power. He triumphantly carried the day by some seven millions of votes—almost the unanimous voice of the French people.

Thus, in less than half a century, after having twice tried the Republican system of government, and, in both cases, having overdone by deplorable excesses the experiment of Political Liberty—more specially during the years of terrorism of the first Republic—France, by a regular reaction, went back to the other extreme, and reestablished arbitrary power not, in the two instances, upon the principle of the Divine Right of the ancient Monarchy, but on that of the Sovereignty of the people, as expressed by the certain will of the whole nation. But ABSOLUTISM, whether the outcome of Divine Right or of popular sovereignty, is always the same and steadily works against the true principles of Political Liberty.

It is a great mistake to suppose that ABSOLUTISM is possible only under monarchical institutions. The terrorist republican epoch, in France, from 1792 to 1795, was ABSOLUTISM of the worst kind, really with a vengeance. As much can be said of the present political situation in Russia, which has substituted REVOLUTIONARY ABSOLUTISM to that of the decayed Imperial regime, suddenly brought to a tragic end by the pressure of events too strong for its crumbling fabric, shaken to its foundation by a most unwise reactionary movement which only precipitated its downfall, instead of averting it, as extravagantly expected by the Petrograd Court, which betrayed Russia in favour of Germany, and unconsciously opened the road which led the weak and unfortunate Czar to his lamentable fate.

In my humble opinion, PLEBISCITARY CÆSARISM is not compatible with a system of ministerial responsibility for all the official acts of the Sovereign.

The frequent use of the plebiscit would certainly tend to diminish in the mind of political leaders the true sense of their responsibility. It would too often offer an easy way out of an awkward position without the consequence of having to give up power.

If I understand right the real meaning of the two words: *plebiscit* and *referendum*, the first would be used to try and ascertain how public opinion stands upon any given question of public policy, of proposed public legislation: the second would be employed for the ratification by the electorate of a law passed by Parliament. I have less objection to the second system which, in reality, is an appeal from Parliament to the Electorate. But to the well practised, the adverse vote of a majority of the electors should have the same result as a vote of the majority of the House of Commons rejecting an important public measure upon the carrying of which the Cabinet has ventured their existence.

Without the immediate resignation of the ministers meeting with a reverse in a *referendum*, I consider that ministerial responsibility would soon become a farce destructive of constitutional government. The defeat of a Cabinet in a *referendum* would be equivalent to one in general elections and should bear out the same consequence.

Surely, no one having some clear notions of what MINISTERIAL RESPONSIBILITY means, will pretend for a moment that a Cabinet who, on being defeated in the House of Commons, advises the Sovereign—or his representative in Canada—to dissolve Parliament for an appeal to the people, could remain in power if the Electorate approved of the hostile stand taken by the House of Commons.

I can see no difference whatever in the meaning of an hostile referendum vote and that following a regular constitutional appeal from an adverse majority of the popular House of representatives. In both cases, the downfall of the defeated ministers should be the result.

From the above comments, I draw the sound conclusion, I firmly believe, that any important readjustment of the constitutional relations of the Colonies with Great Britain, should be first ratified by the actual Parliaments of the Dominions and subsequently by the electors of those Dominions. But I am also strongly of opinion that the ratification by the electorate should be taken upon the ministerial responsibility of the Cabinet who would have advised the Sovereign and asked Parliament to approve the proposed readjustment. It would be the safest way to have the Cabinet to consider the question very seriously before running the risk of a popular defeat which would have to be followed by their resignation.

Another most important reason to quiet the fears of our "alarmists" at an impending wave of flooding Imperialism, is that any radical change in the constitutional relations of England with her Colonies for the unity and consolidation of the Empire, should be adopted by the Parliaments and the Electorates of all the Colonies to be affected by the new conditions.

Consequently, from every standpoint the Dominions and the Empire herself are guaranteed against the dangers of rashness in changing the present status of the great British Commonwealth.

Though it may be of little use, and perhaps perplexing, to look too far ahead to try and foresee what the distant future has in store for the generations to come, still a simple call to common sense tells one that the political destinies of any Commonwealth are, in a long course of time, largely and necessarily shaped by the increases in population and wealth, irrespective of the actual more or less harmonious working of present and immediately prospective constitutional institutions.

Broadly speaking, was it to be supposed, for instance, that the two wide continents of America would have, when peopled by hundreds of millions, continued in a condition of vassalage to the European continent, though owing their discovery and early settlements to European genius and enterprise? No doubt the growing national families of the New World would have liked a much longer stay under the roofs where they were born, had they received better and kinder treatment from their fatherly States. But at best the hour of separation would only have come later, postponed as it would have been by the bonds of enduring affection made more lasting by mutual good relations. Do we not see, almost daily, desolated homes often the sad result of senseless misunderstandings, or of guilty outbursts of intemperate passions? Yet, family home life, even when blessed by the inspiring smile of a lovely wife, the sweet voice of a devoted mother, the manly and Christian example of a good father, the affectionate sentiments of well bred children, is far too short under the most favourable circumstances. And why? Because it has to follow the Divine decree ordering separation for the building of new homes, to keep Humanity advancing towards the final conclusion of her earthly existence.

Had the American colonies been favoured by the constitutional liberties the Dominion of Canada enjoys, they would not have revolted and British connection would have endured many years longer. Still, one cannot conclude that those British provinces, realizing the marvellous development all can witness, would have for ever agreed to be satisfied with their colonial status. When they would have grown taller and bigger than the mother-country, most likely Great Britain herself would have taken the initiative of a friendly separation followed by a close alliance which would have perpetuated the familial bond actually so happily restored.

As prophesied by Sir Erskine May, more than half a century ago, in speaking of the probable future of the then British colonies, the American Republic would *have grown out of the dependencies of the British Empire.*

And to-day, when the United States are doing such a gigantic effort, conjointly with the whole British Empire, to save Humanity from German cruel domination, England, to use the very words of the distinguished writer and historian just cited, "MAY WELL BE PROUDER OF THE VIGOROUS FREEDOM OF HER PROSPEROUS SON THAN OF A HUNDRED PROVINCES SUBJECT TO THE IRON RULE OF BRITISH PRO-CONSULS."

The possibilities of the material development of the Dominions of Canada, Australia, New Zealand and South Africa—without counting India and the lesser colonies—on account of their immense natural resources, are such as to justify very great hopes for their future. The time will come when they will number together a much larger population than the United Kingdom. Will the British Empire, as foreseen by one of the greatest political minds Canada has produced, declared by his chief and worthy opponent the equal to the celebrated William Pitt, then develop into a grand Commonwealth of nations.

If so, as wrote Sir Erskine May, England "*will reflect, with exultation, that her dominion ceased, not in oppression and bloodshed but in the expansive energies of freedom, and the hereditary capacity of her manly offspring for the privileges of self-government.*"

Several generations will certainly rise and disappear before such an important question, looming far off in the future, is likely to be—if ever—raised requiring a practical solution. But foreseeing such a distant possibility, it is still more our bounden duty to be true to our present and prospective obligations for many years to come, as foreshadowed by the actual course of events shaping themselves in the sense of the consolidation of the Empire which may never be really dissolved even by the separation of her manly *offspring*. Family bonds, strengthened by deep affection, are not broken because the faithful boy, grown up a healthy and strong man, leaves to go under his own blessed roof, taking with him to his last day the cherished recollections of the happy days he has passed in the equally blessed parental home.

One of our most ardent desires must be that our successive generations of children be so well trained to the intelligent and patriotic use of Political Liberty, as to accumulate, in due course of time, an admirable heritage of sound principles of self-government enriched by the honourable examples of our faithful loyalty to the Mother land never grudged to her, but given with overflowing measure, not only as a matter of duty, but also as a reward from grateful subjects for the regard and respect always paid to their constitutional rights and privileges.

If such is ever the natural outcome of our political achievements, the vast Empire reared with such a great success would truly survive separation, being merely transformed into a splendid galaxy of independent States still bound together by the strong ties created by centuries of reciprocal devotedness. It would constitute a real league of nations working in concert and with grandeur for the peace and the prosperity of the whole world.

A MACHIAVELLIAN PROPOSITION.

On reading Mr. Bourassa's pamphlet entitled:—*Yesterday, To-day, To-morrow*, I discovered what I have qualified a *Machiavellian proposition*. What *Machiavellism* means is well known. It expresses the views of that most corrupt and contemptible politician and publicist, called MACHIAVEL, born at Florence, in 1649.

At page 140 of the above mentioned pamphlet, Mr. Bourassa wrote:—

"I WILL SPEAK MY MIND OPENLY—*je vous livre toute ma pensée*—: IF IN DEFAULT OF INDEPENDENCE, I CLAIM IMPERIAL REPRESENTATION, IT IS BECAUSE IT WOULD WEAKEN THE MILITARY ORGANIZATION OF ENGLAND,—*l'armature de guerre de l'Angleterre*—PRECIPITATE THE DISSOLUTION OF HER EMPIRE, HASTEN THE DAY OF DELIVERANCE, FOR US AND FOR THE WHOLE WORLD."

Such are the loyal sentiments expressed by the "Nationalist" leader. He clamours for the Imperial representation of the Colonies, for the solemnly avowed object to use the privilege for the destruction of the Empire. To achieve this end he declares that the military power of England must first be weakened.

No wonder then that he started his "Nationalist" campaign by fighting with all his might the two successive proposals of contribution to the great military naval fleet of Great Britain.

No wonder that he opposed Canada's intervention in favour of England in the South African war.

No wonder that from the outbreak of the hostilities, in 1914, until the day when he was shut up by the Order-in-Council censuring all disloyal speaking and writing detrimental to the winning of the war, he has tried to move heaven and earth to prevent Canada's participation in the conflict.

He tells his countrymen that if he has become a convert to Imperial representation—in other words, Imperial Federation—it is because he considers it would be the best way of ruining the Empire and of delivering, not only Canada, but the whole world from British domination.

For fear that the French Canadians, whom he especially wished to influence, would not be very easily caught in the disloyal trap, he tries hard to prevail upon them by the following reasons:—

"If we are not sufficiently clear-sighted and energetic to work for this salutary object by the most constitutional, the most British, means at our disposal,

others, happily, will do it for us.

"The English-Canadians, the Australians, the New Zealanders persistingly claim representation in the government of the Empire. When the war is over, their claims will be reaffirmed with increased ampleness and energy. The Indians (les Hindous) themselves will do the same. Shall we remain alone to rot stupidly (croupir béatement) in colonial abjection."

Without the slightest doubt, there are many English-Canadians, Australians, New Zealanders, South Africans, Indians, in favour of Colonial Imperial representation. The number is increasing and likely to increase. But Mr. Bourassa is absolutely, I might as well say, absurdly, mistaken, if he really believes that they do so for his own purpose of destroying the British Empire. They want the very reverse: their object is TO CONSOLIDATE THE EMPIRE, not TO DISSOLVE HER. They will not accept as a very flattering compliment Mr. Bourassa's charge that their desire to strengthen the British Commonwealth proves that they prefer to continue *stupidly rotting in colonial abjection* rather than work for their deliverance from British domination.

But what in the world has brought the "Nationalist" leader to the conclusion that the surest way to save Canada from the peril of Imperialism was to secure Imperial representation for the treasonable purpose, on entering the fort, to pull down the flag and destroy the whole Empire? To frighten his French Canadian compatriots with terror at the slightest move in favour of an increased Imperialism, he waves before them, with wild gesticulation, any and every extravagant writings he lays his hand on preaching a ridiculous expansion of Imperialist aspirations. He is perhaps the only man in Canada who has read a most absurd work which he pretends to have been written by a General named Lea, and from which, in horror stricken, he summarized a few unbelievable views.

Mr. Bourassa said that General Lea, *gifted with an astonishing foresight, predicted all that was happening in Europe and in the world. The General,* again affirms Mr. Bourassa, *has proved in a striking way that if England wishes to maintain her Empire and to continue exercising her domination over the world she must make the sacrifice of her political liberties and of those of her Colonies, abolish the Parliamentary and Representative Governments and resolutely adopt the ironed regime of the Romans of old, of the Germans of the present day.*

Once so brilliantly inspired, General Lea went on in a splendid manner. He added, says Mr. Bourassa, *that England must transform her Empire into a vast armed camp, must keep in her own hands all the powers of command, must subdue all the non-British races to the supremacy of the Anglo-Saxons united together by the unique thought of dominating the world by brutal force.*

These views—so says Mr. Bourassa—are to be found in a book entitled: "*The Day of the Saxon.*" If they have been really expressed with the full sense given to them by Mr. Bourassa's translation into French, I cannot say less than that they are most absurd, most extravagant. The Nationalist leader would have proved himself a much more sensible, a wiser man, if, laughing at such senseless notions, he had refrained from quoting those lines for the purpose of telling the French-Canadians that like all non-British races on earth they were doomed to be devoured—flesh and bones—by the voracious Anglo-Saxons bent on swallowing humanity. And to save them from such a cruel fate, he implores them to clamour for Imperial representation with the criminal intent of betraying their trust, and to use the honourable privilege they would be granted to ruin the Empire they would swear to maintain and defend. So far as the political program of General Lea is concerned, we have not yet learned that its benevolent author was doing much in the war to carry it out. If I had the honour to meet the General, being presented, I presume, by Mr Bourassa, I would ask him, first, when and where he has discovered that England was *dominating the world.*

I know that there exists a great England holding a large situation on earth. Her Empire extends to almost a fourth of the globe. Her Sovereignty reigns over nearly four hundred million of human beings; a truly beneficient Sovereignty, because it rules according to the wishes, to the opinions of its subjects, managing their own affairs in virtue of the freest political institutions in the whole world.

I know of no England dominating, or even aspiring to dominate, the world. Such an England only exists in the heated imagination of that General Lea and in the minds of all those, like the Nationalist leader, who are, or feign to be, tortured by the bugbear of military Imperialism of the old Roman ironed type.

As long as three-fourths of the earth will remain independent of the British Empire, under numerous sovereignties, England's pretended domination of the world will ever only be an extravagant dream.

Wishing England *to continue her domination of the world*, General Lea, no doubt to please Mr. Bourassa, was bound to suggest the means to do so. Let us analyze them.

1.—England *must make the sacrifice of her political liberties and of those of her Colonies.*

2.—She *must abolish parliamentary and representative governments.*

It is beyond conception that Mr. Bourassa should have for one minute seriously considered such absurd notions.

I would enjoy attending large public meetings in Great Britain, where General Lea would propose to British free men the sacrifice of all their political liberties, to witness the rather warm reception he would be favoured with. I am sure he would have to rush out of the halls much faster than he would have walked in.

Where is the sane man who really believes that, dreaming of a domination of the world by *brute force*, British free men would consent to do away with their Parliamentary system *to transform the whole of the Empire into an armed camp*? Such a proposition was sheer madness, a most foolish talk, unworthy of the slightest attention from sensible people. Mr. Bourassa was very wrong in giving it publicity, and very unwise, to say the least, in using it to frighten his French-Canadian compatriots by blandishing before their eyes that ridiculous specimen of the phantom of Imperialism.

Is it to be supposed for one single instant that the British people, so rightly proud of their political liberties, and of their representative government, which after centuries of efforts and trials they have successfully brought to such perfection, basing its future permanency on the solid rock of ministerial responsibility, would consent to sacrifice them for the sake of a vain, a ridiculous, an odious and impracticable scheme *to dominate the world by brute force*?

It is ten times worse than madness to believe that the British people who have torn away from the British soil the last root of ABSOLUTISM, would, for any earthly reason, renounce their most legitimate conquests, to rebuild, on the burning ruins of their most sacred rights, an ironed political regime of the old Roman or present German type! Is it to be believed that they would agree to replace, on the glorious Throne which they protect with all the might of their loyal affection, their present constitutional Sovereign by a new Nero or another Wilhelm II?

If it is with the purpose of preventing such a dire calamity that the Nationalist leader became a convert to Imperial Federation, he is absolutely losing his time and his energy in promoting such a regime. If ever Imperial Federation becomes a fact, we can all rest perfectly assured that the new Imperial Parliament will not vote their own destruction to be replaced by an autocratic and tyrannical government.

I hope that Mr. Bourassa is the only believer, all over Canada, in the assertion of General Lea that England's aspirations is *to dominate the world by brute force*. It is a most injurious, I can say, calumnious, charge. All know, or should know, that England was the first nation to completely abolish slavery over all her Empire; that has granted, in the largest possible measure, Political Liberty to all her Colonies; that guarantees to all races the same rights and privileges, never interfering in colonial internal management. He is wilfully guilty of a calumnious charge the man who accuses the British race to aspire to dominate the world by an *ironed regime*, when he should know that Great Britain ran the risk of a crushing defeat, in refusing to organize a standing army of several millions of trained officers and men.

A TREASONABLE PROPOSAL.

The Nationalist leader wants the French-Canadians to support his scheme in order *to work for the salutary object of demolishing the British Empire by the so very constitutional means of Imperial Federation.* How he has failed to realize the infamous kind of suggestion he was making will always be a wonder to all those reading it.

If, sooner or later, Great Britain and her Colonies are politically organized as an Imperial Federation, the Province of Quebec will have several French-Canadian representatives in the new Greater Imperial Parliament. The Nationalist leader wants those French-Canadian Members to go to London pledged to destroy the Empire to which they will have to swear allegiance and fealty before crossing the threshold of the House of Commons and taking their seats. Does he not understand that any French-Canadian doing what he wishes and recommends would deliberately perjure himself? Does he not comprehend that he was paying a rather poor compliment to his British countrymen from Canada, Australia, New Zealand and India, when he affirmed, without the shadow of truth, that they would elect to the Imperial Parliament members holding the mandate from them to work for the dissolution of the Empire?

I notice, with surprise, that in the enumeration he has drawn of the future destroyers of the future federated British Empire, he has not convened his friends, the Boers, to his holy task. Does he not consider them as *farsighted* and *energetic* as the others he has pompously mentioned with such childish illusion. Or, has he not, unconsciously, paid them the high compliment to suppose that they would be unable to accomplish the treasonable act which, with confidence, and even certainty, he expects from the others. Our countrymen, the Boers of South Africa, have, by a large majority, become so loyal to the Crown, to the Empire,—and they have so gloriously proved it since the outbreak of the war—that it is manifestly evident that they are very well satisfied with their present position, that they have dispelled from their minds all bitter recollections of the struggle which, a few years ago, finally brought them within the Empire they are doing such a noble effort to maintain and save from the German tyrannical grasp.

The following views, recently expressed, in London, by Mr. Burton, Minister of Railways and Harbours in the Government of South Africa, a leading

154

public man of the far away sister Dominion, is refreshing reading after Mr. Bourassa's outrageous outburst above quoted. He said:—

"One of the motives which prompted South African support of the British cause was the fact, which appealed not only to the English-speaking population, but moved the Dutch population—the fact that the British cause had embraced all the progressive peoples of the world. It was not Britain's wealth, or influence, or power that appealed to them; it was the priceless privilege of the maintenance of our constitutional liberties. He could illustrate their attitude by a single incident which had come within his own experience in connection with a Transvaaler, born and bred, whom he had questioned as to his future in the military service in which he was an officer. The officer replied that he had been through the German South-West African campaign, that he was going through the German East African campaign, and when that was done he intended making for Flanders. He added: "I mean that as a man I could not act otherwise in view of the treatment dealt out to us by Great Britain. If she had not done what she did for us I should not have stirred hand or foot.""

No one need be surprised that the South African Dominion is suffering a little from the "Nationalist" fever, a disease infesting many countries, in various degrees, and with time cured by the safe remedy of the sound common sense of the people. We know too much about it ourselves, after nearly eighty years of free responsible government, to wonder at the fact that a small minority of the Dutch South Africans—from the Boer element—is not yet fully reconciled with their lot under the British Crown. They apparently dream of Republicanism, in sullen recollection of a recent past which only some of the present generation still regret, but which the next will strive to cherish only as the stepping stone to their actual status so full of good promises for their future. The few South Africans suffering from this virus are almost exclusively recruited amongst the populations of the late Republics of South Africa. The people of the provinces of Natal and Cape Colony, with a long experience of British rule, have no faith in the "republican nationalism" desired by some, which does not in the least appeal to their good sense and their sound political foresight. Mr. Burton believes *"that the instigators of the movement are looking for votes more than for anything else."*

Mr. Burton, moreover, truly said:—

"It was part of the history of all countries that what was called "Nationalism" made a powerful appeal to the finer classes of young men. It was an admirable sentiment, but what was complained of in South Africa was that the sentiment was expended upon a wrong conception of "nationalism" and what nationhood should be. In South Africa it was restricted, it was sectional, and

practically racial. The energy and activity displayed were being spent upon a mistaken cause."

Every word of this quotation applies with still greater force to the "nationalism" of the Province of Quebec.

Mr. Burton goes on saying:—

"It was the cause of South Africa first—as it should be—but it was more than that. It was South Africa first, last, and all the time, and South Africa alone. He and those who were associated with him could not accept that view. It would mean ruinous chaos in South Africa. They had obligations to Great Britain. It was not merely that they had received recognition from the beginning that their Constitutional cause was just. It was not merely that Great Britain in its relation with South Africa had been actuated by that beneficent influence which the British system of liberty effected under the sway of its flag throughout the world, but it was that the people of the Union realized the true inward significance of the struggle in which the Empire was engaged. They knew that the world's freedom was at stake, and with it their own. The people in South Africa had long ago awakened to this great fact, and they were realizing it more and more as the war went on. When he had spoken of putting "South Africa first" as the motto of a party he wished it to be understood that he and the people of South Africa generally accepted it, as every nation was bound to accept it. But they also realized that their future as a nation and their freedom as a nation were at stake, and that their interests were bound up with those of the British Empire.

"It was because they realized that fact that the Government of the Union had in these troublous times nailed its flag to the mast. It was the honourable course, the right course, and they had stuck to it through good report and ill report, and through much trial and sacrifice. His last message as representative of the Union Government was: Upon that attitude of the Union Government they might depend to the very last. They might be forced—he did not see any present prospect of it—to abandon office, but so long as they were in office they would adhere absolutely in the letter and in the spirit to the undertaking they had given and would continue in the path they had followed hitherto."

Sensible, truly political and patriotic, noble words, indeed. Are they not the complete expression of the powerful wave of enthusiasm which spread throughout the length and breadth of the whole British Dominions overseas, when, after exhausting to the last drop her efforts to maintain peace, Great Britain, in honour bound, threw her gallant sword in the balance in which the destinies of the world were to be weighed during the frightful years of the most terrific thundering storm ever witnessed by man?

How weighty those words are is evident. They are still more so by the fact that they positively and firmly express the views and sentiments of the two most trusted and illustrious leaders of the Boers, who, both of them, took a very prominent part in the South African war, as generals commanding the forces of the South African Republics: General Botha and General Smuts.

General Botha is, and has been for several years, the Prime Minister of the South African Dominion. General Smuts is minister of Defence in General Botha's Cabinet. He is the representative of the Government of the Union of South Africa in the Imperial War Cabinet. In June, 1917, he was, moreover, "invited to attend the meetings of the British War Cabinet during his stay in the British Isles."

Both General Botha and General Smuts have often spoken about the present relations of their great Dominion with England. The press of the whole British Empire has published their speeches, most favourably commented by that of the Allied nations. In every case, they were brilliant with true and staunch loyalty, worthy of the real statesmen the speakers are, in every sense fully up to what could be expected from the illustrious military and political leaders of a valiant race deserving the respect of all by her heroism of the past and her loyalty of present days.

If ever Mr. Bourassa, as I hope he will, reads the above quoted lines, I am sure he will find therein every reason to be satisfied with his decision not to call upon the South Africans to join with him and those he has summoned, in the unworthy task of bringing on Imperial Federation for the very treasonable purpose of destroying the British Empire. For once, his judgment did not fail him.

Nobody knows if representatives from the whole present colonial Dominions and India will ever sit, in London, as members of a new Imperial Parliament. It is most unlikely, at all events, that any one, merely to please Mr. Bourassa, will help building such a political structure with the criminal and treasonable purpose of throwing it at once to the ground with a tremendous crash. But we can all safely join in the affirmation that in the event of such a great historical fact being accomplished as that of a federated British Commonwealth, the representatives of the Colonies overseas will meet in the Imperial Capital to do their duty with loyalty and honour. I have no hesitation whatever to pledge my word that the French Canadian representatives in London would be amongst the most loyal to their Sovereign and to the Empire, the most true to their oath.

I solemnly protest against the injurious imputation the Nationalist leader has addressed to my French Canadian compatriots in charging them with the desire *to rot stupidly in colonial abjection.* Let us repulse the unfounded accusation from an elevated standpoint. I feel the utmost contempt for all kinds of narrow prejudices, of blind fanaticism. Nations, like individuals, all pursue Providential destinies in this human world. There is no more abjection in the colonial status than in any other. Canada is a British colony by the decree of Providence. Every nation—like every individual—has duties to perform in any situation she may occupy in the course of historical events. Abjection is not the result of the faithful discharge of duty, however trying the circumstances may be. It would be in its violation with the guilty intent to betray.

A hundred times better it is to remain a colony as long as the Supreme Ruler of the world will so order, than to attempt to break through by the dark plot of an infamous conspiracy.

Let our destinies follow their natural development, striving to the best of our ability and patriotism to have them to achieve the happy conditions which we enjoy. Any man aspiring to a legitimate influence on the mind of our compatriots, must encourage them, by words and deeds, to faithfully accomplish their daily task in showing them the advantages of their position. Inconveniences are the outgrowth of any political standing. In the true Christian spirit, trials are everywhere to be met with. Sacrifice, when necessary, ennobles national as well, and as much, as individual life.

It is very wrong on the part of any one to trouble the mind of our compatriots in purposely exhibiting to their view discouraging pictures of the difficulties of their situation. Their national existence is not, never will, never can be, exclusively rosy. Be it as it may, who can pretend, in good faith, that there exists, on the surface of the globe, a population, all things considered, happier than our own. Our race freely grows on a fertile and blessed soil which she cultivates with her vigorous and intelligent daily toils, which she waters from the sweat of her brow, to which she clings by all the affections of her heart, by the noblest aspirations of her soul. On week days, proudly working on her domains; on Sundays, kneeling before the Altars of her Church, fervently thanking Him for past graces and gifts, she prays to the Supreme Giver of all earthly goods to continue to favour her with peace, with order, in the legitimate enjoyment of her liberties, together with the moral, intellectual and material progress she is striving to deserve.

Guilty is the man who tortures them with chimerical aspirations, who advises them to conspire against the legitimate authority which she must, and will, respect in spite of the seductions attempted to have her to fail in her duty.

CHAPTER XXVIII.

OUTRAGES ARE NO REASONS.

The failings of human nature, the differences of temper, of the qualities and defects of heart and soul, are such that harmony and good-will amongst men in private life are too often difficult to secure. The Divine precept, so frequently broken, should, however, always rule the relations between man and man. It should, with still more constant application, rule the relations between different races Providentially called to live together on the same soil, under the same Sovereign authority, enjoying the same institutions, the same liberties, protected by the same flag. That the house divided against itself is sure to fall is true of the nation as well as of the home. National and family happiness and prosperity are alike dependent on the feelings of real brotherhood which prevail in both. Any good hearted man appreciates how much kindness of speech, courtesy of dealings, cordiality of manners, contribute to reciprocal good-fellowship, brotherly in the home, inspiring in the daily intercourse of citizens, patriotic in the nation at large. The more a Sovereign State is inhabited by numerous ethnical groups, like the British Empire and the American Republic, the more important it is that the freedom of expressing one's opinion on all matters of public interest should be used with fairness, with respect for those holding different views, with due regard for the feelings which are the natural outcome of racial developments, of cherished recollections, of legitimate hopes.

Such are the principles, I am most happy to say, that I have admired and try to practice in the exercise of my rights as a citizen of the Province where I saw the light of day, of Canada where I have lived and hope to live all my years, of the British Empire whose loyal subject I have been and am determined to remain to my last moment.

How then could I have helped being shocked when I came to read the following lines I translate as follows from page 121 of Mr. Bourassa's pamphlet:—"*Yesterday, To-day, To-morrow*":—

"*Were the French Canadians to persist in their obstination to rot in colonialism and to consider that it is for them the happiest and the most glorious condition of existence, the English Canadians would force them out of it. Our countrymen of the British races have grave defects: they are* IGNORANT, PRETENTIOUS, ARROGANT, SHORT-SIGHTED, DOMINEERING. *They are, more than ourselves*, ROTTEN WITH MERCANTILISM. *They seem to have lost some of the best qualities of the*

English people, to have developed their faults and acquire many of the VICES NATURAL TO THE WORST CATEGORY OF YANKEES. *But they have not,* LIKE US, *totally* ABANDONED *the* PROUD CHARACTER *and the* PRIMORDIOUS RIGHTS *of the British peoples. When the war is over, they will claim, like the Australians, the New Zealanders, and the Indians (les Hindous), a readjustment of the powers of government.*"

Thus, in a few lines the Nationalist leader, in appealing to his disordered imagination, has succeeded in slapping, in one single stroke, with dynamical outrages, the faces of the English-speaking Canadians of the three great British races, of our neighbours, the Yankees, and of his own compatriots, the French-Canadians. How could he expect that such vitriolic language would promote, in the Dominion, that harmony of feelings never before so essential as at the very time he was writing that injurious paragraph of his work, surely not Intended to help winning the war so full of the greatest consequences, for good or ill, for the World, the British Empire, Canada, and our own Province of Quebec.

So far, Mr. Bourassa, having gone back on the admiration he was wont to profess for England, in his early youth, had reserved all his assaults for the English people. But the heart of man, once under the sway of an unlimited and unsatisfied ambition, is bound to drop to the lowest depths of the extremist's aberration. In the above quotation, he fires his battery of *Kruppic* dimensions—loaded with poisonous invectives, at the THREE GREAT BRITISH RACES, ENGLISH, SCOTCH AND IRISH, living in Canada.

Had his charge been intended for the English race alone, he would have been very particular in so saying. But, let there be no mistake about it, he deliberately wrote *our countrymen of the British races*. Wanting, I suppose, to prove his impartiality, he remembered that the United Kingdom is peopled by three illustrious races represented all over the globe by many millions of worthy sons, everywhere to be found hard at work for the intelligent development of the resources of the countries they live in and are rearing their children. More than four millions of them are Canadians by birth or born in Great Britain. Many more numerous they are in the United States where they form the solid stock upon which the future of the Republic is firmly grounded.

With the same thrust, Mr. Bourassa strikes at the Yankees who, we may hope, have not trembled too much at the blow. He charges them with having infested his poor *countrymen of the British races* with *many of the vices natural to the worst category of* "YANKEEISM." Kind, cordial, courteous, indeed he was in such a mood of tender sympathies for the Canadian British races and their contagious cousins the Yankees of the most corrupted class!

However, the finest flower of the whole *bouquet—the rose par excellence*—is the one he has gallantly presented to his French-Canadian compatriots. He tells them with the sweetest tones of his charming voice that they are pleased and happy to rot in "*colonialism*." But, evidently wishing to speak to them a few encouraging words, he mildly reminds them *that they are less rotten with "mercantilism" than their countrymen of the British races.*

A man can be suffering less than his more sickly brother without, for all that, being in very good health. It is a poor consolation for the French Canadians to hear from the Nationalist leader that they are less infested with the mercantile virus than their brothers of the British races.

All those who have followed with some attention Mr. Bourassa's course for the last twenty years, know that he is an equilibrist of the first class. Having favoured the French Canadians with the flattering compliment as above, he turns about and lashes them with the sweeping slap that, contrary to the stand the Canadians of the British races cling to with an obstination which he deigns to approve, they, the degenerated French Canadians whom he pities so much, "*have totally abdicated their proud character* of old *and the primordial rights of British subjects.*"

So, in Mr. Bourassa's opinion, his French Canadian compatriots are infested to a high degree both with the *colonialist* and *mercantile* corruptions. Hence, his fear that they are threatened with a premature national death if they do not at once listen to his brotherly warnings.

I have already answered the Nationalist leader's charge that the French Canadians are stupidly rotting in "COLONIAL ABJECTION." The same reasons refute his assumption that "COLONIALISM" is an abject status for a people.

A people, a race, who would enjoy living under the German autocratic colonial rule—for which the Nationalist leader has so little dislike—would indeed prove some disposition to *rot stupidly in abjection.* But the divers peoples, the different races, who appreciate all the beneficent advantages of the present British colonial rule, are of very superior stock. They know, from the clearest conception, that Monarchical democratic institutions are as much different from Imperial autocratic tyranny, as true broad patriotism is far above narrow and fanatical "Nationalism."

I have only to say a few words about the "ROTTENNESS OF MERCANTILISM" against which, according to Mr. Bourassa, the French Canadian are not sufficiently protected.

Going back to my recollections of the last sixty years, if there is a complaint which through all my life I have heard almost daily, with deep regret, it is that the French Canadians were not striving with sufficient energy and perseverance to achieve a better and larger position in the business world. Their leaders, religious, political and civil, to induce them to increased exertions, have always pointed to the example given them by their countrymen of the British races: by the clear headed and far-seeing English business man, the sturdy and hard working Scotch, the enterprising and witty Irish. Thank God, I have well enough understood my duty to do my humble but patriotic share to favour this progressive movement. Never, in so wisely advising the French Canadians, any one supposed for a minute that he was leading them to the infested pond of *mercantile corruption*. The change wished by all was becoming more urgent. All were looking for the best means to carry it out. Our leaders, having at their head, by right and merit, our religious chiefs under the authority of a prince of our Church, his Eminence the Cardinal-Archbishop of Quebec, took the initiative with an ever increasing interest in the success they considered so important.

The establishment of a permanent school of high commercial education and of several technical schools was most favourably approved. Political economy is even, in a certain measure, taught in several of our classical colleges for secondary education. The necessity for our young men of knowing the English language, to succeed in commercial, industrial and financial pursuits in Canada and in the neighbouring Republic, is more and more generally admitted. The French Canadians, fully enjoying the undoubted right to do so, aspire to achieve an advantageous and honourable position in commerce, in industry, in finance, in transportation, in mine working. The more we realize this goal of our legitimate ambition, the more we are also intensifying our efforts to promote agricultural progress and the improvement of our country roads.

If, in all the branches of our national activity, we obtain the success we hope for, one single man alone amongst us shudders at the idea that the French Canadians will blindly destroy their race with a mortal dose of the cursed "MERCANTILISM" so dishonourable to the British races.

And Mr. Bourassa, instead of heartily joining with all the leaders of his race— Cardinal, Archbishops, Bishops, priests, statesmen, political men, judges, professional men, merchants, manufacturers, financiers,—to favour, as much as possible, the commercial and technical training of his compatriots, sneers at such efforts which, in his candid opinion, are only plunging them in the irremediable depths of "MERCANTILE CORRUPTION"!

Are not such abominable teachings a curse to all those of the race to which they are addressed with an unsurpassed cynicism?

CHAPTER XXIX.

How Mr. Bourassa Paid His Compliments To The Canadian Army.

With a most admirable unanimity—*nemine contradicente*, as Parliamentary procedure says—the Canadian Parliament decided at once, at the very outbreak of the hostilities, to organize a great army to go and defend the Empire of which the Dominion is an important component part, and Civilization in peril from the Teutonic crushing wave of barbarism, let loose over Belgium and France. In the most evidently constitutional ways, the Canadian people, as a whole, as they had the right and the bounden duty to do, approved the decision of Parliament.

When Mr. Bourassa issued the pamphlets referred to, some four hundred thousands volunteers had already enlisted. A large number of them—over one hundred and sixty thousands had reached the western front—some the eastern —where they fought valiantly, heroically, on French soil, against the German hordes. Thousands of them had fallen on the field of honour, resting with imperishable glory, for them and for us all, in that ancestral land which we, and ever will, cherish.

More than one hundred and twenty-five thousands were on British soil, being trained for the military operations of the following spring.

The rest of the army, in numerous thousands, was still with us, getting organized for the noble task, and waiting to cross over the Atlantic to go on the field of battle.

The Canadian army had in every way merited the respect and the admiration of all their countrymen who were very happy to so testify.

However, in this admirable concert of praise and grateful congratulations, a very discordant note was one day heard resounding from the lowest inspiration of the human heart vibrating with feelings of shameful contempt. It is found at page 105 of the pamphlet previously quoted, and reads as follows in its naked outrageous language:—

"In Canada, a militarism is being forged unparalleled in any civilized country, a depraved and undisciplined soldiery, an armed scoundrelism, without faith nor law, as refractory to the call of individual honour as to the authority of its parading or patronage officers."

For all the treasures of the world, I would not agree to bear before my countrymen the responsibility of such injurious words addressed to the Canadian army whose valour is doing so much for our national honour.

In one single masterly stroke of his poisoned pen the Nationalist leader decrees that the Canadian army is far below the worst type of German and Turkish soldiery, that no other civilized country is cursed with such a degraded, undisciplined, dishonoured militarism.

For God's sake, whence and where has such an outrageous outburst originated? From what dark corner has the electric current been poured out with such infernal fury?

I shall not pretend that all our volunteers, from first to last, had reached the saintly state of soul of their inexorable judge. As a rule poor mortals do not jump, by a single effort, up to that degree of Christian perfection shining with the great virtues of humility, charity, justice —by words and deeds, We must not suppose that many of our heroic volunteers had deserved, like their trusted friend and admirer, Mr. Bourassa, to be canonized during their life time. That some of them, whose past was perhaps not a very strong recommendation, have enlisted with the laudable purpose to rehabilitate themselves in their own self-estimation and in that of their countrymen, it is very likely. Far from blaming them for so doing, we must congratulate them and encourage them to persevere in the glorious task which will entitle them to the everlasting gratitude of their country. Such has been the case in the armies of all nations for many centuries past.

Fortunately, far better and much more authorized judges of the devotion, courage and patriotism of the volunteers of the great Canadian army, as well as of the cause for the triumph of which they have offered, and in so many cases, given their lives, were easily found. They wrote and spoke with no uncertain voice.

In a letter approving the publication of a very interesting pamphlet, entitled: —"War controversy between Catholics"—"La controverse de guerre entre Catholiques,"—His Eminence Cardinal Begin, Archbishop of Quebec, said: —

"Attentively read, as it deserves to be, this work will help to understand and to love to the limit of devotion, (jusqu'au dévouement) the beauty and the sovereign importance of the great cause—the protection of the world threatened by Germanism—for which our soldiers are so valiantly fighting together with those of England, France and Belgium.

"I pray God to bless those brave warriors and to grant peace to the Christian world by the reestablishment of Justice and Right."

What an encouraging contrast! On the one hand, a publicist, with the fury of its resounding organs, so widely used, vowing to eternal damnation, *the armed scoundrelism which Canada is* forging, with conditions inferior to Teutonic and Turkish barbarism, considering that it has reached the lowest depth of "*a degradation unparalleled in any civilized country.*"

On the other, the Head of the Catholic Church in Canada, Cardinal Begin, blessing in the name of God Almighty *our brave warriors who fight so valiantly with those of England, France and Belgium*, because *they love with true devotion the beauty and the sovereign importance of the great cause* to the triumph of which they sacrifice *their lives—the protection of the world threatened by Germanism.*

On Thursday, October 26, 1916, Archbishop Bruchesi, of Montreal, present at a funeral service, in Notre-Dame Church, attended by many thousands, for the glorious victims of the sacred duty of defending the cause of the Allies, eloquently said in part:—

"They (our heroes) had voluntarily enlisted. Two years ago, they organized their Battalion, the glorious 22nd. They enlisted, conscious that they were defending the most just of all causes, that of Civilization, of Right, of Humanity. They enlisted with the conviction that they would serve the interests of their country, for, when oversea, they knew that they were defending Canada. They were young and strong; one could not see them without admiration.

"They have made their country's name and their own grand. They have for all times immortalized themselves in History, and, by them, Canada has been immortalized.

"The war is not over; it goes on horribly, but our hearts are hopeful. It is impossible that they should triumph the men who, during forty years, have prepared for the greatest war and who, during two years, have torn the world asunder and flooded the earth with blood. Impossible that they should triumph the men who have declared this war without a right to avenge, without a grievance to redress, without being menaced in any way. Impossible that they should triumph those who have torn, like a scrap of paper, a pact upon which the nations relied, having faith in the pledged word. Impossible that they should triumph those who have invaded the territory of valiant Belgium, whose only fault was: TO REMAIN TRUE TO HER HONOUR. *They shall not triumph those who, on account of their military service, have made this war a carnage and a butchery without precedent in History. I believe in God of all Justice. Humanity wanted a suffering which purifies, but when mothers shall have wept long enough, God will have His Divine word heard.*

"When this great work is accomplished, and when we shall sing the TE DEUM *of thanksgiving, we will be able to say that Canada, that all the Provinces of Canada, that our Province of Quebec, have deserved their share of glory."*

On Tuesday, November 28, 1916, at a funeral service in the Quebec Basilica, addressing the large audience rallied to pray for the dead heroes, Reverend Mr. Camille Roy, one of the most distinguished professors of the Quebec Seminary, said in part:—

"They went, our officers and soldiers, to serve a great cause. Several reasons, perhaps intermingled in their conscience, have inspired their courageous decision....

"But dominating, penetrating them all, purifying what in them was too personal and restricted, was the thought that in doing all this they were going to fight with heroic brothers and employ their strength to defend what is most venerable on earth: outraged justice.

"Perhaps they ignored historical secrets and diplomatic complications, but they knew the war brutally declared, the treaties torn away, Belgium violated, and agonizing, France mutilated and invaded, England, herself, chased over the moving frontier of her oceans invaded; they knew the destroyed homes, the profanated Cathedrals, the brutally murdered old men, women and children, and the flood of barbarians rushing in tumultuous waves over the fields of the sweetest country. They knew that, over there, two nations to whom we are attached by our political, or by our national, life, wanted the support of their sons far away, that they had to battle for sacred interests in a war requiring an endurance commanding an incessant renewal of our energies; and then, without halting to consider if they were obliged to it by laws, they have answered the most pressing call of their souls, and have freely made the devoted sacrifice."

What other edifying contrast between the appreciation of the part played by the Canadian army by three intellects, one overpowered by an inexplicable hostile passion, the two others, inspired by the noblest sentiments, rising to the sublime conception of the great sacrifice accepted by our brave volunteers, which they express by eloquent words who moved the hearts and brought *abundant and warm tears to the eyes of those who* heard or read them.

Where one only sees *depraved* beings more contemptible *than all those which any other country* could produce or *forge*, the two others, so much superior in every way, admire, the first, THOSE WHO WENT TO DEFEND THE MOST JUST OF ALL CAUSES, THAT OF CIVILIZATION, OF RIGHT, OF HUMANITY; the second, THE SUPERNATURAL BEAUTY OF SACRIFICE THAT THEIR BROTHERS IN ARMS HAVE MADE OF

The pamphleteer cruelly attacks those who, to-morrow, will face with unfaltering courage the guns of the enemy to defend Civilization and avenge the martyrs of barbarity.

The sacred orator blesses the mortal remains of our sons who have fallen on the field of honour, on the soil of France, where our forefathers were born and bred, with the fervent prayer of their grateful country that knows they died heroically "FOR A GREAT CAUSE" TO DEFEND WHAT IS MOST VENERABLE ON EARTH: "OUTRAGED JUSTICE."

The following pages from a very eloquent Pastoral Letter by Bishop Emard, of the diocese of Valleyfield, will, I am sure, be read with most respectful interest by all. They are as follows:—

"Dear Brethren, we certainly have the right, and we even consider that it is for us all, citizens of Canada, loyal subjects of England, a duty to demand from God the success of the arms of our Mother-country and of her Allies in the present war. If we are not called upon, as a matter of faith, to pass judgment on the true causes of the war, and to divide the responsibilities respecting the calamity which covers Europe with blood, we are surely allowed to think and to say that all the circumstances actually known sufficiently prove that right is on the side of the peoples who have checked the invasion, and discouraged the overflowing of the enemy from his territory, in order that the sentiment of justice may serve to support the devotion of our soldiers, in this great conflict, called the struggle of Civilization against barbarism.

"The Church of Christ, always the same by her doctrine, has been marvellously constituted by the Divine Wisdom, to adapt her externally everywhere and always, to the infinitely varied circumstances consequent on the diversity of peoples, of governments, of social relations. She has never ceased to practice, by Her Pastors and her faithful children, the great lesson given by Christ: **"Render therefore to Cæsar the things that are Cæsar's and to God the things that are God's,"** and to claim with the Apostle all the rights as well as accept all the duties of citizens and subjects."

After recalling that from the day *Divine Providence, in Her mysterious designs,* allowed Canada to pass from the French to the English Sovereignty, *the Church, by Her Bishops, has declared that, henceforth, it was the duty of the French Canadians to transfer to the British Crown, without reserve, the cordial allegiance which the King of France had hitherto received from them,* and that since then until the present days, the Canadian Episcopate has remained true to his course, Bishop Emard proceeds as follows:—

"We are then, very dear Brethren, in perfect communion of sentiments, action and language, with our venerable predecessors of the Canadian Episcopate, in asking you to-day to address to Heaven fervent prayers for the complete and final success of England and her Allies in the frightful war which is covering the earth with such unheard of horrors."

The Clergy, never forgetting Peter's word respecting the submission all are in duty bound to practice towards Kings as well as towards all those holding civil power, was always faithful in obeying the Episcopal directions never ceasing to deserve the eulogium which the Bishops expressed to the Pope in their favour.

"The French-Canadian people, so taught by words and examples, have given in all our history the admirable spectacle of a constant fidelity which circumstances more than once rendered highly meritorious. Such are the true religious and national traditions of our country. They have in our own days, as in the past, found the exact expression suggested by the situation.

"On the other hand, it appears to us a well established fact, and the most serious minds so proclaim everywhere, that the British Empire, together with France, martyred Belgium and their Allies are actually struggling for the defence of the peoples' Rights and true Liberty. (Card. Begin.) Therefore, very dear Brethren, it must be acknowledged that Canada, herself threatened by the possibilities of a war fought with conditions heretofore unknown, has acted both wisely and loyally in giving, in a manner as generous as it was spontaneous, all the support in her power to the mother-country, England.

"The Catholics, and especially those of French origin, have not remained behind in this manifestation of true patriotism. If it was well to make a comparison between the other groups, from the standpoint of the free and generous participation of all to the European war, it would be necessary, in the respective figures obtainable, to take into account several elements which are perhaps not sufficiently considered.

"But this is not the real question. It is sufficient to show and to note for historical authenticity that, with the encouragement and the blessings of their Pastors, and true to their constant tradition, the Canadian Catholics, as a whole, have, in this frightful conflict proved the perfect loyalty which is the sound expression of true patriotism, and which is blessed by the Church and by God.

"Thousands and thousands of our young men, for a large number of them at the cost of particular and most painful sacrifices, and in many cases, without being able to give to their race the benefit of their chivalrous devotion, have gone, oversea, to fight and die for the cause which was proved to them noble and urgent.

"Moreover, all over the country, the courage of our soldiers was echoed and answered by many active and important works characterized by charitable solidarity, and this universal co-operative and sympathetic movement must be supported by the sentiments of faith and piety.

"Since we are, at all costs, engaged in a disastrous war, the causes of which we have not to discuss and judge, but the consequences of which will necessarily reach our country, and since our Canadian soldiers are battling under the British flag, with the clear conscience of an honourable duty loyally and freely accepted, it is just, it is legitimate that our prayers do accompany them on the very fields of battles to support their courage, and that these prayers ascend to Heaven to implore victory for our armies."

Evidently the venerable Bishop of Valleyfield is far from believing, like the publicist whose errors we must all deplore, that in organizing a powerful army *"to go overseas to fight and die for the noble and urgent cause so proved to them,"* the Canadian Parliament *"were forging for us a militarism without parallel in any other civilized country, a depraved and undisciplined soldiery, an armed scoundrelism, without faith nor law."*

The blessings of the Head of the Canadian Church and those of the whole Episcopate have consoled our brave volunteers for the outrages thrust at them, and have inspired them with the great Christian courage to forgive their author. The only revenge they have taken against their accuser has been to defend himself and his own against the barbarous Germans.

CHAPTER XXX.

RASH DENUNCIATION OF PUBLIC MEN.

A long experience of public life, whether by daily observation, begun in my early youth, when the Union of the Provinces was finally discussed, carried and established, or, subsequently, during many years of active political life as a journalist and member of the Quebec and Ottawa representative Houses, has taught me to judge the actions of responsible men, whether ministerialists or oppositionists, with great fairness and respectful regard. At all times the government of a large progressive country peopled by several races, of different religious creeds, is a difficult problem. It should not be necessary to say that in days of warlike crisis, of previously unknown proportions, like the present one, the task becomes almost superhuman. Anyone taking into serious consideration the very trying ordeal through which, for instance, the rulers of Great Britain and France have been, and are still passing, since early in 1914, cannot help being indulgent for those who have the weighty and often crushing burden of the cares of State. Let so much be said without in the least contesting the right of free men to their own opinion about what is best to be done. But it was never more opportune to remember that the honourable privilege of constitutional criticism must have for its only superior object the good of the country by improved methods.

We have reason to congratulate ourselves that this sound view has widely prevailed rallying almost as units great nations,—our own one of them— previously much divided in political thoughts and aspirations, for the noble and patriotic purpose of winning a disastrous war they were forced to wage, in spite of their most determined efforts to prevent it.

Public men, nations rulers, like all others are human and liable to fail or to be found wanting. Unconscious inefficiency, however desirable to remove, cannot be fairly classed on the same footing as guilty failures. The first may, more or less, injure the bright prospects of a country; the second stains her honour which an exemplary punishment can alone redeem.

But it is said with much truth that there are always exceptions to a general rule. That of the human heart to be fallible in public life, as well as in other callings, has met with only one solitary exception in Canada: the saintly Nationalist leader who will never have his equal, "nature having destroyed the mould when she cast him."

Considering the outrageous language he thrusted at the Canadians of the three

British races and at our heroic volunteers, it is not to be supposed that he was so tender-hearted as to spare the public men, not only of Canada, but of all the Allied Nations.

When he affirmed that the real and only cause of the war had been, and was still, the voracious greed of capitalist speculators, especially of the two leading belligerents, Great Britain and Germany, united together to profit to the tune of hundreds of millions out of the production of warship building and materials of all sorts, was he not charging all the statesmen and leading politicians of all the peoples at war, of having bowed either consciously to the dictates of traitors to their countries, or of having been stupidly blind to the guilty manipulations of financial banditti?

It would take many pages only to make a summary of the injurious words he has addressed to the Canadian public men of all shades of opinion—with the only exception of the Nationalist—on account of the support they have given, in one way or another, to the Dominion's participation in the war. He qualified as a *Revolution* the policy by which we willingly decided to take part in the wars of the Empire whenever we came to the conclusion that England was fighting for a just cause.

On the 23rd of April, 1917, he wrote as follows:—

"Very often we have shown the evident revolutionary character of the Canadian intervention in the European conflict."

After repeating his absolutely absurd pretention, according to the sound principles of Constitutional Law, that Canada could have intervened in the war as a *"nation"* he found fault with all and every one because *"we are fighting to defend the Empire."* He went on and said with his natural sweetness of language:—

"The politicians of the two parties and the whole servile and mercenary press have applied themselves to this revolutionary work.... For a long time past the party leaders are the tools of British Imperialism and of BRITISH HIGH FINANCE.*"*

And not satisfied with having thus slashed all the party leaders, all the chiefs of the State, he turns round, in an access of passionate indignation, and charges not only all the leading social classes, but even the Bishops, the worthy leaders of the Church, as the accomplices of the Imperialist revolution. He thrusts the terrible blow as follows:—

"But what the war has produced of entirely new and most disconcerting, is the moral support and complicity which the "IMPERIALIST REVOLUTION" *has found in all the leading social classes.* BISHOPS, *financiers, publicists and*

professionals went into the movement with a unity, an ardour, a zeal which reveal the effective strength of the laborious propaganda of which Lord Grey has been the most powerful worker prior to the war."

So that there should be no mistake about its true meaning, he favoured his readers with a very clear explanation indeed of what, in his opinion, has transformed our meritorious and loyal intervention in the war into a guilty revolutionary movement. He wrote as follows:—

"But what the Imperialists wanted, and what they have succeeded in obtaining, was to bind Canada to the fate of England, in the name of the principle of Imperial solidarity and—as we shall see in a moment—to the cause of 'UNIVERSAL DEMOCRACY'*."*

Thus, in the Nationalist leader's opinion, it is a great crime to help England and her Allies to win a war the loss of which would most likely have destroyed the British Empire, involving our own ruin in the downfall of the mighty political edifice to be replaced, in the glorious shelter it gives to human freedom, by the triumphant German autocratic rule and its universal domination. It is, to say the least, an extravagant notion to pretend that the war has afforded the Imperialists the opportunity—eagerly seized—*"to tie Canada"* hand and foot, *"to the fate of England."*

If I am not mistaken—and I am positively sure I am right in so saying— Canada was bound to the fate of England the very day when—by Providential decree, in that instance as well as with regard to everything earthly—she passed under British Sovereignty. The worthy leaders of our Church so considered—and have since unanimously considered—at once taking the sound Christian stand that the French Canadians were, in duty bound, to accept their new political status in good faith, and to loyally support their new mother country whenever circumstances would require their devoted help, whilst revering the old as every child must do, if he is blessed with a good heart, when separated by unforeseen events from the home of his happy youth.

I must acknowledge that with some of our French Canadians of the first class and standing, the word "Democracy" savours with soreness. Well read in all that pertains to the great epoch of the first French tremendous Revolution, they abhor, with much reason, the extravagant and false principles of the BOLSHEVIKISM of those days, which culminated in the frightful period of the "terrorism" which, for three long years and more, kept its strong knee on France's throat, her fair soil flooded with the innocent blood of her children. They are apt to be laid to the confusion that democratic government is in almost every case, if not always, synonymous of revolutionary institutions, in as much as it cannot, they believe and say, be otherwise than destructive of the principle of "Authority," certainly as essential as that of "Liberty," both as the necessary fundamental basis of all good governments.

Knowing this, the Nationalist leader, who has evidently abjured his liberalism of former days, which he was wont to parade in such resounding sentences, multiplies his efforts to capture the support of the few members of our most venerable Clergy whom he supposes labouring under the aforesaid delusion. He would not lose the chance of trading on their feelings and sincere conviction, in boldly declaring that his good friends, the cursed Imperialists, had managed to drag the Dominion through the mire of the European war by blandishing before the eyes of the Canadian people, so enamoured of their constitutional liberties, the supposed dangerous spectre of *"universal democracy."*

If, in reality, democratic government could not help being either the "French revolutionary terrorism," of 1792-95,—which even frightened such a staunch friend of Political Liberty as Burke—or the Russian criminal bolshevikism of our own trying days, we would be forced, in dire sadness, to despair of the world's future, as Humanity would be forever doomed to ebb and flow between the sanguinary "absolutism" either of "autocratic" or "terrorist" tyrants.

Happily, we can, in all sincerity, affirm that such is not the case. Is it not sufficient, as a most reassuring proof, to point at the wonderful achievements of free institutions, first, under the monarchical democratic system of Great Britain and her autonomous Dominions; second, under the republican regime of the United States.

After many long years of earnest study and serious thinking, I cannot draw the very depressing conclusion that the two basic principles of sound government—Authority and Liberty—cannot be brought to work harmoniously together for the happiness and prosperity of nations, as far as they can be achieved in this world of sufferings and sacrifices. Such a conclusion would also be contrary to true Christian teachings, the Almighty having created man a free being with a responsible and immortal soul.

Nations who, forgetful of the obligations of moral laws, indulge in guilty abuse of their liberties, are, sooner or later, as individuals doing alike, sure to meet with the due Providential punishment they have deserved. But, also like individuals, they can redeem themselves in repenting for their past errors, due to uncontrolled passions, and by resolutely and "FREELY" returning to the path of their sacred duty.

The Nationalist leader also deplores, as one of their guilty achievements, the fact that the *"war had ended all equivocals and consummated the complete alliance of the two parties*," to favour, as he asserts, of course, the enterprises of the dreaded Imperialism.

True to the kind appreciation he has pledged himself to make of the inspiring dark motives actuating the conduct of public men, he sweetly added:—

"The truce arrived at in 1914 could not, it is true, resist the thirst for power. "Blues" and "Reds" have recommenced tearing themselves about patronage, places, planturous contracts and "boodle." But with regard to the substantial question itself, and to the Imperialist revolution brought on and sanctioned by the war, they have remained in accord."

It could not strike such a prejudiced mind as that of the Nationalist leader, that political chieftains, and their respective supporters, could conscientiously unite to save their country, their Empire and the world from an impending terrible disaster, and yet freely and conscientiously differ as to the best means to achieve the sacred object to the success of which they have pledged, and they continue to make, their best and most patriotic efforts.

The public men, and even the private citizens, who, not believing that he speaks and writes with Divine inspiration, dare to differ from the Nationalist leader, cannot, in his opinion, do so unless influenced by unworthy corrupt motives. And he further draws the awful conclusion *"that it is his duty to note the ever increasing revolutionary character that the European war, as a whole, is assuming on the side of the Allies."*

To support this last and absolutely unfounded charge, he positively asserts that the joint *"policy of the statesmen, politicians and journalists, has much less for its object to liberate oppressed nations like Belgium, Servia,* IRELAND, *Poland and Finland, from a foreign yoke, than to overthrow in all the countries, allies or enemies, the monarchical form of government."*

And then follows a most virulent diatribe by which he points, in support of his wild conclusion aforesaid, to the Russian revolution, charging *"the officious and reptile press of the Allied countries to have joined in spreading the legend that it had been precipitated by German intrigues at the Court of the Czar, and to have accused the ill-fated Emperor to have been the spy and the accomplice of the enemies of his country."*

At this hour of the day, in the turmoil of flashing events perhaps never before equalled in suddenness, pregnant with such alarming, or comforting, prospective consequences, it is much too early to attempt passing a reliable judgment on the true causes which produced the Moscovite revolution so soon and so dastardly developed into criminal "bolshevikism." The question must be left for History to settle when peace is restored and the sources of truth are wide opened to the impartial investigations of high class historians.

However, enough is known to prove that Mr. Bourassa's charge is altogether unfounded. Anyone conversant with Russian history for the two last centuries, is aware that German influences and intrigues have always played a great part in the Capital of that fallen Empire. From the very beginning of the war, it became evident that they were actively at work at the Petrograd Court, thwarting the Emperor's efforts and those of his advisers, military and civil, he could trust, to be true to the cause he had sworn to defend with France and England.

The Nationalist leader, I hope, is the only man still to wonder at this, after all that has been discovered proving what Germany has tried to bribe the political leaders and the press of the Allies, with too much success in France, England and the United States.

Russia has been for too many years the favourite soil where Germany was sowing her corrupt intrigues, to let any sensible man suppose that she would kindly withdraw from the preferred field of her infamous operations, at the very time she was exerting herself with such energy, and at the cost of so many millions, to extend her vast spy system almost all over the earth,— Canada included—debauching consciences right and left.

Is it unfair to say, for instance, after the event as it developed, that Roumania was prematurely brought into the war in consequence of the dark German machinations at Petrograd, with the evident understanding that the military operations, both on the Teutonic and Moscovite sides, were to be so conducted as to rush poor Roumania into a most disastrous defeat, in order to feed the Central Empires with the products of the fertile Roumanian soil?

No representative man of any consequence has pretended that the unfortunate Czar was himself a party to that treason of the Allied cause. He has likely been the victim of his own weakness in not using what was left to him of his personal autocratic power to silence the sympathies of the friends of Germany at his Imperial Court, and even in his most intimate circle, rather than exhausting it in a supreme, but doomed, attempt at checking the rising tide of popular aspirations sure, as always, to overflow to frightful excesses, if unwisely compressed.

Almost daily witnessing the successive miscarriages of so many of the Russian military operations, too often by the failure of the ammunitions, supplied to such a large extent by the Allies, to reach the Russian soldiers, or by other inexplicable causes, it is not surprising that the people at large became suspicious of their government which they soon believed to be under German tutorage.

The rapid, almost sudden, overthrow of the Russian autocratic Empire can be accepted as evidence that the movement in favour of a change which would more efficiently conduct Russia's share of the conflict, was widespread. The goal it aimed at, once reached, and Russia proclaimed a Republic, with a regular *de facto* government under the leadership of abler men, whose patriotism was proved by their words, but more surely by their deeds, France, England, Italy and the United States cannot be reasonably reproached with having unduly opened diplomatic relations with the new Moscovite authorities.

Unfortunately, once successful in her intrigues at the Petrograd Court, soon to fall under the weight of popular exasperation, Germany tried her hand in a triumphant, but shameful, way with the fiery sanguinary and treasonable element always to be found operating in the darkest corners for their own criminal purposes. The calamitous outcome has been "bolchevikism" betraying their country in the light of day, without blushing, without hiding their faces in eternal shame, and signing, with their hands stained with the blood of their own kin, the infamous treaty of Brest-Litovsk dismembering poor Russia, scattering to the winds her fond hopes of a grand future at the very dawn of the better days promised by a free constitution, and plunging her in the throes of German autocratic domination.

With regard to the Nationalist leader's rash denunciation of public men, I have only a few more words to say. My personal recollections going back to the early sixties of the last century, for several years free from all party affiliations, unbiassed by any sympathies or prejudices, I consider it my duty to say that, on the whole, Canadian public life, as well as British public life, is honourable and entitled to the respect of public opinion. Out of hundreds and thousands of politicians, both in the Motherland and in our own Dominion, there may have been failings. It would be useless, even pernicious, to point at them. The revulsion of public feeling towards the fallen for cause, and the severe judgment of misdeeds by the impartial historian, has been the deserved punishment of the few who have prevaricated. I prefer by far to take my lofty inspiration from the galaxy of faithful public servants who, from all parties, and from various standpoints, have given the fruits of their intelligence, of their learning, of their hard work—and in many cases—of their private wealth, for the good of their country. In the course of the last fifty-five years, I have known hundreds of our public men who lived through, and came out of, a long political life getting poorer every day without being disheartened and retiring from the public service to which they were devoted to the last. Need I point, as examples, to the cases of several men who, departed for a better world, Parliament, irrespective of all party considerations, united to a man to vote a yearly allowance of a few hundred dollars to save their surviving widows and children from actual want and destitution!

Just as well as the Canadians of the three British races, and the gallant volunteers of our heroic army, Canadian and British public men can rest assured that from the high position they occupy in the world's estimation, they are far above the fanatical aspersions of the Nationalist leader blinded by the wild suggestions of an inexhaustible thirst of rash condemnation.

CHAPTER XXXI.

Mr. Bourassa's Dangerous Pacifism.

Two historical truths, undeniable, bright as the shining light of the finest summer day, which have triumphantly challenged the innumerable falsehoods to the contrary constantly circulated by Germany, even prior to the outbreak of the hostilities, are:—

First, that all the countries united under the title—the Allies, have been energetically in favour of MAINTAINING THE PEACE OF THE WORLD, when it became evident, for all sensible people, that Germany was eagerly watching her opportunity to strike the blow she had prepared for the previous forty years on such a gigantic scale.

Second, that, once engaged in the conflict against their deliberate will, and in spite of their noble efforts to prevent the war which they clearly foresaw would be most calamitous, they have always remained the staunch supporters of the RESTORATION OF PEACE upon the two *sine qua non* conditions of JUSTICE and DURABILITY.

To achieve these two objectives, they have been fighting for now more than four years, at tremendous cost of men and treasures, and they are determined to fight until victorious.

They would all lay down their arms to-morrow, if the results so important for the future of Humanity could be secured with certainty.

Like all great causes, PEACE WITH JUSTICE AND DURABILITY has had its TRUE and its FALSE friends.

The TRUE friends of PEACE were those who realized from the very beginning of the frightful struggle that it was perfectly useless to expect it, if the disastrous Prussian Militarism was to be maintained and allowed to continue threatening Civilization.

The TRUE friends of PEACE were those who pledged their honour not to sheathe the sword they had been forced to draw before Germany would acknowledge that she had no right to violate solemn treaties, and would agree to redeem the crime she had committed in invading the neutral territory of Belgium which she trampled under her ironed heels and crucified.

The TRUE friends of PEACE were those who determined to bring Germany to renounce the abominable principles she has professed, training the mind of her peoples to believe and proclaim that MIGHT is RIGHT and the only sound basis of INTERNATIONAL LAW.

The TRUE friends of PEACE were those who, however anxious they were to have it restored as soon as possible—fervently praying the Almighty to that purpose—, knowing what are the principles of International Law recognized by all truly civilized nations, could not forgive Germany, UNLESS SHE SINCERELY REPENTED, the barbarism she displayed in her murderous submarine campaign, and practised in Belgium, Northern France and in every piece of belligerent territory her armies occupied.

The TRUE friends of PEACE were those who clearly understood that to meet the two essential conditions of JUSTICE and DURABILITY, it was PRACTICALLY IMPOSSIBLE to secure it by a compromise which could not, by any means, protect the world against further German attempts at universal military domination.

The FALSE friends of PEACE were those who said and wrote, in sheer defiance of truth, that the Allies, more especially England and Russia, were as much responsible for the war as Germany herself.

The FALSE friends of PEACE were those who falsely alleged that the Allies were preventing it by their repeated declarations that their principal war aim was to destroy, not only the German Empire, but also the German race, thus wilfully and maliciously pretending that to battle for the abolition of Teutonic militarism, weighing so heavily on all the nations, was equal, in guilty knowledge, to fighting for an enemy's race destruction.

The FALSE friends of PEACE were those who were ready to sanction, at any time, a compromise between HEROIC and criminal war aims, which would leave future generations to the tender mercies of a Sovereign Power straining every nerve to dominate the world by the foulest means ever devised.

The FALSE friends of PEACE were those whose daily effort was to dishearten their countrymen from the noble and patriotic task they had bravely undertaken with the strong will to accomplish it at all costs, knowing, as they did, that it was a question of life or death for human Civilization.

"Defeatists," as they are called, to mean the shameless supporters of PEACE negotiations to be opened by the Allies acknowledging their defeat and the victory of Germany, there were, and there are, in all the "Allied" belligerent nations. No one need be too much surprised at the hideous fact. In all countries, at all times, under the direst circumstances, when it is most important, in very distressing hours, that all be of one mind, of one heart, to save the nation's existence, are to be found heartless, low minded, cowardly beings, ready to betray their countrymen rather than stand the strain of their due share of sacrifices, or, which is still far worse, for corrupt motives, to deliver them over to the enemy.

"Defeatists" we have had, we have yet, in Canada, in the Province of Quebec. Most happily, they are few and far between.

Imbued with the false notions he has so tenaciously ventilated respecting Canada's participation in the war, it is no wonder that the Nationalist leader was sure to be found at the head of the small group of PACIFISTS, at almost any cost, mustered amongst the French Canadians. A sower of prejudices, he was bound to watch with eagerness the growing crop of ill-feelings he was fostering.

Those of us who oppose all, and any, participation by the Dominion in the wars of the Empire, be they even so just, so honourable, so necessary, under Mr. Bourassa's deplorable leadership, were naturally supporters of any kind of "PACIFISM."

I will not classify the Nationalist leader and his dupes as "*defeatists*," who were ready to accept peace as the consequence of defeat. The real "*pacifists*," so far as it is possible to ascertain their views, unable, consciously or not, to see any difference in the respective responsibilities of the belligerents in opening the war, consider that they are equally guilty in not closing it.

Most happily, such a disordered opinion is shared only by a small minority. It can be positively affirmed that public opinion, the world over, outside the Central Empires and their swayed allies, is almost unanimous that Germany, through her military party and the junkers element, is responsible for the dire calamity she has brought on Humanity. The question of the restoration of "PEACE" must be viewed from this starting point—the only true one.

The standpoints of the TRUE and the FALSE friends of PEACE being so far apart, the conclusions they draw are naturally widely different.

CHAPTER XXXII.

A MOST REPREHENSIBLE ABUSE OF SACRED APPEALS TO THE BELLIGERENT NATIONS.

I cannot qualify in milder words the use Mr. Bourassa has made of the solemn appeals His Holiness the Pope of Rome has, at different dates, addressed to the belligerent nations in favour of the restoration of peace. I bear to the Head of the Church I am so happy to belong such a profound respect and devotion that I will scrupulously abstain from any comment of the Sovereign Pontiff's writings and addresses. I have read them several times over with the greatest attention and veneration, so sure I was that, emanating from the highest spiritual Authority in the world, they were exclusively inspired by the ardent desire to promote a recurrence to good-will amongst men, in obedience to the Divine precept.

Having to reproach the Nationalist leader with having abused of the weighty words of His Holiness, to support his own misconceptions of duty as a loyal British subject and a Christian publicist, I will refrain with great care from writing a sentence which might be construed as the shadow of an attempt to do the same.

I will take from Mr. Bourassa's own comments of the Sovereign Pontiff's appeals, the two conclusions upon which he lays great stress, and which clearly summarize the convictions of His Holiness Pope Benedict XV.

Praying with all the powers of His heart and soul for the orderly future of the world, the Sovereign Pontiff implored, in the most touching terms, the belligerent nations to agree to a "JUST AND DURABLE PEACE."

As it was certain, even if He had not said so with such pathetic expressions, His Holiness drew the saddest possible picture of the untold misfortunes war, carried on in such vast proportions, was inflicting upon the peoples waging the struggle.

I will only quote the few following words from the first letter of His Holiness, dated July 28, 1915:—

"It cannot be said that the immense conflict cannot be terminated without armed violence."

No one can take exception to this truism, authoritatively expressed under circumstances greatly adding to its importance and to its solemn announcement. It is just as true to-day as it was,—and has been ever since,—

when the whole world was passing through the crucial ordeal of the days during which England and France were almost imploring Germany not to plunge the earth into the horrors of the war she was determined to bring on.

The questions at stake could then have been easily settled without "ARMED VIOLENCE," if the Imperial Government of Berlin had listened to the pressing demand of Great Britain in favour of the maintenance of peace.

It is scarcely believable that the Nationalist leader has abused of those weighty words to the point of attempting to persuade the French-Canadians that the Allies, even more than the Rulers of the Central Empires, have refused to listen to the prayers of the Pope. In January last, he published a new pamphlet, entitled "THE POPE, ARBITER OF PEACE," in which he reproduced from "Le Devoir" his numerous articles, from August 1914, on the intervention of the Sovereign Pontiff in favour of the cessation of the hostilities, and on the current events of the times.

The oft-repeated diatribes of Mr. Bourassa against England were bound to be once more edited in the above pamphlet. Their author, in a true fatherly way, not willing to allow them to die under the contempt they deserve, would not lose the chance to have them to survive in tackling them with his comments on His Holiness' letters.

This pamphlet, the worthy sequel of its predecessors which, for the good of Mr. Bourassa's compatriots, should never have seen the light of day, would call for many more refutable quotations than I can undertake to make in this work. A few will suffice to show the deplorable purport of the whole book.

In his letter dated, July 28, 1915, the Pope wrote:—

"In presence of Divine Providence, we conjure the belligerent nations, to henceforth put an end to the horrible carnage which, for a year, dishonours Europe."

Positively informed about the horrible crimes committed by command of the German military authorities in Belgium, and Northern France, and by the ferocious Turks in Armenia, well might His Holiness say that Europe was being dishonoured by such barbarous deeds. If the military operations had been conducted by the nations of the Alliance in conformity with the principles of International Law, most likely the Pope would not have used the same language. For, however much to be regretted are the sufferings inseparable from a military conflict carried on with the utmost regards for the fair claims of human feelings and justice, it could not have been pretended that such a war was a dishonour for the belligerents on both sides, especially when fighting with an equally sincere conviction that they are defending a just cause.

Referring to recent history, none asserted, for instance, that the Russo-Japanese war was a dishonour to Europe and Asia. It was fought out honourably on both sides. Peace was restored without leaving bitter and burning recollections in the minds of either peoples. And when Germany dishonoured herself and stained Humanity with blushing shame, both Russia and Japan joined together to avenge Civilization.

Let us now see how Mr. Bourassa distorted the words of the Pope so as to use them for his own purpose of misrepresenting the true stand of the Allies, and more especially of England.

The first sentence of his article dated, August 3, 1915, to be found at page 11 of the pamphlet, under the title: *"The Pope's Appeal,"* reads thus:—

"The anniversary of the hurling of the sanguinary fury which makes of Europe the shame of Humanity has inspired the Rulers of peoples with resounding words."

And after eulogizing the Pope's intervention, he adds:—*"that men will not hear his voice, drunk as they are with pride, revenge and blood."*

This may be cunningly worded, but it should deceive nobody.

One cannot help being indignant at the contemptible attempt to place the Allies on the same footing as the Central Empires with regard to the responsibility *in hurling the sanguinary fury in 1914.*

The plain, incontrovertible, truth is that the outbreak of the war was a shame, not for Humanity, the victim of Teutonic treachery, but for Germany herself; whilst the sacred union of Belgium, France, England and their allies to resist the barbarous onslaught hurled at them all, was an honour for Civilization and the promise of an heroic redemption.

At page 12 of the pamphlet, he closes the first paragraph with the following words:—*"since the fatal days when peoples supposed to be Christian hurled themselves at one another in a foolish rage of destruction, of revenge and hatred."* In French, it reads thus:—*"depuis le jour fatal ou les peuples soi-disant chrétiens se sont rués les uns contre les autres, dans une rage folle de destruction, de vengeance et de haine."*

Read as a whole, with the full meaning they were intended to convey, those words constitute a daring falsehood. Historical events of the highest importance cannot be construed at will. There are facts so positively true, and known to be such, that they should preclude any possibility of deceit.

It is absolutely false that, *on a fatal day* of mid-summer, 1914, *peoples hurled themselves at one another.* What really took place, in the glaring light of day, was that Germany, fully prepared for the fray, *hurled* herself at weak Belgium, throwing to the waste basket the scraps of the solemn treaties by which she was in honour bound to respect Belgian neutrality. She had first opened the disastrous game by *hurling* her vassal, Austria, at weak Servia.

Rushing her innumerable victorious armies over Belgian trodden soil, she *hurled* herself at France with the ultimate design to *hurl* herself at England.

That in so doing, Germany was *raging* with a *foolish* thirst of *destruction, of revenge and hatred*, is certainly true. But Mr. Bourassa's guilt is in his assertion that the victims of Germany's *sanguinary fury* were actuated by the same criminal motives in heroically defending their homes, their wives, their children, their all, against the barbarians once more bursting out of Central Europe, this time bent on overthrowing human freedom.

Is the respectable citizen who bravely defends himself against the ruffian who *hurls* himself at his throat, to be compared with his murderous assailant?

But England was not alone in *hurling* herself at Germany, as Mr. Bourassa so cordially says. Without a word, even a sign, by the only momentum of her *furious outburst of foolish destruction*, she was followed by the whole of her Empire. How much we, Canadians, were, for instance, deluded, the Nationalist leader is kind enough to tell us in his ever sweet language.

When the Parliament of Ottawa unanimously decided that it was the duty of the British Dominion of Canada to participate in the war; when Canadian public opinion throughout the length and breadth of the land, almost unanimously approved of this loyal and patriotic decision, we, poor unfortunate Canadians, thought that we were heartily and nobly joining with the mother-country to avenge "OUTRAGED JUSTICE," to rush to the rescue of violated Belgium, of France, once more threatened with agony under the brutal Teutonic ironed heels, of the whole world—Mr. Bourassa's commanding personality included—menaced with the HUNS' DOMINATION.

How sadly mistaken we were, Mr. Bourassa tells us. According to this infallible judge of the righteousness or criminality of historical events, we were labouring under a paroxysm of passion—*of a rage of foolish destruction, of vengeance and hatred*.

Once overpowered by this vituperative mood of calumnious accusations, the Nationalist leader slashes England, as follows,—page 18—:—

"England has violently destroyed more national rights than all the other European countries united together. By force or deceit, she has swallowed up a fourth of the earthly globe; by conquest, and more especially by corruption

and the purchase of consciences, she has subjugated more peoples than there were, in the whole human history, ever brought under the same sceptre."

Thus, in Mr. Bourassa's impartial estimation, the depredations and slaughters of the hordes commanded by Attila, the savagery of the Turks of old and present days, the crimes of Germany in this great war, are only insignificant trifles compared with the horrors of British history. Shame on such outrageous misrepresentation of historical truth.

Mr. Bourassa accuses England to have *by force or deceit swallowed up a fourth of the earthly globe.* Considering the happy and flourishing condition of the vast British Empire, the Nationalist leader, as every one else, must admit that England is endowed with great digestive powers, as she does not show the least sign that she suffers from national dyspepsia from having swallowed up a fourth of the universe. Her national digestion is evidently sound and healthy, for instead of weakening and decaying, she grows every day in strength, in stature, in freedom, in prestige, and, above all, in WISDOM.

The Nationalist leader has thought proper to express his formal hatred of militarism. One would naturally suppose that, in so doing, he should have pointed at the worst kind of militarism ever devised—the German type of our own days. Let no one be mistaken about it. At page 58 of his pamphlet, Mr. Bourassa bursts out as follows in the top paragraph:—

"As a matter of fact, of all kinds of militarism, of all the instruments of brutal domination, the naval supremacy of England is the most redoubtable, the most execrable for the whole world; for it rules over all the continents, hindering the free relations of all the peoples."

Was I really deluded when I felt sure that in peaceful times, British naval supremacy on the seas was not interfering in the least with the freest commercial intercourse of all the nations, whose mercantile ships can, by British laws, enter freely into all the ports of Great Britain? Mr. Bourassa's assertion to the contrary, I shall not, by the least shadow, alter my opinion which is positively sound.

From the above last quotation, I have the right to infer that Mr. Bourassa is very sorry that, in war times like those we have seen since July 1914, British naval supremacy is sufficiently paramount to protect the United Kingdom from starvation, to keep the coasts of France opened to the mercantile ships of the Allies and of all the neutral nations, to "rule the waves" against both the German military and mercantile fleets, chased away from the oceans by the British guns thundering at the Teutonic pirates on land and sea. If he is, he can be sure that he is alone to cry and weep at a fact which rejoices all the true and loyal friends of freedom and justice.

Mr. Bourassa cherishes a wish that will certainly not be granted. He will not be happy unless England agrees to give up her naval supremacy to please Germany. Let him rest quietly on his two ears; the dawn of such a calamitous day is yet very far distant.

At the end of page 12, Mr. Bourassa asserts that *the Germans proclaim their* RIGHT *to "Germanize" Europe and the world, and that the English imperiously affirm their* RIGHT *to maintain their Imperial power over the seas and to oppose "Anglo-Saxonism" to "pan-Germanism."*—

I have already refuted the Nationalist leader's pretention, and informed him that England, no more than any other country, has no "Sovereign rights" on the seas outside the coastal limits as prescribed by International Law. He appears totally unable to understand the simple truth that Great Britain's sea supremacy is nothing more nor less than the superiority of her naval strength created, at an immense cost, out of sheer necessity, to protect the United Kingdom from the domination of a great continental power.

Does he not know that, in the days prior to England's creation of her mighty fleet, she has been easily conquered by invaders? Is he aware of the great British historical fact called the Norman Conquest? Has he never heard that before starting on his triumphant march across Europe, culminating at Austerlitz, the great Napoleon had planned an invasion of England, with every prospects of success, if he had not been deterred from carrying it out by the continental coalition which, calling into play the resources of his mighty genius, he so victoriously crushed and dispersed? Has he never read anything about panic stricken England until she was relieved from the dangers of the projected invasion?

Does he not realize that, unless they were madmen, no British ministers will ever consent to renounce their "UNDOUBTED RIGHT" to be ever ready for any emergency, to save their country from enslavement by would-be dashing invaders? It is the height of political nonsense to suppose that responsible public men ever could be so blind, or so recreant to their most sacred duty, as to follow the wild course recommended by extravagantly prejudiced "Nationalists."

The man who would throw away his weapons of defense would have nothing else to do but to kneel down and implore the tender mercy of his criminal aggressor. Truly loyal subjects of the Empire cannot clamour to bring England down to such an humiliating position. They know too well that if ever matters came to so disastrous a pass, Great Britain could easily be starved into irremediable submission with the consequent and immediate destruction of the whole fabric of the Empire. A Nationalist, yawning for such an end, may suggest the best way to reach it. But no loyal man, sincerely wishing the maintenance of the great British Commonwealth, will ever do so.

No wonder that he who came out openly in favour of Imperial Federation for the express purpose of ruining the Empire, endeavours to achieve his most cherished object in first destroying British naval supremacy on the seas. Imperial Federation would then no longer be necessary for the consummation of his longing wishes.

Freedom of the seas and British naval supremacy are not antagonistic by any means, as I have previously well explained. It is an unanswerable proposition —a truism—to say that supremacy on the ocean will always exist, held by one nation or another. The Power commanding the superior naval fleet will for ever be supreme on the seas. It is mere common sense to say so. Mr. Bourassa would vainly work his wind-mill for centuries without changing this eternal rule of sound sense.

If, by whichever cause, England was to lose her sea supremacy, it would at once, as a matter of course, pass on to the next superior naval Power.

In a subsequent chapter on the after-the-war military problem, I shall explain the way or ways, by which, in my opinion, the question of the freedom of the seas, so much misunderstood, could be settled to the satisfaction of all concerned.

With regard to the supposed conflict of "anglo-saxonism" and "pan-germanism" I will merely say that it is only another sample of Mr. Bourassa's wily dreams.

As I have already said, this last pamphlet of the Nationalist leader is, for a large part of it, but the repetition of his diatribes so often *hurled* at England. I will close this chapter by quoting from page 57, the following paragraph which summarizes, in a striking way, the charges Mr. Bourassa is so fond to *hurl* at the mother-country. It reads thus:—

"What has allowed England to bring Portugal into vassalage? to dominate Spain and keep Gibraltar, Spanish land? to deprive Greece of the Ionians and Cyprus Islands? to steal Malta? to foment Revolution in the Kingdom of Naples and the Papal States? to run, during thirty years, the foreign policy of Italy and to throw her in Austria's execrated arms? to take possession of Suez and to make her own thing of it? to chase France from the Upper Nile, and subsequently from the whole of Egypt, to intervene in the Berlin treaty to deprive Russia of the profits of her victory, to galvanize dying Turkey, to delay for thirty years the revival of the Balkan States and to make of Germany the main spring of continental Europe? In a word, what has permitted England to

rule the roost in Europe and to accumulate the frightful storm let loose in 1914? Who? What? if it is not the "naval domination" of England ever since the destruction of the French and Spanish fleets at Trafalgar."

It would be most difficult to condense more erroneous historical appreciations and political absurdities in so few lines.

Many will be quite surprised to learn, from Mr. Bourassa's resounding trumpet, that England had been for many years gathering the storm which broke out in 1914. So far all fairminded men were convinced that this rascally work had been done by Germany, in spite of England's exhortations to reduce military armaments.

In all sincerity, I am unable to understand how Mr. Bourassa can expect to successfully give the lie to such incontrovertible truths as the guilt of Germany in preparing the war she finally brought on more than four years ago, and as the unceasing determination of England to maintain peace.

CHAPTER XXXIII.

A CASE FOR TRUE STATESMANSHIP.

Whatever the TRUE and the FALSE friends of PEACE may hope and say, it is perfectly useless to close our eyes to the glaring fact that its restoration can only be the result of military effort combined with the highest practical statesmanship. After all what has happened, and the oft-repeated declaration of the Rulers of the belligerent nations, it would be a complete loss of a very valuable time to indulge any longer in the expression of views all acknowledge in principle, but which no one, however well disposed he may be, is actually able to traduce in practical form.

When writing my French book, in the fall of 1916, reviewing the situation as it had so far developed, I said:—

"All are most anxious for peace. However it is infinitely better to look at matters such as they are. It is evident that the military situation does not offer the least hope that the war can be immediately brought to an end. Successes have been achieved on both sides. But nothing decisive has yet happened. The armies are facing one another in defiant attitude. The belligerent nations, on both sides, have yet, and for a long time, great resources in man-power and money."

"If Germany, which should first give up the fight in acknowledging her crime, is obdurate to final exhaustion, how can it be possibly expected that the Allies who were forced to fight, will submit to the humiliation and shame of soliciting from their cruel enemy a peace the conditions of which, they know, would be utterly unacceptable. Consequently they must with an indomitable courage and an invincible perseverance go on struggling to solve, for a long time, the redoubtable problem to which they are pledged, in honour bound, to give the only settlement which can reassure the world."

I am still and absolutely of the same opinion. The present military situation has certainly much improved in favour of the Allies since 1916. However, looking at the question, first, from the standpoint of the developing military operations, there is no actual, and there will not be for many months yet—more or less—practical possibility of a satisfactory peace settlement.

Secondly, looking at the question from the standpoint of true statesmanship, it is very easy to draw the inexorable conclusion that, again, there is not actually the least chance of an immediate restoration of peace.

Statesmen, responsible, not only for the future of their respective countries, but, actually, for that of the whole world, are not to be supposed liable to be carried away by a hasty desire to put an end to the war and to their own arduous task in carrying it to the only possible solution:—A JUST AND DURABLE PEACE.

A broad and certain fact, staring every one, is that the Berlin Government will not accept the only settlement to which the Allies can possibly agree as long as her armies occupy French and Belgian territories. If Mr. Bourassa and his "pacifists" friends—or dupes—have really entertained a faint hope to the contrary, they were utterly mistaken.

Present military events, however proportionately enlarged by the increased resources, in man-power and money, of the belligerents, are not without many appropriate precedents. History is always repeating itself. Great Powers having risked their all in a drawn battle, do not give in as long as they can stand the strain, considering the importance of the interests they have at stake.

For the same reason above stated, but reversed, the Allies will not negotiate for peace before they have thrown the German armies out of French and Belgian soil, and repulsed them over Teutonic territory. I do not mean to say that peace must necessarily be proclaimed either from Berlin or from Paris. But it will only be signed as the inevitable result of a final triumphant march on the way either to Berlin or to Paris. There is no possible escape from the alternative. In such matters, there is no halfway station.

CHAPTER XXXIV.

AFTER-THE-WAR MILITARY PROBLEM.

Two of the most important propositions of His Holiness the Pope more especially deserve earnest consideration. They are indeed supported by the Allies who are purposely fighting for their adoption.

In his note of the first of August, 1917, addressed to the Rulers of the belligerent nations, the Pope says in part:—

"AT FIRST, THE FUNDAMENTAL POINT MUST BE TO SUBSTITUTE THE MORAL FORCE OF RIGHT TO THE MATERIAL FORCE OF ARMS."

No truer proposition could be enounced. If Germany had put this principle into practice, she never would have violated Belgian territory.

When England protested against the proposed invasion of Belgium, she did so in obedience to the sacred principle enunciated by the Sovereign Pontiff. She strongly insisted to the last minute that *the moral force* of solemn treaties should prevail upon *the material force of arms*.

In a letter dated October 7, 1917, His Eminence Cardinal Gasparri, Secretary of State to His Holiness, addressing the Archbishop of Lens, wrote as follows respecting conscription:—

"The Holy See, in his Appeal of the first of August, did not consider, out of deference for the leaders of the belligerent peoples, that he should mention it, preferring to leave to themselves the care of determining it, but for him, the only practical system and, moreover, easy to apply with some good will on both sides, would be the following: to suppress, with one accord between civilized nations, military obligatory service; to constitute an arbitration tribunal, as already said in the Pontifical Appeal, to settle international questions; finally, to prevent infractions, to establish universal "boycottage" against any nation attempting to reestablish military obligatory service, on refusing either to lay an international question before the arbitration tribunal, or to abide by its decision."

Cardinal Gasparri then points to the ante-war British and American systems of military "voluntarism", in the following terms:—

"As a matter of fact, omitting other considerations, the recent example of England and America testifies in favour of the adoption of this system. England and America had, in effect, voluntary service, and, to take an efficient part in the present war, they were obliged to adopt conscription. It proves that voluntary service well supplies the necessary contingent to maintain public order (and is public order not maintained in England and America just as well, if not better, than in the other nations?) but it does not supply the enormous armies required for modern warfare. Consequently in suppressing, with one accord between civilized nations, obligatory service to replace it by voluntary service, disarmament with all the happy consequences above indicated would be automatically obtained without any perturbation of public order."

"For the last century, conscription has been the true cause of calamities which have afflicted society: to reach a simultaneous and reciprocal suppression will be the true remedy. In fact, once suppressed, conscription could be reestablished only by a law; and for such a law, even with the present constitution of the Central Empires, Parliamentary approbation would be required (which approbation would be most improbable for many reasons and above all on account of the sad experience of the present war); in this way, what is so much desired, for the maintenance of agreements, would be obtained: the peoples' guarantee. If, on the other hand, the right to make peace or war was given to the people by way of **referendum**, or at least to Parliament, peace between nations would be assured, as much at least as it is possible in this world."

It should be very gratifying indeed to all the loyal subjects of the British Empire to ascertain, from the declarations of Cardinal Gasparri, that the Pope is in so complete accord with England on this the most important question to be settled by the future peace treaty.

As proved in one of the first chapters of this work, the Government of Great Britain, supported in this course by almost the unanimous opinion of the peoples of the United Kingdom, was the first to suggest the holding of the Hague conferences to consider the best means to adopt to favour the world with the blessings of permanent peace. Their own view, which they forcibly expressed, was that the surest way to reach that much desired result was to limit the military armaments, both on land and sea. For more than twenty years previous to the war, they pressed, and even implored, for the adoption of their program.

I have also proved how obdurate Germany was in resisting England's propositions, and her successful intrigues to thwart Great Britain's efforts to have them adopted and put into practice.

England's policy has not changed. On the contrary, it is more than ever favourable to the limitation, and even to the complete abolition, of armaments, if one or the other can be achieved. It is the principal war aim of

Great Britain, only coming next after her determination to avenge Belgium.

The future peace of the world could no doubt be well guaranteed by a large measure of disarmament. But it would certainly be much more so, if complete abolition could be obtained by an international agreement binding on all nations, with, of course, the allowance of the necessary forces required for the maintenance of interior public order.

The whole world can safely depend on the strenuous support of England for either the limitation or the abolition of armaments whenever the question is seriously taken up for consideration.

Evidently the problem will be difficult to solve. However, it should not be beyond the resources of statesmanship which, assuredly, ought to rise superior to all prejudiced aspirations after the terrible ordeal Humanity will have experienced during the present war.

The maintenance of internal public order, and permanent preparedness for foreign wars, are two very different questions to examine. The first can safely be left to the care of every nation sure to attend to it if willing to maintain her authority. The second has a much wider scope and will tax the ability of statesmanship to the utmost limit.

Will the great civilized nations decide, when the war is over, to completely abolish conscription to return to voluntary military service within a very limited organization, thus doing away by a bold and single stroke with a system which, for more than a hundred years, has been the curse of continental Europe?

Or will they, at least as an initial attempt, come to the conclusion to only limit armaments, maintaining compulsory service for the reduced strength of the armies?

If armaments are either abolished, or merely reduced, will they be so on sea as well as on land? I would answer at once:—of course, they should.

Looking at the question from the British stand-point—and I can also say from that of the United States—it should be easily solved.

Public opinion in Great Britain and all over the British Empire, as well as in the United States, has always been against conscription in peace times, until the present war.

Not exactly foreseeing the full extent of the effort she would be called upon to make, England entered into the conflict determined to meet the requirements of her military situation out of the resources of voluntary enlistment. Canada, joining in the struggle, did the same. Both have done wonderfully well during the three first years of the prolonged war.

I can, without the slightest hesitation, positively assert that public opinion, in the whole British Empire, and, not only in the United States, but in the whole of the two American continents, is, as a matter of principle, as much hostile to compulsory military service as it was before the present war, and would exult at its complete abolition as one of the happiest results of the gigantic contest still going on.

It is to be deplored, but still it is a fact, that great questions of public interest too often cannot be settled solely in conformity with the principles they imply.

If Great Britain, if the United States, if Canada, could consider the question of conscription exclusively from their own stand-point, they would most surely decide at once, and with great enthusiasm, to abolish the obligatory military service they have adopted only as a last resort under the stress of imperious necessity.

Moreover, I have no hesitation to express my own opinion that whatever will be the military system of continental Europe after the war, the British Empire and the United States will certainly not be cursed with permanent conscription. They are both so happily situated that, in peace times, they cannot be called upon to go very extensively into the costly preparedness which the European continental nations will have again to submit themselves to, if they are not wise enough to put an end forever to the barbarous militarism they have too long endured for fear of Teutonic domination.

Under the worst European situation, England, with a territorial army of a million of men ready to be called to the Colours, or actually flying them, backed by her mighty fleet maintained to its highest state of efficiency, could always face any continental enemy. And such an army of a ready million of well trained officers and men, voluntary service would easily produce.

If future conditions would require it, Canada herself could do her share to prepare for any emergency by reverting to voluntary enlistment, but in improving the service so as to produce more immediate efficiency.

Very apparently, the United States will come out of the present conflict with flying Colours and will dispense with compulsory service under any circumstances in the peace days to follow.

What then will the continental powers do? Blessed they will be, if they make up their mind to do away, once for all, with a system which has crushed the peoples so unmercifully.

To speak in all frankness, I believe it would be almost vain, however much desirable it is, to indulge in fond hopes of the complete abolition of militarism on the European continent. The canker is too deep in the flesh and blood of nations to be extirpated as if by magic. Such a reversal of conditions grown to extravagant proportions, during more than a century, will not likely be accomplished at the first stroke. Let us all hope that, at least, a good start will be made by a large limitation of armaments which may, with time, lead to the final achievement for which the whole world would be forever grateful to the Almighty. I have positively stated that extravagant militarism should be discontinued on sea as well as on land. Such has been the policy of England for many years past. I have proved it by the diplomatic correspondence between Great Britain and Germany, and the solemn declarations of all the leading British statesmen for the last quarter of a century. How persistingly England has implored Germany to agree with her in stopping that ruinous race in the building of war vessels, we have seen.

So, the assent, may more, the determination of England to adhere to her old and noble policy, is a foregone conclusion.

The closing sentence of the last quoted paragraph of Cardinal Gasparri's letter expresses the opinion that "*the right to make peace or war should be given to the people by way of referendum, or at least to Parliament.*"

The system preconized by the Eminent Cardinal has been in existence in England for a number of years; ever since the day when complete ministerial responsibility was adopted as the fundamental principle of the British constitution. That system was carried to the letter by Great Britain with regard to her intervention in the present war.

The right to declare war and to make peace is one of the most important prerogatives of the British Crown. This prerogative of the Crown, like all the others, is held in trust by the Sovereign for the benefit of the people and exercised by Him ONLY UPON THE ADVICE AND RESPONSIBILITY OF HIS MINISTERS.

In conformity with this great British constitutional principle, what happened in London, in August, 1914? The then Prime Minister, Mr. Asquith, in his own name and in those of his colleagues, advised His Majesty King George V. to declare war against Germany because she had invaded Belgian territory in violation of the treaties by which these two countries were, in honour bound, to protect Belgium's neutrality. They were constitutionally responsible to the Imperial Parliament and to the people of the United Kingdom for their advice to their Sovereign.

In his admirable statement to the British House of Commons, Sir Edward Grey, Secretary of State for Foreign Affairs, said:—

"*I have assured the House—and the Prime Minister has assured the House more than once—that if any crisis such as this arose, we should come before the House of Commons and be able to say to the House that it was free to decide what the British attitude should be, that we would have no secret engagement which we should spring upon the House, and tell the House that, because we had entered into that engagement, there was an obligation of honour upon the country."*

The British House of Commons, had they considered it to be their duty, had the right to disapprove the foreign policy of the Cabinet and to censure the ministers for the advice they had given, or had decided to give, to the Sovereign. On the other hand, the House of Commons had the right to approve the stand taken by the Government. They did so unanimously, and were most admirably supported by the people.

I must say that I consider it would be very difficult, if not absolutely impracticable, to have questions of war or peace dealt with by way of *"Referendum."* Crises suddenly created lead almost instantly to declarations of war. But this outcome could hardly be so rapidly produced that Parliament could not be called to deal with the emergency.

How could France have been able to oppose the crushing German invasion, in 1914, if her Government and her representative Houses had been obliged to wait for the result of a *"Referendum"* whether she would fight or kneel down?

But the whole world—outside the Central Empires and their Allies—witnessed with unbounded delight the spontaneous and unanimous decision of the heroic French nation to fight to the last. She threw herself with the most admirable courage against the invading waves of Teutonic barbarism, and succeeded by the great and glorious Marne victory in forcing them to ebb, thus giving England and the other Allies the time necessary to organize and train their armies which, by their united efforts will save Civilization from destruction and the world from the threatened German domination.

CHAPTER XXXV.

THE INTERVENTION OF THE UNITED STATES IN THE WAR.

The hostilities, once opened as the direct consequence of Germany's obduracy, many of the most influential leaders of public opinion in the United States foresaw that the conflict taking such a wide range, the great American Republic was most likely to be, sooner or later, involved in the European struggle. They were of two classes. Those out of office, holding for the time no official position, were, of course, not bound to the same careful discretion in judging the daily developments of the military operations, and their far reaching consequences, as those who were at the helm of State.

In appreciating the course followed by the United States since the war commenced, it must never be forgotten that if an autocratic Empire, trampled upon by a domineering military party, can be thrown in a minute into a great conflict, a Republic like that of our powerful neighbours cannot be dragooned into any hasty action. In a free country, under a responsible government, public opinion is the basis of the success of any important official decision.

The political men and the numerous publicists who incessantly called the attention of our neighbours to what was going on in Europe and on the seas, have rendered a great service in moulding public opinion for the grand duty the Republic would eventually be obliged to accomplish.

Having ourselves decided to participate in the war at once after its outbreak, and deeply engaged in the task, we, Canadians, felt somewhat uneasy about the apparent determination of our neighbours to stand aside, and let the European Powers settle the ugly question. As a rule, we were all wishing to see the United States joining with the Allies in the fray.

Once again, we had some black sheep with us. Whilst all the loyal Canadians were anxiously waiting for the day when they would applaud the American Republic's declaration of war against Germany, our Nationalists were getting more nervous at the increasing signs of the growth of public opinion amongst our neighbours against the criminal German cause and the crimes by which the Teutons were supporting it. Their leader, Mr. Bourassa, was doing his best to persuade the Americans that they had much better to remain out of the struggle. He expected he would succeed, as he had done in the Province of Quebec, in influencing, by his erroneous theories, many of the French Canadian element in the United States.

The wish being always father to the thought, Mr. Bourassa easily came to the conclusion that Mr. Wilson, the president of the United States, was decidedly opposed to any intervention of the Republic in the war, and would prevent it at all hazards. How prodigal he was of his eulogiums, of his advices, to the American "pacifists," with the President as their leader, to know one has only to read his newspaper "*Le Devoir.*"

How disappointed, how crest-fallen, he was when he discovered how much mistaken he had been!

When Mr. Wilson, who had long been waiting for the right hour to strike the blow at the Teutonic autocratic attempt at domination, rising grandly to the rank of a great statesman, supported by the splendid strength of the public opinion he had wisely and skilfully rallied in favour of the decision he had taken, was a sad day for our Nationalists and their heart-broken leader. Blind, prejudiced, as they were, meekly pandering to pan-Germanism which they considered as the best antidote to the Anglo-Saxonism they abhor, they could not understand that the Lusitania horror, the slaughtering of hundreds of American citizens in violation of all the principles of International Law, the crimes of the Teutonic submarine campaign more than justified the intervention of the United States in the war.

What our neighbours have done since they have joined with the Allies, what they are doing and promise to do, is worthy of all admiration. Like the British Empire, like France, the United States have given the inspiring example of a most enlightened patriotism, of a splendid unity of purpose, of a boundless confidence in the triumph of the cause of Justice and Right.

Such a grand spectacle of true national unity offered a striking contrast with the sad exhibition of the narrow Nationalism Canada has had to endure without, however, hindering to any appreciable extent our loyal and patriotic effort to help winning the war.

Mr. Bourassa, who had been out of his natural vituperative tune in complimenting Mr. Wilson on his supposed peace proclivities, was sure to turn his guns against the President of the Republic the moment he boldly and energetically took his stand against German barbarism as exhibited since the beginning of the war. Mr. Wilson had especially protested against such outrages as were perpetrated on the seas by Teutonic orders. He had repeatedly warned the Berlin Government what the inevitable consequences of such proceedings would be, and going to the full length of what friendly relations between two Sovereign States could permit, had demanded that an end be put to a kind of warfare most formally condemned by International Law, contrary to all justice, to all human notions of civilization.

When the cup of German iniquities overflowed with new crimes, American reprobation was also raised to the high water mark. Indignation was at the height of its exasperation. Public opinion had rapidly rallied and ripened at the horrible sight of so many American citizens, women and children, murdered in mid-ocean, their dead bodies floating over the waves, and their souls from above crying for vengeance.

Then the President, Congress, statesmen, politicians, publicists, loyal Americans numbering almost a hundred million, all of one mind, of one heart, pledged their national honour to avenge the foul deeds of Teutonic barbarity, and to do their mighty share in rescuing Freedom and Civilization from the threatening sanguinary cataclysm which was cruelly saddening our times and darkening the prospects of our children.

How powerfully, how grandly, how admirably they have kept their word, all know. The laws necessary to prosecute the war with the utmost vigour were unanimously passed by Congress. The organization of the man-power of our neighbours has been made on a grand scale. The calls to the financial resources of the Republic have been patriotically answered by the people who poured out billions and billions of their hard earned and prudently saved money to support the national cause so closely identified with that of the Allies. Besides spending innumerable millions for their own gigantic military effort, the United States are lending billions of dollars to their associates in the great struggle to curb down German autocratic criminal ambition.

The universe, as a whole, gratefully applauded the magnificent effort of the leading nation of the New-World in defending the old continents of Europe, Asia and Africa against the new invasion of the Huns.

The only shadow to this ennobling picture is that which our Nationalists, from this side of the boundary line, try to breathe on it, expecting that their treacherous whisper will find some echo amongst the French Canadian and the German elements of the Republic.

The following lines are a sample of the kind words Mr. Bourassa has addressed to Mr. Wilson—the warrior—not the pacifist. On August 30, 1917, respecting the answer of the President of the United States to the Pope's appeal in favour of peace, he wrote in a gentle mood:—

"Truth and falsehood, sincerity and deceit, logic and sophism are sporting with gracefulness in this singularly astonishing document. One would imagine that the President, persuaded that the European Governments are playing an immense game of "poker" having the life of the peoples at stake, wanted to go further and to prove to them that at such a game the great American democracy is their master. Perhaps did he believe that the "bluff" outbidding would succeed in tearing to pieces the mask of falsehoods, of

ambiguities and hypocrisy, by which the national Rulers are blinding the
peoples in order to lead them more readily to be slaughtered."

On perusing such outrageous writing, one cannot help being convinced that
Mr. Bourassa considers all the distinguished and most patriotic political
leaders who, for the last four years, have guided with so much talent and
devotion France, the British Empire, and their Allies through the
unprecedented crisis they have had to face, are a criminal gang of murderers.

So, in Mr. Bourassa's kind opinion, when Mr. Wilson and all the members of
the two Houses of Congress, with a most admirable unanimity of thought and
aspirations, called upon the American nation to avenge their countrymen,
countrywomen and children, murdered on the broad sea, they were criminally
joining with European Rulers in a game of "bluff", going further than all of
them in order to tear to pieces the falsehoods and hypocrisy they were using
to blind their peoples to the facile acceptance of the slaughtering process. A
very strange way, indeed, of unmasking others' hypocrisy by being more
hypocritical than them all.

The next day, in a second article on the same subject, the Nationalist leader
said:—

"Since the outbreak of the war, more especially since the exhausted peoples
have commenced to ask themselves what will be the result of this frightful
slaughter, the supporters of war to the utmost have tried hard to create the
legend that Germany wants to impose her political, military and economical
domination over the whole universe. To this first falsehood, they add another
one, still more complete: the only way to assure peace, they say, is to
democratize Germany, Austria and all the nations of the Globe."

Two falsehoods no doubt there are, but they are not asserted by those who
affirm Germany's aspiration at universal domination, and who believe that if
true free democratic institutions were to replace autocratic rule in many
countries, peace could be much more easily maintained. They are circulated
by those who deny that such are the two cases.

Whose fault is it if the almost universal opinion, outside the Central Empires
and their few allies, is that Teutonic ambition, for many years past, has been
to dominate the world?

Whose fault is it if, for the last forty years, autocratic rule has once more
proved to be the curse of the nations which it governs, and of the peoples it
subjugates?

Has not Germany only herself to blame? If she had respected the eternal
principles of Divine Morals; if she had been contented of her lot and mindful

of the rights of other nations; if she had been guided by the true law that Right is above Might; if she had followed the ever glorious path of Justice, she would not be presently under the ban of the civilized world rising in a mighty effort to crush her threatening tyranny out of existence.

So much the worse for her, if she falls a victim to her insane ambitious dreams and to the atrocious crimes they have inspired her to commit. In her calamity, the Nationalists' sympathies will avail her very little, as they will everywhere meet with the contempt they fully deserve.

At page 116, in a virulent charge, Mr. Bourassa says that Mr. Wilson *though a passionate and obstinate pedantic of democracy, is as much of an autocrat as William of Prussia.*

Blinded by his fanatical antipathies towards every one and every thing, directly or indirectly, favouring England, the Nationalist leader fails to see any difference between the man who blasphemously claims by Divine Right the power to hurl his whole Empire at the throat of staggering Humanity, to satisfy his frenzied lust of domination, denying to his subjects any say whatever in the matter, and the responsible chief of State who, holding his temporary functions from the expressed will of the people who trusted him, calls upon that same nation to avenge the murder of a large number of her citizens, of her women and children, and the barbarous crimes committed in violation of her Sovereign Rights.

If Mr. Bourassa is conscious of the enormity of the stand he has taken, and of the views he has expressed, he is indeed much to be blamed; if he is not, he is greatly to be pitied.

At page 109 of his pamphlet—entitled:—"*The Pope, arbiter of peace*," Mr. Bourassa has written the following monstrous proposition, after having said that peace must be restored "*without victory*":—

"*The more the results of the war are null, for both sides, the more chances there are for the peoples, astounded at the frightful uselessness of those monstrous slaughters, to protect themselves against a new fit of furious folly. To become odious to men, war must be barren.*"

So Mr. Bourassa has emphatically proclaimed that the war must be barren of any practical results, that the extraordinary sacrifices of lives, of resources of wealth, must be without reward of any kind; that the world must return to the ante-war conditions. And this, he asserts, would be the best means of preventing a renewal of the monstrous slaughters which have been the outcome of Germany's horrible attempt at dominating an enslaved Humanity.

In all sincerity, it is very difficult to suppose that the exponent of such outrageously abominable views is conscious of what he says.

A red hot "pacifist," Mr. Bourassa clamoured as best he could for "PEACE WITHOUT VICTORY," claiming that it was *the only kind of peace that could be "just and durable."* The time was when he pretended—surely without any show of reason—that such was the sort of peace Mr. Wilson wanted and suggested.

Even as far back as December 31, 1915, Mr. Bourassa, no doubt desirous of giving full vent to his new year's wishes to all, had written:—

"In spite of the lies, of the impudent "bluff," of the sanguinary appeals and of the false promises of victory of the partisans of war to excess, in all the warring countries, popular good sense commences to discern truth.... The more victory (the issue) *will be materially null and sterile for all the nations at war, the more chances there will be that peace will be lasting and that the peoples will be convinced that war is not only an abominable crime but an incommensurable folly."*

Evidently it had already become a hobby on the brain of the Nationalist leader. He dogmatically proclaims that war between peoples—not the wars formerly fought by mercenary armies,—is a *crime,—abominable,—*and a *folly,—incommensurable.*

True it is on the part of a State tramping upon all the principles of Justice and of International Law to gratify her guilty ambition.

But honourable, glorious, is war on the part of peoples rising in their patriotic might to resist a sanguinary enemy, to defend their countries, their homes, their mothers, their wives and their children from oppression, to stem the conquering efforts of barbarous invaders.

No doubt it was a crime on the part of Germany to break her pledged honour by solemn treaties, and to violate Belgium's territory.

No doubt it was a crime for Germany—and one abominable—to overrun Belgium, spreading everywhere desolation, devastation, incendiarism, murder.

But can it be said that the admirable and heroic resistance Belgium has opposed to her tyrannical invaders was a dastardly crime?

No doubt it was a crime—and one most abominable—for Germany to order the sinking of the Lusitania and hundreds of merchant ships, without the warning required by the Law of Nations, murdering by hundreds non-combatants, children, women, and old men.

But can any one be justified in asserting that, after exhausting, for the redress of such abominable wrongs, all the resources of diplomacy, the United States were committing a crime when they accepted the criminal teutonic challenge and decided to join with the British Empire, with France, Italy and their Allies, to rescue human Freedom and Civilization from the impending destruction?

It is an aberration of mind—incommensurable in depth—for a publicist, or any one else, to be so blinded by prejudices, so lost to all sense of justice, as to place on the same footing, on the same level, the assailant and he who defends his all, the murderer and the victim.

I positively affirm that I am not actuated by the least ill-will or ill-feeling against the Nationalist leader, in judging his course and his views as I do. Thank God, I know enough of the teachings of Christianity to wish good to all men. But I cannot help being deeply sorry and deploring that one of my French Canadian compatriots is buried in such mental darkness as to be unable to perceive the difference—incommensurable—there is in the present war between the hideous Teutonic guilt, and the commendable and meritorious defence by the Allied nations of the most sacred cause on earth: —outraged Justice.

And with all sincerity, I express the profound wish that during the prolonged recess the timely war measure adopted to censure and prevent all utterances detrimental to the best Canadian effort in the conflict, the Nationalist leader has the pleasure to enjoy, he will reconsider the whole situation and his opinions—too much widely circulated. Is it yet possible to hope that, at last, he will see the dawn which will lead him to the full light with which the great and noble cause of his country and of the world is shining?

It is no surprise that such opinions utterly failed to have any echo amongst the liberty loving people of the neighbouring Republic. They died their merited shameful death before crossing over the boundary line, buried deep under the heap of the profound feelings of reprobation they provoked.

The Nationalist leader even missed the mark where he felt sure his shot would strike. We can rest assured that the large majority of the United States Germans, by birth or origin, would not change the responsible President of their new country for the autocrat Kaiser from whose absolutist power so many of them fled to breathe freely in the new land of promise it was their happy lot to enter.

Mr. Bourassa met with a complete failure in his expectation to arouse the feelings of his compatriots over the frontier against the intervention of the Republic in the war.

It has been a profound satisfaction for us, French Canadians, to learn that from the very moment war was declared by the Republic against Germany, the French Canadian element in the United States has been to the forefront of the most loyal of our friendly neighbours in fighting the common enemy.

The French Canadians of the United States, either by birth or origin, have wisely turned a deaf ear to the Nationalist leader's seductive but prejudiced theories, to the wild charges he was wont to level at all the national rulers of the Allies, and, as a final attempt, at those of the American Republic. They have rallied to their Colours with enthusiastic patriotism.

They have nobly done their duty. They are doing it, and will continue to do so to the last: to the final victory for which they are fighting with the patriotic desire to share in the glory of the triumph of their country.

CHAPTER XXXVI.

THE ALLIES—RUSSIA—JAPAN.

Since its outbreak the great war has, and, before it is over, will have, played havoc in many ways in the wide world. Criminal aspirations have been quashed, extravagant hopes shattered, an ancient throne overthrown almost without a clash, an autocrat sovereign murdered, another forced to abdicate and go into exile.

In the open airs, on land, over the waves, under sea, the fighting demon has been most actively at work, ordering one of the belligerent, eager to obey, to spare no one, young, weak or old. Death has been dropped from the skies on sleeping non-combatants, assassinating right and left. On the soil Providentially provided with the resources necessary to human life, homes have been ruined, their so far happy owners brutally murdered. On the ocean the treacherous and barbarous submariner, operating in the broad light of the day, or in the darkness of the night, has sent, without remorse, to the fathomless bottom, thousands and thousands of innocent victims, children, women, old men, wounded soldiers spared on land but drowned at sea.

Viewed from the height of a much nobler standpoint, the war has developed a superior degree of heroism perhaps never equalled. Belgians, Serbians, Poles, Armenians have endured, and are still suffering, their prolonged martyrdom with a fortitude deserving the greatest admiration.

The nations united to withstand the torrent of German cruel and depraved ambition are writing, with the purest of their blood, pages of history which, for all times to come, will offer to posterity unrivalled examples of the sound and unswerving patriotism which has elevated them all to the indomitable determination to bear patiently, perseveringly, all the sacrifices, in lives courageously given, in resources profusely spent, in taxation willingly accepted and paid, in works of all kinds cheerfully performed, which the salvation of human Liberty and Civilization shall require.

The collapse of the ancient and hitherto mighty Empire of Russia will undoubtedly be one of the most startling events of the "Great War." For the present, I shall not comment, on the causes of this momentous episode, incidental to the wonderful drama being played on the worldly stage, more than I have done in a previous chapter. Still the important change it has made in the respective situation of the belligerents, with the prospective consequences likely to follow, one way or the other, calls for some timely consideration.

Evidently, the downfall, first, of the Imperial regime, second, of the *de facto* Republican government by which it was replaced, throwing the great Eastern ally of Great Britain, France and Italy under the tyrannical sway of the "bolchevikis" terrorists, most considerably altered the relative strength of the fighting power of the belligerents. Very detrimental to the Allies, it was largely favourable to the Central Empires. The "Triple Entente" as first constituted, was much weakened by the desertion of one of the great partners in the heavy task they had undertaken, whilst the "Triple Alliance" was strengthened in a relative proportion, at least for the time being and the very near future.

Evidence, incontrovertible, is coming to light, proving what had been soundly presumed, that "bolchevikism" was not merely the result, as in other instances, of the violence of sanguinary revolutionists overpowering a regular progressive movement of political freedom and reform, but that it has been the outcome of German intrigue easily succeeding in corrupting into shameless treason the "bolchevikis" leaders.

As a Sovereign State, as an independent nation, Russia was, in honour bound, pledged not to consent to a separate peace, and to make peace with Germany only with conditions to which all the Allies would agree. Acceptance of, and concurrence in, all peace agreements, were the essential clause of the pledge Great Britain, France and Russia had reciprocally taken in going to war with the Central Empires. With this sacred pledge Italy concurred fully on joining the Allies.

To that solemn pledge, the American Republic has emphatically assented when she threw her weighty sword in the balance against blood stained and murderous Germany.

The "bolchevikis'" treacherous government repudiated the solemn engagement of their country, threw her honour to the winds, sold her dearest national interests by the infamous Brest-Litovsk treaty. Betrayed Russia was out of the war, leaving her Allies to their fate.

From a military point of view, the consequences were easily foreseen. Freed from the danger of further attacks on the eastern front, both Germany and Austria could send their eastern armies, the first, on the western front in France, the second, on the Italian front. Germany, only requiring a sufficient force to keep down trodden Russia under the yoke treacherously fastened on her neck by the traitors who had ignominiously sold their country to her enemy, and anxious to profit to the utmost by her success in coercing the Russians to agree to dishonourable peace conditions, hurried more than a million men over to the western front. Austria did likewise, sending a large force with the hope of smashing the Italians out of the fight.

Those were no doubt very anxious days. All remember how the Italian army lost in a very short time all the ground they had so stubbornly conquered.

Germany made formidable preparations to strike, in the very early spring of the present year, a decisive blow by which she fully expected to reach and take Paris. We shall never forget the feverish hours we lived when came the successive reports of the crushing advance of the Teutonic hordes so close to the illustrious capital of France.

For a while, it seemed to be—and really it was—a renewal of the first terrific invasion of northern France, in 1914. Fortunately, it was Providentially decreed that the second onslaught was to meet with a second Marne disaster. The Huns were forced to retire after a tremendous loss of men and war materials, the allied armies, brilliantly led and fighting heroically, redeeming all the lost territory and, at the moment I am writing, moving steadily towards the German frontier.

The great good luck of the Allies, treasonably sacrificed by the Russian bolchevikis terrorist government, was the solemn entry of the United States into the European conflict.

Preparing for the grand effort which she confidently expected would be final, Germany rashly decided to resume her barbarous submarine campaign, positively determined to criminally violate all the principles of International Law regulating warfare on the seas. That outrageous decision was her fatal doom.

Its direct result was to bring the American Republic into the war. And then the whole world was called upon to witness, with unbounded delight, the very impressive spectacle of millions of fighting free men being successfully transported over the sea, and landed on the French soil, to join the grand army which, for the last four years, had been resisting the full might of the autocratic forces.

However difficult it is to foretell what the political developments of the present deplorable Russian situation will be, still it is not illusory to believe that, history once more repeating itself, the present sanguinary Russian regime will hasten its well deserved ignominious downfall by the very brutal excesses it multiplies in its delirious tyranny. There are too many elements of the immense population of Russia favourable to an orderly and sensible government, to suppose that they will long fail to gather their strength in order to redeem their country's honour, and to remove from power the traitors who are the shame of their fair land. When the infallible reaction sets in, it will increase the more in momentum that it will have been longer repressed by foul means.

The most important point of the present Russian situation to consider is that of the best initiative the Allies could, and ought to, take respecting the military question.

Many are of opinion that it would be possible, for the Allies, to help Russia out of the present difficulties by an armed support. Such views have been more especially expressed in the United States. Could they, or can they be carried out? I must say that in a large measure I share the opinion of those who would give an affirmative answer to the question.

It is well known that the matter has been most seriously considered by the Allies, and a favourable solution seems on the way of a satisfactory realization.

To the armed intervention of the Allies in Russia, following closely upon the infamous Brest-Litovsk peace treaty, there was a very serious obstacle of German creation.

It was evident, at the very start, that if intervention there was to be, the one Ally to play the most important part in the great undertaking would be Japan.

The British statesmen who, several years ago, brought about the treaty of alliance between Great Britain and Japan have deserved much from the Empire and from the world generally. Surely they had a clear insight of the future. True to her treaty obligations Japan at once sided with Great Britain in the war. All those who have closely followed the trend of events since the outbreak of the hostilities, know how much Japan has done to assist in chasing the German military and mercantile fleets from the high seas, more especially from the Pacific ocean. Canada owes her a debt of gratitude for the protection she has afforded our western British Columbia coast from the raids of German war ships.

Foreseeing that the proximity of Japan to eastern Russia was an inducement for the Allies to decide upon an armed intervention which, starting from Siberia, might roll westward over the broad lands leading back to the European eastern war front, Germany lost no time in trying to poison Russian public opinion against the Japanese. Her numerous representatives and agents told the Russians that if they allowed Japan to send her army on Russian territory, they would be doomed to fall under Japanese sway. They recalled the still recent Russo-Japanese war, amplifying the supposed aims of Japan so as to stir up the national feelings of the Russians. Such a cry, assiduously and widely spread, was no doubt a dangerous one.

Under those circumstances, Japan wisely decided to remain in the expectation of further developments before moving. She took the safe stand that she would intervene only upon the request of the Russians themselves, pledging her word of honour that her only purpose would be to free Russia from German domination, and that she would withdraw from Russian territory as soon as complete Russian independence would have been restored and the treacherous Teutonic aims foiled.

Evidences are increasing in number and importance that the Huns' propaganda in Russia against Japan is being successfully counteracted by the good sense of the people, realizing how much their vital national interests have been trampled upon by Germany in imposing her peace conditions on their country betrayed by the bolchevikis rulers.

An armed Allied force has been sent to, and has been, for some weeks, operating, in Siberia so far with commendable results.

For one, I have most at heart an expectation which I would be most happy to see realized. It seems to me that there ought to be a chance, nay more, a possibility, for the Allies to organize, between this day and next spring, a strongly supported intervention in Russia. In that event, Japan of course, would take the lead. She could rapidly send to help the Russians to resume their part in the war against Germany at least a million of men; two millions if they were needed. As a guarantee of Japan's good faith, the Allies, more especially the United States, could send over contingents to Siberia.

There is no doubt whatever that so supported, the revulsion of Russian public feeling, once set in motion, would soon overwhelm the bolchevikis. A sensible and patriotic government, once at the helm of the state, could easily and rapidly reorganize a powerful army out of the numerous available millions. The financial aspect of the question would certainly be the most difficult for Russia to meet, after the exhaustive strain she has had to bear. But however great their moneyed effort, the United States could yet do a great deal to help Russia financially.

Will the hopes of so many be realized, and will Russia, resuming her place of honour in the glorious ranks of the Allies, be found battling once more with them when together they will finally crush the German tyrannical militarism? God only knows, and time will tell.

CHAPTER XXXVII.

THE LAST PEACE PROPOSALS.

I was writing the last pages of this work when the surprising news was flashed over the cable that Austria-Hungary had taken the initiative of suggesting peace discussion, which proposition she had communicated to all the belligerents, to the neutral governments and even to the Holy See. Without delay the rumour proved to be true. The very next day the full text of Austria's communication was published all over the world.

I have read it with great care and, I confess, with profound amazement.

From several stand-points, this document is astonishing and weighty: astonishing as it reveals more than ever before the astuteness of the inspiration which dictated it; weighty because it derives its importance from one of the most serious situation of the world's affairs ever recorded in History.

It is difficult to suppose that the Austrian Government really expected that their move would be considered as the outcome of their own initiative. Not the hand, but the sword—the dominating sword—behind the Throne is clearly visible.

The carefully drafted document, issued from Vienna, was evidently dictated from Berlin. It is stamped with the Teutonic seal.

After the experience of the last four years—I can safely say of the last half century as well—over credulous is he who believes that, swayed as she has been by her overpowering northern neighbour, Austria would have dared to address such a proposition to the Allies if she had not been asked by Germany to do so.

It is rather amusing to read the news cabled from Amsterdam, Holland, on the 20th of September, that an official communication issued in Berlin said that the German Ambassador in Vienna that day presented Germany's reply to the recent Austro-Hungarian peace note. The purport of the note was that Germany agreed to participate in the proposed exchange of views. This is indeed high class cynicism.

The document would certainly call for somewhat lengthy and strong comments, but they can be dispensed with after the curt, sharp and decisive reply it has elicited from those it was intended to seduce and deceive.

President Wilson was the first to answer a positive, a formidable NO, which, thundered out from Washington, was echoed with equal force in London, Paris and Rome. So that the astute attempt to deter the Allies from the glorious course they were forced to adopt by Germany, and by Austria herself, was doomed to failure, and bound to meet with the contempt it deserved.

But a few remarks expressing the retort that strikes one's mind on reading the Austrian communication, are in order and had better be made. The whole stress of the document is that peace should be restored as soon as possible on account of the sacrifices and sufferings war nowadays entail, and in conformity with the unanimous wishes of the peoples engaged in the conflict.

Did Austria ever suppose that, when she addressed that sadly famous and outrageous ultimatum to Servia, dated the 23rd of July, 1914, which she well knew would bring about the cataclysm she now feigns to deplore —and which Germany and herself were longing for—the war would be only a child's play, a game of golf, or something of the kind? Was Austria at that time cherishing the kind feelings of the German Kronprinz who, on being asked by an American lady, in a social event, at Berlin, why he was so desirous of seeing a great war, replied that "*it was only for the fun of the thing?*"

That war, when once declared, would have terrible consequences, would cost millions of dear lives, would cripple many more millions for the rest of their earthly days, would cost innumerable millions—even billions—of hard earned money, would destroy an immense amount of accumulated wealth, would delay for years the onward march of Humanity towards more and more prosperous destinies, was not only long foreseen before it broke out, but was positively known to be pregnant with all such disasters.

But what was not foreseen, not known, nor imagined as at all possible, after nearly twenty centuries of Christianity, was that, war being on, Germany, the Power responsible for it, guilty of the crime of having let loose the frightful hurricane, would multiply the horrors inseparable from military operations, with unconceivable barbarous acts condemned by all international, moral and Divine laws.

It was not foreseen, nor supposed possible, that heroism would be challenged by murder, that the glorious defenders of their country's rights would have to fight against sanguinary savages obeying the barbarian orders of a modern Attila.

It was not foreseen that hundreds of children, women, old men, wounded soldiers, would be assassinated on the open sea and sent to their eternal watery graves.

So far as the horrors of regular warfare were concerned, they were, as I have just said, very well known. And was it not on account of this knowledge that Great Britain and France had exhausted all their efforts in favour of the maintenance of peace?

Was it not out of this knowledge that England had, for more than twenty years, implored the Berlin Government to agree at least to partial disarmament, to discontinue, or, at the least, to reduce war ship building operations?

When Austria, bowing herself down to the ground under the German tyrannical lash, unjustly and cruelly declared war against weak Servia, she knew what the horrors of the conflict could not fail to be. How is it that at that time she was not moved by the sympathetic feelings expressed in her recent appeal for peace negotiations?

How is it that Austria, and her inspiring angel, Germany, are getting so nervous about the misfortunes of war, just at the time when they are forced to admit that they are utterly unable to realize the aims for which they brought on the frightful struggle?

How is it that those who could order with clear conscience and fiendish delight the violation of Belgium guaranteed neutrality, the sinking of the Lusitania and so many other ships carrying non-combatants, children, women and old men, the murder of so many innocent victims, the Belgian deportations, the destruction of the monuments of art—the work of human genius—are suddenly moved to pity just as they see the hand writing on the wall warning them that their days of foul enjoyments are at end?

How is it that the voice who dictated the following sentence was not silenced and choked by the abominable lie it contains? How is it that the hand that wrote it was not instantly dried up at the impudent falsehood it expresses?

Austria's official communication says in part:—

"The Central Powers leave it in no doubt that they are only waging a war of defence for the integrity and the security of their territories."

But why is it that the Central Empires are now only waging a defensive war, if it is not because after having opened the game with the certainty of crushing their opponents by the tremendous power of their formidable military organization, they are getting beaten and overpowered by the unrivalled heroism called forth by their criminal attempt at destroying weak nations and enslaving Humanity?

The Austrian and German Governments wilfully forget that the important point is not to consider who are the belligerents that are NOW forced by the

213

fortune of arms to wage a defensive struggle. It is to ascertain who started the conflict of an OFFENSIVE war.

To that question, the voice of the truly civilized world has answered with no uncertain sound. It was given, and ever since most energetically emphasized, the very day the first Austrian shot was fired at Belgrade, the first thundering German gun and the first German soldier ordered to cross over the Belgian frontier.

The Austrian tentative peace document pretends "that all peoples, on whatever side they may be fighting, long for a speedy end to the bloody struggle."

This is so evidently true that the writer of the communication might very properly have dispensed with asserting it.

But have the Austrian and the German Governments forgotten that the peoples were equally longing for the maintenance of peace during the many years of intense war preparation prior to the outbreak of the hostilities in 1914?

If they are not yet aware of it, the Central Empires must be taught that the Allied nations have another longing than that for peace, to which they have given precedence and for which they will continue to fight strenuously until it is fully gratified. They long for an honourable, a just and lasting peace. They long to see once more the old landmarks of Civilization and Political Liberty emerging safe and radiant from the waves of Teutonic Barbarism. They long, and most earnestly, for peace restored under such conditions as will put an end to extravagant, ruinous and autocratic militarism, which will henceforth relieve the peoples from the drastic obligation of maintaining, at a cost more and more crushing, an ever increasing military organization for fear of being suddenly subjugated by an ambitious foe bent on dominating the world.

Using the very words of the most admirable speech addressed by President Wilson to the United States Congress, on the 11th of February last, the Allied Nations long for a peace which will provide "that peoples and provinces are no longer to be bartered about from sovereignty to sovereignty as if they were mere chattels and pawns in a game, even the great game now for ever discredited of the balance of power; but that every territorial settlement involved in this war must be made in the interest and for the benefit of the populations concerned and not as a part of any mere adjustment or compromise of claims amongst rival states."

The Allied peoples are longing for a peace by which "all well defined national aspirations shall be accorded the utmost satisfaction that can be accorded them without introducing new or perpetuating old elements of *discord, and antagonism that would be likely in time to break the peace of Europe and consequently of the world."*

The *pacifists* of the Allied nations who have, like the Nationalist leader and his henchmen in the Province of Quebec, clamoured for peace by compromise, must have had a few hours of delightful enjoyment after reading Austria's communication. It is evidently the echo of their oft repeated views and has been carefully drafted to stir them to further exertions in favour of a settlement which will gratify their ill disguised Teutonic sympathies.

Austria's document is a plea intended to be strong for peace by negotiations irrespective of the war situation and its probable result.

This is the kind of peace dear to the heart of the Nationalist leader and his friends. The newspaper *"Le Devoir"* is their daily organ in Montreal. A Sunday paper called *"Le Nationaliste"* is the weekly edition of the daily organ.

By what mysterious inspiration was *"Le Nationaliste"* able to forestall the publication of the Austrian peace document by an article in its issue of Sunday, the 13th of August, which summarizes the leading reasons given by the Government of Vienna to induce the Allied Governments to agree *"to a confidential and unbinding discussion"* of the conditions of peace, *"at a neutral meeting place?"*

Since the official publication of the document, our Nationalists, who had been subdued by the Order-in-Council tightening the censure of disloyal writings and speaking, and reduced to the necessity of merely whispering their fond hopes of an early peace which would relieve the Central Empires, Turkey and Bulgaria from the deserved chastisement of their crimes, are getting again more outspoken in the expression of their views and of their Teutonic proclivities. The street corner propaganda is being resumed with more discreet vigour than formerly when loud talk was considered safe. New efforts, better guarded against a compromising responsibility, to instil the virus in the body politic, are tried over again. They creep in a few newspapers well known for their hardly disguised hostility to the cause of the Allies and to the participation of Canada to its defence. All this under the hypocritical cover of a longing for the restoration of peace and the cessation of the sacrifices the country is still making for the victory for which all loyal British subjects are praying and doing their best to secure.

Germany has prudently—cowardly is the more proper word—remained behind, satisfied, for the time being, to play the part of prompter to her vassal, Austria. But, however desirous of remaining free to repudiate publicly, if considered more advisable, Austria's move, she could not help showing her

215

hand. She betrayed herself by the peace offer she has had the outrageous audacity to make to Belgium she has barbarously crucified.

And what are the terms of this astonishing proposal? I will mention only two of them.

First: "THAT BELGIUM SHALL REMAIN NEUTRAL UNTIL THE END OF THE WAR."

That Germany should have decided to address such a demand to Belgium is truly inconceivable. Has she forgotten the days when Belgium was neutral, and determined to remain so, under the joint protection of England, France and Germany, bound by solemn treaty to uphold Belgian independence? Does she not realize that if Belgium has not been neutral up to this day, she has been the cause of it in tearing to pieces the *scrap of paper* which should have been the sacred shield of the nation she criminally martyred? After having violated Belgium's frontier, overrun her territory, destroyed her happy homes, murdered by thousands her children, her women, her mothers, her old men, ransomed her to the tune of hundreds of millions, without granting her liberty, shattered her monuments of arts, she has the impudence to ask her to betray those who hastened to her defence, and who are pledged to require the restoration of her complete independence with due reparation as one of the essential conditions of peace. A more brazen outrage cannot be imagined. It is on a par with that addressed to England whose neutrality Germany wanted to secure at the cost of her honour in betraying France.

What was the true object of Germany in making such a proposition? Was it not to protect herself against the increasing likelihood that the Allied army would soon be able to enter on German soil by passing through Belgium. But in that event, so much to be hoped for, there would be that difference that whilst Germany invaded Belgium in sheer violation of her solemn treaty obligations, France, England and the United States would honour themselves in turning the guilty invaders out of the soil they have sullied by their hideous presence and their horrible savageness.

The second German peace proposition to Belgium reads as follows:—"*That Belgium shall use her good offices to secure the return of the German colonies.*"

And such a request is made by the Power that, in spite of the treaties it was in honour bound to respect, ordered the German army to conquer Belgium in a dastardly rush, in order to reach France at once and crush her out of the conflict before she could be helped by Great Britain and her Colonies! Incredible indeed!

Germany and Austria knew very well that their proposals would be indignantly and contemptuously rejected. But they had a twofold object in making them. First, they wanted to stir up their own peoples to further efforts in carrying on the struggle by throwing upon the Allies the apparent responsibility of refusing even a confidential and unbinding discussion of the question of the restoration of peace.

Second, they were anxious to make a strong bid for the support of the *pacifists* of the Allied countries.

How much will they succeed in galvanizing the enthusiasm of their peoples for another grand effort, remains to be seen.

So far as their attempt to move our *pacifists* to exert themselves in favour of a peace by compromise, it has already met with a complete failure. Our Nationalist *pacifists* are getting so few and so far between, that they will most likely once more disappear and give up the street propaganda.

On completing the reading of the official communication of Austria, President Wilson at once gave his reply, authorizing the Secretary of State to issue the following statement, dated the 16th of September and published broadcast on the next day:—

"*I am authorized by the President to state that the following will be the reply of this Government to the Austro-Hungarian note proposing an unofficial conference of belligerents:*

"'*The Government of the United States feels that there is only one reply which it can make to the suggestion of the Imperial Austro-Hungarian Government. It has repeatedly and with entire candor stated the terms upon which the United States would consider peace and can and will entertain no proposal for a conference upon a matter concerning which it has made its position and purpose so plain.*'"

On the eleventh day of February, 1918, President Wilson, instead of addressing as usual a message to the two Houses, went personally to meet the Senate and the House of Representatives, in Congress assembled, and, in a most admirable speech, replied to the then recent peace utterances of Count von Hertling, the German Chancellor, and Count Czernin, the Austro-Hungarian Foreign Minister, fully explaining the only principles by which the Government of the United States would be guided when peace negotiations do take place. This most important statement is published as an appendix to this book. It is worthy of the great statesman who made it, and deserves the most attentive reading on account of the lofty views and noble principles it expresses, of the large issues it involves and of the ardent patriotism it inspires.

The prime ministers of Great Britain and France have signified their entire assent to the energetic stand taken by President Wilson in the above quoted reply to Austria's peace communication.

The whole British Empire, France, the United States and Italy are a unit in refusing to consider for a moment Austria's cynical peace proposals.

Belgium, from the cross of martyrdom to which the Huns' barbarity has nailed her, has summoned all her wonderful courage, in her long and cruel agony, to repudiate with scorn the infamous German proposition to betray those who are pledged to be her saviours.

Consequently, the peace offensive, so cleverly planned by Germany and opened by her contemptible Austrian satellite, has met with as dismal a failure as the military offensive launched on the twenty-first day of March last, with such superior numerical forces, and unbounded confidence that this gigantic effort would at last smash the Allies' resistance.

Just as the Teutonic hordes are hurled back by the matchless strategy of the Chief Commander of the Allied armies and their incomparable heroism, the Austrian peace offensive communication is returned to their authors a miserable "*scrap of paper*".

And the grand and noble fight will go on until Germany is brought to her knees and forced to recognize that "THE RESOURCES OF CIVILIZATION ARE NOT YET EXHAUSTED."

The modern Huns are doomed to a very sad awakening from their dream of universal domination.

Germany has challenged the world to a deadly struggle. She must bear the consequences, however sad they may be. Four years ago, anticipating a crushing victory, she exulted over the early fall of her enemies, madly certain that in a few weeks they would kneel down crying for mercy. She trusted her all to the fortunes of war. They will at last go against her. She would have been cruelly triumphant. Will she be cowardly in defeat?

Austria has blindly served Germany's criminal ambition. She must abide by the result of her blindness.

Both carried away by passion, they forgot that there would be a terrible reckoning day for their atrocious crime. It is near at hand, and they cannot avoid being called to a severe account for their foul deeds.

Kaiser Wilhelm II will soon find out that Divine Justice is very different from what he fondly believed. He will receive the proper answer to his blasphemous appeals to the Almighty to bless with success his guilty ambition to dominate the world. He will learn that from above the innocent victims whom he has mercilessly sacrificed to his lust of autocratic power, have cried for vengeance and have been heard. He bears the guilt of blood and sacrilegious war. He shall receive his deserts in due time.

CHAPTER XXXVIII.

NECESSARY PEACE CONDITIONS.

It can be positively affirmed that, taking no account whatever of the treasonable views of the *defeatists*, and no more of the disloyal opinions of the *pacifists*—because they only deserve absolute contempt and reprobation —the peoples called the Allies have been long ago, are now, and will remain to the last, unanimous on the essential PEACE CONDITIONS without which all the sacrifices they have made and are making would be a total irreparable loss.

It has been proclaimed with the highest authority, and universally approved, that henceforth PEACE MUST BE JUST AND DURABLE. Such it should always have been.

The principle is no doubt very easily enunciated. It is applauded by all and every where, even by Germany and Austria. The great, the insuperable, difficulty is to agree upon SUCH CONDITIONS as will PERMANENTLY, and to the COMPLETE SATISFACTION OF ALL CONCERNED, bless the world with the maintenance of a TRULY JUST AND DURABLE PEACE.

It is better to admit at once that the very moment the question is considered, the presently contending belligerents are as far apart as the two poles of the earthly globe.

It is extremely easy to prove it.

No one now ignores—or at least should fail to realize—what kind of peace would be accepted by Germany as JUST AND DURABLE.

To be satisfied with a settlement of peace, Germany would require the sanction by her opponents of her right to maintain, develop and strengthen her MILITARISM so threatening to the universe.

At the time she was exulting over the great and crushing victory which she was sure to have within her powerful grasp, in debating with her vanquished enemies, the conditions of peace, Germany, elated as she would certainly have been by her triumph, would have positively claimed the annexation of Belgium and of all the northern part of France by right of conquest. She would not have been less exacting than she was, in 1870, when in the face of indignant but powerless Europe, she stripped France of her two fine and wealthy provinces, Alsace and Lorraine.

She would have claimed the right to supersede England as mistress of the seas,—German supremacy replacing the British and henceforth ruling the waves.

She would have claimed the annexation of Russian Poland, and that of Servia to Austria.

She would have claimed the recognition of her imperial paramount power over the Balkans, which she would have united under the direct sway of her ally and vassal, Bulgaria.

Victorious over all continental Europe and equally over Great Britain, she would most likely have claimed the cession to her of the great British autonomous Colonies for the purpose of pouring over to Canada, Australia and South Africa her increasingly overflowing population. And to better achieve that most coveted result, she would have destroyed at once the free institutions they enjoy under the British Crown to replace them by her autocratic rule.

In one of his illogical pamphlets, abounding in extravagant views, the Nationalist leader has denied with scorn that Germany had ever intended to acquire Canada by force of arms. He supported his assertion by the declaration made to the contrary by a German Minister. But he failed to explain that this German public man said so only when the Berlin Government had fully realized that they could not succeed in breaking asunder the mighty British Empire. The Teutonic declaration was hypocritical, intended to deceive, and to supply our Nationalist *"pacifists"* with what would seem a plausible argument to cover their sympathies for the gentle cause of the tender hearted Huns. It is very easy to disclaim any aspiration to possess what one is sure never to get.

Triumphant Germany would have bargained very hard to lay her powerful hand on the great Indian Empire.

She would have dismembered Russia, as she has effectively done—at least temporarily—by the infamous Brest-Litovsk treaty.

She would have strongly supported Austria in destroying for ever Italy's legitimate aspirations to round off her national territory by the annexation of that part of Austria's possessions called *The Trentino*, which is hers by nature.

Following the precedent she had laid down, in 1870, after her triumph over France, Germany would undoubtedly have exacted from her fallen enemies, billions and billions of dollars as indemnities of war.

And Germany, with such a peace treaty imposed to her despairing enemies with her sanguinary sword at their throat ready to murder them—as she did at Brest-Litovsk—would have swayed the world with her UNIVERSAL

DOMINATION.

But I hear—I must say without being the least frightened—the thundering clamour of the Nationalist leader crying that Germany does not NOW claim such peace conditions as above enumerated.

Very true, and why?

Only because she is no longer able to exact and impose them!

In 1914, Germany being victorious over all Europe, England included, after a four months overpowering campaign, as she expected, would certainly not have been satisfied with less than the conditions just specified. They were the goal for which she had been strenuously preparing for fifty years, her success, in 1870, being the preliminary opening of her conquests.

To bring Germany to renounce—temporarily—to her fond hopes of domination, it has required the heroic efforts and the untold sacrifices, in men and money, which Great Britain, her Colonial Empire, France, Italy, Belgium, Japan, betrayed Russia, and, LAST BUT NOT LEAST, the United States, have made during more than the last four years and which they are pledged to make until a successful issue.

The kind of peace as above would have been what can be very properly called —Germany's "OFFENSIVE PEACE." In Germany's opinion this would have been the just and durable peace dear to her so kind heart.

But having failed to carry the tremendous victory for which she had so powerfully prepared, Germany would NOW likely agree to negotiate what can be as properly called a "DEFENSIVE PEACE."

By "DEFENSIVE PEACE", I mean Germany negotiating NOW with her opponents with the determination to repulse, as much as possible, their just claims, to prevent them to the utmost limit to reap the legitimate fruits of their admirable endeavours, to thwart the realization of their noble aspirations to protect the world hereafter against her guilty and barbarous militarism.

Germany—I mean, of course, the Teutonic Imperial Government—has yet given no sign of a change of mind on the vital points at stake in the consideration of the restoration of peace. If the fortune of arms was once more to favour her armies, her blood stained for Colours, she would, to-morrow, be as mercilessly exacting as she would have been, in 1914, had she triumphantly entered Paris inside of two months after her challenge to the civilized world.

Germany is surely not a convert to sound Christian principles. She will not repent for her crimes. She does not feel the tortures of remorse at her foul deeds. She would certainly be a relapser, in the near future, if the Allies, unwisely heeding the clamour of the *"pacifists"*, imprudently gratified her ACTUAL wish for a peace compromise.

And before long Humanity would be forced to go again, in much aggravated conditions, over the way of the cross she has been threading along for nearly five years, steeped to the knees in the blood of millions of her heroic sons, with a reorganized Germany this time straining all the Huns' accumulated power to lead Civilization to her Calvary.

With God's grace, that shall not be. Five years of martyrdom have deserved and will receive JUSTICE.

After having explained what Germany, from her stand-point, considers a JUST AND DURABLE PEACE, let us see what such a peace means from the Allies' stand-point.

Every free man has a right to his own opinion. However, he must never forget that Liberty of opinion does not mean—never meant—absence of knowledge, ignorance of the basic principles of political society.

I do not hesitate to expound what the real conditions of the coming peace MUST BE to make it JUST AND DURABLE.

Let the inveterate opponents of Political Liberty say what they please, it is undeniable that the present war has rapidly developed into a deadly conflict between Autocratic Power and Political Freedom.

Consequently a peace patched up to uphold Autocracy and destroy free institutions could not be JUST and DURABLE.

Under the dominating circumstances of the present struggle, to bring it to a satisfactory conclusion, peace, to be Just and Durable, must be restored with all the necessary guarantees that Political Liberty will hereafter be safe against the foul attempts of military despotism.

This *sine qua non* condition is general in its nature and equally interests all the contending Allied nations.

Let us now consider the peace conditions which, though of general importance so far as they are NECESSARY for its permanency, are essential from the particular stand-point of each one of the Allies separately.

I shall begin the review by considering the particular case of Great Britain.

To be JUST and DURABLE for the British Empire, the future peace treaty must not be so drafted as to supersede British sea supremacy by that of Germany.

The question of what is to be done with the great German African Colonies, conquered by the South African Dominion army, is next in importance to England's sea supremacy, from the British Empire stand-point.

Germany, very far from foreseeing what was to happen, deliberately opened that question when she precipitated the present conflict by coercing Austria to crush weak Servia, herself challenging Russia and France, and thundering at Belgium in violation of her most sacred treaty obligations.

Great Britain, as in honour bound, standing by Belgium, was forced to fight with Germany. The great autonomous Colonies nobly rallying to her support, the South African Dominion, Boers and British admirably united for the purpose, undertook for her share to conquer the German African Colonies. She has grandly succeeded.

If, as we all hope, the Allies are finally victorious, would it be just to relinquish Great Britain's right over the German African Colonies, more especially if the South African Dominion is strongly opposed—as there is no doubt she will be—to their retrocession?

And what about Belgium and France? No peace treaty could be called JUST nor could be DURABLE, which would not completely restore Belgium's independence; which would not oblige Germany to indemnify Belgium for the damages wrought upon her, more especially those which were inflicted to the Belgian weak but heroic nation out of sheer barbarous destruction.

To France, the northern part of her presently occupied territory, together with Alsace and Lorraine, MUST be restored.

The Germans are loudly crying that in exacting the restoration to France of the provinces of Alsace and Lorraine, the Allies would be partly dismembering the German Empire.

Quite so, and why not? Does the victim of the highway man lose the right to claim his property from the ruffian who has stolen it by brutal force?

In 1870, under the circumstances all know, Prussia imposed upon France the cession of Alsace and Lorraine, rounding off the territory of the new German Empire.

France naturally smarted under the cruelty of the condition which she could not help accepting. For many years she cherished the hope that the lost provinces would ultimately return to the parental home.

But it is well known how TIME is an efficient cure of many ills. France's yearning for the restoration of Alsace and Lorraine had gradually subsided. The general opinion was spreading that the Alsace-Lorraine matter was more and more becoming a finally settled question.

Before the war, no Power, European or American, would have countenanced France in any attempt to break peace to run her chance of reconquering Alsace and Lorraine. France knew it perfectly well and at last bowed to her fate.

Who has reopened the closed question of Alsace and Lorraine? Is it not Germany herself?

Great Britain, Russia, the United States and Italy, who would not have supported France in an OFFENSIVE WAR with the objective of getting back her lost provinces, are now a most determined unit in favour of the restoration of Alsace and Lorraine to France as a result of the DEFENSIVE war Germany forced her to wage.

That would be JUSTICE pure and simple: the peace treaty MUST do it.

Germany having run the risk of reopening the Alsace-Lorraine acute question, the Allies MUST close it anew but this time against the Huns.

Germany MUST also pay for the devastation she has savagely spread in France.

I stand firm for a final settlement of the Austro-Italian too long pending question by giving to Italy the Trentino territory to which she has an evident national claim supported by the best of geographical conditions.

Servia's independence MUST be once more secured, and Poland SHOULD be resuscitated.

The United States part in the war is truly a grand, a noble one. They have no particular territorial interest to serve. Their only object is the general public good. They will be the benefactors of Humanity in claiming for their Allies the above enunciated conditions without which no JUST and DURABLE peace can be expected nor obtained.

It is most important to caution the public against the insidious clamours of our *"pacifists"*, trying again to deceive the people by asserting that Germany is ready to negotiate for peace on fair terms.

The Huns will acquiesce only to such peace terms as they will be forced to.

The Allies are better to be guided in consequence in their unfaltering determination to realize a JUST and DURABLE peace by a GLORIOUS VICTORY.

225

CHAPTER XXXIX.

CONCLUSION.

My ardent desire to speak the plain truth and only the truth, is just as strong to-day as it was when, in concluding my French work, I summarized the situation such as it was at the end of the year 1916, to show the hard duty incumbent on all the Allies, Canada included. It has been perhaps still more intensified by the outrageous efforts of those amongst us whose sole object has been, since the outbreak of the hostilities, to discourage our people from the herculean task they had bravely undertaken.

Two years have since elapsed—years full of great events, and of untiring heroism on the part of the glorious defenders of Justice and Right—and I do not see the slightest reason to modify the conclusions I then arrived at as a matter of strict duty. Unworthy of public confidence is the man who, pandering to the supposed prejudices of his countrymen, refrains out of weakness, or of more guilty considerations, to tell them what they are bound to do for their own country, for their Empire, for the world, in the supreme crisis of our time.

True every one is longing for the restoration of peace. But few are those who, even before being tired of the war, were ready to curb their heads under the German yoke, are now praying for a compromise between the Allies and their enemies. There are some left, it is sad to admit. Everywhere they are chased by the indignant public opinion daily growing more determined that millions of heroes shall not have given their lives in vain, that millions of others, wounded on the fields of battles, shall not, until the last of them is gone for ever, be the betrayed victims of Teutonic dastardly ambition.

True, peace is sorely wanted, and would be welcomed by the thanksgivings to the Almighty of grateful peoples, who have borne with undaunted courage such untold and admirable sacrifices to uphold their Rights and their Honour. But it cannot be sued for by the nations whom Germany wanted to enslave by the might of her crushing militarism operating under the dictates of a new code of International Law of her own barbarous creation.

Thank God, the flowing tide of unlimited Teutonic ambition let loose over the world, more than four years ago, has met with inaccessible summits where love of Justice, respect of Right, devotion to human Civilization, obedience to Christian Law, heroism of sacrifices, were so deeply entrenched, that they could not be reached and conquered. From this commanding altitude, they not only continue to defy the tyrants bent on dominating the universe, but they are mightily smashing their power.

From the overshadowing point of view which cannot be forgotten, or wilfully abandoned, nothing has changed since the German Empire, in her delirious aspirations, challenged the world to the almost superhuman conflict by which she felt certain to succeed in realizing her fond dream of universal domination.

At the outbreak of the war, ever since, to-day, to-morrow, there were, there are and there will be but three alternatives to the restoration of peace:—

1.—A victorious German peace imposed on beaten and cowed belligerents: the peace of the "*defeatists.*"

2.—A peace by compromise, patched up by disheartened "*pacifists,*" lured by cunningness, winning where force would have failed to succeed, to agree to conditions pregnant with all the horrors of a new and still greater struggle in the near future.

3.—A peace the result of the indomitable courage and perseverance of all the nations who have joined together to put an end to Germany's ambition to rule the world, and to destroy the instrument created for that iniquitous purpose: Prussian militarism.

There could be a fourth alternative to peace, but it would be possible only by a miracle which, we can grant without hesitation, the world has perhaps not yet deserved.

It would be peace restored by the sudden conversion of Germany to the practice of sound Christian principles, acknowledging how guilty she has been, repenting for her crimes, agreeing to atone for them as much as possible, and taking the unconditional pledge to henceforth behave like a civilized nation.

All must admit that there is not the slightest hope of such a move from a nation whose autocratic Kaiser, answering, in February last, an address presented to him by the burgomaster of Hamburg, thundered out, in his usual blasting manner, that the neighbouring peoples, to enjoy the sweetness of Germany's friendship, "MUST FIRST RECOGNIZE THE VICTORY OF GERMAN ARMS."

As an inducement to the Allies to bow to his wishes, he pointed to Germany's achievement in Russia, where a beaten enemy, "*perceiving no reason for fighting longer,*" clasped hands with the generous Huns. The world has since learned with appalling horror with what tender mercy the barbarous Teutons reciprocated the grasping of hands of defeated Russia, tendered to them by the "bolshevikis" traitors.

The Allies had then to select one of the three above mentioned alternatives.

They have made their choice and they will stick close to it until it is achieved by the victory of their arms.

Knowing as they do that the future of their peoples, and that of the whole world, are at stake, they will not waver in their heroic determination to free Humanity from Germany's cruel yoke.

Viewed from the commanding height it requires to be worthily appreciated, the joint military effort of the Allies offers a truly grand spectacle, daily enlarging and getting more gloriously magnificent.

All the Allies—every one of them—are doing their duty and their respective share in the great crisis they are pledged to bring to a triumphant conclusion.

Belgium and Servia were the first to be martyred, but the hour of their resurrection is getting nearer every day.

France, the British Empire, the United States, Italy, have done and are doing wonders. There can, there must be no question of appraising their respective merit with the intention of giving more credit either to the one or to the other. With the greatest possible sincerity, I affirm my humble, but positive, opinion that each one of the Allies has done and is doing, with overflowing measure, all that courage could and can earnestly perform, all that patriotism and the noblest national virtues can inspire.

France has been heroic to the highest limit.

The British Empire—Great Britain and her Colonies—has been grand in her unswerving determination to fight to a finish.

The great American Republic is putting forth a wonderful exhibition of pluck, of strength, of boldness, of inexhaustible resources.

Italy has stood nobly with her new friends ever since she broke away from the Triple Alliance, to escape the dishonour of remaining on good terms with the Central Empires in the shameful depth of their ignominious course. She has bravely gone through days of disaster which she has heroically redeemed.

All the Allies, bound together by the most admirable unity of purpose, only rivalling in the might of their respective patriotic effort, having nobly *"chosen their course upon principle,"* can never turn back. They must move steadily forward until victorious. They are indomitable in their decision not to live, under any circumstances, *"in a world governed by intrigue and force."*

Echoing the wise and inspiring words addressed by President Wilson to Congress, on the eleventh of February last, we can affirm that the *"desire of enlightened men everywhere is for a new international order under which*

*reason, justice and the common interests of mankind shall prevail. Without
that new order the world will be without peace, and human life will lack
tolerable conditions of existence and development."*

A most encouraging achievement was realized, a few months ago,
emphasizing to the utmost the unity of purpose of the Allies. Every one of
them have millions of men under arms and at the front. It is easily conceived
how tremendous is the task of properly directing the military operations of
such immense armies, unprecedented in the whole human history. Most
patriotically putting aside all national susceptibilities, the statesmen governing
the Allied nations acknowledged the necessity of supporting unity of purpose
by unity of military command. Their decision was heartily approved and
applauded by all and every where.

It is important to note the great difference between the standing of the two
groups of belligerents with regard to the leadership of the armies. Whilst the
Powers dominated by Germany, and fighting with her, are coerced to endure
the Teutonic military supremacy of command, those warring on the side of
France have all most cordially agreed to the appointment of a Commander-in-
Chief out of the profound conviction that unity of command was more and
more becoming a necessity for the successful prosecution of the war.

Since this most urgent decision has been taken, events have surely proved its
wisdom and usefulness. Evidently, the same as unity of purpose, to bear all its
fruits, must be wrought out by statesmanship of a high order, unity of military
command, to produce its natural advantages, must be exercised with
superiority of leadership.

Great statesmen, in a free country, are successful in the management of State
affairs, just as much as they inspire an increasing confidence in their political
genius, developed by a wide experience, honesty of purpose, a constant
patriotic devotion to the public weal.

Great military leaders can do wonders when their achievements are such as to
create unbounded reliance on their ability. Superiority of command, proved
by victories won in very difficult circumstances, is always sure to be
rewarded by an enlightened enthusiasm permeating the whole rank and file of
an army, and trebling the strength and heroism of every combatant.

Added to the widespread renewal of confidence produced by the timely
decision of the Allies to rely on unity of military command, is the reassuring
evidence that the Commander-in-Chief to whom has been imposed the grand
task of leading the unified armies to a final and glorious triumph, is trusted by
all, soldiers and others alike.

The cause for which the Allied nations are fighting with so much tenacity and courage being that of the salvation of Civilization, threatened by a wave of barbarism equal at least to, if not surpassing, any to which Humanity has so far survived, all must admire the wonderful spectacle offered by those millions and millions of men, under arms, from so many different countries, united, under one command, into a military organization which can most properly be called the GRAND ARMY OF HUMAN FREEDOM.

It has been said by one who has presided over the destinies of the American Republic, as the chief of State, that peace must be dictated from Berlin. Can we really hope to behold the dawn of such a glorious day? It is hardly to be supposed that Germany would wait this last extremity to realize that she must abandon for ever her dream of universal domination, relieve the world from the enervating menace of her military terrorism, and redeem her past diabolical course by the repentant determination to join with her former enemies to deserve for Mankind long years of perpetual peace with all the Providential blessings of order, freedom, truly intellectual, moral and material progress.

When the Kaiser ordered his hordes to violate Belgium's territory, to overrun France in order to crush her out of existence as a military and political Power, preparatory to their triumphant march to St. Petersburg, in his wild ambition, which he made blasphemous by pretending that it was divinely inspired, he felt sure that his really wonderful army, which he believed was, and would remain, matchless, would in a few weeks enter Paris.

What a reverse of fortune, what a downfall from extravagant expectations, would be a return of the tide which, after flowing to the very gates of Paris, spreading devastation and crimes all over the fair lands it submerged, would ebb, broken and powerless, to Berlin, bringing the haughty tyrant to his knees before his victors!

If such a day of deliverance is Providentially granted the world, having deserved it by an indomitable courage in resisting oppression, history would again repeat itself but with a different result. The French "TRICOLORE" would once more enter proud Berlin, but this time it would not be alone to be hoisted over the conquered capital of the modern Huns, scarcely less savage than their forefathers. It would be entwined with the "UNION JACK" of Great Britain and Ireland, the "STARS AND STRIPES" of the United States, the Colours of Italy, and, I add with an inexpressible feeling of loyal and national pride, with the Dominion Colours so brilliantly glorified by the heroism of our Canadian soldiers who have proved themselves the equals of the bravest through the protracted but ever glorious campaign, unfolded with those of Australia and South Africa into the glorious flag of the British Empire.

When after the glorious battle of Iena, the great Napoleon, who could have ruined for ever the rising Prussian monarchy, entered Berlin at the head of his victorious legions, the new Cæsar, then already the victim of his unlimited ambition, represented, though issued from a powerful popular movement, triumphant absolutism.

In our days, on entering Berlin, as the final act of this wonderful drama, the entwined Colours of the Allies would symbolize Human Freedom, delivering Germany herself and the whole world from autocratic rule.

Such a memorable event taking place, and rank with the most remarkable in the world's history, the great satisfaction of all those who would have contributed to its achievement, would be that the joint Colours of the Allies would not be raised over Germany's capital to crush the defeated nation under despotic cæsarism, but to deliver her from autocratic tyrannical rule. Waving with dignity over the great Empire they would have freed from the thraldom of absolutist militarism, they could be welcomed as the promise of the renewal, for her as well as for her victorious rivals, of the reign of Justice, of Christian precepts, of Right, Order and Peace, of honest and productive Labour, of science applied to works creative of human happiness instead of diverting the marvellous resources of the great modern discoveries to criminal uses for the calamitous misfortune of the peoples.

I will close this work with the expression of two of the wishes I have most at heart, cherishing the confident hope that they will be realized.

England, France and the United States, fighting as they do for the triumph of such a sacred cause, should emerge indissolubly united from the great struggle they have pledged themselves to carry to a successful issue. I cannot conceive that so many millions of their heroic defenders will have given their lives only for a temporary achievement, soon to be forgotten. They will be gone for ever. Their sacrifices will be eternal. They must bear permanent fruits. United in death, buried together in the soil of France flooded with their blood, from their glorious graves they will implore their surviving countrymen to remain shoulder to shoulder in peace as they are in war. Their holocaust should be the holy seed from which loyal amity ought to grow ever stronger between the future generations of their countrymen who could not testify in a more eloquent and noble way their everlasting gratitude for the glorious heritage of permanent freedom they will have derived from their heroism.

A most enthusiastic daily witness of the immortal deeds of the millions of our brothers, sons and friends, fighting with such splendid courage in the land of my forefathers for our common cause, how often have I, for the last four years, ardently vowed to God from the very bottom of my heart, deeply moved by the reports of their noble achievements, that those who will rest for ever in the ground over which they fell heroically, may enjoy from above the inspiring spectacle of the union for the permanent triumph of Liberty and Christian Civilization, of the great nations for whose grand future they gave their lives!

I also most earnestly hope that the more fortunate of our defenders who will return either safe from the fields of battle, or proudly bearing the glorious wounds which will have crippled their bodies, but not their hearts, will enjoy from the sanctuary of their homes, made comfortable by their grateful compatriots, the profound satisfaction to see the holy union cemented on the thundering firing line perpetuated for the lasting prosperity and happiness of Mankind.

The last shadow of the recollections of the feuds of past ages between England and France should be forever sunk in patriotic oblivion, buried deep beneath the glory both valorous nations will have jointly reaped in their mighty efforts to rescue the world from the frightful wave of barbarism which they will have forced to recede.

All the well wishers of peaceful and happy days for future generations are very much gratified at knowing that in joining with the Allies in the mighty struggle they were carrying with such undaunted courage, the great American Republic was also inspired by a feeling of gratitude for France in remembrance of what she has done to help her to achieve her independence. Let us behold anew the inscrutable designs of Providence. Nearly a century and a half has elapsed since France, England and her American Colonies seemed to be for all times irreconcilable opponents. What a change in Destiny! Years have rolled by. New and unforeseen conditions have been developed the world over. Gradually two great currents of thoughts and aspirations have been flowing with increased strength preparing a formidable clash which was to threaten Civilization with utter destruction.

Autocratic ambition was for many long years challenging Political Liberty to a deadly conflict. At last from the cloudy sky came the flash of lightning, and the thunderbolt was on the earth shaking it to its depth by the tremendous shock.

Germany, having fired the wonderful autocratic shot, fully expected that her rivals would be thunderstruck beyond possibility of resurrection. But to her great dismay, the friends of Political Liberty the world over rallied as one man to its defence. And Germany trembled at seeing England burying for ever all ill-feelings against France, her ancient foe, rushing to her support with millions of her brave sons, after having drawn around her ally the protecting chain of her matchless fleet.

232

Another very discomforting surprise was in store for the cruel Huns. The American Republic, grateful to France for past services, was also moved by renovated feelings of affection for the mother-country from whom she had parted without disowning her. Determined to be at the forefront of the battle for the triumph of human Freedom—after unsuccessfully exhausting every means of bringing Germany to her senses—she clasped hands with England and France and valiantly rallied to their sides to share the merit and the glory of saving Political Liberty from the terrible Teutonic onslaught.

In my humble but sincere and profound opinion, the present spectacle offered to the world's admiration by the sacred and mighty union of the British Empire, France and the United States, every patriotic home of theirs thrilling with undiminished enthusiasm for the success of their heroic efforts, is a truly grand one inspiring unbounded faith in the future of Humanity. Let no one forget for a moment that the present war, certainly NATIONAL so far as the existence of each one of the Allied States is concerned, is, above all preeminently a world's conflict which favourable issue deeply concerns the destinies of all the peoples of the earthly globe.

The whole question is whether autocratic tyranny will henceforth rule the world, or if Humanity will yet enjoy the blessings of Liberty, of free institutions!

In all hearts must abide the supreme desire that when peace is restored with all and the only conditions to which they can agree, the British Empire, France and the American Republic will forever remain united to promote the prosperity and the welfare of all the nations of the earth, large, middle-sized or small. The duty of those of Imperialist proportions will be as hitherto performed by England and the United States in their democratic way, to protect the independence of the small States, never aspiring to any territorial acquisitions but those accruing to them with the full and free consent of the new populations asking the protection of their ægis and the advantages of their union.

When I consider the grand and magnificent part the three above named leading nations can play for the happy future of Humanity, by working hand in hand, and shoulder to shoulder, for general peace, order and prosperity, my heart is full with the ardent desire to witness them accepting that glorious task with the stern determination to accomplish it to its better end. In spite of the vicissitudes and the failings of their past, they have done a great deal for the general good. They can do still more in the future. Like everyman bearing with fortitude the trials of life with the worthy design of profiting by the experience thus acquired to elevate himself to a higher conception of his duty, the British Empire, France and the United States will undoubtedly emerge from behind the dark clouds of the present days with aspirations ennobled by the sacrifices they are making, purified by the sufferings and the holocaust of so many of their own, with a stronger will to help working out the world's destiny by maintaining permanent peace and good-will amongst men. If they pursue that dignified course of high ideals they will fully deserve the admiration and the gratitude of all those who will benefit by their examples, and reap the abundant fruits of their devoted and enlightened leadership.

It is one of the blessings of true Political Liberty, when duly understood and intelligently practised, to produce a class of politicians and statesmen of wide experience, of commanding character, of high culture, of great attainments, with a superior training in the management of public affairs, who are readily acknowledged as national leaders by the people who confidently trust them, reserving, of course, their constitutional right to call new men to office whenever they consider in the public interest to do so. Those trusted leaders do not claim, as the German autocratic Kaiser, the power, by Divine Right, to do anything they please, asserting that in every imaginable case they do the will of the Almighty.

When charged with the Government of their country, they understand very well that their duty is to manage the national affairs under their responsibility, first, to the Divine Ruler, as any other man in any other calling; secondly, to those who, having required their services, have the constitutional right to call them to account for their stewardship.

Just as confidence is the basis of sound national credit, trust, on the part of the people, and responsibility, on that of the national leaders, are the two cornerstones of free institutions.

Great Britain,—and her great autonomous Colonies also—for many long years past, have been most fortunate in the choice of the national leaders whom they have successively entrusted with the affairs of State.

In that momentous occurrence, more than four years ago, when the whole question whether Great Britain would go to war, or not, was laid before the Imperial Parliament supported by the strongest possible reasons in favour of the decision to accept the challenge of Germany, and fight with the firm determination not to sheathe the sword before victory was won, no British public man would have dared, like the German Emperor, to claim, by Divine Authority, the right to violate the solemn treaties the provisions of which his country was in honour and duty bound to carry out to the very letter.

The commanding parts national leaders play in a free country, in consequence of the public confidence they inspire and enjoy, can have their counterparts in the great society of nations.

Whatever shall be the final settlement of all the difficult matters brought up for solution by the war, it is certain that the management of the world's affairs will be well served by the legitimate influence of great nations whose leadership will be beneficial just in proportion as it is itself directed by the true principles of political Freedom, and an uncompromising respect of the rights of weaker nations always entitled to the fairest dealings on the part of their stronger associates in the great commonwealth of Sovereign States.

There cannot be the slightest doubt that the British Empire, France and the United States, until Providentially ordered otherwise, will hereafter be the three leading nations of the world. Their union maintained sacred in peace, as it is in war, will be the safest guarantee that the days of autocratic domination have ended. Henceforth the tide of political Freedom will flow with increased rapidity and strength. The only danger ahead, against which it is always wise to provide with due care and foresight, is that which would be the result of abuse and wild expectations always sure to react in favour of absolutist principles. Political Liberty and Order, Governmental Authority and Freedom, both well directed, must work hand in hand for the national welfare.

The British Empire, France and the American Republic are free countries. More and better than any others they should and must, by example and friendly advice, lead the peoples in the successful practice of self-government.

Considering more especially the part the British Empire will be called upon to play in the reorganized world, freed from autocratic terrorism, we must not lose sight of the much larger place England's great autonomous Colonies will occupy in the broadened English Commonwealth. We, Canadians, together with our brethren from Australia, New Zealand and South Africa, will have done our glorious share to win the war. We shall have to perform with equal devotion the new duty of sharing the British Empire's task in gradually elevating the nations to an enlightened practice of Political Liberty.

Evidently to do so with the success this noble cause will deserve, we must first strive to utilize our admirable free institutions to the best advantage, for ourselves, for our own future, and for the grand destinies of our Empire.

As an instrument of good government our constitutional charter is almost perfect, as much so as any thing worldly can be. Let us never forget that the best weapon for self-protection may become useless, or even dangerous for us, if not handled with the required intelligence, justice and skill. We would lose all claims to contribute guiding others in the enjoyment of free institutions if we, ourselves, were mistaken in the proper working of our own constitution from a misconception of its literal wording or of its largeness of spirit. We must never challenge the truth that "spirit giveth life."

More than ever the supreme difficulties of governing numerous racial groups, issued from ancient stocks so long divided by endless feuds,—the result of the many sudden changes of territorial limits to be wrought by the restoration of peace—will be very hard to settle satisfactorily. The task will require the constant effort of statesmanship of a high order.

Many of those who will hereafter be trained to self-government will look to us for their guidance. We must give them the inspiring example of fair play, of justice for all, of unity of purpose and aspirations in the diversity of ethnical offsprings.

Need I say that the most urgent duty of all fair minded Canadians is, and will ever be, to heartily join together, to bless our dear country with concord, good feeling, harmony and kindly dispositions to grant an overflowing measure of justice to all our countrymen of all origins and creeds.

Writing this book with the express purpose of explaining and strongly disapproving the deplorable efforts of a few to deter my French Canadian compatriots from doing their bounden duty through the dire crisis we are all undergoing, I will close these pages by calling anew upon my English speaking countrymen not to judge them by the sayings and deeds of persons who can at times somewhat stir up dangerous prejudices, but who are utterly incompetent to lead them as they should and deserve to be. Silenced at last by a patriotic measure to censure any disloyal expression of sentiments, matters have easily resumed their regular and honourable course. All loyal citizens, throughout the length and breadth of the land, have, I am sure, much rejoiced at the loyalty with which the French Canadians, of all classes, religious, social, commercial, industrial, financial, agricultural, have united to obey a statute of military service to which many of them did not agree, as long as they had the constitutional right to differ from the opinion of the large majority of our people, but to the successful operation of which they rallied the moment it was the law of the land. The worthy leaders of our Church strongly recommended obedience to the decision of the constituted authority, firmly condemned any guilty attempt at disturbing public order, and ordered all the members of their flocks to fervously pray the Almighty for PEACE WITH VICTORY FOR THE ALLIES.

Our "pacifists at all hazards" once more silenced, this time by the very religious leaders under whose ægis they had shamefully tried to shield themselves, the patriotic impulse was moved to most commendable action. Without waiting for the call of the law, hundreds of young men from the better classes, from the universities and other educational institutions, well educated, voluntarily enlisted and rallied to the Colours. At least as much as in the other provinces, the class of our young manhood called by law heartily responded, all the real leaders of public opinion uniting to give the only advice loyal men could express.

For one, I was most happy to ascertain how favourably western public feeling was impressed by the new turn of thoughts and events in the Province of Quebec. The reaction of sentiments operating both ways,—in Ontario, the western Provinces and Quebec—augurs well for the final abatement of the excitement which for a time menaced our fair Dominion with regrettable racial strifes so much to be deprecated.

It can be positively affirmed that the whole people of Canada, east to west, north to south, are now more than ever a unit in their patriotic determination to fight the war to its final victorious issue. To this end the two millions of French British subjects in Canada, in perfect communion of thoughts and aspirations with the two millions of the neighbouring Republic's subjects of French Canadian origin, are loyally doing, and will continue to do, their share. Their representatives at the front are gloriously fighting the common enemy. Their valour and their achievements during the Allies' offensive so masterly planned and carried out by the Commander-in-Chief, Foch, have been worthy of their victories at Ypres, Vimy, Courcelette, Passchandaele. Many have, during the last three months, given their lives for the cause they defend. Many more have been wounded and are anxiously waiting their cure, when possible, to return to the field of honour. Daily reports from the front tell of their enthusiasm, of their bravery, of their heroism!

The French Canadians—I have no hesitation whatever in vouching for it— will continue to bear stoically with the sacrifices of so many kinds the conflict imposes upon them. Though smarting, as all others, under the burden, yet they cheerfully pay the heavy taxes required from the country to meet our national obligations the outcome of the war.

So all is for the best under the strenuous present conditions of our national existence.

In closing, I pray leave to reiterate, from the Introduction to this work, the following lines expressing my most sincere and profound conviction:—

I hope,—and most ardently wish—that all my readers will agree with me that next to the necessity of winning the war—and may I say, even as of almost equal importance for the future grandeur of our beloved country—range that of promoting by all lawful means harmony and good will amongst all our countrymen, whatever may be their racial origin, their religious faith, their particular aspirations not conflicting with their devotion to Canada as a whole, nor with their loyalty to the British Empire, whose grandeur and prestige they want to firmly help to uphold with the inspiring confidence that more and more they will be the unconquerable bulwark of Freedom, Justice, Civilization and Right.

May I be allowed to conclude by saying that my most earnest desire is to do all in my power, in the rank and file of the great army of free men, to reach the goal which ought to be the most persevering and patriotic ambition of loyal Canadians of all origins and creeds.

And I repeat, wishing my words to be reechoed throughout the length and breadth of the land I so heartily cherish:—I have always been, I am and will ever be, to my last breath, true to my oath of allegiance to my Sovereign and to my country.

APPENDIX—A.

PRESIDENT WILSON'S SPEECH

To The United States Congress—11th Day of February, 1918.

On the above mentioned date, Mr. Wilson, the President of the great American Republic, delivered the following speech to the Congress, in Washington. This noble and statesmanlike utterance met with the unanimous and enthusiastic approval of the members of both Houses, and was highly applauded, not only in the United States, but over all the truly civilized world. It reads thus:—

"On the eighth of January, I had the honor of addressing you on the objects of the war as our people conceive them. The Prime Minister of Great Britain had spoken in similar terms on the fifth of January. To these addresses the German Chancellor replied on the 24th and Count Czernin for Austria on the same day. It is gratifying to have our desire so promptly realized that all exchanges of view on this great matter should be made in the hearing of all the world.

"Count Czernin's reply, which is directed chiefly to my own address, on the eighth of January, is uttered in a very friendly tone.

"He finds in my statement a sufficiently encouraging approach to the views of his own government to justify him in believing that it furnishes a basis for a more detailed discussion of purposes by the two governments. He is represented to have intimated that the views he was expressing had been communicated to me beforehand and that I was aware of them at the time he was uttering them; but in this I am sure he was misunderstood. I had received no intimation of what he intended to say. There was, of course, no reason why he should communicate privately with me. I am quite content to be one of his public audiences.

"Count von Hertling's reply is, I may say, very vague and very confusing. It is full of equivocal phrases and leads, it is not clear where. But it is certainly in a very different tone from that of Count Czernin and apparently of an opposite purpose. It confirms, I am sorry to say, rather than removes, the unfortunate impression made by what we had learned of the conferences at Brest-Litovsk. His discussion and acceptance of our general principles leads him to no practical conclusions. He refuses to apply them to the substantiate items which must constitute the body of any final settlement. He is jealous of international action and of international council. He accepts, he says, the principle of public diplomacy, but he appears to insist that it be confined at any rate in this case, to generalities and that the several particular questions of territory and sovereignty, the several questions upon whose settlement must depend the acceptance of peace by the twenty-three states now engaged in the war, must be discussed and settled, not in general council but severally by the nations most immediately concerned by interest of neighbourhood. He agrees that the seas should be free, but looks askance at any limitation to that freedom by international action in the interest of the common order. He would, without reserve, be glad to see economic barriers removed between nation and nation, for that could in no way impede the ambitions of the military party with whom he seems constrained to keep on terms. Neither does he raise objection to a limitation of armaments. That matter will be settled of itself, he thinks, by the economic conditions which must follow the war. But the German colonies, he demands, must be returned without debate. He will discuss with no one but the representatives of Russia what disposition shall be made of the peoples and the lands of the Baltic provinces; with no one but the Government of France the "conditions" under which French territory shall be evacuated and only with Austria what shall be done with Poland. In the determination of all questions affecting the Balkan states he defers, as I understand him, to Austria and Turkey and with regard to the agreements to be entered into concerning the non-Turkish peoples of the present Ottoman Empire, to the Turkish authorities themselves. After a settlement all around effected in this fashion, by individual barter and concession, he would have no objection, if I correctly interpret his statement, to a league of nations which would undertake to hold the balance of power steady against external disturbance.

"It must be evident to everyone who understands what this war has wrought in the opinion and temper of the world that no general peace, no peace worth the infinite sacrifices of these years of tragical suffering, can possibly be arrived at in any such fashion. The method the German Chancellor proposes is the method of the Congress of Vienna. We cannot and will not return to that. What is at stake now is the peace of the world. What we are striving for is a new international order based upon broad and universal principles of right and justice—no mere peace of shreds and patches. Is it possible that Count von Hertling does not see that, does not grasp it, is in fact living in his thought in a world dead and gone? Has he utterly forgotten the Reichstag resolutions of the 19th of July, or does he deliberately ignore them? They spoke of the conditions of a general peace, not of national aggrandizement or of arrangements between state and state. The peace of the world depends upon just settlement of each of the several problems to which I adverted in my recent address to Congress. I, of course, do not mean that the peace of the world depends upon the acceptance of any particular set of suggestions as to the way in

240

which those problems are to be dealt with. I mean only that those problems, each and all, affect the whole world; that unless they are dealt with in a spirit of unselfish and unbiassed justice, with a view to the wishes, the natural connections, the racial aspirations, the security and peace of mind of the peoples involved, no permanent peace will have been attained. They cannot be discussed separately or in corners. None of them constitutes a private or separate interest from which the opinion of the world may be shut out. Whatever affects the peace affects mankind, and nothing settled by military force, if settled wrong, is settled at all. It will presently have to be re-opened.

"Is Count von Hertling not aware that he is speaking in the court of mankind, that all the awakened nations of the world now sit in judgment on what every public man, of whatever nation, may say on the issues of a conflict which has spread to every region of the world? The Reichstag resolutions of July 19 themselves frankly accepted the decisions of that court. There shall be no annexations, no contributions, no punitive damages. Peoples are not to be handed about from one sovereignty to another by an international conference or an understanding between rivals and antagonists. National aspirations must be respected; peoples may now be dominated and governed only by their own consent. "Self-determination," is not a mere phrase. It is an imperative principle of action, which statesmen will henceforth ignore at their peril. We cannot have general peace for the asking, or by the mere arrangements of a peace conference. It cannot be pieced together out of individual understandings between powerful states. All the parties to this war must join in the settlement of every issue anywhere involved in it because what we are seeking is a peace that we can all unite to guarantee and maintain whether it be right and fair, an act of justice, rather than a bargain between sovereigns.

"The United States has no desire to interfere in European affairs or to act as arbiter in European territorial disputes. We would disdain to take advantage of any internal weakness or disorder to impose her own will upon another people. She is quite ready to be shown that the settlements she has suggested are not the best or the most enduring. They are only her own provisional sketch of principles, and of the way in which they should be applied. But she entered this war because she was made a partner, whether she would or not, in the sufferings and indignities inflicted by the military masters of Germany, against the peace and security of mankind; and the conditions of peace will touch her as nearly as they will touch any other nation to which is entrusted a leading part in the maintenance of civilization. She cannot see her way to peace until the causes of this war are removed, its renewal rendered, as nearly as may be, impossible.

"This war had its roots in the disregard of the rights of small nations and of nationalities which lacked the union and the force to make good their claim to determine their own allegiances and their own forms of political life. Covenants must now be entered into which will render such things impossible for the future; and those covenants must be backed by the united force of all the nations that love justice and are willing to maintain it at any cost. If territorial settlements and the political relations of great populations which have not the organized power to resist are to be determined by the contracts of the powerful governments which consider themselves most directly affected, as Count von Hertling proposes, why may not economic questions also? It has come about in the altered world in which we now find ourselves that justice and the rights of peoples affect the whole field of international dealing as much as access to raw materials and fair and equal conditions of trade. Count von Hertling wants the essential basis of commercial and industrial life to be safeguarded by common agreement and guarantee, but he cannot expect that to be conceded him if the other matters to be determined by the articles of peace are not handled in the same way as it was in the final accounting. He cannot ask the benefit of common agreement in the one field without according it in the other. I take it for granted that he sees that separate and selfish compacts with regard to trade and the essential materials of manufacture would afford no foundation for peace. Neither, he may rest assured, will separate and selfish compacts with regard to the provinces and peoples.

"Count Czernin seems to see the fundamental elements of peace with clear eyes and does not seek to obscure them. He sees that an independent Poland, made up of all the indisputably Polish peoples who lie contiguous to one another, is a matter of European concern and must of course be conceded; that Belgium must be evacuated and restored, no matter what sacrifices and concessions that may involve; and that national aspirations must be satisfied, even within his own empire, in the common interest of Europe and mankind. If he is silent about questions which touch the interest and purpose of his Allies more nearly than they touch those of Austria only, it must, of course, be because he feels constrained, I suppose, to defer to Germany and Turkey in the circumstances. Seeing and conceding, as he does, the essential principles involved and the necessity of candidly applying them, he naturally feels that Austria can respond to the purpose of peace as expressed by the United States with less embarrassment than could Germany. He would probably have gone much farther had it not been for the embarrassments of Austria's alliance and of her dependence upon Germany.

"After all the test of whether it is possible for either Government to go any further in this comparison of views is simple and obvious. The principles to be applied are:

"First, that each part of the final settlement must be based on the essential justice of the particular case, and upon such adjustments as are most likely to bring a peace that will be permanent.

"Second, that peoples and provinces are not to be bartered about from sovereignty to sovereignty as if they were mere chattels and pawns in a game, even the great game, now for ever discredited, of the balance of power; but that,

"Every territorial settlement involved in this war must be made in the interest and for the benefit of the populations concerned and not as a part of any mere adjustment of compromise of claims amongst rival states; and,

"Fourth, that all well defined national aspirations shall be accorded the utmost satisfaction that can be accorded them without introducing new or perpetuating old elements of discord, and antagonism that would be likely in time to break the peace of Europe and consequently of the world.

"A general peace entered upon such foundations can be discussed. Until such a peace can be secured we have no choice but to go on. So far as we can judge, these principles that we regard as fundamental are already everywhere accepted as imperative except among the spokesmen of the military and annexationist party in Germany. If they have anywhere else been rejected, the objectors have not been sufficiently numerous or influential to make their voices audible. The tragic circumstance is that this one party in Germany is apparently willing and able to send millions of men to their death to prevent what all the world now sees to be just.

"I would not be a true spokesman of the people of the United States if I did not say once more that we entered this war upon no small occasion, and that we can never turn back from a course chosen upon principle. Our resources are in part mobilized now, and we shall not pause until they are mobilized in their entirety. Our armies are rapidly going to the fighting front, and will go more rapidly. Our whole strength will be put into this state of emancipation—emancipation from the threat and attempted mastery of selfish groups of autocratic rulers—whatever the difficulties and present partial delays. We are indomitable in our power of independent action, and can in no circumstances consent to live in a world governed by intrigue and force. We believe that our own desire for a new international order under which reason and justice and the common interests of mankind shall prevail, is the desire of enlightened men everywhere. Without that new order the world will be without peace, and human life will lack tolerable conditions of existence and development. Having set our hand to the task of achieving it, we shall not turn back.

"I hope that it is not necessary for me to add that no word of what I have said is intended as a threat. That is not the temper of our people. I have spoken thus only that the whole world may know the true spirit of America—that men everywhere may know that our passion for justice and for self-government is no mere passion of words, but a passion which, once set in act, must be satisfied. The power of the United States is a menace to no nation or people. It will be never used in aggression or for the aggrandizement of any selfish interest of our own. It springs out of freedom and is for the service of freedom."

APPENDIX—B.

On the 18th of September, 1918, the Secretary of State made public the official text of the letter he sent, to Mr. W. A. F. Ekengren, the Swedish Minister, in charge of Austro-Hungarian affairs, conveying President Wilson's rejection of the Austrian peace proposals. It reads as follows:—

"Sir,—I have the honor to acknowledge the receipt of your note, dated September 16, communicating to me a note from the Imperial Government of Austria-Hungary, containing a proposal to the Government of all the belligerent States to send delegates to a confidential and unbinding discussion on the basic principles for the conclusion of peace. Furthermore, it is proposed that the delegates would be charged to make known to one another the conception of their Governments regarding these principles, and to receive analogous communications, as well as to request and give frank and candid explanations on all those points which need to be precisely defined.

"In reply, I beg to say that the substance of your communication has been submitted to the President, who now directs me to inform you that the Government of the United States feels that there is only one reply which it can make to the suggestion of the Imperial Austro-Hungarian Government. It has repeatedly, and with entire candor, stated the terms upon which the United States would consider peace, and can and will entertain no proposal for a conference upon the matter concerning which it has made its position and purpose so plain.

"Accept, sir, the renewed assurances of my highest consideration.

"(Signed), ROBERT LANSING,

"Secretary of State."

Lightning Source UK Ltd.
Milton Keynes UK
UKHW040705300622
405186UK00001B/227